ForeWord Reviews book of the Year

Winner of the 2014 Epic eBook Award

"Mesmerizing! The story is so alarmingly plausible you'll never look at the horizon the same way again!" – *Nick Nickles, Senior Intelligence Specialist, U.S. Department of Justice*

"A fascinating and exciting novel ... how to prevent a real life catastrophe of major proportions." – *Dr. Carolyn Shoemaker holds the record for Near Earth Object discoveries including comet Shoemaker-Levy*

"Action, philosophy ... a hero who thinks more of others than himself and F-18 fighters – what more could you ask for in an adventure novel?" – Hall of Fame Astronaut Ken Bowersox, shuttle and International Space Station Commander

"Stevens tells a story that is both deeply personal and global at the same time. The tension started on the cover and never let up. This is a book that opened doors long closed. Don't expect to sleep until you finish." – *Stuart Frisch, Israeli Special Forces, counter-terrorism expert, co-founder Obsidian Strategies*

"Engaging from the very start, it was a thrilling, thought provoking adventure into a new world!" – *Cherry Meadows, international motivational speaker*

"In the vein of the Dan Brown novels, this is a page-turner that sucks you in, but differentiates itself by having much stronger intellectual 'chops,' and more complex, soulful characters." – *Christian Johnson, international photographer*

"Another master story teller has emerged. Dave Stevens has used a tantalizing blend of science and philosophy to move forward a gripping plot. What a wild and fulfilling ride."
– *Dan Smith, President DES Incorporated*

"I could not put it down. It's thought provoking, emotional and even a little humorous. Why are our world leaders not talking about these issues?!" – *Julie Atlas, President of The Wave Agency*

"I enjoy Tom Clancy, Robert Ludlum and Dan Brown, but there is a definite difference when reading someone who has actually lived the life they are writing about." – *Tim Hendricks, CEO, author and international speaker*

"Highlights a real-life threat facing all of us, and packages it into a highly entertaining action adventure." – *Dr. Ed Lu, former astronaut and CEO of the B612 Foundation*

"Fascinating. Technically accurate and frighteningly plausible." – Professor Joe Veverka, former Chairman Cornell Astrophysics, Principle Investigator NASA Stardust mission

"Inspiring, thought provoking and impossible to put down. A compelling book and should make a blockbuster film." – Fred Miller, Executive Producer of Academy Award nominated **For All Mankind**

"Thrilling, technically astute and knowledgeable of the inner workings of an elite club. Commander Stevens' stories about naval aviation and 'black' programs can only come from someone who's 'been there, done that.'" – Vice Admiral Joe Dyer, former Chief Test Pilot of the Navy and COO of iRobot

IMPACT

Book One of the Fuzed Trilogy

David E. Stevens

Second Edition

CFP

Originally published as Resurrect in the UK by Monarch Books
(a publishing imprint of Lion Hudson plc)
Cambridge Free Press

ISBN 978 0 69240 222 1 Print
ISBN 978 0 85721 341 9 Kindle

Published in association with Terry Burns
Hartline Literary Agency
www.hartlineliterary.com

DEDICATION

This book is dedicated to the men and women of the B612 Foundation and the cadre of scientists and professionals who have the vision to see the future and the courage to change it.

ACKNOWLEDGMENTS

This book wouldn't have been possible without the help of so many. My wife, Lilli, was the ultimate encourager *and* subject matter expert. Terry Burns, one of the top-ranked Literary Agents in the U.S., saw something in the rough manuscripts and was a patient teacher. My editor, Normandie Fischer, taught me what I should have learned in English class, Ryan Deken was great at asking "Why this?" and Garrett Johnson provided video magic. A special thanks to Fred Miller and Rick Eldridge for their belief, wisdom and guidance.

The accuracy of this story hinges on the expertise of many, from astrophysicists to physicians, astronauts to admirals. A huge thanks to my subject matter experts who gave generously of their time: Vince Battistone, Chris Boblit, Ken Bowersox, Teri Burns, Winston Broad, Naomi Chuckwuk, Reed DeVries, Nikko Dutton, Joe Dyer, Susan Dyer, Jim Eisenbeck, Tommy Harper, Amy Hunter, Jay Jost, Kristi Kyle, Ed Lu, Neil Mammen, John Marshall, Jerry and Cherry Meadows, Adrian Melott, Jeff Moore, Bill Napier, Jim Roberts, Brett Sappington, Dan Smith, Scott Straub, Jerry Steel, Dale Stevens and Joe Veverka. A few remain unnamed due to the sensitive and dangerous work they do every day.

I also want to thank the awesome friends and reviewers who helped me craft a better story. They include: Joe and Linda Baggett, Stan Boyd, Jackie Bray, Albert Comulada, Victoria Comulada, Mike Craddock, Lori Davidson, Lou and Carol Deken, Lori Derr, Susan Dyer, Julie Eisenbeck, Lester and Margaret Eisenbeck, Susan Femino, Ken and Lisa Farnham, Rob Gryger, Lesia Harper, Laura Stevens-Hawkins, Kathy Heard, Tim Hendricks, Chandler Johnson, Christian Johnson, Judy Johnson, Kevin Johnson, Rob King, Leslee Kitchings, Tracy Kuhar, Mike Lee, Sheila Mannion, Nancy Mayhew, Steve McQueen, Gene Mixson, Molly Mueller, Mary Ann Moore, Catherine Murray, Richard Mustakos, Ellen and Patrick O'Neil, Mike Pasternack, Lee Person, Cletus Pew, Betsy Smith, Ray Stone and Bart Waggoner.

I

RE-ENTRY

His thoughts became less distinct and his vision began to fade.
As he looked up at the stars ... his heart beat its last beat.

1

THE END

He awoke in pervasive nothingness. It was neither dark nor light, silent nor loud. It just ... was. He tried to move, but didn't know how. "Where am I?"

The nothingness swallowed his question, but he began to see images. Unfolding at incredible speed was a cascade of sights, sounds and smells: *Legos – skinned knee – captured frog – classroom – soccer – emergency room – girls – speeding ticket ...* As time advanced, the pace slowed, and he became immersed.

A teenager competing in his first karate tournament, he glanced from his opponent to a cute girl in the audience ... and found himself flat on his back. His instructor leaned over him with a wry smile. "Andy, this ain't a beauty pageant. You really gotta focus."

Two of his friends stared down three large locals across a pool table. Before it came to blows, he slid in with drinks and defused the confrontation. One of his inebriated friends said, "Thanks, dude. That could've gotten us thrown out of flight school."

In a training flight debrief, the Squadron Commander pointed at him. "Our *new guy* got a perfect bull's eye," he shook his head, "on the wrong target." Looking right at him, he added, "Son, we don't need to deploy with a pilot that's *dazed and confused.*"

A senior pilot sitting next to him slapped him on the back. "Our FNG just scored himself a new call-sign – *Confused!*"

The Skipper laughed but shook his head. "It's too long." He thought for a moment and then with a half-smile, added, "*And* he *did* get a bull's eye." On the whiteboard, he wrote, "*Fuzed.*"

Strapped into an F-18 fighter on the aircraft carrier's catapult, he watched a wave break over the bow. The typhoon had taken an unexpected turn and with aircraft struggling to land, the airborne jets were running dangerously low on fuel.

He was the emergency tanker. His Super Hornet carried a refueling package and extra fuel tanks under each wing. Snapping his oxygen mask on, he saluted the Catapult Officer and was hurled into the typhoon.

He rendezvoused with and tanked five jets. After they were safely aboard the carrier, *he* was the last aircraft airborne. But the typhoon went from bad to nightmare, with sea and sky merging into a violent visceral black.

On his radio, the Landing Signal Officer said, "302, paddles. Storm's tossing the carrier around like a bathtub toy. Visibility's almost zero. What's your state?"

With 1400 pounds of fuel left, he replied, "One point four."

Paddles said, "Dang, Fuzed, you gave away all your gas." There was a pause. "You only got enough for one approach. The helos are grounded. Fly your needles and *do … not … go … high!* Do you understand?"

He replied, "Roger that." With no recovery helicopter, ejecting into the typhoon was a death sentence. He flew the instrument approach as if his life depended on it. It did, but with the turbulence, it was like trying to fly a rollercoaster.

Thirty seconds to touch down, approach control said, "302, three-quarters of a mile, call the ball."

He saw nothing and said, "302, clara, zero point eight." Clara meant he couldn't see the ship – or anything beyond the fighter's nose – and 800 pounds of fuel meant he was minutes from engine flameout.

With wind whistling in the background, he heard paddles say, "302, keep it coming. Fly the needles!"

His radar altimeter warned him he was less than 200 feet above the ocean. Seconds to impact, he was still blind and once again called, "302, clara!"

He had to abort the approach or crash into the ship or sea. As he started to add power, he heard paddles yell, "We see ya! Come left! Come left! Easy with it!"

The ship emerged like an apparition through thick, oily

sheets of rain. He was too high and too far right. Yanking the throttles back, he slapped the stick hard left. His wing dipped, dumping lift and dropping the fighter like an express elevator.

At the same time, an ocean swell heaved the ship up to meet him.

Slamming onto the flight deck with a bone-jarring impact, the tires exploded and the fighter bounced back into the air. He jammed the throttles into afterburner, knowing he'd have to climb and eject. But the tip of his tail hook caught the fourth and final steel cable, ripping him violently from the typhoon.

Pilot to crash-test dummy in two seconds, he sat motionless on the flight deck still clenching the stick and throttle, and pleasantly surprised to be aboard and alive. Before pulling the engines back to idle, they flamed out.

The flight crew chained his jet to the deck where it sat.

As soon as it was secure, he climbed out of the cockpit and staggered across the storm-blasted flight deck to the nearest hatch. He was drenched with rain and sweat as he stepped inside, closed the heavy metal hatch and breathed a sigh of relief. But as he turned around, he was confronted by an intimidating six-foot-three, muscular black man with a shaved head.

Commander Joe Meadows said, "That was the worst damn landing I've ever seen!" Grinning from ear to ear, his Squadron Commander slapped him on the back, adding, "Awesome! Fuzed, you saved a lot of pilots' butts out there. I'm proud of you and I'm going to get you that Test Pilot School slot you wanted." He gave him a half-smile. "Just don't forget, sometimes, little details – *like fuel* – can be important."

He saw three gold stripes on his own uniform's sleeve, as he shook hands with an admiral who said, "Congratulations, Fuzed. The Robotic Fighter project you're taking over is one of the most important black programs we have." With a wry smile, he added, "The bad news is … it'll eventually put all us pilots out of a job."

The minister said, "May I present Commander Andrew and Mrs. Kelly Logan." They walked out of the front of the church and under a ceremonial arch created by two rows of Navy officers holding crossed swords over their heads. At the end of the arch, his best man gently swatted his new wife on the backside with a sword. "Welcome to the Navy, ma'am." And to him, "About *flippin'* time, Commander!"

As they got into the limo, his wife, smiling through tears, said, "Thank you for letting us do a church wedding!"

As he kissed his wife goodbye, she said, "Happy first anniversary!" With a challenging smile, she added, "Remember ... you said after a year we'd talk about having kids?"

Seeing his expression, her face fell, but she just said, "We'll talk when you come back from California. Love you."

At sunset, 30-foot blue-white blowtorches drove his 20-ton fighter down the runway like an angry rhino on crack. The Super Hornet was clumsy and ungainly on the ground, but as it leaped into the air, it transformed into a graceful bird of prey.

It was a routine flight, but it was great to get away from his desk and ... other decisions.

He was delivering a brand new 50-million dollar F-18 Super Hornet to its squadron home on the West Coast. The Boeing plant, where the fighter was assembled, adjoined St. Louis International. Sharing the airport with airliners, the overworked air traffic controllers wanted the small, fast moving jets out of their crowded airspace as soon as possible. Happy to oblige, he yanked the Hornet's nose into a 60-degree climb, his afterburner departure dominating the twilight sky like a brilliant comet.

As he raised the landing gear, he caught something out of the corner of his eye – a tiny brown blur of motion and what felt like a slight vibration.

The red-tailed hawk tucked its wings and dove ... too late. Expiring in an explosion of feathers, it struck a fuel line in the landing gear bay at 200 miles per hour.

2

FIRE

He checked his engine instruments carefully. Everything looked fine.

Passing 10,000 feet, he pulled the engines out of burner and reduced his rate of climb. Slewing the cursor on his radar with his throttle-mounted mouse, he realized he was just working on his office computer like everyone else. His "office chair," however, was a thinly padded ejection seat sitting a few feet in front of hundreds of twirling, titanium turbine blades. His "suit" was made of green, fire-resistant Nomex, and over it, he wore a G-suit zipped tightly around his stomach and legs. Designed to force blood back to the brain during high-G maneuvers, they looked more like green cowboy chaps than high-tech clothing. He imagined strapping into a fighter might not be that different than saddling up a high-strung bronco. In addition to a wild ride, both were capable of ejecting their riders.

He checked in with Kansas City Center for his final cruise altitude.

They responded, "Hornet Zero Seven, climb and maintain flight level four seven zero."

He repeated the altitude back with a "roger." Technically, the correct response was "wilco," meaning, "will comply." Like most pilots, he never used it ... probably just an inherent dislike of being compliant.

Leveling off at 47,000 feet, he relaxed and enjoyed the view. His accommodations might have been Spartan, but unlike many offices, his had a window, and what a window it was. The fighter's bubble canopy gave him a panoramic view with only a centimeter of Plexiglas separating him from the cold, thin, 600-mph air.

Cruising nine miles high on a twin-turbine Harley, he

chased the setting sun across the continent. The sun always won, but flying close to the speed of sound, he gave it a run for its money, stretching a 15-minute sunset to an hour. With 80% of the atmosphere below him, the brilliantly compressed colors spanned the spectrum. Above him was the simple dead, dark black of space. Stars stared down unblinking, having lost their atmosphere induced twinkle. The black dome ended in a narrow strip of deep iridescent purple. The purple feathered into infinite shades of blue, from the darkest navy across a band of powdery sky-blue, into a brief gasp of turquoise. Finally, an explosion of brilliant yellows, fluorescent oranges and deep, rich reds cut the horizon like a rip in the heavens. He savored the beauty and solitude, knowing there'd be few of these moments in the years ahead.

A familiar female voice broke his reverie. Bitching Betty – the pilot's nickname for the warning system – spoke when the computer detected an emergency requiring immediate action. In her calm, sultry voice, she shared the worst words in her limited vocabulary – "Engine Fire Left, Engine Fire Left."

His first reaction was disbelief, followed by a curse as he slammed the left throttle off. Jabbing the Fire Warning light, he cut fuel flow to the engine. Then he punched the fire-extinguisher button, releasing a flood of Halon gas.

He held his breath. It seemed like an eternity, but it was only seconds before the fire light extinguished. Breathing again, he saw his now single engine jet was losing airspeed rapidly. He pushed the nose down into a descent.

Kansas City Center called, "Hornet Zero Seven, we show you descending out of your assigned altitude. Say intentions."

"Center, Zero Seven, had a fire. I'm now single engine and declaring an emergency. Need to land as soon as possible."

"Zero Seven, say fuel remaining and souls on board."

"Souls on board" was standard aviation terminology, but it always gave him the creeps. "I have plenty of fuel, and it's just me. Need a vector to the nearest field with 7,000 feet of runway."

The Center Controller came back quickly. "Closest field is Kansas City, 10 degrees right of your nose, 70 miles. You're cleared direct."

He turned to the new heading and scanned his displays. The

right engine and hydraulics looked good. He had plenty of fuel, but automatically checked – 6,000 pounds. Wait ... it couldn't be that low already. As he watched, the digital indicator dropped to 5,900. It suddenly made sense. Here was the fire's source – a massive fuel leak.

He timed the drop and did a quick calculation. He was pleased he could remember how to multiply. IQ dropped as adrenaline rose, particularly, when the calculation showed only minutes of fuel remaining.

"Center, Hornet Zero Seven, looks like the fire was caused by a fuel leak. I have, maybe, 10 minutes left. Need something closer. I'll take *anything* with even 3,000 feet of runway."

The Controller, now sounding a bit more stressed, said, "Standby, Zero Seven."

Edging the throttle up, he increased his airspeed and descent. He was in a race, stuck between the proverbial rock and a hard place. With his jet hemorrhaging fuel, the last thing he wanted to do was run the remaining engine *hotter.* But it was either burn it or lose it.

"Hornet Zero Seven, there's a small airport on the outskirts of the city, 52 miles from your position. It has a 6,000-foot runway."

"I'll take it."

"Hornet Zero Seven, turn right to two-niner-five. Descend at pilot's discretion. We're clearing all traffic between you and the field. Destination weather is broken to overcast with a 1,500-foot ceiling."

He pushed the fighter into a steeper descent, accelerating to 450 knots. It was more like a dive-bombing run than a landing approach. He scanned his fuel gauge for the umpteenth time – might have just enough to make it.

Descending into the clouds, he left the heavens above – for the darkness below. As he transitioned to flying by instruments, he was thankful for his Heads-Up Display. The green flight symbols appeared to float 10 feet in front of the windscreen, allowing him to keep his eyes out of the cockpit. Referred to by fighter pilots as PFM, the technology *was* pure magic.

Betty, with no apparent concern, said, "Fuel Low, Fuel Low."

He punched through the bottom of the overcast layer,

leveling off 1,200 feet above the ground. Below the clouds, it was dark, but Approach Control had lined him up perfectly. He could see the runway lights six miles off his nose.

The Approach Controller gave him the tower frequency and added, "Good luck."

He thanked her, switched to the tower and pulled the throttle to idle to slow down. As he checked in, the tower immediately cleared him to land. He realized he didn't even know the name of the airport, but it was in the middle of suburban sprawl. Like an illuminated net, he saw an ever-expanding grid of street and house lights spread below him as far as he could see. Ahead of him were the flashing red lights of a crash truck flanking the runway.

Slowing to 250 knots, he lowered his gear and flaps. Only four miles from the runway – he was going to make it.

But as the landing gear came down, both engine fire lights illuminated. Looking up into his canopy rear-view mirrors, he saw flames clearly visible between the fighter's twin tails. Opening the landing gear doors must have pushed air into the engine bay, reigniting the fuel. His fire extinguisher was empty and the jet could explode any second. The emergency procedure for this situation was clear and simple – eject. But he was over a populated area and so close to the runway.

He coaxed his fighter. "Come on baby. We're almost there." The fire trucks would be ready to spray him down after he landed.

Less than a minute from touchdown, he felt the jet decelerate. He immediately jammed the throttle forward ... nothing! The fuel gauge said he still had 1,000 pounds of gas!

As Betty casually added, "Engine Right, Engine Right," his last engine flamed out and he realized the fire must have burned through the rest of his fuel lines.

Only two miles from the runway ... but it might as well have been two-hundred. Twenty-ton fighters made lousy gliders.

Everything began to move in slow motion. In 15 seconds, his beautiful new jet would slam into the ground, creating a fireball that would blow burning titanium and graphite across several acres. But there were too many lights below; each was someone's home, someone's life and family. The small airport was in the middle of suburbia. He couldn't eject yet.

He saw a small, dark area a half mile to his left. No lights meant no houses. The floating green symbol in his HUD projected his flight path or, in this case, impact point. He *might* have just enough altitude to glide the burning fighter into the dark area.

He banked the jet away from the runway, but as the engine spooled down, the hydraulic pressure that powered his flight controls began to falter. The fighter responded sluggishly, as if angry with him for heading away from the runway. He had to use exaggerated stick inputs to control the dying jet.

To slow his descent, he held the nose up, but the Hornet began to buffet as it approached stall speed. If it stalled, it would roll over and tumble to the ground. There were houses on each side, and under his nose was a brightly lit and occupied soccer field. He fought his instincts and pushed the stick forward, increasing his descent to maintain flying speed. As he dropped through 200 feet, Betty pointlessly shared, "Altitude, Altitude."

Like blood from a severed artery, red hydraulic fluid sprayed across the wing as the fire burned through the hydraulic lines.

Betty spoke her final words, "Flight Controls, Flight Controls."

With no hydraulics, the jet began an uncontrolled roll to the right.

He slammed the stick left, but knew it was futile. His Hornet had bled out – she was dead.

Letting go of the useless stick, he pulled the yellow and black handle between his legs.

The canopy blew off the top of the jet. Shoulder, waist and leg restraints yanked him against the seat, and with the force of several sticks of dynamite, the ejection charge detonated. His spine compressed as the seat blasted up the rails like an artillery shell. Clearing the cockpit, its rocket motors ignited, firing him into the night. His last thought – trees!

The rocket-propelled seat tried to right itself as it accelerated away from the almost inverted jet, but the angle was too great, the altitude too low. The seat ripped through the top of the forest at 150 miles an hour, breaking branches and bones. Its barometric sensor quickly deployed the parachute – which immediately shredded in the treetops. The chute's tangled shroud lines slung him against tree trunks like a puppet on the end of a string. His unconscious body finally slid to the forest floor like a battered ragdoll. Shock constricted arteries as his heart struggled against the massive internal hemorrhaging.

Less than a quarter mile away, the fighter followed its pilot into the ground. Rolling thunder echoed through the woods as the young soccer players froze in their tracks. They watched the boiling cloud of orange and white flame rise above the forest.

He opened his eyes and saw treetops silhouetted against the low clouds. Illuminated from below, the clouds had a soft orange glow – reflecting the flames from his fighter's funeral pyre. A few stars peeked through holes in the overcast sky, and, faintly, he heard sirens in the distance. Otherwise, it was the peaceful quiet of an early spring evening before the crickets awoke.

He couldn't move. Completely paralyzed, he felt nothing – no pain or physical sensation, only the metallic taste of blood.

He knew he was dying.

With surprising calm and clarity, he realized he'd had an incredible life; he'd done things most people only dreamed of.

His thoughts went to Kelly. Not just his wife; she was his best friend. He wished he could see her one more time.

Like his father, the pragmatic scientist, he didn't see sufficient evidence for the existence of a God, but he also knew lack of proof didn't prove anything. He'd soon find out.

His thoughts became less distinct and his vision began to fade. As he looked up at the stars ... his heart beat its last beat.

3

DEPART

At midnight, a dark sedan pulled up in front of a small house in a suburban neighborhood. Two Naval officers in uniform got out. Led by a Captain, they walked to the front door and rang the doorbell. A pretty, redheaded woman in a bathrobe greeted the Captain by name and invited them in. Her smile faded as she saw his expression.

Do you know what happened?

Suddenly conscious, he couldn't see or feel anything ... but remembered everything.

He heard the voice again. *Do you know what happened?*

"I waited too long to eject. I thought I was....." He couldn't hear his own voice.

You have a decision to make. Doctors can't save your body, but you can be given a new life, a new mission.

"I don't understand. Am I on life support?"

The voice ignored his question. *If you accept, you can never go back to your old life. Those you knew will believe you died.*

He had to be in bad shape. "I know I may not have long but I need to know I'm not making some kind of contract I ... I don't understand."

You will be free to act in any way you wish, but no one can ever know you're still alive ... no one.

He had a million questions but he was out of time. With death the alternative, the decision was obvious. He should feel sad or frightened, but he felt nothing, no emotion at all. It was as if he were choosing a cell phone plan.

As he said, "OK," his consciousness faded.

A flag-draped casket sat on a stand in a cemetery. Arrayed around the casket, in neat rows of folding chairs, were family and close friends. Surrounding them, and filling much of the small cemetery, was a sea of formal, white uniforms with colorful ribbons, contrasted by an equal number of dark suits and dresses.

A Navy color guard silently removed the flag from the casket and slowly, with great ceremony, folded it into a neatly tucked triangle. They handed it to a Navy Captain standing at attention. A large and imposing figure, he wore a formal dress-white uniform with a chest full of medals and ribbons. Accepting it, he slowly stepped to the widow's side. Dropping to one knee and speaking to her softly, he presented her with the flag.

As she accepted it, four F-18 fighters approached the cemetery at low altitude. They flew in a tight "V" formation, one fighter to the left of the lead aircraft, and two to the right. Just before they reached the cemetery, the second jet on the right side abruptly pulled straight up and away from the formation. The single jet flew off toward the sunset, leaving an obvious hole. Breaking the solemn silence, the "missing man" formation flew over the cemetery. The widow, stoic to this point, looked up with tears streaming down her face.

He woke up. He still couldn't see, but he could sense his own breathing and heartbeat.

He had so many questions. "You guys were able to patch me back together?" The response was immediate.

Yes.

"But why can't I see anything?"

Your body is adapting.

"Adapting to what?"

You will have enhanced abilities.

"Enhanced? What does that mean?"

Your abilities will not be unique, but they will be rare.

"How rare?"

One in one hundred million.

He repeated, "A hundred million?" Many possibilities ran through his mind, but he remembered a course he took in college given by the famous Professor Carl Sagan. Sagan introduced them to Occam's Razor. Dating back to the fourteenth century, it simply stated that all things being equal, the solution with the fewest assumptions was probably correct. He knew the state-of-the-art in robotics. There was no way. They were decades away from building a bionic "Six Million Dollar Man." Genetic science, however, had advanced to the point where it was possible to clone almost anything. No doubt, that included *human* parts. He ventured, "You're some type of ... classified agency with advanced medical technology?"

There was no response.

He was about to ask again, but wasn't sure he wanted confirmation he was a lab rat. He'd try a different approach. "What's our mission? What are we doing?"

What's the biggest threat to life on earth?

He was talking to a flippin' fortune cookie. "That's easy ... *we* are."

Silence.

"Are you talking about ... mass extinctions?" He paused. "We're facing some kind of natural disaster?"

Yes.

"What is it?"

You'll learn soon enough, but first there are some rules we must cover.

"Wait. So, the name of your agency is classified, but what do I call you?"

Whatever you wish.

Frustrated and feeling a little rebellious, he said, "When I was a kid, I pretended to have an *invisible* playmate. Called him Jesse."

Silence.

He thought it was pretty funny. Clearly they didn't. "What are the rules?"

You can never return to your old life. Your friends and family will believe you're dead and buried.

He had pushed those thoughts aside, but realized he was being told he couldn't see his wife. Slowly, he said, "My wife ... she's OK?"

It has been difficult for her, but she's strong and has moved on. Success in your new life may save hers.

"Moved on? I don't understand."

It's time for you to return and learn.

"Return to what?"

You can ask for guidance any time.

"Guidance? For what? You haven't told me what we're facing or what I'm supposed to do!" As his awareness faded, he had an ironic and terrifying thought. He had been the program manager for robotic fighters. What if he was about to become one, a biological drone ... and Jesse was his controller.

4

RE-ENTRY

A high-pitched hum penetrated his sleep. He was *so* tired; it was too much effort to swat the insect away. He tried to ignore it and stay in his warm, comfortable half-dream state, but the hum wouldn't go away. It grew louder and became more pervasive like the relentless noise of summer cicadas.

Frustrated, he finally opened his eyes – to blurry white squares. He blinked. The white squares slowly came into focus as acoustic ceiling tiles. The annoying sound clarified into a combination of electronic beeps, clicks and voices.

For a terrifying second, he couldn't remember anything, not even who he was. He felt as if he were falling, spinning out of control. He closed his eyes tightly.

After a few seconds, the spinning stopped and his memories began to filter back. He remembered. He remembered everything. He remembered that he no longer had any history, family or friends.

He opened his eyes again. In contrast to his fuzzy emotional state, his senses were razor-sharp. The lights were overly bright, colors artificially vivid. It was as if someone had maxed out the color and contrast settings on a TV. He could read the ridiculously tiny print on the needle disposal box mounted on the wall. He heard several voices outside what was obviously a hospital room, but he not only heard them, he could differentiate conversations.

"... her oxygen is 95%, but we still need to watch ..."

"... finished prepping the girl in room three for surgery ..."

"... pretty comfortable for stilettos, and they were like 50% off ..."

His vision and hearing were extremely sensitive, almost overwhelming. He propped himself up on his right elbow and immediately felt dizzy and queasy, reminiscent of the alcohol-induced spins following a good squadron party. His body responded to commands, but sluggishly, as if he'd had a head-to-toe Novocain injection. Lifting his left hand, he saw an IV attached. He turned his hand over and examined it.

"Look familiar?"

Startled, he looked up to see a woman in blue scrubs standing in the doorway. She watched him for a moment and then entered the room, looking concerned.

He finally realized her comment had been in jest, and he must look like a deer-in-the-headlights. He asked the obvious. "Where am I?" It came out as a raspy whisper.

Looking relieved, she said, "You're at Kansas City Medical Center. How are you feeling?"

He was in a public hospital? His voice was still hoarse but getting stronger. "What day is it?"

Pointing at a large digital clock and calendar on the wall, she said, "Monday, March 23rd."

It had only been a few days since the crash. But as he looked at the calendar display closer, he blinked. That couldn't be! It was a few days ... and one year! What happened? Where was Jesse or his team?

Again, she asked, "How are you feeling?"

"Huh?"

"Are you in any pain?"

Frowning, he finally looked back at his nurse, really seeing her for the first time. She was early thirties, athletically slim and attractive with dark eyes and blondish hair. Shaking his head, he said, "No." He cleared his throat. "I'm just a little ...."

"Disoriented?" she finished.

He nodded. As his voice grew stronger, it became stranger. His inflections and accent were the same, but his voice sounded ... different.

"That's understandable. You've been unconscious for a few days. What's your name?"

That was a good question. For some reason, he was on his own right now. He needed time to figure out what was happening. The best answer was probably closest to the truth. He cocked his head to one side and said, "I'm ... I'm not sure."

With a professional smile, she said, "Well, I'm Elizabeth, your ICU nurse." She spoke slowly, as if he were a child. "Don't worry, we'll figure out what yours is." She patted him on the shoulder. "Probably just temporary amnesia. I'm going to let your doctor know you're awake. Be right back."

After she left, he wanted to get to a bathroom mirror. He lifted his sheet and discovered that in addition to the IV, he was tethered with EKG leads and a catheter. He wasn't going anywhere.

His nurse returned almost immediately with a doctor in tow.

"I'm Dr. Tracy Dutton, your Neurologist."

He gave her a small smile. "Hi, I guess I'm ... not sure."

"How are you feeling?"

"Fine."

"Do you hurt anywhere?"

"No."

"Do you know what happened to you?"

"No." That was the truth.

"Do you know where you are?"

He nodded toward his nurse. "She said I'm in Kansas." He frowned. "How did I get here?"

The doctor exchanged a quick glance with the nurse. "A few days ago you were found by the side of the road without any clothes." Continuing, she asked, "Do you know if you're allergic to anything?"

He looked down. That didn't make any sense at all. Why would they leave him like that? He frowned shaking his head. Where were they? Where had *he* been for the past year?

Looking back up, he said, "I'm ... I'm sorry. What did you say?"

He saw compassion on the nurse's face as the doctor slowly repeated the question.

He replied, "Allergies? I ... I don't know."

With a slight frown the doctor said, "I'm going to check a few things, OK?"

He nodded dumbly.

She shined a penlight into each eye and asked him to watch her fingertips as they moved. She had him move his hands and feet, squeeze her fingers, and then tapped him on the knee. Pulling up a chair, she asked, "Can you remember anything at all from your past?"

He was hungry. "I like hamburgers."

She smiled. "We'll have food sent up right away."

Trying to avoid more questions, he pointed to his IV. "May I get ... unhooked?"

"Now that you're awake, I don't see why not. Elizabeth will take care of that."

She asked a few more questions, made some notes and left.

—✻—

Elizabeth followed Dr. Dutton into the hall. Once outside the room, Dutton spoke quietly. "He checks out OK, but the amnesia worries me. Keep an eye on him."

Elizabeth nodded. She'd been thinking the same.

Returning to his room, she said, "Let's get you mobile." She put on latex gloves and pulled a cart over. "We'll start with the IV."

He nodded, looked down at the needle in his arm and then looked away.

Why were men so squeamish when it came to blood and needles? While he carefully studied the wall, she studied him. He had short, curly, dark hair with unusual, almost red, highlights. A strong jaw gave him a good masculine face, very handsome but approachable.

Finishing with a Band-Aid, she said, "That takes care of the IV. Now, we'll remove your EKG leads."

He looked back at her with some relief and smiled. His eyes were gray – no, actually, they were a color she'd never seen. They looked as though someone had mixed all the eye colors in a blender, sort of a steel-gray with flecks of brown, green, and blue mixed in, beautiful and intense.

She opened the top of his gown and pulled the EKG leads off his chest, remembering how surprised she was that he had no scars. After arriving without an identity, they checked every square inch of his body for identifying marks. His skin was perfect. It wouldn't have been out of place on a child, but even children usually had scars. He didn't even have any dental work. "Just one more thing and you'll be free." She knew removing the urinary catheter was going to be uncomfortable and awkward. Distracting him, she said, "I don't know if you are ... or were, into tech stuff, but everyone's talking about the new app that's being released by iMagination tomorrow. It's supposed to work on any device and across every operating system."

Grimacing, with one eye closed, he asked, "What does it do?"

She continued casually, "Everything. It's supposed to be the ultimate personal digital assistant and eclipse Siri." She smiled. "It combines GPS, calendar, language translator, video phone, search engine, practically every app ever invented into one seamless program." She shrugged. "Kind of the mother of all apps."

Clenching the bedrail, he whispered, "Expensive?"

"They're offering it for free ... at least for now. I'm sure once we're all addicted to it, they'll charge for upgrades, like everything else."

As she finished and cleaned him up, she thought he definitely had the body of a professional athlete. He could have been Michelangelo's model for *David*, except David wasn't quite as buff ... in some areas. "OK, we're done."

He nodded without making eye contact.

"I'll put in an order for some food. Other than hamburgers, is there anything else you'd like?"

He shook his head.

Pulling her gloves off, she said, "I'll be right back." Despite her reassurance, amnesia was *not* common, particularly with no sign of trauma. She had watched his face when he'd learned how they'd found him. He'd been genuinely surprised and confused. She tried to imagine what it would be like to lose her identity. Her heart went out to him. An amnesiac with perfect health, the body of an athlete, and no identifying marks or history, he was the most *interesting* case she'd ever seen.

As she left, he let out a relieved sigh. *That* was uncomfortable and made more so because she was a beautiful woman. Making sure no one was around, he slid his feet to the floor. Standing up slowly, a wave of vertigo swept through him. He steadied himself against the bed rail, waiting until it passed. Then, carefully, he let go of the rail and stretched. He actually felt remarkably well. The little ache he'd always had in his back from soccer and karate tournaments wasn't there. His right knee, hurt in a hard skydiving landing, didn't twinge at all. In fact, he felt better than he could remember. He navigated carefully into the small bathroom, closed the door and went straight to the mirror over the sink.

He froze.

Someone else stared back. He actually tilted his head to prove it was really him. He wasn't sure what he'd expected ... but not this. They'd *totally* altered his appearance. Only his six-foot-plus height remained. His skin was a perfect tan, right between the whitest white guy and the blackest black guy. The face in the mirror was no super model, but he'd definitely traded up and looked a few years younger, mid-thirties.

He pulled his hospital gown off and studied his upper body in the mirror. Wow. He'd always played sports, but now he looked like an Olympic athlete. He didn't have huge, bulging muscles, but they were well developed and proportioned with little body fat. If he hadn't seen his face, he'd swear his body belonged to a twenty-year-old. The small mirror only reflected the top half of him. He stepped back and looked down.

Involuntarily, he exclaimed, "Oh, my God!"

He wasn't circumcised anymore! For some reason, this was the biggest shock of all.

There was a loud knock at the door. Elizabeth's voice asked, "Are you alright? Do you need help?"

"Ah ... no. Everything's fine ... in here ... thank you."

"Alright."

Looking back in the mirror, he quietly asked himself, "Why ... would they have reversed...?"

The truth finally sank in. Glancing at his hand as he flexed his fingers, he said quietly, "They didn't *enhance* your body ... they *replaced* it." He frowned. "That's not possible. Even if you cloned a human body, you can't just stuff someone's consciousness into it." He looked back at the mirror. "Can you?"

The answer frowned back at him.

Stepping closer to the mirror and leaning forward, he carefully studied the shape of his eyes, nose and cheekbones. He examined his skin color, hair, and the proportions of his body. He shook his head as if to knock the thought loose, but the evidence was there. Into the mirror, he said, "You, my friend, look like you have a grandparent from every continent." He frowned and added, "Jesse and friends clearly don't have any ethical issues with creating a genetic Frankenstein."

He put his hospital gown back on but looked back in the mirror one more time. With a slight headshake, he said to his reflection, "If they're this cavalier about *creation* ... how concerned might they be about *termination?*"

5

IDENTIFY

Elizabeth grabbed a quick lunch in the cafeteria with two other nurses.

Between mouthfuls, a young nurse named Leslee Wong, asked Elizabeth, "So? What do you think?"

"About what?"

"How many mysterious John Doe patients do we have?"

Elizabeth shrugged. "He seems pretty normal."

"And very cute." Frowning, Leslee asked, "Think he was abducted by aliens?"

Lesia Rabb, a beautiful Queen Latifah look-a-like, and the ICU Charge Nurse, laughed. "More like a brainwashed government agent."

"My mom doesn't care who I marry, but Dad insists on a nice Chinese guy." Staring at the ceiling, Leslee added, "But I bet I could get a guy like this by him."

Lesia shook her head and winked at Elizabeth. "Sorry Leslee, he's clearly a brother, with some mixed blood. If no one claims him, I may have to take him home and train him."

"But you're married," Leslee said with a sincere frown.

"Oh yeah."

Elizabeth smiled. She wasn't surprised they found him attractive, but she *was* surprised that each assumed he was primarily of her race. She too had assumed he was Caucasian with some mixed ancestry.

Walking back to the unit with Lesia, Elizabeth said, "He really is a fascinating mixture, isn't he? It adds to the mystery and makes him – the case – very interesting."

Lesia looked at her with raised eyebrows and a slight smile.

He sat up in his bed with his arms crossed staring at the wall, thinking. His appearance actually made a weird kind of sense. They improved food crops and livestock by combining different genetic lines. If you were trying to cull the best attributes from the population – the one in a hundred million abilities Jesse mentioned – you'd have to pull genes from every race. His old body had already been a combination of French, English and Irish with African and Native American in the mix, but now he was sure he was all that and more. If nothing else, he'd have fun filling out the forms that ask for ethnic background.

He looked up as Elizabeth came into his room.

"Remember anything?"

"Nothing new."

As she took his vital signs, she said softly, "John Doe is a bit impersonal. Is there something you'd like us to call you?"

To be on the safe side, he decided to use his middle name, Joshua. When he was young, his mother called him Josh almost exclusively.

"Uh ... *Josh* sounds familiar."

"Josh it is."

Seeing the needle in her hand, he asked, "Think they'll run out of things to test before I run out of blood?"

She shrugged with a smile. "It's possible."

He wasn't going to watch her draw blood, so he studied her. With a cute, dimpled smile, she had the proverbial girl-next-door beauty, mixed with exotic, dark eyes. About five-foot-nine, she looked like a natural blonde, but with a surprisingly dark olive complexion. It was hard to tell with scrubs, but she looked like she had a trim, athletic body with curves in the right places. She also carried herself with confidence, which he always found attractive. As she pulled her gloves off, he saw a wedding ring.

Finishing up, she said, "All the tests so far indicate you're in exceptionally good health." She leaned over conspiratorially. "In fact, better health than all of the hospital staff."

He nodded but his eyes unfocused as he thought, *Great. I have an enhanced body, and I'm sitting on its butt.* He had to get out of here.

Misinterpreting his expression, she said, "It must be awful to lose your identity."

He smiled. "Probably somewhere between losing your mind and your car keys."

She laughed.

"So what's the staff's theory on me?"

"Oh, you *don't* want to know."

"I could use some humor right now."

She raised one eyebrow. "You sure?"

"Please."

"Well ... let's see. You were in a witness protection program that went bad. You were a troublesome CIA agent whose memory was erased. Hmmm ... oh yeah, you're a secret sleeper agent planted by a foreign country."

Laughing, he asked, "How'd they come up with that one?"

"Well, you have a nice mocha complexion," she smiled, "and you're not ..." She suddenly appeared uncomfortable. "I mean you're ..." She blushed.

He wanted to help but had no idea where she was going.

Finally, she blurted out, "You're not circumcised."

It was his turn to blush.

Continuing quickly, she said, "You were unconscious for several days. You got a lot of attention because of the mystery and, of course, the nursing staff knows what you look like in your birthday suit."

He had unconsciously pulled his bed sheet up.

Clearly suppressing a laugh, she added, "Sorry ... TMI." Saving him from further embarrassment, she continued, "The other ideas go from being neuralized by the "**Men In Black**" to alien abduction and clone experiments."

He laughed, but then stopped. He realized the last one might actually be correct.

She looked at him curiously. "You OK?"

With complete honesty, he said, "I'm sorry. The ideas really are funny, but I realized I can't be sure that one of them might not be true." Quickly changing the subject, he asked, "What about you Elizabeth? Where are you from?"

"Oh, we don't need to talk about me."

"Well ... right now, we can't really talk about where I'm from."

She gave him a touché smile and said, "I was born in Austin,

Texas, the oldest of several brothers and sisters. My childhood was good, if a little boring."

"Why did you go into nursing?"

"I actually started out as a computer major. My dad had a computer repair business, and I spent hours on his lap learning from him. Loved helping people with their computer problems, but realized most computer jobs don't interact with people. I like helping people directly, so I tried nursing. Love it."

"Miss computers?"

"No, I still help my friends with them and like to play with the latest tech."

"Kids?"

She looked down and said softly, "No." She paused. "I ... I was married for a few months, but he died in a motorcycle accident."

"I'm so sorry."

"It's been over a year. I don't think about it much anymore." She paused. "I'd better get on with my rounds."

Not wanting her to leave on that note, he read her nametag, and asked, "Is Edvardsen Scandinavian?"

"Yes, it's my maiden name."

"That would explain the blonde hair but...."

"Yeah, I know." She laughed. "The skin and eyes don't match. I think I have some relatives from India."

"Well, the combination works beautifully."

She smiled. "Thanks. I need to get back to work. Is there anything I can do for you?"

"You already have."

They locked eyes for a fraction of a second and then she said, "They'll be moving you out of ICU soon, but I'll check-in with you before then."

As Elizabeth updated his chart on the computer in the hall, she thought, he was a nice guy, good sense of humor and easy to talk to. The bad news was that there was something seriously wrong with his brain, or ... he was hiding something, something bad enough he'd be willing to give up his identity. In either case, he'd make a lousy romantic interest. She shook her head. *Now where did that come from? Probably just Florence Nightingale syndrome*

... but her intuition told her there was something else.

As she walked down the hall, she saw Dr. Dutton talking to the hospital administrator, Ned Brockmeyer. Hearing him ask about their John Doe, she joined them.

Dutton was saying, "We ran the entire alphabet soup of tests: CT, MRI, EEG, etc. They all came back normal." She corrected herself. "No, actually, they all came back perfect."

Brockmeyer smiled. "Hope his insurance is equally healthy. Have the police identified him yet?"

Dutton shook her head. "No. His fingerprints haven't turned up anything. They're checking DNA."

Brockmeyer frowned. "Great, that means a huge diagnostic bill and no insurance."

"The next step is to bring in a psychiatrist," Dutton added. "Severe emotional trauma can also cause amnesia."

"A psychiatrist?" Brockmeyer shook his head sharply. "Absolutely not! That's just more charges we'll never get reimbursed for. He's taking up a bed that could be used by ... other patients."

Elizabeth knew Brockmeyer meant "insured" patients. The rumor was that Brockmeyer modeled himself after Donald Trump. Looking down on his comb-over hair, he looked like a Trump mini-me, except he was shorter, balder and less sensitive.

Dutton nodded in agreement. "You're right of course." Looking thoughtful, she asked, "If he turned out to be some kind of terrorist, the hospital wouldn't be held liable ... would we?"

Brockmeyer frowned and with an exaggerated sigh, he said, "OK, we can have a shrink check him out, but I want you to make sure Homeland Security is involved. If he turns out to be dangerous," he smiled unpleasantly, "it'll be their problem."

As Brockmeyer scurried off, Dutton winked at Elizabeth.

Josh devoured the food they brought up. There were no TVs in ICU and he'd already figured out all the controls on the automated bed. He was playing with the blood pressure monitor when Elizabeth returned. She was a welcome diversion even though he suspected she was just going to draw more blood.

With a smile, she started, "Good news, since all your tests are negative, they're bringing in a mind specialist."

He frowned. "A psychiatrist?"

"Well, yeah, but it's Dr. Sheri Lopez!"

He looked at her blankly.

"Sorry. She's a well-known psychiatrist and bestselling author. She even had her own daytime TV talk show. You don't recognize the name at all?"

"No." He honestly didn't, but he'd never watched much TV.

"She'll be in tomorrow morning."

He nodded, wondering if a psychiatrist would see through his amnesia claim.

"They're moving you to a regular room in a few hours."

He'd no longer be under Elizabeth's care and probably wouldn't see her again. She was the closest thing he had to a friend. "Thanks. Thanks for taking care of me."

She smiled. "You're a lot noisier than most of my Neuro patients." Winking, she added, "I'll check in on you after you're relocated."

After they moved him to a regular hospital room and found him a bathrobe, he watched the news networks. Interspersed between the moral and legal tribulations of celebrities, he tried to pick up a little information about his missing year. He also discovered his new body needed only a few hours of sleep.

Jesse indicated they'd given him the ability to communicate at any time. He had no idea how, but with their obviously advanced medical technology, some type of communication implant was possible. It was late at night and the nurse had made her rounds.

He made sure no one was outside in the hall. Feeling stupid, like trying to make a phone call without a phone, he said, "Jesse, this is ...." He stopped, realizing he wasn't even sure what to call himself anymore. Since it felt like he was talking on a radio, he decided to use his call sign. "Jesse, this is Fuzed, over. Can you read me?" He tried one more time.

Then he shook his head, realizing how ridiculous it was. He knew no one was going to answer him. They'd probably contact him after he was released from the hospital. He had to get out ... but not in a bathrobe.

6

PSYCH

Early the next morning, a woman entered his room. Petite and professional, she had black hair, a nice tan and dark, penetrating eyes. With a stylish sports jacket and silk blouse, he suspected her clothes weren't from Wal-Mart. As he shook her hand, the diamond encrusted Rolex confirmed it.

"Hi, I'm Dr. Sheri Lopez."

He nodded. "So far, I'm Josh. Glad to meet you, Dr. Lopez."

"Call me Sheri." She paused. "Do you think that's really your name?"

He'd never been a good liar. The best strategy was to stay as close to the truth as possible.

"It feels familiar."

She nodded. "I've reviewed your medical tests. There's no indication of disease or physical trauma. In fact, you appear to be exceptionally healthy. There could be some hidden trauma or drug causing this, but retrograde amnesia also occurs from traumatic emotional events."

He just nodded.

"I'd like to give you some psychological tests and see where that takes us."

He had no grounds to say no. "Sure."

He spent the rest of the morning taking written, verbal and visual tests. Since none of the questions referred to his past, he answered honestly.

She finished up and said, "I'll be back in the afternoon with the results."

Intelligent and confident, it was clear to him why she was successful. What wasn't clear was why a celebrity psychologist was involved in a John Doe case.

At lunchtime, Elizabeth dropped by carrying a small bag. "Found some of the books you were looking for."

He smiled. "Thank you. You and the rest of the staff have been amazing."

"Yeah, well, when they release you, they'll present you with an *amazing* bill." She gave him a mischievous smile. "Your amnesia might come in handy." Looking more serious, she asked, "Do you know what you're going to do when you get out?"

He was sure Jesse's team would contact him, but it wouldn't hurt to have a backup plan. "Guess I'm going to need a job."

She nodded. "I did a little checking around. There's an opening in the hospital ... well hospital grounds maintenance. With your vocabulary, you probably have advanced education..."

He interrupted, "I have no known education, skills or references. Working outside would be perfect, in case I turn out to be a lunatic."

Laughing, she said, "You do have references. You were friendly and kind to everyone here. If most of us were in your shoes ... well, it speaks a lot for your character."

He couldn't help but notice her eyes smiled when she did.

She bit the side of her lip and asked, "Do you have a place to stay?"

He shook his head.

Looking at the floor, she said, "Because, I suppose, well, I mean ... look, I have a, uh, guest bedroom in my condo ... I mean just until you get on your feet." She knocked a plastic cup off his bedside table with the book bag. Bending over to pick it up, she dropped one of the books. As she stood up, he saw she was blushing. She suddenly looked very vulnerable and *very* beautiful.

He smiled. "That's the best offer I remember getting in my entire life." That broke the tension, and he added, "That's incredibly kind but the hospital staff would warn against it, and they'd be right. I can't even vouch for me."

With a challenging smile, she said, "It's a three-bedroom condo, I have another roommate and I'm a Texas girl, armed and dangerous."

Before he could reply, she set the books on the table and turned to go. As she left, she glanced back and said, "I'll bring you that job application."

A couple hours later, Lopez returned. "Any new memories?"

He shook his head.

She sat down in the chair next to him. "I've gone through your test results."

Setting the book he was reading aside, he nodded.

"They suggest you're very intelligent." She glanced at the paper in her hand. "You have an IQ *over* 160, and the tests indicate you're emotionally stable." She paused. "There was a slightly elevated sense of paranoia ... but that's probably not unusual in your situation." She continued, "If you were applying for a high-level federal job, you'd be accepted based on these results. You're very healthy in every area, including most aspects of your memory ... except for your identity."

She stopped and looked at him closely.

Was her comment about federal jobs on purpose? Was she connected to Jesse? He matched eye contact but said nothing.

When it was apparent she would say no more, he said, "Thank you for working with me." Fishing, he added, "With your reputation, and going along with my *elevated* sense of paranoia, am I just an interesting ... case?"

She smiled. "As they say, just because you're paranoid, doesn't mean everyone isn't out to get you." It morphed into a professional smile as she added, "Of course, that's not the case."

She glanced at the book next to his bed, and he saw recognition on her face as she realized it was her book.

Shaking her head with a wry smile, she added, "*As you know,* my area of expertise is mass psychology, and you never know when a case might make a good book." She paused, and looking serious, added, "There's one thing left to try. I'd like to put you under hypnosis."

He couldn't risk it. Narrowing his eyes, he shook his head. "Doc ... I gotta tell you, hypnosis gives me the creeps. I'd really rather not."

"I really think it could help." She waited.

He said nothing.

She shrugged. "I'm sorry ... then there's really nothing else I can do for you."

She stood up, and he stood up with her. As they shook hands, she said, "If you change your mind, I'd be happy to work with you." She gave him her business card.

Cocking his head slightly, he asked, "If you don't mind my asking, what's your theory on my situation?"

Frowning, she answered slowly, "I don't know. I know you didn't just get a bump on the head, but I suspect your situation isn't of your own doing." With a raised eyebrow, she added, "At least not entirely."

He believed she was telling the truth, but – like him – only part of it.

Right after Lopez left, Elizabeth knocked on his door. She came in with a large, white, plastic trash bag and some papers. "The staff brought in some clothes that might fit."

"Thank you."

"And here's the job application, but I already talked to the maintenance department head. You start first thing tomorrow."

"Tomorrow? How'd you pull that off?"

"They were shorthanded and just had someone quit."

"But I have no references or records."

She smiled. "I pointed out that *also* meant you have no criminal record." She shrugged. "And he's a friend."

"Thank you."

She smiled and looked at her watch. "Gotta run."

After she left, he went to the bathroom and tried on the clothes. Some were obviously new. He suspected Elizabeth had bought them. He was certain of it when he found $100 in the pocket. He'd make it up to her.

As he came out of the bathroom, an older nurse presented him with the release paperwork.

He signed the paperwork, including a promise to pay. Looking at the wheelchair she brought with her, he shook his head. "I won't need that."

"Hospital policy for all patients upon departure," she said flatly. She dismissed all his arguments with a will of iron.

Finally, he took his white plastic bag full of his worldly possessions, sucked in his ego and slid into the wheelchair. Pushed down the hall by a woman twice his age, he said quietly, "And the warrior charges forth to save the world."

7

SCHIZOPHRENIA

Outside, it was a cold overcast day. His highly attuned senses amplified the sights, sounds and sensations. He savored the cold breeze on his face and the simple sounds of the streets. He looked around expecting someone from Jesse's team to pick him up. After 30 minutes, he decided to go for a walk. Maybe they didn't want to contact him near the hospital.

He set off toward the downtown part of the city. Having seen a map of the area at the information desk, he realized he could still see it in his head. Apparently, he now had a photographic memory.

As he walked, he had a subtle sensation that he was being watched. At any moment, he expected a car to pull up and take him to Jesse.

Two hours later, he was still walking. He was clearly on his own for now. Not only was he homeless but, without any identification, he was technically an illegal alien. Time for plan B.

He found a discount store and bought a simple duffel bag and basic toiletries. To stretch his money, he ate the cheapest fast food.

It was late. He found a comfortable chair in a nice hotel lobby. Fortunate not to look like the homeless person he was, he caught a few hours of sleep.

Early the next morning, he shaved in the hotel lobby bathroom and walked back to the hospital.

As Elizabeth promised, they started him working immediately. His job consisted mostly of grounds work. Because it was spring, he did a lot of mulching and watering, which he actually enjoyed. If the world didn't end, he might like a garden someday. He continued to expect contact at any moment but there was nothing.

The hospital had an area with computers that patients and visitors could use. Employees weren't supposed to use them, but the woman in charge knew of his situation and looked the other way.

First, he searched all the social media sites for his wife Kelly. She had been a Facebook fiend, so he was surprised when he found no sign of her there or anywhere else. That concerned him. Next, he checked the news to see if there were any potentially cataclysmic, natural disasters facing humanity. Again, he found nothing beyond the usual issues. Frustrated, he decided to take another walk around the city after work. He was still certain someone would contact him or he'd catch sight of his watchers.

Over the next three days, he slept where he could, often in the hospital waiting rooms. Every evening after work, he tried to get a few minutes on the computer. Then he'd walk the city streets, continuing to feel as if he were being watched. As his cash dwindled, his frustration and confusion grew.

His fourth night out in the city, he thought he had identified one of his watchers. He was sick of being the mouse. He darted around a corner into an alley. Hiding behind a dumpster, he waited. After a minute, he heard a car stop at the entrance to the alley. He jumped out from behind the dumpster and ran toward the car. It was a black sedan with tinted windows. As he approached, it pulled out with a squeal of tires. Angry and pumped up with adrenaline, he pursued on foot. He knew he was running faster than he'd ever run in his previous life. He actually caught up to it as it stopped at a light, but as he got closer, it ran the red light and accelerated away. He was fast, but he was no bionic man and no competition for the Ford.

His frustration and confusion turned to depression. It had been almost a week. The time with Jesse and even his previous life began to feel unreal. It was like waking up after a particularly vivid dream. His memories remained clear, and yet, every morning he shaved someone else's face. What if the face in the mirror was real, but his memories were illusions. With no confirmation of Jesse or his past existence, he began to question his sanity.

He used the hospital computer to Google mental illnesses. On the Mayo Clinic site, he read the symptoms of Paranoid Schizophrenia – "Hallucinations and voices, often focused on the perception that the individual is being singled out for harm. They may believe that the government is monitoring every move they make. It is often accompanied by delusions of grandeur. The delusional conviction of their own importance, power, or knowledge, or that they have a special relationship with a famous person or deity." That pretty well summed up his situation.

He had to find something to verify his sanity. He remembered his wife's email and phone number. Ignoring Jesse's warning, he tried to email her, but it bounced back. He used a hospital phone to call her, but got, "You have reached a non-working number." It was as though she'd never existed.

It was three in the morning. The waiting room he often slept in was empty. He went to one of the hospital's family bathrooms, locked the door and splashed water on his face. Occam's Razor said the solution with the fewest assumptions was probably correct. Looking in the mirror, he quietly asked himself, "Which is more likely? A – I'm a test pilot, brought back from the dead by a voice in my head to save the world. Or ... B – I'm a fruitcake with raisins for eyes."

He sighed and shook his head. Still a couple days from his first paycheck, his $100 was gone. He was penniless, hungry, depressed and ... probably insane. His memories, even his appearance, might be just another delusion. He felt like the little Russian dolls that nested inside each other. Split one in half, and inside was another identical but smaller doll, inside that another, and another. He was afraid inside the last doll ... there would be nothing.

There was one chair in the bathroom. He sat in the Thinking Man pose, staring at the beige industrial tiles on the wall. He softly said to no one. "I was a Navy Commander, a test pilot, a husband ... wasn't I?" He looked down at his dim shadow cast on the nondescript linoleum at his feet. He felt like he was perched on the edge of a greasy, black pool of insanity. It would be so easy ... to let go and slip in. He slid off the chair onto his knees. With his elbows resting on his thighs, he bent over, head in hands.

Softly, he said, "My God, I can't live like this."

After a few seconds, he closed his eyes and slid toward the black pool.

Josh.

Josh.

It finally registered. He bolted upright, looking around he sputtered, "Jesse! Jesse, is that you?"

Yes.

He stood up and automatically put his finger to his ear as he realized Jesse's voice must be coming from an implant. He said, "Thank God you're talking to me again! I was convinced I was completely insane and you were nothing but a delusion!" His relief was short lived and turned to anger. "Where the hell have you been? Why'd you dump me on the road with no clothes?!" He started pacing. "What kind of Mickey Mouse operation is this?!"

He shook his head. "What if ... what if I just decide to ignore you?" He couldn't sit by and watch the world die, but the rebel in him had to know he wasn't just some type of biological drone.

That's your choice.

He heard the relaxed voice of a patient teacher. After several deep breaths, his anger subsided and he sighed. "I'm ... I'm sorry. I know you were probably trying to give me time to adapt, but this transition has been tougher than I thought."

He took another deep breath and finally said, "OK ... now what?"

First, you must know what you face.

"Yes ... I still have *no* idea why I'm here."

What destroys the most life?

"I've been thinking about that. Most mass extinctions were caused by volcanoes and asteroid impacts, but they're very rare."

Rare?

"There haven't been any big ones in recorded history." He stopped, realizing the absurdity of his statement. With a laugh, he added, "Guess, by definition, recorded history would start after one." He paused. "But we haven't had any major impacts in thousands of years."

On Earth.

Confused, he repeated, "On Earth?" Then tentatively asked, "Impacts on *other* planets?" He thought for a moment. "Comet

Shoemaker-Levy hit Jupiter when I was a kid. I also remember reading that the probability of dying from an asteroid impact is higher than being killed in a plane crash." With a wry smile, he added, "Not good – been there done that."

What would happen if a comet struck Earth?

He had a passion for astronomy and with his new abilities could recall anything he'd ever read. "A Shoemaker-Levy sized comet could kill billions."

Two years.

"Two years?! To an impact?"

Yes.

He just stood there, as it sunk in. Finally, he asked, "What part do I play?"

Adapt and learn all you can.

That wasn't what he wanted to hear. Sensing the conversation was over he said, "Wait ... how do I contact you?"

Talk to me.

Frowning, he said, "I was thinking more like an 800 number." Unconsciously, he put his hand to his ear and said, "That's creepy on several levels." He paused. "Hey, what about the guys you assigned to watch me?"

No one was assigned to watch you.

He frowned again. Slowly, he said, "Look, I understand why this is covert and hasn't been released to the public, but someone *is* watching me. If it's not your people, you may want to find out who they are."

There was no response.

He sighed and shook his head. "OK, so, when do I meet the rest of the team?"

When you're ready.

It was clear the conversation was over. One of the black programs he'd worked with had been building insect-sized drones. Needing more power than batteries could supply, they had been trying to scale-down the nuclear power source used on deep-space probes. Looking in the bathroom mirror, he put his hand to his ear again. The possibility of having plutonium in his head wasn't exciting.

Then he had another thought. He asked his reflection, "If they implanted you with a communication device ... what else might you be carrying?" Robotic fighters were always outfitted with self-destruct mechanisms. He said softly, "*Click* – rogue operative suffers fatal aneurism?"

8

FUZE

He finally received his first paycheck. It wasn't much more than minimum wage, and they were *conveniently* deducting a portion of his hospital bill. It was barely enough to cover basic needs – food and a phone with Internet access. He wasn't sure what Jesse meant by "adapting" but they were clearly leaving him on his own for now, and he needed to maintain his cover for whoever was watching him.

He never realized how important an identity was, until he didn't have one. With no birth certificate or Social Security number, he was an illegal alien. He smiled. But where would they deport him?

The first step was to open a bank account.

The bank clerk asked, "What's your name?"

He couldn't use his real last name. All he could think of was his old call sign. He coughed and said, "Josh, uh Josh *Fuze*."

"How do you spell that?"

"J O S H."

She shook her head. "No, I mean your last name."

"Uh, F U Z E." He wasn't even sure it was a real last name, but it was definitely appropriate. His body was clearly a *fusion* of genes from every race. With a slight smile, he realized he was GMO, but his smile faded as another image appeared in his head. It was the mechanical *fuze* on a bomb – counting down to Armageddon.

The driver's license was more difficult, but one of his fellow employees from El Salvador helped him with a "workaround."

He spent all his free time online. There was nothing about a new comet, but he plowed through everything he could find on Near Earth Objects, orbital mechanics *and* ... abnormal psychology. He was painfully aware that with Jesse still nothing more than a voice in his head, *crazy* was still a viable explanation.

He shook his head and said quietly to himself, "Insanity is preferable to a reality involving a million-megaton impact." He sighed. "But until they put me in a padded cell...."

He needed help. Clearly, Jesse wasn't ready to bring him in yet and trying to do serious research on his phone wasn't sufficient. Elizabeth was into computers. Maybe she had an old laptop he could borrow. Regardless, he owed her and could use a friend right now.

After work, he went up to Neuro ICU. One of the nurses pointed him in the right direction.

He saw her in the hall. "Hi, Elizabeth. I want to thank you for everything you did for me. Got my first paycheck and was wondering if I might be able to take you out to lunch or something ... some time ... I mean if you're not busy ..."

Before he could stumble through, she said with a smile, "Sure, my place for dinner, say seven?" She wrote her address and number on a small piece of paper, handed it to him and said, "Gotta go."

As she turned and left, he smiled like a teenager who successfully invited a date to the prom.

———✳———

As Elizabeth walked down the hall, Lesia, who'd overheard the conversation, fell in alongside. Elizabeth glanced sideways at her friend.

Lesia said nothing but raised her eyebrows in question as they walked.

Elizabeth said, "I'm just curious. Everyone loves a good mystery."

Lesia's expression didn't change.

"It's not like it's a date. I just didn't want him to spend money on an expensive restaurant." Seeing Lesia wasn't buying it, she stopped and turned to her. "Look, I've been around him enough to know he's a good guy."

Shaking her head, Lesia said, "Honey, *he* doesn't even know if he's a good guy." She softened. "He probably is, but did it ever occur to you that whatever happened to him might have been *intentional*, and whoever did it might still be around?"

Elizabeth sighed and shook her head.

"Elizabeth, it's so good to see you taking an interest in men again. It's *long* overdue and he's cute as a bug, but you know you shouldn't have invited him to your place on a first date."

Elizabeth started to protest about the date, but saw the "don't even go there" look.

Lesia took one of her hands. "Sweetie, I'll tell you what. I'll just happen to be in your neighborhood around seven. I'll call. If you don't answer and say, 'Lesia, you're the best,' you'll have extra dinner guests."

Elizabeth hugged her and said, "You *are* the best."

"Josh Fuze. Josh Fuze." he repeated it several times, trying to get used to his new identity. "Josh" was easy; "Fuze" took some getting used to.

As an amnesiac, his dinner conversation topics would be limited, so he surfed the Internet for "Year in Review" articles. He discovered the world was wound tighter than when he left. Dozens of countries were involved in military actions, standoffs or rising tensions. Terrorism continued to pop up like metastasizing cancer cells. The only bright spot was a European Union Vice-President from Turkey named Doruk Turan. Turan was apparently having success in ridding Europe of terrorism, but the rest of the world wasn't getting better. He shook his head. He had doubts about whether the human race could survive even without a comet.

Elizabeth's condo was only a few miles away. As he walked there, it was getting dark and there were few people on the streets. Looking around to make sure no one was near, he used proper radio etiquette, and quietly said, "Jesse, Josh, can you read me, over?" He immediately received a reply.

"Jesse, I'm maintaining my cover, learning as much as I can, and playing nice with the other kids. How much longer before you bring me into the team?"

What have you learned?

"The impact threat's well documented." He shook his head, adding, "We've known about this risk for decades, and we've been playing Russian Roulette." He paused. "I'm also surprised how many people think the world would be better off without a dangerous species like us." He smiled. "Crazy, but it does make you wonder about us sometimes, doesn't it?"

What is the most powerful force in the universe?

He shook his head with a smile. "Back to fortune cookies." He took a deep breath. "Well ... in physics, the Strong Nuclear Force is hundreds of times stronger than gravity. Guess that's why they call it the strong force."

What does it do?

"Holds atoms together."

Can it organize itself?

"Uh ... no."

Can it organize its environment?

"No."

Can it replicate?

"Of course not. You're talking about *life*, aren't you?" He thought for a moment. "The Strong Force holds atoms together, but *life* actually organizes them, grows and reproduces. I understand where you're going, but it's kind of an apples-to-oranges comparison, isn't it?"

How many planets in the solar system have life?

"We don't know. Aside from Earth, Mars probably had microbial life. A couple of Jupiter's and Saturn's moons are possibilities."

How common is the Strong Nuclear Force?

"Uh ... universal."

How common is life?

"If our solar system is any indication, probably pretty rare."

How common is sentient life?

"Intelligent life? Probably extremely rare."

Life is rare. Sentient life is the most incredibly rare and precious force in the universe.

Josh nodded, but continued to play devil's advocate. "Yeah, but just because we're rare doesn't make us *good*. I mean, Polio's rare. Mankind's done a lot of awful things."

Would you kill a three-year-old because he hit his sibling?

"Of course not, but they're children. We're not. And we don't just destroy ourselves; we drive other species to extinction."

The human race is the only life capable of protecting all other life on Earth.

Josh frowned and actually stopped walking. He'd only thought about the comet killing people. Nodding he said, "The impact that killed the dinosaurs wiped out three quarters of all species."

If the species you drove to extinction could speak from the grave, what would they say?

He started walking again. With a slight smile, he said, "You mean would they vote us off the island?" He shrugged. "Guess if we were *really* able to stop an apocalyptic impact, we'd make up for a lot of past sins."

Life is tenacious and will find a way under the most extreme conditions, but only if it has time to adapt. Catastrophic events don't allow that. Only sentient life can intervene.

It was hard to believe Jesse might just be a figment of his imagination. He was too good a teacher. Josh pictured him as a gray-haired professor sitting in a big leather chair with a headphone and mic. Looking up, he realized he'd arrived at Elizabeth's condo. He found himself surprisingly nervous ... for multiple reasons.

9

ELIZABETH

Elizabeth's condo was part of a high-rise complex sitting on top of a small hill overlooking the city. The building wasn't new but looked nicely maintained.

Josh took the elevator to the fifth floor, found her number and rang the doorbell.

As Elizabeth opened the door, he realized he'd never seen her in anything but scrubs. Framed in the doorway, he saw a beautiful woman with blondish shoulder-length hair wearing a white silk blouse and perfect fitting jeans that confirmed curves in all the right places.

"Hi, Elizabeth."

She smiled, and said, "You look great with your clothes on."

A woman coming up the hall glanced up quickly with raised eyebrows.

Elizabeth stammered, "I mean you look good without your bathrobe on."

The woman looked straight ahead.

Elizabeth shook her head, laughing. "You know what I mean. Come on in."

As soon as he was inside, a blonde Cocker Spaniel walked up to him with its stubby tail wagging. He bent down to play with it. "What's his name?"

Elizabeth corrected, "*Her* name is Toto."

"I thought Toto was a terrier."

She just looked at him.

Smiling and shaking his head, he said, "Oh yeah, I forgot … we're in Kansas."

Classical music played in the background as she showed him around. The furniture was simple but expensive teak sitting on thick cream-colored carpet, contemporary but comfortable. On the far side of the living room were giant windows and sliding glass doors that opened onto a balcony, giving her fifth-floor home a beautiful view of the city lights. The living room opened onto a large study with several floor-to-ceiling bookcases. Sitting on a teak desk were two huge monitors.

"Video games?"

"I have an Internet business on the side and some real estate."

His impression of her went up still another notch.

They spent the next hour enjoying a simple but delicious dinner. He asked her about herself and her job. She told him many funny, and a few sad, stories from her profession. Finally, he asked, "If you had all the time in the world what would you do?"

"That's easy. I *love* to travel. I want to see the whole world, the more exotic the better. I've been to Canada, Mexico and the Caribbean, but I've only been to Europe once."

"Why haven't you traveled more?"

"For years, I used credit cards to rack up airline miles. I have enough to fly around the world many times." She paused, looking pensive. "Before I was married, I thought it would be great to travel with my husband. Then, after ... well, it's not the same traveling by yourself." Shaking her head sadly, she looked back at him. "That's just an excuse, isn't it?"

Instead of answering, he gently said, "I'm so sorry."

She looked down at the table. "He went out for a motorcycle ride ... and I never saw him again." Glancing at a picture on the coffee table of a good-looking young man, she said softly, "The accident was terrible. They had to ... identify him with dental records."

Josh suddenly realized he was witnessing the same anguish his wife might have experienced. He'd been robbed of one of the few benefits of death – not being around to worry about those you left behind.

By tacit agreement, they moved to less painful topics.

Finally, she said, "I've never talked this much about myself in my life." Playfully, she added, "Amnesiacs make perfect dinner guests."

He laughed. He also realized he'd broken a stereotype. There was an inside joke about fighter pilots on first dates. After totally dominating the conversation by talking about flying, the fighter pilot finally smiles benevolently and says, "Well, enough about flying. Let's talk about ... me."

Elizabeth said, "Now, I want to know how *you* think." She paused. "What do you want to do when you grow up?"

"Save the world."

Her cell phone rang. "I'm sorry, Josh; I really need to take this. Someone was ... uh, facing a small crisis and needed to be checked on."

He nodded. "Sure."

She answered, "Hi. ... Yes, fine. ... Yup. ... You're the best! Love you girl. Bye."

He asked, "Is she OK?"

Smiling warmly, she said, "Yes ... she's doing great." She paused. "Let's see, where were we? Oh yeah, save the world." With a slightly challenging smile, she asked, "And how are you going to do that?"

He smiled back. "I'm still working on it."

"Not sure everyone thinks we should be saved." She paused. "Why is human-race-bashing so chic nowadays?"

He shrugged. "I don't know. Maybe we give ourselves too much credit for being *all-powerful* destroyers. We forget that for most of our existence, *we* were the endangered species."

She gave him a questioning look.

"For millennium, the climate's driven the rise and fall of civilization with ice ages, floods and droughts. *We* didn't cause that ... not back then. It's only in the last century or so we've turned the tables and messed with the climate."

She frowned.

He smiled. "Yeah, I know, the climate will probably have the last laugh, but the point is – it's our usual arrogance that we believe we're the *bane* of all life on the planet. We didn't invent uranium. We just dug it up and concentrated it. On a geologic scale, the human race looks like nothing more than a temporary infection – a simple case of acne on the face of the earth. And, unfortunately for us, it's an infection that can be cleared up with a nuclear war or ... extraterrestrial impact."

With a half-smile, she said, "And this is supposed to make me feel better about humanity *because* ...?"

Laughing, he said, "Sorry, that's the dark side. On the other hand, we have incredible potential. As a global civilization, we're babies."

Elizabeth giggled. "I like the idea of being a baby better than acne." She added, "But it's hard to see us as babies." She waved her hands toward the cityscape, accidentally knocking her empty wine glass off the table.

With astonishing speed, Josh caught it before it hit the floor. Looking up, he smiled and said, "There's a law of physics that deals with something called entropy. It says the universe, and everything in it, tends toward disorder over time. Everything will eventually scatter, run down and burn out as time goes on."

She nodded.

"We see it in our daily lives. Unless we add *energy* by putting stuff away, our home becomes more and more disorganized. Eventually, we have chaos, with everything randomly scattered throughout the house."

Smiling wryly, she said, "What a relief. I thought it was just my housekeeping."

He smiled. "Yet life creates order out of chaos, and sentient life can even organize its surroundings and create incredible things."

Looking thoughtful, she said softly, "When I think about the universe, I feel small and insignificant. But when you explain it this way, I know that despite all our shortcomings, *we* are one of the most amazing things in it." She frowned. "I think entropy applies to people too. If we don't constantly add positive energy, people become *dark* just like the universe."

He nodded. "Never thought of it that way, but you're right."

Carefully stacking their plates and glasses, she gave him an impish smile, and said, "Second Law."

"Pardon me?"

Taking the plates into the kitchen, she said over her shoulder, "Entropy, it's the Second Law of Thermodynamics."

He shook his head with a half-smile and quietly said, "So much for impressing the little woman." He picked up the silverware and followed her to the kitchen, further reducing entropy.

After putting everything in the dishwasher, they moved out onto the balcony. Leaning on the railing, they looked down across the twinkling carpet of lights. It was a beautiful view on a crisp spring evening. Shivering slightly, Elizabeth stood close. Turning to him, she said, "I really like your view of the world."

Looking down into her eyes, he couldn't help but say, "I really like the view from here."

She tipped her head up and kissed him. He kissed her back, putting his arms around her. Her scent was amazing. Physically, he felt like he was on his first date, and realized his new body had twenty-year-old hormones.

Unlike his first date, however, he felt remorse as Kelly's face flashed into his mind. He couldn't convince himself their marriage was no more. He stopped before his hormones got the best of him.

As they separated, he said, "Elizabeth, I ... I really should be going." Trying to keep it light, he added, "I know I'm still on double-secret probation."

She looked at him carefully, obviously trying to read him. Finally, she said softly, "Yes. I didn't realize it was so late." With that, she went with him to the door. He thanked her for a wonderful dinner, leaned forward, and kissed her on the cheek.

After he left, Elizabeth sat down on her couch with a slight frown. It'd been an incredible evening. She was certain he was attracted to her and there was real electricity when they kissed, but then ... he shut down. There was something wrong, something he wasn't telling her.

Lesia was right; this *was* a date, and the first she'd had since her husband died. She picked up the framed picture of her husband from the side table. As ridiculous as it was, she realized part of her had been expecting him to walk through the door at any moment, telling her it had all been a terrible mistake.

Looking at the picture, she shook her head. "You're not coming back." The words sounded as if they were coming from someone else. She repeated them. "You're dead. You're never coming back." For some stupid reason she began to cry. She was angry with herself but couldn't stop. She cried hard. She cried like she did when she was a little girl.

Finally, it subsided ... and with it, her mourning. She set her husband's picture back on the table and stood up. Very slowly, she slid the wedding ring off her finger and gently laid it in a drawer.

Her dad had always said she was stubborn as a post. Instead of feeling sorry for herself, she was going to get to the bottom of this mystery. She would find out who Josh really was.

10

MISSION

Elizabeth woke up the next morning determined. Lesia was right, even if Josh's situation wasn't his fault, he was probably bad news but there was only one way to find out. He said he spent a lot of time on the Internet, presumably to find his identity, but with limited access, he was obviously frustrated.

Before starting her shift, she stopped by the maintenance office and asked where he was working. She found him sitting on the ground working on an automatic sprinkler head. As she approached, he was intently studying a small part in his hand and gently shaking his head. She stopped in front of him.

Startled, he looked up and then smiled.

She asked, "Fix it?"

"Uh ... think so." As he stood up, he tossed the part into a toolbox, adding, "But I sometimes have *spare parts* when I'm finished."

Biting the side of her lip, she took a deep breath and quickly said, "If you need the Internet to save the world, I have two powerful computers with high speed access. Can't use both of them at the same time ... you're still welcome to rent one of the rooms at my condo until you find a place."

He looked surprised and started to say something, but then stopped.

"Look Josh, I heard you've been sleeping in the waiting room. This is purely a logical business arrangement for both of us."

He sighed and with a slight shake of his head, said, "Actually ... that would be awesome. I have money for rent but it's not a lot. I may have to pay by the week."

She handed him a key. "We'll work something out."

As Elizabeth started her shift, Lesia came over smiling. "How'd dinner go?"

"We talked for hours. Amnesia or not, he's very intelligent and has amazing insight."

Lesia said, "And...?"

Elizabeth gave her a wry smile. "You mean did we end up in bed?"

Lesia just shrugged.

"No, he was a gentleman." She smiled. "We had a romantic moment on the balcony." She paused and frowned. "Then he suddenly pulled back and said he had to go."

Lesia frowned. "Why are the cute ones always gay?"

Elizabeth laughed. Shaking her head, she said, "We kissed. Trust me, he's not gay, but...." Looking more serious, she stared past Lesia. "He's holding something back." She paused. "I'm going to let him use my computer to help him find his identity." Her eyes unfocused, as she added, "There's just ... something about him."

This time Lesia laughed. "Oh honey, my first child was the result of those *exact* same words. But it's not like you gave him the key to your condo."

Elizabeth's eyes got wide.

Lesia frowned. "Tell me you didn't."

Her silence said it all.

Lesia grabbed both of Elizabeth's hands. "What am I going to do with you? You need to be careful. He may not be a sex fiend but that doesn't mean he's not dangerous."

Elizabeth said, "It's OK; I'm armed, I have a dog and another roommate."

Frowning, Lesia said, "Roommate?"

"Amber Wilcox. She has boyfriend trouble and is staying with me temporarily. We'll be safe."

"Amber from X-ray?"

Elizabeth nodded.

Lesia laughed and said softly, "Yeah, but will *he* be safe?"

"What?"

"Never mind." Still holding Elizabeth's hands, she clearly noticed the missing wedding ring and softened. "I can't tell you how good it is to have you back among the living. I'm thankful to him for that, but baby girl, you need to shop around. Why don't you go out with Terry Burns? He's the nicest single doc in the hospital, and I know he likes you."

Elizabeth didn't say anything.

Lesia shook her head. "OK, but would you do me a favor?" She gave her a meaningful look. "You need to talk to Dr. Lopez. She evaluated him and I'm sure she'll share some professional insight."

With a resigned sigh, Elizabeth said, "OK." Hugging Lesia, she added, "Thanks for looking out for me."

Josh had to admit, he was not only excited about uninterrupted computer access, he couldn't wait to sleep in a bed again. After work, he rode home with Elizabeth in her Jeep.

As they went inside, Elizabeth said, "It's a three-bedroom, two-bath condo, so you'll have to share the bathroom with Amber, my other roommate. Amber works at the hospital too. She's just staying with me until she can get a new apartment – boyfriend issues."

Sitting in a leather recliner, positioned directly in front of a large TV, was a cute twenty-something, wearing a headset, 3D glasses and actively working a controller.

Elizabeth said, "And *this* is Amber."

Amber glanced up briefly, waived and refocused on the battle.

Elizabeth rolled her eyes with a smile. "We don't want to bother her. She's protecting the world from brain-sucking aliens in still *another* online tournament." They moved on to his new bedroom. It was small with no window and nothing but a bed and side table.

"Sorry, it's pretty tiny."

"Yeah, it'll be a tight fit with all my stuff." He winked.

Smiling, she said, "I've got a quick meeting I need to go to. Help yourself to anything in the kitchen."

After she left, it took 30 seconds for him to hang his two shirts and set up house. As he came out of the bedroom, Amber finished her game and took off her headset and glasses. Five-foot-nothing with short, dark, spiky hair, she was actually very cute.

She offered her hand and said, "Hi, I'm Amber."

"I'm Josh. So, did we win?"

She smiled. "Yup. I'm really not a video game junkie but we have a group that plays together." She paused. Looking at him curiously, she asked, "So you, like, really have amnesia?"

He frowned. "Ah, yeah."

"That's so crazy. Does it ... hurt?" She moved closer, unconsciously extending a hand toward him as if to touch a bug.

"Only when people mention it."

She pulled her hand back.

He smiled. "I'm kidding. I feel great."

Returning his smile, she said, "You look great." She paused. "Are you and Elizabeth ... uh ... like a thing?"

He smiled. "No she's just kind enough to take in strays."

"Strays unite!" She gave him a high five. "Elizabeth's such an angel. She's *always* helping people. I just broke up with my boyfriend because he turned out to be a little psycho." She shook her head.

Frowning, he said, "Sorry to hear that."

"It's OK." She smiled. "Hey, I'm going out to meet some friends for drinks, wanna come?"

"Appreciate the invite, but I've got some computer work to do tonight."

After Amber left, he jumped on the computer. With an extremely high-speed connection, he dove into his research. Slowly, he began to realize the magnitude of what they were attempting. He also learned that detecting an undiscovered comet two years out was extremely difficult.

He looked down at the dog. "Toto, Jesse's organization has access to more than just advanced medical technology." He frowned. "What they're trying to do is next to impossible." He shook his head. "Who does he really represent?"

Toto didn't respond.

In science, the first task was to define the boundaries of the problem. In this case, it was a comet – already inbound – on a collision course. He studied every idea ever proposed for asteroid or comet deflection. There were many clever concepts, but the "already inbound" part eliminated all but one of them due to lack of time.

He told Toto, "Sir Arthur Conan Doyle said, once you

eliminate the impossible, whatever remains, no matter how improbable, must be the truth." After the Cold War, the grand scheme of an impenetrable ballistic-missile shield had slid to the back burner, but missile defense was alive and well. Several of his former military colleagues were pursuing the classified technologies. He pulled up the "Missile Defense Agency" website. Pointing to if for Toto's benefit, he said, "This may explain Jesse's interest in me."

11

ASSAULT

It was early evening. He was online reading about high-energy laser physics, when Elizabeth came home. After a quick hello, she sat next to him and worked on the other computer. Even when she was quiet, which wasn't often, he found it ... uncomfortable having her so close.

As he sat there trying to concentrate, the front door flew open. Turning around, they saw Amber rush in out of breath and in tears. She tried to close the door behind her, but a man stuck his foot in the door and forced it open. She screamed, "Seth, leave me alone! You have no right to be here!"

Josh was on his feet. He quickly sized up the situation. The man was mad and big, over six-foot-four with a 70-pound advantage on Josh, and all of it appeared to be muscle.

Amber continued to back away as the man slowly advanced. "Amber, you're coming home with me!"

"I'm never coming with you. It's over."

He could see anger rising in the man's eyes. Josh moved forward and motioned Amber back, saying softly, "Seth, let's talk about this."

Seth glanced at him and then yelled at Amber, "Are you sleeping with him too?!"

"This is Elizabeth's friend, I just met him today!"

With steel in her voice, Elizabeth said, "Get out of my house or I'm calling the police."

Toto started barking but smartly stayed behind Josh.

Seth ignored them and continued to advance on Amber, yelling, "You're coming with me!"

Josh stepped between them.

Seth put his hand on Josh's shoulder and tried to push him

61

out of the way.

Using a martial arts hold, Josh grabbed Seth's hand. Gripping it tightly around the thumb side, he twisted it back toward the door.

Seth grunted in pain as he stopped.

Twisting it further, Josh was able to push Seth backwards. "Seth, let's talk about this."

No longer focused on Amber, Seth came at Josh with a hard right hook.

As Josh's adrenaline rose, he felt like the world slowed down. It was easy to dodge the blow and step inside the swing. He hit Seth with a lightning fast punch to his neck and carotid artery. The softening blow, as intended, staggered the big man.

Once again, Josh tried to talk to him, but it became clear he was beyond reason.

Seth's face contorted in rage as he pulled a knife from his pocket.

Josh saw a six-inch blade.

Amber screamed as Seth lunged at him.

Amazed by the speed of his own reflexes, Josh blocked the thrust with ease, knocking the knife from Seth's hand. Spinning inside, he punched Seth hard in the solar plexus.

But the blow only slowed the big man slightly. Recovering, Seth screamed and attacked with blind fury.

As he charged, Josh grabbed the front of his shirt and put his right foot against Seth's hip. Dropping himself to the floor on his back, Josh pulled Seth over the top.

Seth's momentum pivoted him in a perfect 360-degree flip. The huge man slammed onto his back with a satisfy crash, smashing a coffee table.

Josh rode him through the flip, ending up on top of Seth.

With the wind knocked out of him, the big man was stunned.

Josh grabbed the back left side of Seth's collar with his right hand, and did the same with his left hand. Crossing his arms over Seth's throat, he created a chokehold.

As Seth recovered, he tried to grab at Josh's arms.

Josh simply pulled both sides of Seth's collar toward each other, cutting off the air and blood flow until Seth began to lose consciousness.

Easing up a little, Josh leaned in and did his best **Dirty Harry** impression, whispering, "Do you feel lucky?"

Seth struggled feebly.

Josh increased the pressure. "Do you want to live?"

Seth finally stopped struggling and after a few seconds gave him a choked, "Yes."

Josh slowly reduced the pressure. "You and I are going to go out in the hall and have a little talk."

Seth nodded.

Slowly releasing the hold, he stood up and offered Seth his hand.

Still breathing heavily, Seth tentatively took it.

Josh helped pull him to his feet and guided him out the front door. On the way out, he picked up Seth's knife.

Josh shut the door behind them and said softly, "Seth, you can't go around beating up women. It's not right, it's not legal and it won't score you many repeat dates."

Seth looked surprised.

"Do you care for Amber?"

Seth almost cried, "Yes. I love her."

Josh put his hand on Seth's big shoulder and very quietly said, "OK, I'm going to give you a choice. If you go get a therapist and *seriously* work on your anger management issues, I promise to put in a good word for you with Amber. Can't promise what she'll do, but it's your only chance of ever having a relationship with her ... or anyone." He paused, looking serious. "Or ... if I see your face anywhere near her before then, the best possible outcome for you will be jail. Do you understand me?"

Seth nodded. Then, looking Josh in the eye, said, "If I get help ... you'd ... you'd really put in a good word for me?"

Josh gave him a hard look. "I could have broken your neck and been done with it." He shrugged with a half-smile. "But I like helping people. Prove you've gotten help and I'll put in a good word ... I promise."

Seth gave a heavy sigh. "OK ... I will."

Josh handed him his knife back and patted him on the back. As he watched Seth leave, he let out a relieved sigh and knocked on the door.

It opened tentatively with Elizabeth and Amber peeking out. Seeing him, they opened the door and leaned past him to look down the hall.

As they all stepped inside, Amber, with wide eyes, said, "Wow."

Elizabeth nodded. "Ditto."

He was feeling pretty impressed with himself until he noticed a Taser pistol in Elizabeth's hand. He looked from the Taser to the smashed table and said, "Sorry about that. I'll pay for it."

Elizabeth smiled. "You kidding? You just paid for your month's rent."

He shared his conversation with Seth, adding, "My 'Dr. Ruth' may not take. Amber, you need a restraining order and a gun or..." he nodded toward Elizabeth's hand, "one of those."

Amber, still watching him with wide eyes, just nodded her head.

Elizabeth and Amber went to bed. Josh stayed up. He had to admit he was as surprised and impressed by his performance as they were. In his past life, he had a black belt in karate with some judo and jujitsu training, but he'd never been competitive in tournaments. Josh loved to play but didn't have the speed or "win at all cost" attitude to compete professionally. What he did have was a knack for understanding people. He was president of his fraternity not because of his looks or popularity, but because he was good at breaking up fights and working with sororities. The psychology and martial arts moves he used with Seth weren't new to him, but the speed of his new body and mind was nothing short of amazing. With adrenaline flowing, his body was so fast that it felt as if everything around him was moving in slow motion.

A sound came from the kitchen. He relaxed when he heard the sound of clinking glasses. Looking up, he saw it was Amber with a bottle of wine in one hand and two glasses in the other.

Smiling, she said, "I never thanked you for what you did. That was like so amazing."

He smiled back. "You're welcome but anyone would have done the same." As he took one of the offered glasses, he noticed she was wearing a man's large button-down dress shirt as a nightgown.

She shook her head as she poured the wine. "No. I've been in these *situations* before and no one did anything." She drank half her glass and looked up at him with big eyes. "I've never had a knight in shining armor defend me." Smiling, she said, "A toast, to a real gentleman."

As she raised her arm to toast, Josh couldn't help but notice the shirt was barely buttoned and she wore nothing under it. The irony wasn't lost on him. He was admiring what he shouldn't, while being toasted as a gentleman.

She drank the rest of her wine and put her hand on his knee. "After the battle, may I give my knight a back rub?"

He so missed human touch and was tempted, but knew where it would lead. Amber was cute, but not his type and he was still in love with his wife. Before he could formulate a reply, they both heard someone in the kitchen.

Elizabeth appeared in her bathrobe.

Amber removed her hand from his leg, and said, "I was just thanking Josh for saving my butt."

Glancing at Amber's shirt, that didn't quite cover her butt, Elizabeth said, "Yes ... I can see that."

Amber faked a yawn. "Well ... it's late. Guess I better turn in." She leaned forward and kissed him on the cheek. With a smile, she took the bottle and her glass and said, "Goodnight."

Elizabeth watched her leave. Then turned to him with a raised eyebrow. "So, how's the *research* going?"

"A bit ... awkwardly." He winked at her and added, "Thanks."

She winked back. "Night, Josh."

The next morning Josh was up early. He'd just gotten out of the shower and was shaving when he heard a knock on the bathroom door. Before he could answer, Amber walked in.

"Morning, Josh. Hope you don't mind but I'm running late for work again."

Wearing only shaving cream, he managed, "Uh ... morning." He watched her walk behind him in the mirror, peeling off her nightgown as she went. Dropping it on the floor, she stepped into the shower with nothing but a smile.

He grabbed a towel and wrapped it around his waist, but couldn't help but laugh. This sort of thing *never* happened to him in his old body.

After he got to work, they had him out mowing the grounds with a large industrial riding mower. He immediately had the feeling he was being watched, but this time he was certain he'd identified the car. It was parallel-parked on the other side of the street.

He drove the mower all the way around the hospital so he could come up on the suspect sedan from behind. As he approached, he could just make out a man in the driver's seat through the tinted windows. Without thinking it through, he drove the large mower across the street and stopped it inches from the front bumper of the car, blocking it in.

Startled, the driver tried to back up, but he was too close to the car behind him to get out.

Josh jumped off the mower and went to the driver's door. It was locked. The car surged forward, hitting the mower and sliding it sideways to make room. Then backed up, hitting the car behind.

Josh knew he wouldn't get another chance. With adrenaline flowing, he used a martial arts kick to shatter the window on the back door.

The car started pulling out.

There wasn't time to open the rear door, so he dove part way through the broken window and reached for the driver. With his head and shoulders inside and his feet dragging, the car pulled out. Josh got his hand under the driver's chin and forced the man's head up so he couldn't see. The car accelerated erratically and then jumped a curb and hit a telephone pole.

The airbag deployed as the impact threw Josh from the car. He hit the sidewalk and rolled. Ending up on his back, he decided to stay still and play possum.

The driver stumbled out. Wearing a golf shirt, jeans, and a black windbreaker, the man in his mid-twenties pulled a pistol out of a shoulder holster.

Josh kept his eyes mostly closed as the man moved toward him. He stopped outside of Josh's reach ... but not outside the range of his legs. Once again, time slowed and with a lightning-fast scissor kick, Josh swept the man's feet from under him. As he fell, Josh was on him with phenomenal speed. He knocked the man's pistol loose and in seconds had him in a wrestlers hold, yelling, "Who are you?!"

The man surprised him by saying, "FBI! FBI!"

Josh carefully reached in and pulled the man's wallet out. Throwing it open on the ground, he saw a badge and FBI ID.

With a heavy sigh, he carefully let the agent out of the hold. As the man sat up, Josh picked up the wallet and gun and handed them to him. Shaking his head, Josh asked, "Why have you been following me?"

The man stood up and put his wallet away but held on to the pistol. "Homeland Security Joint Terrorism Task Force, and you're under arrest for assaulting a federal officer."

12

PROBE

Josh avoided arrest by pointing out to the young FBI agent that he'd have to explain how he damaged hospital property *escaping* from a surveillance subject, not to mention losing his weapon.

Josh's boss, however, was less understanding. With the mower damaged and no police report explaining the incident, his boss suspended him and told him he'd probably have to fire him.

Home early, he had the condo to himself and called Jesse. Frustrated, he said, "Just had a run-in with the FBI." He shook his head. "You've been evasive about who you are and who you represent. I haven't questioned it because you obviously know what you're doing or I wouldn't be here, but this is crazy. I need to know exactly who you work for."

Why?

Indignant, he said, "So I can make sure I'm working for the right side!"

What's the right side?

He stopped and realized with the human race at stake, was there a "right side"?

Do you have a problem with the mission?

Frowning, he shook his head. "No, no of course not." Regrouping, he said, "I just don't like being kept in the dark. You obviously have access to amazing technology. What do you need me for?"

When children are learning to walk, do you grab them every time they lose their balance?

He sighed and under his breath, said, "Here we go again." Shaking his head, he finally said out-loud, "No."

Why?

"Because they'll never learn to walk." He understood the

analogy. "But I'm not a toddler."

I wasn't referring to you.

He frowned. "You mean humanity?"

Yes.

He paused to consider that, and then said, "OK ... but isn't it a bit late for *us* to be learning to walk?"

Humanity is still very young.

"In comparison to what?!"

He sensed the conversation was over, and, once again, Jesse hadn't answered his questions ... or had he. It wasn't just what Jesse said, it was how he said it. Josh shook his head. It was almost as if Jesse had a perspective outside of .... No, no he wasn't ready to go there ... not yet.

Still suspended, he didn't have to go to work the next morning and it was also Elizabeth's day off. He'd been up for an hour when Elizabeth came out of her bedroom and into the kitchen. He noticed she was wearing a short silk bathrobe. Peeking out from underneath was a black negligee. Unlike Amber's shirt, the robe did its job, properly covering everything. He could see a lot less of Elizabeth than Amber, but for some reason Elizabeth was more distracting. She was also barefoot. He liked women in high heels, but for some reason, he found barefoot women particularly attractive. He wished she didn't keep her condo quite so warm.

She asked, "Do you want some breakfast? I'm going to make some anyway."

"No, thanks, I'm fine." He tried to angle himself so that she wouldn't be in his direct line of sight.

After a few seconds, she said, "Josh ... is there any particular reason the kitchen faucet is disassembled?"

He totally forgot. "Oh, sorry. It was dripping, so I thought I'd fix it. After I took it apart, I realized I ... needed a couple extra parts." He needed extra parts because one of the micro springs had shot out of the valve and he hadn't been able to find it. Taking things apart to see how they worked was fun, but he had a tendency to lose interest when it came to minor details – like putting them back together.

He realized he and Elizabeth were opposite personalities, just as he and Kelly had been. Kelly was outgoing, loved people and lived in the present. She saw the trees but sometimes missed the forest. He, on the other hand, was reserved, task-oriented and lived in the future. He saw the forest but sometimes ran into a tree. Kelly had been his perfect complement: fascinating and frustrating, intriguing and incomprehensible. His secret term of endearment for her was "Kelly Bear," cute as a Koala, with the temper and passion of a Grizzly. Elizabeth looked nothing like Kelly, but she had that same indefinable ... something.

"Ouch!" Elizabeth scared him out of his reverie.

He looked up. "You OK?"

Hopping on one foot, she was trying to look at the bottom of the other foot. Somehow, she made that awkward pose both graceful and sexy.

She pulled something from the bottom of her foot. Examining it with a frown, she added, "Weird. It looks like a tiny metal spring."

Quickly looking back at his computer screen, he added a non-committal, "Hmm."

After pouring herself a cup of coffee, she came over, stood next to him and looked over his shoulder at the computer.

He once read that Americans had larger "personal bubbles" than other cultures. Elizabeth never got the memo.

"What are you working on?"

He pointed to the screen. "It's a diagram of the Oort Cloud at the outskirts of our solar system. It's where dwarf planets and comets hang out."

With her coffee in one hand, she put her other hand on his shoulder and leaned in to look at the screen. He couldn't help but glance down her loosely tied bathrobe and lost interest in astrophysics.

As she looked sideways at him, he quickly looked back at the screen.

"Interesting." She said with the slightest of smiles. Straightening up, she added, "By the way, I had a little talk with Amber. Since Seth knows she's here, we thought it *best* she stay with another friend until she can find a new place. It'll be safer for her and ... others." With a raised eyebrow, she added, "I intended you and Amber to share a bathroom ... just not at the same time."

He stammered, "I can explain...."

She shook her head with a smile. "No need."

He changed the subject. "But ... having just a guy roommate might cause people at work to talk."

Waiving her hand dismissively, she said, "For goodness sake, Josh, this is the twenty-first century ... the people I work with would never question you living here." As she turned and walked back to the kitchen, she added, "Because they already assume we're in a hot steamy relationship."

"Uh ...." he replied wittily as his eyes followed her of their own accord. To himself, he quietly said, "Focus."

After Elizabeth left the kitchen to get dressed, he put the faucet back together and went back to studying the enemy. A mountain moving many times faster than a rifle bullet was awe inspiring and ... terrifying. He was chasing down an interesting line of research, when he heard Elizabeth say something about what a beautiful day it was.

He said, "Uh huh."

A few minutes later, she inserted her face between him and his screen. "Off the computer!"

Startled, he pushed his chair back. She was wearing running attire. "You've been on that thing for six hours." She pointed outside. "It's a perfect spring day with blue skies and summer temperatures. You need to be outside, getting some exercise, vitamin D and color." Her eyes swept up and down him, and with a smile, she added, "Well, at least ... vitamin D."

He really needed to finish, but looking at her expression, he yielded. "OK."

"Go put on your running shoes. We're going to the park."

He said, "I don't have any running shoes."

She held up a pair of brand new ones. "Happy birthday!"

He frowned. "It's not my birthday."

"How do *you* know?" She laughed. "Go get changed!"

They opened the canvas top on her Jeep. Sitting in the warm sun with the wind in his hair, Josh forgot about the comet and just watched the world. They hit a small construction area where they were putting in an entrance to a new mall. The sign said, "Logan Shopping Center." Seeing his old name reminded him of the family he'd lost.

As they arrived at the park, he saw running trails that

wandered through small lakes, athletic fields and woods. Brilliant yellow daffodils were everywhere, punctuated by prolific pear trees in full bloom. The white blossoms made the trees look like giant popcorn balls. Runners, skaters, bikers and kids filled the park. It was a barely controlled cacophony of sound and colorful chaos. *This* – was what he was trying to protect.

Before their run, they stretched against a large oak tree. Elizabeth was exceptionally limber, and could bend herself into impossible but interesting angles. As she touched her toes, he caught a small pin-stripe tattoo just above a truly spectacular empennage.

They ran a trail that wound through the park. He was impressed with Elizabeth's fitness, measured both in her ability to set a fast pace and turn male heads. After three miles, they slowed to a jog.

The sun was beginning to set and there was a large moon just above the horizon.

She stopped to look at it and said, "That's so beautiful." She turned to him, biting the side of her lip. He noticed it was something she did when she was nervous. She'd make a lousy poker player.

Tentatively, she said, "Josh, I don't know what your spiritual beliefs are," she frowned, "Guess you may not either, but I believe there's something bigger than us out there."

Curious, he asked, "What do you believe?"

She looked thoughtful. "I believe there is a God."

He wasn't excited about the topic, but nodded politely.

"And I think to whom much is given, much is required."

Under his breath, he said, "Tell me about it."

"What?"

"Uh, I think you're right about it. Did you grow up in a church?"

"Yeah." Imitating a heavy southern drawl, she said, "I came from one of them there eeeevangelical Christian families." Frowning, she added in a normal voice, "You know I hate that label. In the media, 'evangelical' is interchangeable with 'fanatical.' They act like anyone who actually shares all that 'love your brother, turn the other cheek' crap is a nut job."

He shrugged. "A fanatic is just someone who's more excited

about something than you are."

She smiled. "But if people don't believe in God, why do they get their panties in a wad about religious stuff? Shouldn't they just be amused and ignore it, like we ignore the Flat Earth Society?"

He narrowed his eyes slightly and said, "Unlike the Flat Earth Society, organized religion has had a rather checkered past: The Inquisition, Jihads, etc. A lot of death and destruction occurred because of religions."

Looking very serious, she said, "Really? I think we usually find conflicts are based on three things: territory; 'haves' versus 'have nots'; or just plain prejudice. In most cases, religion is a convenient excuse used to mask empire-building or justify an existing hatred."

Josh frowned. She continued to surprise him.

"Think about it. If religious *differences* were the biggest reason for conflicts, shouldn't Hindus with lots of gods and Christians with just one, be at each other's throats all the time. Instead, we see Muslim against Jew, even though they share many beliefs and prophets. Or, how about Protestant against Catholic in Northern Ireland?"

He nodded neutrally.

She shook her head. "Sorry, Josh, I've been totally lecturing. I want to hear what you believe."

He knew her belief was the result of years of religious indoctrination, but her arguments were surprisingly well thought out. Regardless, he couldn't afford to alienate her.

"I think we're more than just the sum of our parts, and I agree, it's not just all about us."

She gave him a questioning look.

Deflecting, he asked, "What happens when mankind goes gentle into that good night?"

Elizabeth exclaimed excitedly, "You must have read poetry!"

"Ah ... maybe." He added honestly, "Or, I may have heard it in a TV commercial."

She finished with, "It would be very sad if mankind doesn't 'rage against the dying of the light.'"

He nodded. "Yes, but not just for us. We're the only life on Earth that can save all the other life."

"From what?"

He nodded toward the moon and asked, "What do you see on its surface?"

"Green cheese?" she giggled.

He smiled. "More like Swiss cheese."

Still smiling she said, "Craters?"

"Yup."

"So ... you're saying we can save life on Earth from an impact like in the movies?"

"Yes."

She smiled. "Cool!"

He loved her attitude and open acceptance of new concepts. He really wanted to share the truth with her ... but the risk was too high for both of them.

That night, after Elizabeth was asleep, he decided to try cross-examining Jesse again. He called quietly and sensed the communication link was live. "Jesse, I understand your analogy – letting a child learn to walk without catching him every time he falls – but you wouldn't let him learn to walk next to a cliff. Wouldn't a cataclysmic comet kinda fall into that category?"

Yes. That's why you're here.

He shook his head. "That wasn't the answer I was looking for. A minor in Astronomy and access to some defense programs doesn't qualify me to do much. I hope that's not why I'm involved."

You're good with people, and despite your skepticism, your belief is stronger than your fear.

"Belief? What does that have to do with anything?"

Fear is being convinced of a negative outcome that has yet to occur. The opposite ... is believing in a positive outcome that has yet to happen. Without belief, nothing significant is ever accomplished.

"OK, but how is a comet impact going to help mankind 'learn to walk?'"

How do you feel?

"Frustrated with your answers." He shook his head and sighed. "I feel clueless and inadequate."

What else?

He sighed. "I don't know." He gently shook his head. "I guess

... some excitement?"

What causes happiness?

He had no idea where Jesse was going. Sighing again, he said, "Getting something you want?"

Are you happiest when you get something you want or during the pursuit of it?

"We should be happy when we get it, but society is littered with people who reach the top of their game and are miserable." He paused. "We're happiest when we're *pursuing* stuff, aren't we? That explains why I feel excitement ... but I don't think you told me all this to help me 'find myself.'"

Do you think societies are so different?

"You lost me."

What was your nation's finest hour?

Josh frowned. It made him nervous that Jesse referred to the U.S. as 'your nation.'" He shook his head. "I don't know ... maybe when everyone pulled together during World War II, or when we landed a man on the moon?" He paused. "You're suggesting that for a society to be happy, it also needs to have a purpose?"

Yes.

"If that's true, we got a problem. We're usually at our most *purposeful* when we're trying to annihilate each other."

Purpose is often working together to defeat an enemy ... but it can be a common enemy.

He slapped his forehead. "Of course, the comet!" It would give humanity a common goal. "But how do you pull humanity together to fight something they can't see until it's too late?"

Good question.

The next day, Elizabeth was halfway through her shift when Lesia said, "Girl, we need to talk."

Over a cup of coffee in the cafeteria, Lesia said, "He's living with you. Talk to me."

Elizabeth shared what had transpired and Lesia listened quietly, asking for details at several points. Finally, Lesia shook her head. "You know he was suspended from the hospital?"

Elizabeth nodded. "He said he damaged one of the mowers."

"But did he say how it happened?"

Elizabeth frowned and shook her head.

Lesia glanced around. "Someone saw him attack a man in a parked car. Rumor is it was an undercover cop."

Elizabeth looked skeptical but before she could object, Lesia continued, "You said he's spending his time online doing research. What's he studying?"

"I guess he's trying to find his identity and figure out what he's going to do with his life."

"Have you actually seen where he goes online?"

Elizabeth frowned. "Well, no. It's really none of my business."

Lesia gave her the head and finger wag. "Au contraire, girl, it's very much your business. He's going to these sites on *your* computer from *your* home." Her face softened as she continued in a gentler voice. "So you got the hots for this guy, who could blame you? But you still don't know anything about him. Honey, you gotta protect yourself. You're a computer geek; find out what he's doing ... *carefully!*"

Elizabeth nodded.

On the way home, she called Dr. Lopez. Something she had promised Lesia she'd do, but had never done. They talked for 20 minutes.

As soon as she got home, she saw a note from Josh. He'd just taken Toto to the park for a walk and would be back in an hour.

Looking around unnecessarily, she sat down in front of the computer he used.

II

CONSPIRACY

"If asteroids were marbles, they'd fill a dump truck. But if cometary objects were marbles, you'd need a line of dump trucks parked bumper-to-bumper for 200 miles. ... A Halley's Comet-sized impact would be the same as having a global nuclear war ... every day ... for 50 years."

13

CHALLENGE

With cool temperatures and threatening clouds, the park was almost empty. Toto had taken a liking to him, and he really enjoyed going for walks with her. He'd also found a good way to talk to Jesse in public. Slipping an inactive Bluetooth headset in his ear, he said, "Jesse, Josh, can you hear me now?"

After sensing his link was live, he said, "I've read everything I can find on comets. I'm ready to join the team. What's the plan? How are we going to stop this thing?"

What would you do if you were in charge?

"I hate it when you answer questions with questions ... especially questions like that." He took a deep breath. "We need experts and resources."

How would you get them?

"Well, you could do it politically. A world leader could move national resources. Or, you could get an expert who can influence governments."

Do you have to influence publically?

"I guess a lot of important decisions are made behind the scenes."

What's required?

Laughing, Josh said, "I know, I could write a book about our conversations and start a fake religious cult."

Although there was no sound, he was certain Jesse was "laughing." It was just a bright sense of amusement.

While Jesse was amused, he might as well ask – "Hey, how about transferring a hundred million dollars into my checking account?"

Silence.

It was worth a try.

As far as Jesse, he could probably forget Occam's Razor and going with the "fewest assumptions." Instead, it was more like Sir Arthur Conan Doyle's, "Whatever remains, no matter how improbable must be the truth."

He took a deep breath. "Jesse, you aren't part of a U.S. government lab, are you?"

No.

Then who are you? Who do you represent?

All in time.

"That's it? That's all you're going to say?"

Silence.

Sensing the conversation was over, he looked down at the dog. "Toto ... I have a feeling he's not from Kansas anymore."

As they got back to the condo, Josh noticed the silence. The music that usually played in the background was missing. Elizabeth was sitting on the couch looking at him intently and biting the side of her lip.

He gave her a questioning look.

She stood up and came toward him. Taking a deep breath, she said, "Look, Josh, you know more about your past than you're letting on."

He felt a knot in his stomach. "Why do you say that?"

She looked a little sad. "I'm not a psychiatrist, but I've read up on amnesia. It's usually selective to an event or time. It's hard to believe you have all this knowledge ... and don't remember how you got any of it. Lopez also told me you refused hypnosis." She paused. "I watched you take down a 300-pound man without working up a sweat, and I've seen what you're researching online ... U.S. Ballistic Missile Defense, nuclear weapons, high-energy lasers?" She looked directly into his eyes. "Josh, *who* are you and what are you doing?" Her voice was a little raspy.

The knot in his stomach became a pit. He hated emotional conflict. "You're right. I haven't told you everything ... but you wouldn't believe me if I did."

She gave him a steely stare. "You might be surprised. Try me."

Looking down, he said, "I ... I can't."

"Why?" Her voice cracked.

"I can't explain ... it's for your own protection."

"My *protection*, what are you talking about?"

He said, "I'm ... I'm sorry. I shouldn't have come here." Shaking his head as if clearing cobwebs, he continued, "I'm putting you at risk. It was a terrible mistake. I'm ... so sorry, I'll ... I'll leave."

With tears in her eyes, she spun around and went to her room.

He put his few possessions in his duffel bag and left the condo. Sad and angry, he walked across the parking lot.

What are you doing?

Startled, he stopped and looked around. Then realized it was Jesse. Shaking his head, he said, "I'm busy pissing off the only human being willing to help me." He paused. "She knows I'm not being straight with her but I can't tell her the truth; she'll have me committed. Even if she believed me, I can't involve her. It could put her in serious danger."

What happens to her if you fail?

He rarely swore, but let loose a few choice words. Then sighing, turned around and went back.

Inside the condo, he set his bag near the entrance and went to her closed bedroom door. He knocked gently and quietly asked, "Elizabeth, may I speak to you?"

She opened it tentatively and came out.

"Elizabeth, I care about you and don't want you hurt."

With glassy eyes, she gently shook her head frowning. "Don't you understand? You *are* hurting me. Stop trying to do my thinking. Let me decide what I do and don't believe." She looked both defiant and vulnerable.

He took a deep breath. "I'm going to explain as much as I can. Then you can decide if I'm stark raving mad."

She just stared at him.

"The world's facing a cataclysm."

She cocked her head slightly and said, "Those weren't just philosophical discussions." She slowly walked past him toward the living room, then turned and said, "You believe we're going to get hit by an asteroid, don't you?"

Stunned at how quickly she had put the puzzle pieces together, he said, "A comet."

Facing him, she said, "A comet? How do you know?"

"That's the part that's hard to believe."

Uneasily, she said, "What, you think you're ... an alien?"

He smiled. "No, I'm not an alien."

Her eyebrows went up. "An angel?"

He laughed. "No, I'm not *that* deluded. Unfortunately, I'm very human."

Her eyes narrowed as she slowly said, "You believe you're here to ... prepare us for the end?"

"No. No, I'm going to do whatever I can to make sure this *isn't* the end."

She put her finger on her lips and slowly turned away from him. She walked across the living room. Stopping in front of the picture window overlooking the city, she stood silently.

He could see her face reflected in the dark windowpane. She was just staring into the night. In the lengthening silence, he said, "As a nurse, you know schizophrenia is often accompanied by delusions of grandeur."

She said nothing.

The room was painfully quiet. He replayed their conversation in his mind, trying to hear it from her perspective. He realized, at best, he might earn her pity. She hadn't moved. The only sound in the room was a large, decorative clock, loudly ticking off the seconds.

Finally, he realized he had his answer. He picked up his bag and turned to the door. Over his shoulder, he said softly, "I'm ... I'm sorry." Turning the door handle, he glanced back. He saw her spin around to face him. She walked toward him purposefully with fire in her eyes. He paused, bracing for the attack.

Stopping directly in front of him, hands on hips, she said loudly, "Josh, I'm attracted to you, but I'm not a child and I'm not stupid!"

There it was. It hurt, but ultimately it was best for her. Trying not to let his emotions show, he repeated softly and genuinely, "I'm so sorry."

She continued, "What you say is *way* out there!"

He nodded his head in resignation and opened the door. He'd have to start thinking about where to go and what to do if she turned him in.

As he started to leave, she reached in front of him and pushed the door shut. Speaking quickly, she said, "But so is everything else about you. You show up out of nowhere, no fingerprint records, not even dental fillings for heaven's sake. I've seen every square inch of your body. *No one* can make it to your age without a single scar. Your medical reports say you're the healthiest human I've ever heard of. Your numbers are off the charts. That's not explainable by mental illness." She edged closer. With the slightest of frowns, her eyes searched his face. Staring directly into his eyes as if trying to see inside, she delivered the final blow. "Josh, I know who you are ... and who sent you."

His jaw literally dropped. He barely got out a whispered, "You do?"

Instead of answering, she stepped forward and wrapped her arms around him, hugging him tightly. "Yes, Josh, I do."

Dropping his bag, he returned her hug. Looking totally confused, he had no idea what just happened. Could she really know who sent him? No, no ... that's wasn't possible ... he didn't even know. She seemed completely confident with her understanding. He needed to know what she believed, and started to open his mouth to ask, but every endorphin in his body said, 'Shut up.' He just stood there, frozen in time, gently hugging her.

She finally pulled back, wiping her eyes and said, "OK, what do we need to do?"

Close to tears himself, he said softly, "Thank you." He took a deep breath and cleared his throat. "We're on a clock. We have less than two years." Pausing and taking another breath, he added, "I'm trying to work behind the scenes to facilitate the technology required."

All business, Elizabeth said, "What's our first objective?"

Speaking more confidently, he said, "I'm trying to identify which programs have the greatest potential to deflect a comet."

She nodded, "Why can't we go public?"

He laughed. "Well, I'm sure I could convince the tabloids."

"You have no proof?"

"And won't until it's too late."

"Why can't the astronomers find it?"

"We haven't even been able to find all the threatening

asteroids, much less comets."

"What's the difference?"

"There are about two million asteroids orbiting in the Asteroid Belt between Mars and Jupiter."

She nodded.

"But there are hundreds of *billions* of cometary objects, and they live out beyond Neptune. The volume of space they can hide in is a trillion times bigger than the Asteroid Belt."

She frowned, clearly trying to grasp the scale.

He thought for a moment. "If asteroids were marbles, they'd fill a dump truck. But if cometary objects were marbles, you'd need a line of dump trucks parked bumper-to-bumper for 200 miles. And if the Asteroid Belt were the size of a donut, it would take a sphere one mile-wide to hold all the comets."

She whistled softly.

He sighed. "Because comets orbit so far out, they reflect almost no sunlight. That means, unlike asteroids, they're pretty much invisible."

"So it takes longer to find them?"

"With current technology, it's not really possible yet."

She nodded. "So we're not going to see it until it's too late, but how dangerous is it? I mean is it really like in the movies?"

"Worse."

"But isn't a comet made of ice? Won't it melt in the atmosphere?"

"At 30 miles per second, it'll cross the earth's atmosphere in three seconds."

She said softly, "No time to melt." Frowning, she asked, "So what happens if it hits?"

"Depends on how big it is."

She gave him a small smile, "So size *does* matter."

He smiled back. "Unfortunately, yes."

"What if it was like Halley's Comet?"

Staring off into space with little expression, he said, "Halley's Comet is about 11-kilometers across. An impact that size would create a two-hundred-million-megaton explosion."

She gave him a questioning frown.

"That would be the same destructive power as a global nuclear war *every day ... for 50 years.*" Eyes unfocused, he continued, "The firestorm would incinerate the continents on one side of the planet. The shockwave would race through the earth's crust, causing massive earthquakes. Cities not incinerated or blown away would turn to rubble. Tsunamis a half mile high would sweep the globe. The fires would poison the atmosphere, turning day into night for months. What wasn't vaporized, crushed or suffocated, would freeze and starve as the world entered an ice age." He finished with, "We're not just talking about the end of humanity; we're talking about the end of most life on Earth."

Nodding seriously, she said, "Well that kinda sucks."

14

CONSPIRACY

After Elizabeth went to sleep it was very quiet in the condo. With his exceptional hearing, he could hear her rhythmic breathing down the hall. She always slept with her door open. He preferred to sleep with his closed. It was indicative of their personalities. He was private, skeptical and analytical. She was open, trusting and giving. That probably explained why he found her irritatingly attractive. To add insult to injury, she kicked her covers off as she slept. With her "mostly air" nightgowns and his exceptional night vision, he had to keep his eyes forward when passing her door ... most of the time.

Focusing back on the problem at hand, he scribbled some notes on the tablet Elizabeth loaned him, but finally dropped it on the couch in frustration.

Very quietly, he asked, "Jesse, you there?" He sensed the link was open. "Jesse, I've looked at every possible technology for deflecting comets and asteroids. All of them require 10 to 20 years to implement."

There's nothing that can be done?

"There are things that might work from a physics standpoint, but they're not possible from an engineering perspective and there's no time to develop them." He shook his head. "Even if we could, I don't have the knowledge or experience to put together a project big enough to do it." He sighed. "I'm not qualified to do any of this. I'm sorry ... you made a mistake in choosing me. You need to give this mission to someone else."

You have the single most important qualification.

"What ... an Astronomy minor?"

You were willing to give up your life for others.

That caught him by surprise. He shook his head. "Hate to

tell you this, but I didn't *intend* to die."

You could have ejected sooner.

"No! No, I couldn't. I had to stay with the jet. I had to make sure...."

Yes?

"It ... it doesn't matter. It doesn't change the fact that I'm not capable of doing this."

You don't have the knowledge or experience.

"That's what I've been trying to tell you!"

Enlist those who do.

"I can't. Those from my past life, who could've helped, think I'm dead."

You and they have a common friend.

"Common friend? I don't understand." He felt like a slow child. Then it dawned on him. "Wait, you mean – me. *I'm* the common friend." He paused. "I could introduce myself as a friend of my past self. I know things about them that only my former self would know." He shook his head as if to clear it. "Wow. That sounded seriously schizophrenic." He took a deep breath. "OK, but even it that worked, I still need experts beyond my few past friends."

You need leaders of leaders. They will multiply you and do what you can't.

"How would I get them? I don't have anything to offer."

They don't need reward. They require purpose. Capture their minds and hearts.

As the conversation ended, the weight of the world settled on his shoulders. He carefully reviewed everything Jesse had imparted. Blowing out a lungful of air, he said quietly to Toto, "I'm afraid I may be in charge."

Toto cocked her head.

Nodding at her, he added, "Yup ... we are totally screwed."

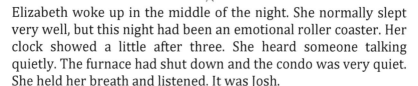

Elizabeth woke up in the middle of the night. She normally slept very well, but this night had been an emotional roller coaster. Her clock showed a little after three. She heard someone talking quietly. The furnace had shut down and the condo was very quiet. She held her breath and listened. It was Josh.

She heard, "... I'm not qualified to do any of this. I'm sorry ...

you made a mistake in choosing me. You need to give this mission to someone else."

There was a pause. Elizabeth knew she was hearing only one side of a conversation. The furnace came back on and she could only hear bits and pieces of what followed.

She was impressed and frightened. Either Josh was some type of modern day prophet with a direct line to the Big Guy, or ... he was textbook schizophrenic. She wasn't sure which she preferred, falling in love with a lunatic or an apocalyptic prophet. She sighed. It didn't usually end well for prophets ... or those around them. At least schizophrenia was treatable. She should have listened to her mom and dated accountants.

After a short fitful sleep, she got up early the next morning and made a pot of coffee. Josh was sitting in front of the computer as usual but he was just staring at a blank screen.

She brought him a cup of coffee, put her hand on his shoulder and said brightly, "So, how do we start?"

It seemed to break the spell. He turned to her with a small smile. "Thanks." He took a big sip of coffee, set it down and rubbed his hands together. "I guess I need to put together a team of experts."

She nodded. "OK."

He paused and then looked directly at her. "This is going to sound a little strange but I had a former life. I was a Navy test pilot."

She just nodded, but when he looked away, she smiled and said under her breath, "A test pilot prophet?"

"What?"

"Nothing. So who do you need on your team?"

"I'd like to start with some of my past military colleagues."

"Can you call them?"

"Uh ... they wouldn't ... recognize me." With the expression of a child asking for a third piece of cake, he added, "I mean, I don't look like I did ... then."

She nodded thoughtfully as if what he said actually made sense.

Encouraged, he pressed on. "Homeland Security and the FBI have taken an interest in me due to my rather odd arrival. Accessing some of the military websites might bring additional attention. I could use your computer expertise."

"What do you need?"

"Can you make sure our visits to certain websites can't be tracked back to your computer?"

She shrugged. "Sure. I can use an IP masking program." Slipping into the computer chair, she added, "Took a course in ethical hacking."

He frowned. "*Ethical* hacking?"

Her fingers flew over the keyboard. "Can't stop the bad guys if you don't know how they do what they do. It was fun and I was actually pretty good at it." After a minute, she said, "OK."

He jumped on the keyboard. After a few attempts to sign into a site, he sighed. "They took me out of the Navy system."

She watched him go to a different website – Boeing.

On his first attempt, he said, "Yes! We're in! They should have shut down my email account a long time ago. Thank goodness for the glacial gods of bureaucracy."

Looking on, she said, "I thought you said you were a Navy pilot. Why are you trying to get into Boeing's site?"

"I was assigned to oversee the development of the next generation of UCAVs at Boeing."

She looked at him blankly.

"Unmanned Combat Aerial Vehicles ... or robotic fighters."

She frowned. "Wouldn't they ... kind of ... put you out of a job?"

He gave her a half-smile. "Unfortunately ... yes."

She nodded. "But at least it keeps our military pilots from getting killed?"

He shrugged. "From a State Department perspective, they're less concerned about dead pilots than captured pilots."

With narrowed eyes, she asked, "Are you trying to get access to classified information?"

He shook his head. "No. This is an unclassified site. It just allows me to send and receive email from inside the system. Despite Hollywood, seriously classified stuff isn't put on computers connected to the Internet."

"Then, what are you trying to do?"

"I'm not going to break in to a classified program," he looked up with a mischievous smile, "I'm going to create one."

She shook her head. "I don't understand."

"Classified, or black programs, are 'need to know.' No matter how high your clearance is, you only have access to information you need for your job. That protects programs if someone talks, but it also means no one can ever *know* about all the black programs out there."

"Aside from *why* you would want to create a black program; how could you do it?"

"I just need to *read* people into the program."

She shook her head again. "*Read* into?"

"That's how you bring people into classified programs. They sign a sheet that says they'll have access to secret information, and if they divulge it, they go to jail."

"So you're going to read people into a program that ... doesn't exist."

"Exactly."

"What if they ask someone else about it?"

He grinned. "That's the beauty. They can't."

"Why?"

"It's a security violation – not to mention bad etiquette – to ask about a black program you're not already a part of."

She frowned. "Well that's kinda weird."

He nodded knowingly. "Welcome to your federal government."

"Are we going to get arrested?"

"I don't think there's a law against *creating* black programs." He shrugged. "At least not yet."

"But how are you going to *create* it?"

Looking serious, he asked, "Do you have PowerPoint?"

She couldn't help but laugh.

After breakfast, she watched him create his counterfeit classified program, hoping she was doing the right thing. After inhaling his eggs, he said, "I'm sorry, Elizabeth, but I could really use more of your expertise. I need to reestablish my security access at Boeing so I can get in to see the people I need." He paused. "But now we're talking about doing something that could get you in trouble."

Still in her bathrobe, she sat down at the computer.

He gave her his username and password.

After studying the site, she said, "There's nothing we can do here. It only allows basic updates. We'll have to talk to someone who can make entries for us on the security server."

Josh gave her a questioning look.

She smiled. "Everyone thinks cyber bandits hack into networks by cracking the encryption. It's not impossible, but it would take weeks of super-computer time."

He frowned. "Then how do they get in?"

She laughed. "The same way every system is cracked – person-to-person."

Josh looked skeptical.

"Here's a classic example. You're at work. You get a call, apparently, from your IT department. They tell you they have to shut down the network for a software upgrade. Of course, you're right in the middle of a big project and your email and presentation programs are network-based. You can't afford to be down that long. The IT person, trying to be *helpful*, tells you they can keep *your* computer up while the rest of the network is down, but of course ... to identify your computer they need your username and password. Voila, they're in!"

Josh nodded. "So, what do we do?"

She winked. "Get me another cup of coffee and my phone."

He sat next to her watching and listening nervously.

She eventually convinced a Boeing computer administrator that Josh's identity got confused with someone who died, making his life very complicated.

In the process, Elizabeth had to ask him multiple security questions from his background. Putting the pieces together, she said, "So 'Fuze' was your pilot call sign?"

"Fuzed."

She looked at him questioningly.

He shook his head. "It's a long story."

She shrugged and then shooed him away so she could work.

After another hour on the computer and phone, she announced, "Commander Josh Fuze has a Boeing badge!"

He came back and gave her a huge hug, saying, "You totally rock!"

Still in her bathrobe and nightgown, she felt his hands and arms holding her tightly through the thin silk. He suddenly released her, looking distinctly uncomfortable.

She smiled, enjoying his discomfort.

Clearing his throat, he changed the subject. "To recruit them, I'm going to have to meet with some of these people, but ..."

Before he could finish, she said, "I have zillions of airline credit card miles. You can use them, but you can't go looking like that." She waved her hand at him. "I'll need to dress you."

He gave her a half-smile.

She rolled her eyes. "I mean get you some real clothes."

Looking serious, he said, "Elizabeth, I can't ..."

She smiled. "Shut up."

15

CAPTAIN

Success hinged on finding a strong, effective leader to pull a team together, a team that would include high-level scientists and engineers. Josh needed an insider with credibility. He needed Navy Captain Joe Meadows. Meadows had been the Squadron Commander of VFA-146, the Blue Diamonds, Josh's first fleet squadron. He'd led them into combat against sophisticated fighters, but later in his career had also successfully led aircraft development programs into combat against the General Accounting Office.

Having commanded the USS Gerald R. Ford – one of the newest aircraft carriers in the fleet – Meadows was on the fast track for admiral. But less than a week after he had taken command, an AMRAAM missile accidentally detonated on the flight deck, destroying three new F-35 fighters. The Navy was one of the last bastions of accountability. The old saying about 'going down with your ship' still applied. Despite completing an outstanding tour as the Ford's Captain, the fire had eliminated any chance of admiral. Meadows could have retired, but they asked him to stay and take over critical classified programs at Naval Air Systems Command. His office was at NAS Patuxent River, Maryland, but he spent much of his time at the contractor facilities where they did the development work. He had satellite offices at the Lockheed Skunk Works in Palmdale and the Boeing Phantom Works in St Louis ... where Josh worked before the crash.

He called him. "Captain Meadows? This is Commander Josh Fuze. We haven't met but I worked closely with Andy Logan on a special project before he died."

"Hi, Josh. What can I do for you?"

"Captain, the reason I'm calling is that Logan recommended you for involvement in a very important program, one that I'd like to talk to you about."

"What type of program?"

"We'll have to talk in person."

"OK, but we'll have to meet tomorrow. I'll be leaving NAVAIR for St. Louis the day after tomorrow."

Josh smiled. "Actually, St. Louis would be great if you can fit me into your schedule."

"Sure. Can you meet me at the Phantom Works around noon on Thursday?"

"Yes sir. I'll see you there."

His next call was to Washington, D.C. He knew the effort would eventually be global and he'd need international and legal expertise. Carl Casey had been the intelligence officer in their squadron and had a degree in International Law. They'd been good friends. After a few tours in the Navy, he'd left and joined the CIA, not uncommon for intel officers.

After a similar conversation, Carl also agreed to see him. Hanging up, he realized he was about to invite a CIA agent into a counterfeit black program. Softly he said to himself, "Oh what a tangled web we weave."

Josh had a moment of déjà vu as his flight touched down in St. Louis. Thirteen months ago, a happily married Navy test pilot took off from this very runway on a simple delivery mission. Under his breath, he said, "I'm back ... minus one jet and a body."

The Boeing Phantom Works was on the far side of the airport. Walking the two miles around the perimeter helped him conserve his limited funds and settle his nerves. He had good reason to be anxious. He was about to meet someone he knew ... wearing a new body. On top of that, Meadows was his only candidate to run the program. Josh, however, had an advantage. Working and living in close quarters, on multiple six-month cruises, ensured familiarity with the quirks, fears and dreams of squadron mates.

He arrived at an inconspicuous-looking, windowless, two-story building. The only thing that hinted at the secrets inside was a tall fence topped with barbed wire and a manned gate. As the guard checked his ID and cleared him in, he silently thanked Elizabeth.

Going straight to Meadows' office, he knocked on the open door. It was a small office, made even smaller by the occupant. A six-foot-three, muscular, 250-pound, black man with a shaved head rose from his chair. Watching Meadows step carefully around his desk reminded him of the classic bull in a china shop. Countering his imposing size were eyes that perpetually smiled, combined with a frequent booming laugh.

As Josh shook Meadows' huge hand, he remembered a barbeque at his skipper's house many years ago. Meadows' three-year-old daughter had been perched on his shoulders. With crayons in each hand, she'd been trying to draw on top of his bald head. He never missed a beat, continuing to carry on conversations while handing her different colored crayons. A patient father translated well into an aircraft carrier captain of 4,000 mostly teenage sailors.

After exchanging pleasantries, Meadows brought up Josh's former self. "It was a real blow when we found out about Andy. We're not supposed to have favorites in a squadron – kinda like kids – but we do, and he was."

It was surreal hearing someone talk about him posthumously.

Meadows continued, "Since he wasn't in a fleet squadron, we had to pull some strings for the missing man formation over the memorial service. It wasn't hard to arrange considering what happened."

Years ago, Josh had flown in a missing man formation for a fellow pilot killed in a crash. Just thinking back on it created emotion ... but this one had been for *him*. He had to stay on task. Humor helped as he remembered his mom scolding him, "You'll be late for your own funeral!"

Meadows shook his head. "I was sure he'd make admiral someday."

Josh smiled. "He talked very fondly of his time in your squadron. In fact, he said he wanted to grow up to be just like you." That was a true statement.

Meadows chuckled. "Well, maybe up to the point where I blew admiral."

"We all know what happened." Josh said with vehemence. "That fire was completely outside your control. I ... had friends who deployed with you and said you were the best skipper they ever served under."

Meadows, looking a little surprised, said, "Well, thanks, Josh, that's good to hear, and that's what's important to me. After the accident investigation was over, that tour turned out to be one of the best of my career. Never been that concerned about promotion as long as I was having fun." With a half-smile, he added, "After the fire, I was freed from *ever* having to worry about my career." He shrugged. "So, what can I do for you?"

"Captain Meadows, I'm familiar with some of the programs you manage. Bottom line, we believe there may be an intersection between one of your programs and ours. I'd like to read you in, if you're game?"

"OK. Is NAVAIR aware of this?"

Josh remembered Meadows' habit of starting sentences with "OK."

"No sir. I'm sure Admiral Hendricks doesn't know about this one yet, it's sensitive even for a black program. As you know, we rarely get recognition for anything we work on in the black world anyway."

Meadows nodded. "In my case, credit doesn't matter. You have my curiosity, but unless it's of strategic importance, I have a pretty full plate."

Josh nodded. "We understand."

Meadows frowned. "OK, that's my other question, who is 'we'? Since you're not in uniform, who are you attached to?"

He could have bought a uniform with the correct insignia and ribbons, but in addition to identifying him as a pilot, some ribbons were what they jokingly referred to as "been there, done that's." They would indicate operations he'd been involved with and places he'd been. He was walking a fine line. He had to be relatable enough that Meadows would accept him as a fellow officer, but distant enough that he wouldn't expect to have common friends. The F-18 community was too small for him to show up wearing wings.

"I miss the simplicity of khakis but I'm on loan to another agency outside the Navy. As I mentioned, it's a bit sensitive."

Meadows smiled. "Yeah, I know." He recited the old joke. "You could tell me but then you'd have to kill me." He paused. "I'd guess your uniform might have included a ... Budweiser? ... But I won't ask."

Josh just smiled back. The Navy SEAL insignia, officially called the Trident, was nicknamed "Budweiser," a corruption of Basic Underwater Demolition/SEAL. With less than 2,500 active SEALS, they were arguably the most elite military team in the world. He felt deceitful by not denying Meadows' assertion, but the ambiguity would help mask his background. He quickly moved on. "Here's the paperwork and the usual signing-your-life-away stuff."

As Meadows glanced over it, he said, "Huh. Did you know Andy Logan's call-sign was Fuzed?"

Josh nodded. "Uh, yeah." Shaking his head casually, he added, "What are the odds?"

Meadows signed the paperwork, and handed it back. "OK, what do you got?"

"Sir, what do you know about comets?"

Meadows frowned. "Probably what everyone knows, they're big snowballs that run around our solar system now and then, putting on pretty displays."

"The team I work with believes they've identified a comet that might be a threat to the earth in a couple years."

Meadows frowned, unconsciously clicking his pen. "Wow. Doesn't take a rocket scientist to see what you're thinking. You believe that something we worked on for missile defense might be used on a comet?"

Josh nodded.

"How likely is this ... threat?"

"Unfortunately, we believe it's probable."

"How much damage could it do if it hits us?"

"If it was as big as Shoemaker-Levy, about five kilometers across, it would be catastrophic."

Meadows stopped clicking his pen. He leaned back, staring through his desk. "Josh, I loved flying fighters. The 'knights of the air' image is overly romantic, but the parallel's real." He looked up. "I was a history major. Just as the knight's armor, skill and chivalry fell to the new technology of the crossbow, so fighter pilots are bowing to the deadly efficiency of UCAVs." He paused. "In school today ... sits the last generation of fighter pilots. Soon there will be no warriors engaging in one-on-one aerial combat."

Frowning, he added, "Logan worked with me on UCAV programs. It's important work in a dangerous world," he sighed, "but making deadlier, robotic weapons ... well, it weighs on you." He smiled. "Who wouldn't want to work on a project like this? Use cutting-edge technology to save humanity and life on Earth."

Josh just said, "Couldn't agree more."

"Besides, I've always been a closet 'Trekkie.'" He paused. "But why is the program classified?"

"Good question." Josh tried to come up with a reason. "Uh, part of it hinges on the use of the advanced strategic defense work. A lot of it is still very sensitive. Part of it is fear of public reaction."

Meadows frowned. "OK. Well, I'll need to share this with some of our mad scientists. Can you read them into the program?"

Josh nodded. "Better yet, we'd like you to take over as the on-site program manager. Then you can take care of the 'read-in' paperwork through your organization's existing system. That'll prevent delays and keep control at your level." Josh held his breath.

Meadows raised his eyebrows. "OK ... I get it. You basically want me to run this thing."

Josh smiled. "Yes sir. You've been handpicked from the very highest level." He thought to himself wryly, he'd flown jets to over 50,000 feet. He read Meadows' body language – he had him.

Meadows nodded. "It's a lot of responsibility." He grinned. "But I'd be honored."

"Thank you, sir."

Tapping his pen against his chin and staring past Josh, Meadows said, "First we need technical leads in astrophysics, engineering and logistics." He paused, looking back at Josh. "This is real? I mean we're talking catastrophic damage and many lives at stake, right?"

Josh said, "I swear; this is as real as it gets and it could potentially be millions of lives."

Meadows nodded. "Then we need the first string, the best and brightest. I know many of the players and I'll research the rest. Be prepared; some of these folks have healthy egos."

With a half-smile, Josh said, "That's why we picked you to lead them."

Meadows' booming laugh filled the small room as he shook his head. "OK, we'll get them read-in and together for a meeting. How about three weeks from now ... by the way, what's the program's name?"

Josh named it on the spot. "Resurrect. Any chance you can get them together sooner?"

"Yeah ... I see the need for speed. Let me see what I can do."

—✶—

Josh headed back to the airport for his flight to Washington. For the first time since his return, he had hope. He felt like he'd been carrying the lives of everyone in the world on his back. Now, at least, he could share the burden with two people. On the other hand, he was frustrated. Even though he'd been careful with his meager funds, he barely had enough to stay in D.C. overnight. He'd have to return to Kansas City and either earn more or beg it from Elizabeth. He knew it was just his ego but he hated asking for money.

While sitting at the gate waiting for his flight, he put on his Bluetooth headset. "Jesse, you there?"

Sensing the link was live, he said, "The meeting went well. I think we have someone capable of leading this thing." He paused. "Hearing about the missing man formation made me finally accept ... I really am *dead* to everyone I know. That'll send a chill down your spine like someone's walking over your grave." He stopped abruptly. "Oh my God ... that might actually be possible."

He shook his head to clear the image and took a deep breath. "I'm trying to save the world with a fake ID and a shoestring budget. If you're not willing to help directly, why can't you at least give me straight answers to my questions? Like who are you and who do you represent?"

It wouldn't help.

"Why, because I'm too dumb to understand?" He looked up and saw the man sitting across from him looking at him oddly. Bluetooth aside, he realized his side of the conversation sounded bizarre. He got up, and went for a walk.

Your nature prevents you from accepting direct answers.

"What do you mean?"

You question everything. For you to accept anything, you have to reason it out for yourself.

Josh smiled. "Mom called me 'Doubting Thomas.' But I don't have a closed mind. I'm willing to accept anything, as long as it's supportable with evidence and logic." He paused. "Even the possibility that you might be from ... elsewhere or ... *elsewhen?*"

Silence.

He sighed heavily. "OK. Would you at least be willing to discuss some basic science?"

Yes.

"What is your perspective on our understanding of physics?"

What do you think?

"See? There you go again!"

We have to start from your understanding.

He frowned. "OK ... *I think* we've figured out most of the laws the universe operates under. We're getting close to a theory that will tie all the forces into one master equation. We have a lot to learn, but we have the basics figured out and mostly need to fill in the details."

What holds the universe together?

"Gravity."

What is the source of gravity?

"Matter – stars, planets, dust and gas."

Is that all?

"Uh ... no. There's also Dark Matter."

What is Dark Matter?

"Well, apparently, there isn't enough visible matter to create the gravity that holds galaxies together. They've calculated that we only see about 20% of the matter in the universe. Therefore, there has to be another 80% that's invisible. We call it Dark Matter."

What is Dark Matter made of?

"There are several theories ... but we're not exactly sure yet."

How does Dark Matter affect the universe?

"It creates a powerful gravitational pull that should slow the universe's expansion." He paused. "But a decade ago we discovered the universe isn't just expanding, somehow the expansion appears to be ... *accelerating.*"

What causes this acceleration?

"Dark Energy."

What is Dark Energy?

"We're not exactly sure."

Silence.

"OK, they're probably called Dark Matter and Dark Energy because we're in the *dark* about them." He understood why Jesse walked him through this. "I admit parts of our science are not exactly intuitive or fully understood."

Silence.

Josh laughed. "All right, all right! I get the point. I claimed we just need to fill in the details. *Minor* details, like we don't know what 80% of the universe is made of. Oh yeah, and the universe is being blown apart by a force more powerful than gravity and we're not sure what it is." He paused. "I guess our understanding of the universe kinda sucks." He sighed. "Can you help illuminate my ignorance a little?"

That's enough for now.

"That's just great! I now know less than I did before I asked."

Taking his Bluetooth off, he realized he had more pressing issues. He was an illegal alien, masquerading as a U.S. military officer ... on his way to CIA Headquarters.

16

INTEL

Josh drove his microscopic rental car from Dulles International to Langley, Virginia. As he approached CIA Headquarters, he saw an SR-71 Blackbird perched on a pedestal. The sleek black reconnaissance jet had long since been retired, but was still, officially, the world's fastest.

He suddenly felt apprehensive. For some reason, the jet began to look sinister, like the raven of Edgar Allen Poe's dark poem. His fear wasn't logical; the CIA dealt with external, not internal threats.

Entering the lobby, he walked across the granite CIA seal seen in so many movies. After checking in with the receptionist, he looked over at the wall of stars. Years ago, Carl had shared with him that each star represented an exceptionally heroic CIA operative killed in the line of duty. There were well over a hundred stars carved into the marble wall. Half remained nameless because their mission, to this day, was too secret to divulge ... he had a new appreciation for their unrecognized sacrifice.

Carl was punctual and met him with a visitor's pass. Once again, he felt strange meeting an old friend who didn't recognize him. He introduced himself and said, "Thank you for seeing me on such short notice."

Carl said, "You've got my curiosity."

As Josh followed him to his office, he realized they were about the same height, weight and hair color. Outwardly, Carl was a relaxed personality who always carried a slight but perpetual smile, as if constantly amused by the world.

Arriving at his office, Carl said, "Have a seat. So, you knew Andy well?"

"Yes, we spent a lot of time together working on black programs." He also knew Carl well. They'd gone on several Western Pacific cruises and had become good friends. Carl was very intelligent and a walking encyclopedia of information on international politics, history and, of course, bad guys and their weapons of choice. He was also conservative, skeptical and a tiny bit paranoid ... the perfect intelligence officer. Josh believed that as their program expanded, he'd need Carl's knowledge and insight.

As Josh sat down across from him, he casually scanned the room. Carl had a very neat office and desk. There were no papers sitting on the desktop and his computer screen was blank. As he looked at the only picture on the desk, he suddenly realized he was looking at *his* wife. It was Kelly, wearing a ... a wedding gown? Wait! This was a wedding picture of Kelly and ... and Carl. His breath caught in his throat as he felt a moment of panic.

Carl noticed his reaction and asked, "Are you all right?"

"Sorry." He lied. "Think I must have caught a bug ... making me a little lightheaded." He regained his composure and clamped a lid on his emotions. He had a job to do, but he had to know the situation or he wouldn't be able to concentrate. He ventured, "Isn't that ... Kelly?"

"Yes. You didn't know? Kelly and I were married about five months ago."

Josh knew the unwritten code. When someone died in the line of duty, the squadron family gathered to help. Although never an expectation or obligation, it wasn't uncommon for a fellow officer to marry the widow of a fallen comrade. "Torn" didn't begin to cover how he felt! His intellectual side understood. His emotional side was horrified. He felt sick to his stomach. All he could do was nod his head.

Carl continued, "I saw Kelly at the funeral and then again at the medal ceremony."

Josh realized this was why he couldn't find Kelly online. The wife of a CIA agent had to keep a lower profile. Trying to focus on something else, Josh asked, "Medal ceremony?"

"You weren't able to attend the ceremony or funeral?"

"Unfortunately, couldn't make it physically but was there in spirit." With dark humor, he realized it was the other way around.

"They gave him the Navy Flying Cross posthumously. As I'm sure you heard, he was trying to land his burning jet at an airport surrounded by neighborhoods. Only one small area wasn't developed – they were building a new shopping center there. He dropped the jet right into the middle of it." He paused.

Josh was surprised. Carl, the hard-boiled analyst, was actually struggling to hold back *his* emotions.

Switching back to his normal self, Carl continued, "The people who live in the surrounding neighborhoods got the shopping center named after him."

Glad to find a diversion, Josh laughed and said, "He always said he wanted to have a business of his own. He would've found that very funny."

"No doubt." Carl smiled. "Then about seven months ago, Kelly and I were thrown together at a squadron reunion. We started dating shortly after. We've always been good friends. I think Andy would have approved."

Josh swallowed hard. His intellectual side was able to squeeze out, "Yes … he would have wanted her to be happy."

He had to concentrate on why he was here. He decided to tell a story that would let Carl know that he had 'known' his former self, and it would take his mind off Kelly. "Logan told me about the time you two were on the USS Enterprise. He said you were in port in Hawaii. You got back to the ship just as the sun was coming up … feeling no pain. Minutes after you hit the rack, they woke both of you. I think he said the squadron officers were scheduled to qualify with pistols at the base range early that morning?"

Carl started laughing. "I totally forgot about that. Skipper thought we were just hung over. The rest of the pilots knew we were still drunk. They were laughing their butts off. We couldn't have passed a Breathalyzer and they put 45 automatics in our hands. The funny part was …"

Josh finished his sentence, "You both qualified 'Expert.'"

Carl, still laughing, added, "And the *skipper* only qualified as a Marksman! He was pissed!"

Knowing Carl was task-oriented, as soon as the laughing died down, Josh moved on. "Carl, the reason I'm here is that we're working on a critical black program of unprecedented scale. We need your expertise, and I trust you based on Logan's recommendation. He would have contacted you."

"What type of program?"

"Well as you know, we have to read you into it first. I'll level with you; we haven't talked to your chain of command." He knew, by nature, Carl would question everything. If he didn't, he wouldn't have been such an exceptional agent.

Carl frowned.

"Carl, this program has nothing to do with terrorists, foreign troop movements or weapons of mass destruction. I won't be asking for any classified information."

"Then why do you need me?"

"Because, according to Logan, you're one of the most brilliant analysts he knew, with an exceptional understanding of global politics and international law."

Relaxing a little, Carl smiled. "International law was my major, and I do work in that area, but there are others with more knowledge and experience."

"Maybe, but not that Logan trusted with something this important." He played his ace card. "Captain Meadows is in charge of the program."

Carl's eyes lit up. "The Skipper, huh? Well, I don't see any downside unless this is going to absorb a lot of time, but I'll have to clear it with my boss."

Josh said, "That's fine, and no, it shouldn't take much time."

There was a pause. Josh pushed on, "Would it be possible to ask while I'm here?"

"Guess this is kind of urgent?"

"You'll understand when you see what we're working on."

Carl picked up the phone and punched a button. "Bob, got a second? ... Have a Navy officer in my office, Commander Josh Fuze. He's a friend of a friend. Wants to read me into a black program to get our agency's perspective on something, is that all right?" ... "No, he said it's just to ask some questions." ... "Yeah, I know if we put any manpower on it, we'll need a charge number." Carl rolled his eyes.

Josh smiled back. Some things never changed.

Carl hung up. "All right."

Josh gave him the paperwork to sign and explained what

they were doing.

Half an hour later, Carl's eyes were wide and he said, "This is big. I'm surprised our agency isn't already involved."

Josh shrugged. "They probably are at the top, but you know the compartmentalization stuff. Sometimes us Indians need to work directly with each other to get things done."

Carl nodded. "Amen. I'm fascinated but a bit skeptical since you can't give me the source."

"I don't blame you, but be honest, how many times has your agency told us in the military that you couldn't release the source?"

"Touché."

"Carl, I'd share it if I could, but you know those lie detector tests." Josh knew from his friend that lie detectors were often a part of their job, understood but resented.

"So what help do you need from me?"

"As our program expands, we'll need your insight into how to work with other agencies and countries, not to mention personnel clearance and international site issues."

Carl nodded. "Fair enough. I'm excited about participating. The only thing that bothers me is the unidentified source. I understand you can't release it but it just sounds too much like ... frozen aliens. God knows we've taken enough hits from the public for that. Some people still think we shot Kennedy."

Josh laughed. "Glad to hear you didn't." Quickly continuing, he added, "Carl, think about it, if our source is wrong, it won't take long to find out. It would be great if we discover there's no imminent threat. In that case, we spend several hundred million *sooner* than we absolutely had to, *but* we're ready for a future contingency. On the other hand, if the source is right ...."

Carl nodded. "You're right, there's really no down side." He laughed. "Unless you're from the Government Accounting Office."

Josh grinned.

They shook hands, but as he was about to leave, Carl asked, "By the way, who's handling your program's security?"

Josh was caught off guard. He'd never thought about protecting *his* program. He'd been more concerned about others protecting their programs from *him*. He replied weakly, "We don't have anyone assigned."

Carl looked at him skeptically. "You don't have experience in the Intelligence and Counterintelligence community, do you?"

He said honestly, "Carl, I got an aerospace engineering degree with a minor in astrophysics, and I've been an operational military officer most of my career. This intel stuff's all new to me, and the people I work for are more of the ... big picture types. That's one of the reasons I came to you."

Carl relaxed and said, "I figured." Smiling, he added, "We gotta fix that and I think I have the perfect guy. He's a friend and former CIA operative, arguably the best in the business at protecting high-value programs and people. He's retiring but I may be able to talk him into one last job."

"Retiring?"

Carl shook his head. "Not because of age. He's in his forties, and," he gave a low whistle, "he's a walking weapon." Frowning, he added, "He was involved in an operation that, through no fault of his, went bad. I think he's just ready to move on. I'll fill you in on the details, if he's available. Course, he's not cheap but I imagine your program has plenty of funding."

Josh nodded, a little nervously. "Yeah, OK. If he's available, bring him to next week's team meeting in St. Louis."

Leaving the CIA headquarters building, he tried not to think about Kelly, but the picture on Carl's desk kept reappearing. As he drove past the shadowy Blackbird on the pedestal, Edgar Allen Poe's dark poem, The Raven, came back to haunt him. Lost love mocked by the evil bird's repetitive "nevermore" repeated in his head.

He blindly followed his phone's GPS to the airport hotel. After checking in and changing clothes, he went for a run. He ran and then ran more. Trying to outrun his thoughts, he ran faster and harder. Oblivious to his surroundings or the time, he ran an Olympic pace.

Reaching total exhaustion, Kelly's face finally faded. He stopped running and looked around tired and confused. It was getting dark. He must have run for a couple hours and had no idea where he was. He wandered aimlessly until he looked up and saw an airliner on approach. He headed in that direction. Somehow, he found the hotel, stumbled to his room and fell in bed. As his head hit the pillow, he was out.

Because of the nature of his job, Carl shared almost nothing about his work with Kelly, to her great frustration. Since Josh knew Logan and recognized Kelly in the picture, he thought it would be safe to mention him, and, he had to admit, he was curious.

"Kelly, I met someone today that you probably know. He used to work with Andy in St. Louis – Josh Fuze?"

Kelly frowned, shaking her head. "Doesn't ring a bell."

"Are you certain? He seemed to know Andy very well."

"I'm pretty sure, but if I met him, I'm sure I'd recognize him."

17

SECURITY

Josh slept for eight hours; the longest he'd ever slept in his new body. He woke just in time to catch his flight back to Kansas.

Elizabeth picked him up at the airport. As she drove him back to the condo, he shared the results of his meetings with Meadows and Casey.

Elizabeth said, "That's fantastic! Who else do you need on your team?"

"Meadows will take care of the scientists and engineers, and Carl Casey's got the international angle and security covered. I think that's it for now."

Elizabeth asked, "What about the public?"

Josh frowned. "The public?"

"Josh, this won't stay secret forever. How are you going to prevent global panic?"

Looking at each other, they simultaneously said, "Lopez!"

Josh pulled out his phone, recalled her telephone number with his photographic memory and texted her.

Elizabeth said, "By the way, I got you a credit card and transferred some funds into your account."

He was about to object, but stopped, knowing it would be nothing more than male ego noises. He just looked at her shaking his head. "Thank you, Elizabeth, I really appreciate this and will repay it with interest."

She just smiled and said softly, "With interest."

He watched her out of the corner of his eye. Elizabeth was everything good about humanity: honest, trusting, positive and confident, beautiful inside and out. She and those like her were enough reason to want to save the human race.

Josh met Lopez the next day for lunch. It turned out they shared a love of Italian food and met at a small local restaurant she liked. As before, she dressed impeccably in a business suit.

"I was surprised to get your call. You look good and I heard you aren't working at the hospital any more. I assume you have your memory back?"

"Yes. Dr. Lopez, I can't tell you everything but I can tell you that I used to be a military officer. I was recruited into a special program, and in the process, became a man without an identity." Everything he said was true, if ambiguous.

She nodded. "Sheri, remember? Well, that would explain it better than alien abduction." With a mock frown, she added, "But alien abduction would have made a better book. So how did you end up in a coma?"

"You wouldn't believe it if I told you. Suffice it to say, it was an unintended but direct consequence of what happened to me. I really was in a state of shock when I arrived and did have to reestablish my identity." Also true, but stated in a way that was open to interpretation.

"You showed signs of emotional trauma." She paused. "But I still don't understand your lack of scars or identifying marks."

"All I can tell you is that my physical condition is a byproduct of what I was working on. I can't say more because of its highly classified nature."

He added, "You may be able to draw your own conclusions." He had no idea what conclusions she'd draw.

Pressing on, he said, "Sheri, I was very impressed with you at the hospital and have since read all your books. You're the best in your field. I'd love to have you join our team."

Looking surprised, she said, "Your team? I don't understand."

"We're working on a project of global importance and need an expert in mass psychology. I believe you are that person. I know you already hold a government clearance, and I'd like to read you into a Top Secret program." He didn't know she had a clearance, but it was a reasonable assumption based on her work.

She shook her head. "I gotta tell you; this isn't at all how I thought this meeting would go. I was expecting to pick up an interesting new patient, or," she raised her eyebrows with a smile, "at least get asked out on a date." Still smiling, she nodded. "But, yes, I guess I would like to know more."

Josh nodded. "By the way, you understand that you cannot share this with anyone else in the government unless they've been read into this program?"

"You mean like my Homeland Security contact?"

This confirmed they commissioned her to examine him at the hospital. "Yes. He hasn't been read-in."

She said, "No problem." She read the paperwork and signed it quickly.

Having finished lunch, he looked around and said, "Can we go for a walk?"

As they walked, he ran through the explanation. Lopez got progressively more excited. Finally, she said, "Wow. A catastrophic comet – I see why you want an expert in mass psychology." She stopped and turned toward him. "Is this for real?"

Looking serious, Josh cocked his head to one side. "Well ... another explanation might be schizophrenia accompanied by delusions of grandeur. *But* ... a leading psychiatrist diagnosed me as sane."

She laughed out-loud, shaking her head.

He smiled. "Don't worry; it'll be easy to confirm that I have a team ... or at least a bunch of fellow lunatics. Can you meet us in St. Louis in four days?"

"I wouldn't miss it."

Josh flew to St. Louis one day before their first team meeting. They were off to a good start, but that's all it was. They had no plan and no funding.

He found a cheap, third-floor, studio apartment near the airport. Elizabeth transferred another few thousand into his checking account without him asking. Between deposits, rent, food and transportation, it was going fast, but he had no choice; he had to be there.

The next day – only 10 days after their first meeting – Meadows pulled his key experts together.

Josh arrived early. He told Meadows he wanted to stay in the background during the meetings. He'd be Meadows' "liaison" with the comet source agency.

Meadows said, "Yeah, I get it. You pass the buck to me and sit back and watch."

Josh smiled. "Absolutely." More seriously, he added, "I have neither the credibility nor experience to lead this type of team."

Meadows looked at him carefully. "You've been in combat?"

Josh nodded honestly.

Meadows continued, "And you're probably a good leader, but you're right. Although you can be young and lead senior people, it takes time to earn their respect."

Josh nodded. "And *time* is something we don't have."

As he finished, Carl arrived, knocking on Meadows' open door. Grinning, Meadows yanked him in and slapped him on the back. Carl introduced a man he'd brought with him. "This is Tim Smith. He's one of the best in the world at security. We were extremely fortunate to get him."

Smith was medium height, medium build, brown hair, brown eyes and regular features. He was remarkable in his un-remarkableness, which was probably an advantage in his line of work. Although, Josh wasn't exactly sure what "his line of work" was.

Meadows said, "Tim, it's great to have you on the team."

With no emotion, Smith asked, "Are you really trying to keep a comet from hitting the earth?"

Meadows said, "We have to." He paused. "Tim, forgive me for my ignorance but what exactly do you do?"

"You protect the earth. I protect you and your team."

Meadows nodded his head but maintained a slight frown. "Protect us from what? I mean who'd be opposed to deflecting a comet?"

Carl said, "Tim's like an insurance policy. You hope you never need him, but if you do, and don't have him, it's too late. Whenever you're dealing with high stakes, you attract attention and not always the right kind."

Meadows looked at Josh.

Josh shrugged.

Meadows said, "OK, what do you need from us?"

"I need the names of everyone involved in the program and permission to talk to them. I will respect their time, but need access. I'd also like to attend your major meetings."

Meadows nodded. "How should we introduce you?"

"Personnel Safety and Security is appropriate."

Smiling, Meadows said, "You know, if you think about it, you may be on the biggest protection project ever."

Smith nodded but didn't smile. "I'd also like your key people to create an authentication phrase that can be used if there's any doubt about the authenticity of an order or directive."

Meadows said, "I hate remembering passwords."

Smith shook his head. "It can be a phrase or even the punch line of a joke. It would only be used once and only in an emergency. It's not to be shared with anyone but your team leaders."

Carl looked mischievously at Meadows. "Josh said Logan told him the story about us qualifying on the pistol range."

Meadows started laughing. "Yeah ... *that* was a high point in your career. I'm surprised you can even remember it. We were lucky you didn't shoot yourself or one of us."

Carl pressed on. "Let's see, my authentication password could be 'Expert.' Yours could be – what was your pistol qualification again – oh yeah, *Marksman.*"

Meadows rolled his eyes. "As my daughter use to say, '*Whateverrrr.*'"

Laughing, Carl and Josh just shook their heads.

Meadows turned back to a very serious Smith. "Sorry, Tim. Promise we'll come up with real authentication passwords. Anything else?"

Smith looked at Carl, and Carl said, "That's right; we'll need an account to charge his services to. You can transfer the funds to a CIA account and we'll disburse them to Tim."

Meadows pointed at Josh. "Talk to my accountant."

Josh nodded nervously. "Ah ... I don't have that information with me right now but I'll get that to you ... soon."

18

TEAM

On the way to the conference room, Carl told them, "After this one, I won't be able to attend future meetings. I'd rather work on this than anything else, but at my level, the CIA policy is clear. Tim Smith can handle any security questions, and I can 'attend' via encrypted conference call if you need me."

They entered the Boeing Phantom Works conference room. A large oval table comfortably sat 12 with another dozen chairs around the perimeter. It only strayed from a conventional meeting room in that it had no windows, was soundproof and shielded from electronic signals.

Lopez was already there and Josh introduced her to Meadows.

They made a stark physical contrast with Lopez's small hand disappearing into Meadows' bear paw, but they had the same highly motivated, outgoing personalities.

Meadows said, "Dr. Lopez, I've read your books! It's an honor to have you on the team."

"Call me Sheri. Captain Meadows, I understand you were the first Commanding Officer of the USS Ford."

Meadows smiled. "Just call me Joe."

With their mutual admiration society, Josh could see they were going to get along very well.

Meadows then introduced Josh and Lopez to the lead scientists and engineers. The senior scientist was NASA astrophysicist Dr. Victoria Chandra. Since astronomy was one of his passions, Josh knew who she was. Before joining NASA, she had done post-graduate work under Professor Joe Veverka, Chairman of Cornell Astrophysics. When Josh was an undergraduate, he'd heard her speak as a guest lecturer. Not only was she brilliant, she had one of the best records for getting unmanned missions to the outer planets successfully. He couldn't imagine anyone more qualified. He even remembered, as a sophomore, thinking she was pretty hot looking. She might not fit Hollywood's definition of beauty, but he'd always been attracted to strong, intelligent women. Now in her fifties, she remained striking, with long, jet-black hair, fine features and dark intelligent eyes. At almost six foot, she was also quite the contrast to the engineer standing next to her.

Dr. Steve Katori, head of Boeing's Missile Defense Division, looked like the stereotypical image of a Japanese scientist. About 60, short and slight of build, he had thick, bushy, white hair and wore black horn-rimmed glasses. Also renowned in his field, his reputation was that of a no-nonsense engineer. He'd lead many programs, from stealth fighters to tactical lasers.

Katori then introduced them to an engineer from Northrop Grumman. The big aerospace contractors often worked together on large projects. Dr. Garrett Cho had been the lead engineer on the Air Force's next-generation Airborne Laser. Mounted in a 747, the megawatt laser could take out ballistic missiles in flight. Cho, in his mid-thirties, wore a Hawaiian shirt and looked like a cross between a sumo wrestler and California surfer. With unruly blonde highlighted hair, he had a strong handshake and grin to match.

Meadows started the meeting. "Thank you for coming on such short notice. I'd like to remind everyone that this is a highly classified program. We want open discourse but only among the participants and in controlled areas. This isn't a formal meeting, so don't be bashful. We need everyone's ideas. Let's kick it off by understanding the threat. Our Chief Scientist, Dr. Victoria Chandra, will explain."

Chandra stood up. "Our job is to find a way to prevent a small comet from striking the earth. Comets, of course, are the worst-case scenario. They come with higher kinetic energy and detection latency than asteroids."

Meadows held up a hand. "Whoa. Dr. Chandra, can you please use simple pilot terms?"

She smiled. "Sorry. Let's start with what a comet is. We often think of them as dirty snowballs composed of rock and ice.

While that's usually correct, we can define them more accurately by *where* they come from rather than what they're made of. Unlike asteroids, most comets live in a region *outside* the orbit of Neptune where Dwarf Planets, like Pluto and Eris, are found."

Meadows nodded. "We hear a lot about asteroids. Aren't comets fairly rare?"

"Actually, it's quite the opposite." If you collected all the asteroids, their combined mass would be less than two percent of the earth ... but if you rounded up all cometary matter, it would be greater than *40 earths.*"

Cho said, "Holy cow!"

Chandra raised her eyebrows at his comment but then smiled. "In fact, dwarf planets are made primarily of ice like comets and have unstable orbits. It's possible that a lot of comets are the result of these little planetoids swinging too close to the sun. The heat and tidal forces from a close pass break them up into a cloud of debris. Many of us believe this shotgun blast of comets might explain earth's periodic mass extinctions." Seeing some blank looks, she added, "Everyone in here has already seen cometary debris. Most meteor showers occur when the Earth passes through old comet trails." Looking more serious, she added, "Unfortunately, because comets are so much further out than asteroids, they're almost impossible to detect until they're inbound."

Meadows said, "You'd think they'd be easy to spot with those tails."

"The tails are caused by gas boiling off the ice from the sun's heat. But that only happens when they get close to the sun."

Meadows frowned. "But we have Spaceguard and other programs to locate these things, don't we?"

"Asteroids, yes; comets, no. Unless a comet has made a loop around the sun, we really have no way to detect it. By the time we see a tail, the comet could be months from impact."

Meadows nodded. "So how much advanced warning do we need to deflect one?"

"Well ... that's what we need to talk about. Surprisingly, it doesn't take much to nudge a comet or asteroid so that it misses us ... *if* we catch it early enough."

Meadows said, "I'll bite, what's early enough?"

"Eight years or more." She paused while the team absorbed this. "Most deflection concepts require a couple years to intercept the comet with a spacecraft, and then mount a small rocket motor or other propulsion mechanism to it. Then, it takes several more years to push it off course. The shorter the time to impact, the more push it takes."

Meadows frowned. "But we won't have eight years if it's a new inbound comet."

"That's correct."

There was some discussion around the table.

Meadows said, "Can we just vaporize it with a nuke?"

Chandra shook her head. "That makes for good movie special effects but it's not as simple as it sounds, and even if we succeed, we may create a bigger problem. Instead of one big comet, we have many smaller ones. We trade a rifle bullet for a shotgun blast."

Meadows nodded. "Are there other intercept options?"

"Yes. We can fill a rocket full of nanoparticles and release them just before impact. The collision of the tiny particles across the comet's surface should impart momentum without fragmenting the comet. If we hit it with enough of them, we can change its trajectory."

Meadows nodded. "Sounds like slowing down a semi-truck with spitballs."

Chandra shrugged.

Meadows took a deep breath. "OK, let me summarize. An intercept mission requires at least eight years, so it won't help with a newly discovered comet on a collision course. Nuking a comet is probably a bad idea. So, that leaves shooting rockets filled with nanoparticles?"

Chandra nodded. "Nanoparticles should work if the comet's small or far enough out that we can hit it with multiple rockets. If it's big or within a couple years of impact, it would require hundreds of rockets."

"Are there any other options?"

She smiled. "Yes." She paused, looking around the room. "We may be able to hit it with an extremely intense beam of focused energy."

Meadows smiled. " Vaporize it with a giant laser beam?"

Dr. Garret Cho laughed. With his booming voice, he said, "That would be totally awesome. Unfortunately, we're a long way from Darth Vader's Death Star. There's nothing – even on the drawing board – with a tiny fraction of the power needed."

Katori, smiling, added, "Yeah, but it would be fun to try."

Katori and Cho started an animated conversation.

Chandra laughed. "What is it with guys and blowing things up?"

With a smile, Meadows said, "We pretty much come out of the womb that way."

Chandra sighed dramatically. "I know. I have two sons." Like a kindergarten teacher trying to corral boisterous children, she said loudly, "As *fun* as I'm sure that would be – and aside from the fact that it's not even remotely possible – there is a simpler, more elegant solution." She paused for effect. As the conversations quieted down, she said, "We don't have to *vaporize* it. All we have to do is *nudge* it."

Frowning Meadows asked, "How can a laser *nudge* something?"

She smiled. "Good question." She looked around. "We melt a tiny part of the surface. In vacuum, liquid goes straight to gas, which creates a small gas plume or jet. That jet acts like a tiny rocket motor. If we hit it enough times we can slow the comet down."

Cho added, "I worked on a NASA project to remove space debris from low Earth orbit using that technique. Hit the junk with a powerful laser pulse and the tiny plasma jet slows it down enough to reenter the atmosphere." He shook his head in disgust. "They canceled it because some countries thought we'd use it to take out their satellites."

Meadows frowned. "I see how it might work on space debris, but a comet?"

Chandra said, "Captain, the earth is a moving target. It orbits the sun traveling 30 kilometers per second. If we can slow the comet down by just a few minutes, the earth won't be there when it arrives. To do that, however, we have to hit it with an intensely focused beam at extreme distance, *and* we have to keep hitting continuously for a year or more. The bigger or closer it is, the more energy we have to hit it with."

Meadows said, "Can we do that?"

Chandra nodded to Katori and sat down.

Katori stood up and said, "As you remember, this is the same general problem we were trying to solve with the Ballistic Missile Defense Program. The idea was to burn an ICBM in flight with a laser. As difficult as that is, it's child's play compared to what we're talking about here."

"Why?"

Katori nodded to Cho. Cho, leaning forward in his chair, said, "We can hit a one-meter target from a hundred kilometers, but hitting a one-kilometer target from a million kilometers requires ten thousand times greater accuracy and more energy. It's like etching your name on the head of a rifle bullet ... after it's been fired at you from London."

Meadows shook his head. "Doesn't sound possible."

Cho smiled. "It's theoretically possible and a wicked cool engineering challenge." He paused. "But it ain't gonna be small."

Meadows raised his eyebrows in question.

Cho said, "The beam collimation – sorry, the accuracy – is directly proportional to the diameter of the beam. This sucker's gonna have to be pretty big." He smiled. "We just need good people and lots of supercomputer time ... a blank check wouldn't hurt."

Meadows looked directly at Katori and Cho. "Seriously, can we do this?"

Katori glanced at Cho. "We need to crunch some more numbers, but ... I think we can."

Nodding excitedly, Cho said, "I know geniuses in the field, that'd give their right arm to play. Throw in a critical deadline and we'll pull in the best and brightest."

Under his breath, Josh said, "Be careful what you ask for."

19

FUNDING

Josh knew that soon, very soon, his team would need real money. There was no faster way to get unwanted attention than diverting government funds from existing programs, but he had no idea where he was going to get the funding. Trying to think positively, he had a flash of illogical insight. He caught Lopez after the meeting and asked her if they could talk privately over dinner.

They found a good Italian restaurant near the airport. Between delicious butter and garlic infused pasta, he asked, "Sheri, how did you become a famous psychiatrist?"

She smiled. "As a child, I was a competitive tomboy. Then I grew up, and ... nothing changed, except the label. I was a 'highly motivated, task-oriented individual.' For women, they often shorten that to one word that begins with a 'B.'" She gave him a wry smile. "I studied psychology, like many, to figure out why I was different. Being competitive, I graduated at the top of my psychiatry class and started a private practice." She shook her head, laughing. "I quickly discovered that I had to work too hard to be sympathetic. I wanted to tell most of my patients to stop whining and deal with it."

He enjoyed watching her eat, suspecting she approached life the same way she attacked food – with gusto.

Wiping butter from the corner of her mouth, she continued, "Anyway, that's what took me into psychology of the masses. It was just as fascinating but a lot less messy. My books became bestsellers and it catapulted me into the spotlight. I honestly don't care what people think of me, but fame does open doors and I've been able to work with some fascinating people."

Josh said, "That's one of the reasons I wanted to talk to you. In addition to your insight, you're obviously well connected." He paused, frowning slightly. "Sheri, you're the only one on the team who's not part of the government or the military-industrial complex. Speed is of the essence here and some things we have to do can be done better and faster ... outside the government."

She nodded as she chased the last slippery shrimp around her plate.

"Can you think of someone in the private sector who might have resources, influence and a particular passion for our cause?"

She looked up grinning. "Like a risk-taking billionaire who's into space stuff?"

Josh smiled, nodding.

"Actually, I know just the guy ... Elton Musk."

Looking surprised, he said, "Seriously?"

"Yup. He's perfect. He's a brilliant entrepreneur and inventor, and, of course, owns the most successful space access company. Musk's got guts and loves a challenge ... and he's kinda cute."

He gave her a raised eyebrow.

"Yeah, we were a *thing* many, many years ago. We're still good friends."

Josh frowned. "Isn't he too much of a public figure?"

She gave him a meaningful look. "Josh, not everyone in the public eye is superficial."

"Sorry."

She smiled. "We both know how to keep a secret. I think he's in the U.S. now. I'll call him; see if I can get you two together."

"That would be awesome. Thank you." He paused. "Sheri."

"Yes?"

"Could you do me another favor and not mention how we ... uh, met to the rest of the team. I'm not trying to hide anything but ..."

She finished, "Discovering that the source of our comet information didn't know who he was a few months ago, might not instill the greatest confidence in the mission?"

He nodded sheepishly.

She put her hand on his arm and winked. "Your secret's safe with me." Still holding onto his arm, she added, "But, someday, I *really* want to know what happened to you."

With a slight smile, he said softly, "Me too."

On the drive back to his apartment, Sheri called.

"Just got off the phone with Elton. Told him he had to see you. Said it was a major secret that I couldn't discuss over the phone. That just made him curious. Can you be in New York City Tuesday?"

"Absolutely!"

"I'll text you the details."

"Sheri, *you* are amazing!"

She laughed. "I know."

Josh returned to his apartment. He normally avoiding talking about anything program-related over the phone, but it had been an incredible day. He was so excited; he had to share it with someone and called Elizabeth. Being careful not to talk details, he said, "The meeting went *extremely* well with a cast of incredible people! I'll fill you in when I see you. On top of everything else, I just had a fantastic dinner with Lopez and she arranged for me to meet with Elton Musk!"

"Elton Musk? That's great."

"It really is! This could be just what we need. Sheri knows everyone. I don't know what I'd do without her. She's an absolutely *amazing* woman!"

Very softly, Elizabeth said, "Yes ... yes, she is."

Thinking of all the work he needed to do before the meeting, he said, "Well, I better go. I'm scrambling to get my cost estimates together, but I just wanted to share that."

She didn't say anything.

"I'm sorry, Elizabeth ... how are you doing?"

"I'm doing fine, thanks." She paused. "This is all very exciting." She paused again. "Well, I ... I better let you go."

As he hung up, he frowned. She hadn't sounded as excited as he thought she would, but he didn't have time to worry about it right now. He needed to schedule a flight and prepare for the meeting.

At the Northrop Grumman lab in Redondo Beach, California, the top secret program briefing began. Dr. Jackie Jones saw that the young engineer giving the brief was clearly nervous. It was his first time to brief the billion-dollar spy-satellite program's status to her – his corporate manager and vice president. This next generation of satellites would use pulsed laser illumination, similar to a camera's flash. If it worked, it would help them capture extreme high-resolution pictures and even video. Their goal was nothing less than facial recognition from orbit, and they had the most brilliant laser physicists and engineers working for them. If they couldn't pull it off, no one could.

Jones listened to the brief intently. After the young engineer finished, she said, "Conner, you did a great job, but where's Dr. Cho?"

"I think he's in St. Louis. They called him in on some special project. He said he'd probably be back in a week or two."

With surprise, she said, "A *week* or two?!"

20

PLAN

It was one week after the first team meeting. As Josh and Meadows entered the conference room, they found Smith and Lopez in an animated conversation. Correction, Lopez was animated; Smith, as usual, appeared emotionless. He reminded Josh of Spock. As they joined them, Lopez, with obvious approval, said, "Did you know Tim has a master's degree in psychology from UCLA?"

Josh thought there was clearly more to Smith than met the eye.

Within a few minutes, the room was full. They'd added several more players. Chandra introduced everyone to Dr. Drake Wooldridge, an astrophysicist and professor at Berkeley who specialized in comets. In his early forties, Wooldridge was tall and slim with a neatly trimmed beard and reading glasses perched on the end of his nose. He looked like a professor, except for his clothes. He wore an expensive suit that appeared to be custom-made.

Josh sensed an underlying excitement and an air of expectancy from the group. Meadows started the meeting by turning it over to Steve Katori, introducing him as the Chief Engineer.

Despite his diminutive size, Katori had a strong voice. "Working with Dr. Chandra and her staff, we've got a better feel for the power and accuracy needed. We'll be handling energies that we've never had to control before and with a huge increase in accuracy. This isn't cutting-edge technology; it's bleeding-edge."

"All right." Meadows smiled. "You've done the proper disclaimers. Can we do it?"

Katori and Cho exchanged grins. Katori, looking like a three-year-old with candy, said, "Yes, by God, I really think it's possible!" Then the engineer returned. "But it would help to know where we're going to build this."

Meadows nodded. "Excellent." He turned to Chandra. "So, where do we put this thing?"

Chandra leaned back in her chair. "Well, we have a two-body problem. Not only is the comet moving, so are we. The perfect solution would be to put it in space, preferably at an orbital Lagrangian point. That way we'd have a stable platform that we could point in any direction."

Meadows asked, "How long would it take to build this type of space-based laser?"

Katori said, "Well, in space, the energy source is the biggest issue. We need thousands of times more power than what even the biggest solar arrays can provide. It'll have to be nuclear. Since there are no space-based, nuclear reactors of that size, we'd have to scale up an existing design."

Meadows said, "That's going to be a lot of weight."

Katori nodded, looking down at his tablet computer. "To boost these components into orbit will take the biggest rockets out there. Even if we commandeer all of the world's heavy-lift capability, it'll still take a couple years."

Josh spoke for the first time, saying quietly, "We don't have that long."

All eyes turned toward him, and Chandra asked, "What do you mean?"

He realized it was time to make a statement that he couldn't back up. "What I'm about to tell you is *highly* classified and must *never* leave this room." He paused. "We believe we may have less than two years to a possible comet impact."

Dr. Drake Wooldridge said, "How can that be? There are no known comets on an intercept course with Earth."

Josh said softly, "No known."

Wooldridge continued but turned to Meadows. "Captain Meadows, I think I speak on behalf of all of us, when I say how excited I am to be part of this project, but I'm an astrophysicist; comets are my specialty. I have access to the biggest and best observatories in the world, and I have extensive connections to the amateur astronomy network. I'm sure I'd know about this kind of threat within hours."

Josh couldn't afford to alienate his astrophysicists by challenging their expertise. "Dr. Wooldridge, you and Dr. Chandra are renowned in your field, and we're honored to have you on the team." He needed, first, to establish some credibility. "The threat has been identified as an extreme low albedo comet."

Meadows interrupted, "A comet with low sex drive?"

There was some muffled laughter.

Wooldridge, with obvious disdain said, "*Albedo* ... not libido."

Josh said, "Dr. Wooldridge, would you mind explaining the concept?"

"Certainly." He automatically slipped into lecture mode. "With cometary objects numbering in the hundreds of billions, we knew we should see hundreds of times more comets sweep through our solar system than we do. About 15 years ago, Dr. Bill Napier and several other astrophysicists proposed a solution. As Dr. Chandra mentioned, comets are dirty snowballs, composed of ice, rock, sand, and in some cases hydrocarbons. As they make trips around the sun, they boil off their surface ice leaving the 'dirty' part of the dirty snowball. In other words, they end up with a fluffy shell of grit and tar that can be blacker than fresh asphalt. This suggests that there is a large population of dark comets zipping by us unseen. The theory wasn't generally accepted until after the Russian Chelyabinsk meteor. Using actual atmospheric impact data from the Nuclear Test Ban Treaty's monitoring system, we realized the impact rate was 10 times higher than we thought. Add to that the discovery that the asteroid that wiped out the dinosaurs may have actually been a comet."

Nodding, Meadows said, "But the dinosaur extinction impact was over 60 million years ago."

Josh threw in, "Chesapeake Bay and the Wooly Mammoth."

Wooldridge and Chandra looked at him with surprise.

Frowning, Wooldridge said, "Yes, during oil exploration in the 1990s, an 85-mile wide crater was found at the bottom of the Chesapeake. Although not as big as the dinosaur killer, it probably destroyed all life on the East coast and shaped the Chesapeake Bay. It was dated to about 35 million years ago." Glancing at Josh, he added, "Although still *hotly debated*, there is *some* evidence to suggest the extinction of the Wooly Mammoth, Saber Tooth cats, etc., along with the demise of the Clovis Indian culture may have been caused by a comet detonation over the Great Lakes. That would have been only about 12,000 years ago." He paused. "I completely agree that low albedo comets may be the largest single threat to humanity. What I don't understand," he glanced back at Josh, "is how anyone could *possibly* have found a new one, particularly a dark comet, two years out."

Josh said quietly, "The information I have, came from ... another source. One that's so highly classified, I can't share it with you at this time. I'm sorry. I would love nothing more than to give you the background. All I can say right now is that we believe our information is ... reliable." He paused. "I wish it weren't."

Wooldridge, with some sarcasm, said, "What are we talking ... aliens?"

There was nervous laughter around the room.

Josh gently shook his head. "I'm sorry. I can't say where the information came from."

Wooldridge started to say something and then stopped.

Josh knew his refusal to explain would force them to draw their own conclusions. They'd probably run the gamut from super-sensitive military space hardware to aliens at Roswell. As brilliant and logical as these people were, they were still driven by emotions. He knew most of them were just excited to be involved with an important purpose. "Dr. Wooldridge, when we can release the source, I promise that you and Dr. Chandra will be the first to be notified."

Wooldridge looked a little uncertain, but sat down.

There was a loud buzz of conversations around the table.

Meadows brought them back. "OK folks, let's focus." Josh admired Meadows' ability to roll with the punches. As things quieted down, Meadows said, "If we're talking two years, boosting a nuclear reactor into orbit will be a challenge."

Chandra added quietly, "It's not two years."

Meadows said, "Pardon me?"

Chandra said, "That's time to impact. We need time to deflect it. Depending on its size and the power of the beam, we'll need to hit it continuously for at least a year. That means we have to be up and operating less than a year from now."

Meadows whistled. "In that case, no matter how much money we throw at it, I don't think we have the infrastructure to put up a space-based system. It hinges on too many undeveloped capabilities, any one of which could stop us in our tracks." There was silence in the room.

Into the silence, Meadows said quietly and with the slightest of smiles, "Dr. Chandra, you've already thought of another way."

Josh knew that Meadows played the 'history major' to make people feel comfortable or force them to explain things clearly. In fact, he was extremely knowledgeable about U.S. space and defense capabilities. Like Josh, he was also very good at reading people.

Chandra and Katori exchanged a conspiratorial glance.

She said, "The system has to be ground-based. That massively reduces the logistics and power issue. *However,* it creates two other challenges. The first is that we'll need more power and beam correction."

Meadows said, "I understand punching a beam through the atmosphere takes more power, but correction?"

"Yes." She pulled glasses out of her pocket and held them up. "It's like wearing glasses for astigmatism. The atmosphere isn't uniform, that's why stars appear to twinkle. We'll need the clearest, driest air possible, and even then, we'll need to apply an 'optical correction' to the beam."

"Clear, dry air ... like on mountaintops where observatories are located?"

"Yes, but that brings us to our second challenge ... the earth rotates. If we put this thing on any existing observatory mountain, half the time, the comet would be on the wrong side of the earth. We'd have to wait until we came around again to continue firing."

Meadows said, "Since we may not get enough funding to stop the earth from rotating, what are you suggesting?"

Chandra smiled. "We need to put the beam projectors on the earth's Poles."

Several conversations started around the table. Meadows held up a hand. When the room quieted down, he said, "Explain."

Chandra continued, "We need as much time as possible with

an unobstructed shot at the comet. From the North and South Pole we can swivel the beam as the earth rotates and fire it 24 hours a day. The Poles also happen to have the thinnest, driest air and least amount of rainfall."

Meadows asked, "Are we talking both Poles?"

Chandra said, "That would be optimal but let's start with one site. It'd be easier to build it on land at the South Pole." She looked directly at Josh. "Unless our source suggests the comet's coming in from above the solar equatorial plane? If that's the case, we'd have to use some type of vessel at the North Pole."

Meadows looked at Josh.

Without even questioning Jesse, Josh suddenly knew the comet was coming in with a slight bias towards the Southern Hemisphere. He said, "South Pole."

Major Wendy Crowell, an Air Force engineer and MIT grad, said, "You have no power there. You'd need a nuclear reactor."

Chandra nodded. "Yup."

Meadows added, "Easier than putting it in orbit."

Crowell continued, "But we don't own the South Pole. How would we get permission to put a reactor there?"

Chandra shrugged and looked at Meadows and Josh. "Not my problem."

More conversations started around the room. Meadows leaned back and whispered to Josh, "Guess I see now why this thing's classified."

He nodded and said into Meadows' ear, "I'll talk to Carl about how to set up operations at the South Pole."

The meeting continued for another hour as they discussed details. Meadows finally wrapped it up.

Grinning, Cho faked a yawn. "Monster lasers, nukes at the South Pole. Hope we have something more interesting to work on soon."

Meadows finished with, "OK folks, great job! I feel good about our progress." Glancing at Josh, he added, "I've been promised we'll have funding authorization ASAP. Dr. Chandra, Dr. Katori, please give me a preliminary schedule and cost estimates as soon as you can, so we can work up a budget. Ladies and gentlemen, we don't have the authority to pull you off other projects, but I'm sure we'll be able to cut through the red tape soon. Off the record, I'd ask you to make this your number one priority.

With notification that a comet was going to hit the world in two years, he expected the mood to be somber. Instead, the atmosphere was more like a good Christmas party. Jesse was right, purpose was critical to happiness.

As Josh was about to leave, Meadows asked to see him, Chandra, Lopez, Katori and Wooldridge in his office.

They went in and sat down.

As Meadows closed the door, he said, "Dr. Wooldridge?"

Looking constipated, Wooldridge said, "Where's the data on this comet? I want to see its coordinates."

Josh asked quietly, "Could you see a dark comet two years out?"

"Of course not! That's my point."

Meadows, looking thoughtful, said, "When I was a young squadron safety officer, I had to take a course in Risk Management. It was very boring, but one thing stuck with me. When you're deciding how much time and money to put into mitigating risk, you look at two things. How likely is it to happen, and how severe are the consequences if it does?" He paused. "Apparently, even a small comet carries more destructive power than the world's entire inventory of nuclear weapons." He paused again. "Dr. Wooldridge, I understand your skepticism, but it seems to me there's a more important question. Why, if we've known we could be blindsided by a catastrophic impact, isn't there already a plan in place to deflect these things?"

Wooldridge said, "Despite the new impact estimates, the youngest impact craters bigger than a kilometer are tens of thousands of years old. The probability of a large impact is still considered very low."

Meadows nodded thoughtfully. "As a history major, I can tell you that there are over 150 great flood legends from across the globe. Since every major culture has one, anthropologists believe they must be based on some type of real event. I'm not a scientist but what could cause a global deluge and obliterate coastal civilizations?"

Chandra said, "It does make some sense. With 70% of the

world covered in oceans, that's where most impacts should occur, and they don't leave obvious craters for us to find." She shook her head. "It wouldn't take more than a one-kilometer-wide asteroid or comet to vaporize cubic miles of ocean and create 500-foot-high tsunamis." With a small smile, she added, "*That* would be enough to wash away a mythical Atlantis and even explain '40 days and 40 nights.'"

Wooldridge frowned. "That's conjecture."

Chandra smiled. "Yes, but IRAS-Araki-Alcock isn't." Looking around, she added, "It was a 10-kilometer-wide burned-out comet – a planet killer – that came within five-million kilometers of the earth. With a surface as black as coal, we didn't spot it until it was *two weeks* from closest approach."

Wooldridge gave a slight head nod and sighed. "It's really a matter of budgets. The government doesn't see it as an imminent threat and hasn't been willing to spend the money."

Lopez jumped in. "The problem is belief. It's hard for the mind to accept anything without personal experience. In the U.S., cars kill about 35,000 people a year. After hundreds of studies, we know seatbelts could have prevented half those deaths, and surveys show almost everyone knows this. Yet 10,000 unbelted people die every year. The problem is that unless you, or someone you know, cracked a windshield with your head, it's just not real. We understand logically but not emotionally." She looked around with a slight smile. "No one knows anyone killed by a comet."

Meadows nodded. Looking back at Wooldridge and then around the room, he said, "I understand it's hard to work without a concrete source." He glanced at Josh and said, "Hopefully we'll have that soon. However, this is something we should have done decades ago. At this point, I really don't care if Josh's source is **Optimus Prime**."

They nodded with some half-smiles.

Meadows continued, "I'll get off my soapbox." He smiled. "I honestly can't imagine a more brilliant team or a program with greater potential to help mankind. It's truly my honor to be able to work with you." He paused looking at each of them. "Let's make this happen."

As the meeting broke up, Wooldridge came over to Josh.

"I'm not only a tenured professor at Berkeley, I went there as an undergraduate." He looked down his long nose at Josh. "Do you have a college degree?"

Momentarily forgetting his need for concealment, Josh said, "Cornell."

Wooldridge, looking constipated again, said, "Well ... at least it wasn't a *state* school, like ...." He waved his hand vaguely in the direction of the others.

Josh knew that Chandra's University of Texas was highly ranked in astrophysics. Wooldridge was simply retreating into the security of his academic credentials. Giving him his due, Josh said, "Berkeley is unquestionably one of the best schools in the world in astrophysics."

"Actually, Berkeley is *the* best in the world."

Josh nodded, "Yes, of course, and I can't tell you how fortunate we are to have someone of your stature on this team. It's truly an honor."

Wooldridge finally smiled. "Glad to be able to offer my expertise."

Josh remembered Meadows' comment about "healthy egos."

After the meeting broke up, Tim Smith came by. With only Josh and Meadows in the office, Smith asked them, "May I talk to you?"

Josh jumped in with, "Sorry, Tim. I know I owe you that account information. I'll get it to you as soon as I can."

Smith shook his head. "No hurry. Even after you get it to the CIA, it'll take a while to get through their system to me." He paused. "Just wanted to let you know I've started my preliminary security investigation of the team members."

Frowning, Meadows asked, "I thought everyone on the team has a Top Secret clearance and a special background investigation?"

Smith nodded. "Yes, but most of them are dated, and I have resources that allow me to go into a little more depth."

Meadows nodded but maintained his frown. "Is that necessary? I've never been big on invading people's privacy unless it's absolutely necessary."

Smith said, "My purpose is simply to identify anyone on the team who might be vulnerable to outside influence such as blackmail, so that we can protect them and the program." He paused. "Captain Meadows, I'm very good at what I do. I've only had one failure in my career, and it was my fault for not knowing who I was protecting."

Josh thought he saw some emotion on Smith's face, but then it was gone. Smith ended with, "I won't let that happen again."

Meadows nodded seriously. "I understand. Do what you feel is necessary to protect the team."

Josh hoped Smith's detailed investigations didn't apply to his employers.

21

BILLIONAIRE

Josh learned that Elton Musk would be leaving New York to open his new launch facility in Ecuador. Sheri had managed to schedule Josh to see him at 5:00 pm, just before Musk departed. To make sure he had plenty of time to get to Musk's Manhattan office, he booked the earliest morning flight.

As he was shaving that morning, he looked in the mirror and said, "Only a couple minor details left to take care of – build a secret nuclear base at the South Pole and find a few hundred million to fund it." He smiled. "Delusions of grandeur, huh?"

As he arrived at the airport, he discovered there were major delays due to a line of heavy June thunderstorms pounding the East Coast. His 7:30 am flight finally left at 12:30 pm. He would still make it but his margin was gone.

It was a rough flight with a lot of turbulence. He felt sorry for the woman sitting next to him. She was clenching the armrest and sweating profusely. He told her he was a pilot and tried to set her at ease by explaining that the pilots would never take them through truly dangerous weather. The rough air was just from the periphery of the storms. It seemed to help.

Then the pilot, in a relaxed Texas drawl, announced they'd be stuck in a holding pattern for 30 minutes. He also said they might have to divert to another airport if the weather didn't improve.

Now Josh began to sweat and clench the armrest. He needed this meeting. The scientists and engineers couldn't keep charging their time to other programs without raising suspicion. On top of that, they needed to buy real pieces of hardware, not to mention building a base in Antarctica. He'd used up or cashed-in all of Elizabeth's free airline miles and had to max out his credit card just to pay for this flight.

He glanced over and realized the woman next to him was watching him closely.

With large eyes, she asked, "Are we going to die?"

He took a deep breath and smiled, confessing his nervousness was simply because he had a critical meeting in New York.

Relieved, she said, "I understand. I do meetings all over the country. Why don't you just text them your situation using the airline's Wi-Fi?"

Of course! He thanked her and texted Sheri.

Sheri replied that she'd call Musk.

Thirty minutes later the pilot updated them. "I'm sorry folks, if we don't get cleared for an approach in a few minutes, we're gonna have to divert to Philadelphia due to fuel."

Sheri texted him back that the best they could do was delay the meeting until 5:30 pm. Musk had to leave no later than 6:00 to catch his flight. Josh looked at his watch; if they didn't start their approach now, he'd never make it. He took a deep breath and made a conscious effort to stop producing adrenaline. He opened his eyes, feeling better.

The pilot came up and said, "I'm sorry folks, looks like we're going to have to divert to ...."

The passengers looked at each other and the woman next to him asked, "You think he forgot where he's going?"

Before Josh could respond, the pilot said, "Sorry. Just got cleared for the approach. Should be landin' at JFK in about 15 minutes. May be a little bumpy. Make sure your belts are cinched tight."

The approach was rough in heavy rain and winds, but they landed with only a few bounces. As soon as the airplane hit the gate, Josh was out and running through the airport. Checking the time, he realized he'd have to take a cab. After paying the fare and tip, he'd be down to his last few dollars. He appreciated the irony. He was there because he needed hundreds of millions, but he'd have to take a bus back to the airport.

He burst out of the terminal into a heavy downpour punctuated by lightning and thunder. He was able to grab a cab quickly but as they entered Manhattan, they hit a huge traffic jam.

Sitting in gridlock, he mapped the destination on his phone. He was only three miles away, but it was 5:15. No way he'd make it. Giving the driver the last of his cash, he jumped out into the deluge and started running. He ran hard, doing four-minute miles through the blowing sheets of rain. He dodged cars like a running back and reached the building at 5:27. Looking like he'd walked out of a swimming pool, and squeaking with each step, he went straight to the lobby information desk and showed his ID. The receptionist said, "Raining, huh?"

Still breathing hard, he replied, "Is it? I didn't notice."

Looking at him strangely, the receptionist directed him to the elevator.

Musk's office was, of course, at the top. Alone in the elevator, Josh caught his breath, closed his eyes and focused on what *must* happen. It was difficult. He was used to planning for the worst-case scenario and having a backup plan. He had no backup plan.

As he stepped out of the elevator, he was breathing more normally and saw the clock behind Musk's receptionist – 5:30.

Noticing his dripping clothes, the receptionist gave him a questioning look.

He shrugged. "Water balloon fight in the lobby."

She smiled. Pointing toward a large ornate entrance, she said, "He'll see you now, Commander Fuze." She winked and said, "I'll get you a towel."

He thanked her and went into the office. As he entered, he had a breathtaking view through floor-to-ceiling windows of a lightning illuminated Manhattan. Beautiful dark cherry wood covered the walls and ceiling with rich maroon carpet underfoot. Books completely dominated one wall. The office was an interesting mixture of old world and new technology: he saw multiple large monitors sitting on Musk's massive cherry desk.

Behind it stood Elton Musk, looking just like the newspaper pictures. "Good to meet you, Commander Fuze."

For some reason he wanted to say, "Bond, James Bond." Instead, still dripping, he said, "Do you need any of your plants watered?"

Smiling, Musk came around his desk as the receptionist came back with a large towel. Wiping his face and hands, Josh

IMPACT

offered one relatively dry hand. "It's Josh, and it's an honor to meet you, sir."

He'd never shaken the hand of a multi-billionaire before. Josh continued, "I admire what you've accomplished, both in the business and engineering world."

"Thank you." Musk paused. "I did a little checking after Sheri set this up. To be honest, my people couldn't find anything on you at all. That's extremely unusual but it also increased my curiosity. Who do you represent?"

"I'm a Naval officer but I'm ... *on loan* ... to another agency, one that I am not at liberty to discuss right now." He continued, "I know your time is valuable but I believe we have something you will find very interesting. Before I share it, do you mind telling me a little bit about your long term goals and what you're ... passionate about?" Josh knew he could use words like passion with successful people like Musk.

Musk started laughing. "So you haven't read the tabloids?"

Josh smiled. "I wanted to hear what your vision really is and see if it intersects with our project." He thought he knew what Musk's passion was but needed to hear it from him, and start building trust. The best way to make friends was to ask people about themselves.

Musk looked at him carefully, as if assessing his seriousness, and then motioned him to a seat. Josh sat on the towel as Musk perched on the edge of his desk. Musk shared some of his long-term business and humanitarian goals, emphasizing that if humanity were to survive, they'd have to expand beyond the earth. He talked about his Mars colonization initiative and the ridicule he'd received from much of the media.

Josh asked him why he thought it so important to make humanity an interplanetary culture. After Musk explained his fear of potential global disasters, Josh knew Musk was his man ... *if* he could convince him. "Sir, I appreciate what you are trying to do more than you know. If I share something with you, will you promise not to divulge it to anyone?"

"Yes, and call me Elton."

Josh pulled out the damp folder with the security paperwork in it. Getting Musk cleared into the program would draw too much attention. Since Musk would never attend

136

meetings at Boeing, no one but Josh would know that he didn't have a project clearance. Accurately, Josh said, "This is just a formality. I know you're a man of your word."

As Musk read over the paperwork, pen in hand, Josh continued, "With knowledge comes responsibility, and with great knowledge comes great responsibility. What I tell you today may change the course of your life and business." He knew that people like Musk responded to challenge and adventure. Security and even safety were often secondary considerations.

Musk signed the paper and handed it back.

Josh asked, "Is this office secure from electronic eavesdropping?"

Musk pressed a button on his desk and said, "It's as secure as our current technology can make it."

A half hour later, Musk was excitedly nodding his head. "I knew something like this would happen someday. I feel like screaming, 'I told you so!' We should have been planning for this decades ago. Our space program would have been light-years beyond where it is today."

Josh nodded. "I know."

Musk shook his head. "But ... I didn't think it would happen this soon." He stood silent for a moment and then looked at Josh. "This has so many implications. Your source ... I'm guessing ... we're not alone?"

"I'm sorry." Josh shook his head. "I've said more than I should have. The question is – can you help us? We're asking you to convert your mission and resources from commercial space access, to protecting the earth from a comet. As if that's not enough, you'll have to do it in total secrecy for a while. I can't even guarantee you'll be fully compensated."

"If what you say is true, it's a simple decision. The alternative is the death of millions or billions including my family." He paused. "I've always known I had a critical purpose and as corny as it sounds, this feels right." He looked back at Josh meaningfully. "*If* I were convinced this is real, I'd have no problem committing my business and personal wealth, but there are a couple things that don't make sense. First of all, why do you need my help? Surely the U.S. government has sufficient resources."

Josh asked, "What do you think will happen when this goes public?"

"Maybe wars will stop and we'll all work together."

"And maybe the world's stock markets will collapse overnight," Josh countered.

Musk looked out the window toward the skyline and nodded. "Yeah, that's possible."

"Only a handful of people know about this. As we speak, experts are trying to figure out how to introduce this to the public without causing panic or economic collapse."

Musk nodded. "Of course! That's why Sheri Lopez is involved."

Josh nodded. "Plus, no matter how many resources the government brings to bear, you know they can never act as quickly as private industry. We're trying to install a nuclear reactor and humongous laser at the South Pole ..."

Musk interrupted, "And if *Commander* Fuze and the U.S. military are tied to a project involving a nuclear reactor and what looks like a giant weapon in Antarctica ...."

Josh nodded. "It could create serious international confrontation. By keeping the funding source private for the Antarctic part of the operation, we have a better chance of maintaining our cover story."

Musk nodded. "I guess that makes sense." He paused. "So – hypothetically – what would you need from me?"

"Your engineering expertise and several hundred million dollars to start building the polar base."

"Josh, one of my hobbies is mountain climbing and I even climbed one in Antarctica. You've picked one of the toughest places on earth to build something."

Josh shrugged. "No choice."

"If I fund this, am I going to be the fall guy if the U.S. denies involvement?"

Josh shrugged again. "Probably." Then he added, "But even if the comet information is wrong, I think history will treat us well for building the first planetary defense system."

"No offense, Josh, but I would've expected a higher-ranking government official, like maybe the President, to have made this request."

Josh smiled. "No offense taken, but you can see the risk involved with a high-ranking official talking to you directly. Because of the incredible sensitivity, few in the government are aware ... even at the highest levels."

Musk frowned and then said wryly, "Makes it a bit difficult to confirm."

Josh had an idea. "Do you know of Dr. Ken Katori from Boeing?

"Yes, he's one of my primary competitors."

"How about Dr. Victoria Chandra?"

"Chandra? Yes, of course. Everyone in the space community knows her or her reputation."

"Ken is our chief engineer and Dr. Chandra is our chief scientist."

Musk nodded slowly, then stared out the window gently drumming his fingers on the desk. After several moments, he turned back to Josh and blew out a lungful of air. "Josh, can you give me a minute? I need to make a quick call."

"Of course." Josh stepped outside his office, and tried not to pace while picturing a positive outcome.

After a few minutes, Musk came out and asked Josh to follow him. They got on the elevator and on the way down, Musk said, "I've scheduled a face-to-face meeting with Dr. Chandra. If this checks out, I have two hard requirements. I want to be part of the Antarctic operation, and I want Christoff Bobinski on your leadership team."

Josh nodded his head. "We need your expertise in Antarctica. You'll have full access there." He frowned. "But who's Christoff Bobinski?"

"A trusted Russian business partner, he is to extreme arctic construction what Red Adair was to oil well firefighting. He's an absolute wizard. You'll need him."

"We can use all the help we can get. I'll run him through our system, and we'll figure out how to get him cleared onto the project."

Musk added, "By the way, I *am* going to get some serious tax breaks with this project, aren't I?"

Josh shrugged. "Doubtful. The IRS hasn't been read into the program."

"Josh, you're not a very good salesman." Laughing he said, "Come on. I'm taking you to my comptroller where you can work the account details so we'll be ready to hook your system to ours. By the way, *do not* tell her that there are no tax breaks; she'll have a nervous breakdown."

They arrived at his comptroller's office, and Musk quickly introduced them. Then said, "I have to go."

As he was leaving, Josh looked at the time and said, "I'm sorry. I made you miss your flight."

Looking back over his shoulder, Musk winked. "Josh, I can't miss my flight. I own the airliner."

Musk's comptroller looked like his grandmother. He sheepishly confessed he had little understanding of how government accounting worked. She smiled and assured him that she had worked with the government and knew what to do. All she needed was a point of contact. He promised he'd get all the information she needed as soon as he returned to St Louis.

As he was about to leave, she handed him what looked like a credit card and a Post It with a handwritten number. She said, "Mr. Musk told me to set up a petty cash fund for quick response needs until we get the final clearance." Looking a little stern, she added, "You can use it as a debit card for whatever you need, but there's only $100,000 in the account." Smiling again, she said, "If you lose it or need the funds replenished, just give me a call."

Like a boy given a puppy by his grandmother, he promised he'd be careful with it and thanked her profusely.

As soon as the elevator door closed, he did a football touchdown dance. This was exactly the outcome he had pictured, except for the *petty* cash fund. He'd just been hoping for bus fare. He also realized he could pay Elizabeth back. As silly as that was in the scheme of things, it bothered him to borrow money from her. What he really wanted to do was treat her to a fancy dinner as soon as he got back to Kansas City and buy her a nice gift. He'd be careful with his funds, but he owed her that. None of this would have been possible without her.

As he got back to the airport, he made a call.

"Carl, can you do me a favor? I need to have an individual checked out before inviting him on the team."

Carl said, "Sure. Where are you now?"

"New York City."

There was a pause. "Can you stop by D.C. on the way back?"

Josh understood. They really couldn't talk about sensitive information over the phone, and Carl hadn't been able to attend the team meetings in person. "Sure, I'll change my flight and can be there tomorrow morning."

"Great. If we don't have to talk details, let's grab lunch at J. Gilbert's around twelve. Do you know where that is?"

"No, but I'm sure I can Google it. See you there."

Josh used his new charge card to change his flight to D.C. He could fly first class now, but wouldn't. He wasn't against having nice things or bothered by people who did. If things worked out, he planned to have some fun, but not now, not yet. He would continue living at his current level, not just to be a good steward of the funds, but because he didn't need distractions. He knew distractions came in many shapes ... but the most dangerous had two legs.

22

REUNION

J. Gilbert's was an elegant steakhouse with rich, dark wood, brick and soft lighting. Before Musk's debit card, even buying a hamburger there would have been a financial stress.

Josh saw Carl sitting at a table with his back to the wall. Classic position for an intelligence guy.

After joining him and ordering drinks, Carl said softly, "Been thinking about the Antarctic site. There was a treaty created in the late 1950s – now signed by over 40 countries including the U.S. Basically, it set aside Antarctica as a scientific preserve, established freedom of scientific investigation, and banned all military activity on the continent."

Josh had looked this up as well.

Carl continued, "Our program would certainly qualify with both the letter *and* the spirit of the law ...."

Josh asked, "But?"

"But, trying to get 40 countries to agree on anything is next to impossible, and certainly not in the time we have." Carl smiled. "This is one of those rare times when I think history will vindicate us for being sneaky."

Josh whispered, "What type of story would raise the fewest eyebrows?"

"This may sound funny coming from our agency, but honesty is the best policy." He winked. "It reduces the number of lies you have to remember."

"Roger that."

Carl asked, "What will the equipment look like?"

"Not really sure but it will be very big with a large optical telescope for tracking."

"Off of the top of my head, I'd go with an astrophysics

142

project." He paused. "Which, come to think of it, it is."

Josh smiled. "Sounds good."

After their drinks arrived, Carl said, "So who do we need to check on?"

"He's an arctic construction expert, but he's a naturalized American citizen."

"Where's he from?"

"I'm afraid it's Russia. His name is Christoff Bobinski."

"Actually, Russians are usually easy to check on. Tim can run the background check. That's one of his specialties."

"I'm sorry, Carl. It never even occurred to me to ask him. I'm embarrassed to say I forget he's even there. He's like a shadow."

Carl smiled. "Being invisible is one of his specialties. If you were aware of him, he wouldn't be as effective."

Josh nodded. "We're also considering working with Elton Musk."

He frowned and then shrugged. "Makes sense; he's the ultimate space entrepreneur."

Josh added, "And he has construction infrastructure. In fact, Bobinski was his idea."

Carl nodded. "This could actually be beneficial. It wouldn't seem odd if he was supporting a space science project in Antarctica." He paused. "Josh, is there any way we could route some of the government funds through him to make it look like *he's* funding the Antarctic part of the program?"

Josh, trying not to smile, said, "I don't see why not."

Carl smiled. "Great. Then I don't see a problem."

Josh was congratulating himself when Carl looked up over Josh's head and said, "Hope you don't mind. I invited my wife, Kelly. Thought you guys might like to meet, having known Andy Logan so well."

Time slowed as he turned around and their eyes met.

As he stood, adrenaline flooded his bloodstream, creating a flash of anxiety that almost made his knees buckle. She looked exactly as he remembered her, down to her clothes and hairstyle. Kelly was an incredibly cute, fair-skinned redhead with a light dusting of freckles. She had beautiful, intense green eyes that matched her passionate personality. They could stare a hole right through you when angry. Caught between conflicting compulsions, he wanted to run away … and hold her tightly.

She offered her hand.

Speechless, he took it, as Carl said, "Kelly, this is Josh Fuze."

Looking directly into his eyes, she said, "Hi, Josh. Glad to meet you. So you knew Andy?"

Jesse's words echoed painfully in his mind. "No one can ever know you're still alive … no one." He managed a nod and a "Good to meet you." Even in his state of shock, he thought that this was just like her, always to the point. Just when he thought it couldn't get any worse, he caught her scent. She was wearing the same perfume, light but unmistakable. It threatened to send him into a memory spiral. Clearing his throat to give him a few precious seconds, he said, "Yes, we worked on some programs together."

Kelly said, "I'm sorry, I don't remember him talking about you, but I know he worked on a lot of those secret squirrel things." She kissed Carl as she sat next to him.

As Josh sat back down, he thought, *This can't be happening!* He *knew* about Carl and Kelly but this … this face-to-face reality. He felt like he was suffocating. With huge effort, he tried to compartmentalize his emotions and maintain his composure. His intellectual mind resurfaced, and he suddenly had a thought. Maybe this surprise meeting was exactly that, but Carl was a brilliant strategist and skeptical by nature. This might be a test, a test to see if he really knew Andy Logan. Good! He needed a challenge to deal with, anything to keep his mind off … them. He had to tread carefully but he had an advantage. He knew as much about Kelly as any man could ever know about a woman.

Before he could come up with a plan, Kelly asked, "Are you married or have any kids?"

Josh said, "No."

"*Were* you married?"

"Yes. Yes, I was. She …." He stumbled. "She remarried."

"I'm sorry. It wasn't that long ago was it?"

"Uh … no." This had to be the oddest conversation in history. He knew she would ask questions relentlessly. It's just what she did. He had to change the subject, if only to maintain his sanity. An idea struck him. Before she could ask her next question, he said, "Kelly, Andy told me a funny story once. You'll have to tell me if it was really true."

She finally looked nervous.

"He said you were at a local lake with your ski boat. You did the romantic thing with champagne at sunset. Then you dropped him off at the dock so he could get the truck and boat trailer. While he was getting the trailer, he said you took the boat out for one last high-speed spin."

He saw her eyes widen with recognition. "Oh no, he told you *that?*" Smiling, she hung her head dramatically.

He knew she liked being the central character in a story, and Carl was enjoying her embarrassment.

"He said he heard you racing off into the night near the shoreline. It was getting dark, and ... wasn't the water level in the lake lower than usual?"

She nodded guiltily.

"If I remember correctly, he said that as he brought the truck down the ramp with the trailer, he heard an outboard motor running at full speed. Then he heard a cough, stutter and silence."

Kelly shook her head. "I didn't know the water was only a few inches deep near the island."

Smiling, Carl added, "Oops."

Josh continued, "He said, in the dark he heard a distant, rhythmic splashing sound. He yelled your name but got no answer. He got worried, jumped in and swam out a couple hundred yards."

Kelly smiled and shook her head.

"As he got closer, he said he could make out the outline of the boat and you swimming in front of it. You were trying to pull the boat in with a rope?"

Kelly protested, "I had to, there was only one paddle. I kept going around in circles."

Carl started laughing.

She added, "He almost drowned laughing at me, so I helped him by pushing his head under. I was *so* mad!" Kelly's eyes flashed, and then she started laughing.

He couldn't help but think how much he missed those laser green eyes.

Rolling her eyes, she said, "I *can't believe* he shared that with you. So your only impression of me is an airhead sailor with a bad temper!"

"No, no, I'm sorry. He told me awesome things about you. This was just one of those stories that kinda sticks with you."

Kelly said, "Yeah, he was always a great storyteller ... like you." She cocked her head to one side. "Josh, it's weird but as you told that story, I *so* heard him. You told it almost exactly like he would've."

Carl nodded. "She's right. You really could be his brother with your speech patterns."

He realized a new voice box didn't change his inflection or idioms. He'd have to be more careful. Truthfully, he said, "That's probably because we both grew up in Northern Virginia."

Carl and Kelly both nodded, but Kelly added, "Did you know his call sign was *Fuzed*, almost like your last name?"

"Yeah. That was a ... cool coincidence." Deflecting, he quickly asked, "So how do you like the D.C. area?"

Kelly said, "It's actually a great place to live, but of course we'll have to start thinking about good school districts now with the baby."

Josh coughed, almost spitting out his water, "Baby?"

She frowned at Carl. "Carl didn't tell you?"

Carl shrugged awkwardly.

She continued, "We have a beautiful, bouncing baby girl." Like any proud mother, Kelly immediately pulled up pictures on her phone.

Carl added, "She's already got her mother's temper."

Kelly smiled, shaking her head. "She's just strong."

Josh looked carefully at the pictures and saw a beautiful, red-haired baby girl. Softly, he asked, "How old is she?"

"Let's see, Caitlin will be seven months next week.

For Josh, time stopped.

23

DAUGHTER

Josh saw a bright flash and for a moment, there were two of him.

Time started moving again but in slow motion. He stood up abruptly, knocking his chair over backwards and rushed to Kelly's side of the table.

Startled, she pushed her chair back. He grabbed her arms just above the elbow and pulled her out of her chair. "Kelly Bear, it's me! It's Andy! I'm alive!" He could see the look of surprise and shock on her face. Still moving in slow motion, he saw Carl stand up out of the corner of his eye, as everyone in the restaurant turned toward them.

Kelly's eyes were wide as she stared intently into his. Then her face turned from surprise to anguish and fear. Backing up slowly, she started shaking her head and sobbing, "No, no...." She looked away from him and swept her hands up between them, breaking his grasp. Her face continued to morph into terrible agony.

He moved toward her but felt Carl's hand in the middle of his chest.

With a look of unadulterated hatred, Carl yelled, "What the hell are you doing? Get away from my wife!" He shoved Josh back against the table almost knocking him down, as Kelly ran from the restaurant.

Suddenly, his perspective flashed forward in time. Like a movie trailer, he saw himself running. He was a fugitive. His program crumbled around him and there was fire everywhere. Then, another bright flash.

He found himself still sitting in his chair at the restaurant, muscles tensed to stand.

"... seven months next week. It's hard to believe she's

already that old, but time flies faster when you're changing diapers." She finished with a smile.

Josh took a cautious breath and tried to relax his calf muscles.

Kelly suddenly tipped her head sideways and said, "Whoa. I just had a total déjà vu moment, like this already happened." She laughed. "I get those all the time, do you?"

He just nodded dumbly, still looking at the picture on Kelly's phone. Finally, he managed to squeeze out, "She's beautiful, just like her mom." Sitting back, he added, "Excuse me, boy's room. Be right back."

As he got up, he heard Kelly whispering to Carl, "I was wrong. I'm sure I *have* met him before."

Inside one of the men's room stalls, he just stood there leaning against the wall trying to breath. It was the same feeling he had after narrowly avoiding a midair collision with another fighter. He did the math again as his overworked adrenal glands quieted. It had to be. Caitlin was his daughter. He shook his head and said softly, "A daughter ... I have a daughter."

It also dawned on him that Carl had asked a very pregnant Kelly to marry him. Josh realized he'd been harboring an illogical resentment toward Carl, but this ... changed things. Carl had done something few men would have done. He felt genuine warmth for his old friend again. He sighed. "Thanks, Carl."

Shredded by so many emotions, he just had to hold it together a little longer. He latched on to something to help him focus. He had a daughter ... a daughter who was going to die in 20 months unless he succeeded.

He went to the sink and splashed water on his face. Wiping it off, he took a deep breath and returned.

As he sat back down at the table, he said, "I realized I never congratulated you on your marriage or daughter."

Kelly smiled. "Andy and I never talked about what would happen if one of us weren't here anymore, but," she paused, "I think he would have approved."

He saw her eyes get a little glassy but she was a strong woman. No tears and she never let her voice inflection change. He appreciated that strength now. He glanced at Carl and then looked her directly in the eye. Slowly but with strength, he said, "I am absolutely certain that Andy wouldn't have wanted it any other way."

With a slightly raspy voice, Kelly said, "Thanks, Josh." Taking a deep breath and wiping her eyes, she escaped into her comfortable cross-examination mode. "So, you're not married now. Anyone in the wings?"

Carl shook his head. "She just meets you and she's already weighing you to decide who she'll introduce you to."

Josh, looking a little uncertain, said, "Uh, actually ... there might be someone." He paused. "She's a nurse in Kansas City, but I don't know if my *occupation* will ultimately work for her."

Kelly laughed. "Military officers and nurses; it's such a cliché. Well, she's in for a wild ride, but if she's got any guts, she won't let you get away. Course, she must be a saint if she's hanging with someone like *you*."

Josh knew he'd been accepted when she was willing to tease him. He pushed his food around the plate, and finally looking at his phone, said, "I'm sorry, but I really have to go. Kelly, it was great to ... to meet you."

They all stood up and Carl shook Josh's hand saying, "I'll get back to you on that security check."

Josh nodded.

Before Josh could offer his hand, Kelly came over and hugged him. He didn't want to let her go ... but matched her hug and politely patted her on the back.

On the drive home, Kelly was uncharacteristically quiet.

Carl finally asked, "You OK?"

Sniffing she said, "I'm sorry. I don't know what's wrong with me. Probably just hormones."

She smiled at Carl and ran her hand through his hair. "Actually ... I'm great." Looking out the window, she said, "I don't know why ... but for some reason I feel like a weight's been lifted off my shoulders." Then she looked back at Carl with a hint of mischief. "And if Josh's current girlfriend doesn't work out, I know just who to introduce him to ... *but* he's going to have to get over his ex first."

"His ex? What are you talking about?"

Looking incredulous, she asked, "Didn't you see his body

language when I asked about his previous marriage?" She shook her head. "He's *totally* not over her!"

Carl frowned. "You deduced that from his *body* language?"

"Well, yeah! He looked like a kicked puppy."

Carl, frowning and smiling at the same time, said, "You're *sure* you don't want a job with the agency?"

She rolled her eyes but grinned. "I'm going to have to meet this girlfriend of his and find out what the real story is."

Josh drove to his hotel completely numb. He went to his room and threw his briefcase on the bed. Standing motionless, he replayed in his mind all that transpired. Kelly kissing Carl ... one of the hardest things he'd ever had to witness. He had fought himself the entire time. Then, the alternate-reality confrontation with Kelly. It was like a bucket of ice water in the face. He still didn't know what had happened but it was painfully real.

When Jesse first told him his old life was gone, he understood ... but not really, not emotionally. Then when Meadows told of the missing man formation, it began to sink in. *He* was the missing man. His death became real, but even then, it was just *him*.

When he saw the wedding picture on Carl's desk, he had run away from the thought – literally. Now he understood what Jesse meant and why he could never go back to his old life. He exhaled unsteadily as he said softly, "I've lost her ...."

Running a hand through his hair, he slammed his fist on the desk, knocking the lamp off. He wanted to scream at Jesse. Rage against the mind-numbing unfairness ... but he was exhausted, emotionally desiccated. His whole body sighed as he dropped into a chair.

Head in hands, he stared at nothing. When Elizabeth told him how her husband died, he knew she had no closure and felt sorry for her. He'd been oblivious to the fact that he had the exact same problem ... the loss of his wife ... and now his child. His anger and indignation deflated into despair. He could never tell Kelly the truth, even if the world wasn't hanging in the balance. She'd been through the grief and mourning. She *had* closure and pulled her life back together with a new husband. If somehow she believed him – he remembered her face in his alternate reality – it would rip her apart. It would be monumentally selfish and hurtful. He must, he would, remain silent. "Kelly," he said with anguish and then softer, "Caitlin ...."

When he was a child, his dad told him men don't cry. He cried ... then slept.

24

LOGISTICS

Josh sat in Meadows' office with Smith. He told them about Musk and Bobinski.

Meadows looked skeptical. "Elton Musk is too much of a public figure. He'll draw the media like a lightning rod."

Josh said, "Maybe, but Lopez is a celebrity too. Along with Musk's engineering expertise and construction connections, Carl suggested we use him to 'launder' our program's money through his company. That should provide some insulation."

Smith nodded.

Meadows said, "That's good but I'm still uncomfortable having him around our team."

Josh knew that without an official clearance, he couldn't get Musk into the building, much less into their meetings. "You're right. We wouldn't have him attend any of our regular meetings. The only place we'd see him would be in Antarctica, which would help support our cover story."

Meadows smiled, nodding. "Probably not a lot of paparazzi there. I assume you're taking care of his clearance and how to route the money through him?"

"Yes sir."

Meadows asked Smith, "What about Bobinski?"

Smith said, "We've checked him out. It wasn't hard. He's a colorful character but appears to be the best in his field."

Meadows asked, "Is he a security risk?"

Briefly looking at Josh, Smith said, "We're all security risks. It just requires the right situation or leverage. Bobinski was a born entrepreneur and became a naturalized U.S. citizen during the Soviet days to escape the communist regime. He still loves his former country and spends a lot of time there. He also has some connections with Russian organized crime."

Meadows said what Josh was thinking, "So, he *is* a risk?"

Smith said, "This may sound strange, but it's the people who don't believe in something that worry us. What we're doing will save both the U.S. and Russia. I don't see any conflict of interest."

Meadows asked, "What about his connections with the Russian mob?"

Smith said, "It would be surprising if he didn't. When the Soviet Union collapsed, it was like the U.S. during prohibition. To get anything done, you had to work with the shadier elements. Since then, the Russian government has clamped down considerably, but organized crime is still an economic reality in some areas."

Meadows said, "So what are you saying?"

"Bobinski is tough and doesn't suffer fools patiently but he has character and even those who don't like him, respect him. He's already a multi-millionaire, so he doesn't need the job. He has no obvious vices aside from a love of a good party and Russian women, and he really doesn't care what other people think of him."

Meadows smiled. "I like him already."

Smith continued, "In other words, he's not a good blackmail target. We also discovered that he once worked on a U.S. government project that required a basic security clearance. It shouldn't be too hard to update it to a higher level. Carl can help expedite that."

Josh finally asked, "Would *you* trust him?"

"Yes." Looking down, Smith added softly, "But I've been wrong before."

—✳—

Elizabeth hadn't seen or heard from Josh since he left for New York two weeks ago. Coming home from work, she was surprised to find a letter from him. She opened it quickly. Inside was a check for $15,000, and a note. *"Here's the $5,000 you loaned me plus interest and reimbursement for the airline miles. Thank you! I couldn't have done it without you. Josh"*

She sat down and said quietly to Toto. "That's it? Thanks for everything?" With a funding source, he didn't need her support anymore. There was nothing more she could contribute to the cause. She had thought – or maybe just hoped – there was more between them. Part of her was hurt and angry with Josh. Still another part was angry with herself for being angry. She knew what was at stake. Her feelings were irrelevant. With a half-smile, she shook her head and asked the dog, "What kind of idiot dates a prophet?" She sighed softly as she dropped the letter in the trash.

Dr. Jackie Jones got Cho's voicemail for the third time. She tried Cho's deputy but got the same response. Finally, she called Conner, the young engineer who did the last program briefing.

Without preamble, she jumped in. "Conner, where the heck is Dr. Cho? We've got a major program status meeting for the National Reconnaissance Office coming up, and I'm looking at some serious schedule slips. He hasn't returned my emails or calls in over a week."

"Sorry, Dr. Jones. He's been gone. He's working on that other program, but I'm putting together the technical and schedule status for you."

"What *is* this other program?"

"I'm sorry, ma'am; I'm not read into it. All I know is that it's very sensitive and he has half the lab involved, but no one's talking."

Jones bit down on her first response, forcing herself to acknowledge it wasn't Conner's fault. "When you talk to Dr. Cho, please have him call me *as soon* as possible."

"Yes ma'am. Would you like to see the charts I'm putting together?"

Jones sighed softly. "Sure, Conner. That would be great."

After she hung up, she called the president of Northrup Grumman.

It was the end of July, one of the hottest days of the year in St. Louis. Insulated from the sweltering heat and humidity, there were almost two dozen people in the cool conference room; all wearing special program badges. Seeing the "Resurrect" name on the badges, Josh smiled. He probably shouldn't have named it that, but the participants probably assumed it was resurrection of the technology from the old Strategic Defense Initiative.

There was a positive tension in the room. Meadows sat at

one end of the table with Chandra on his right and Katori on his left. Lopez, Wooldridge and Cho usually sat in the first tier, spaced around the table. Generally, the second tier was for the more junior personnel. Josh always sat in the second tier near Meadows, trying to keep a low profile. He noticed that Tim Smith also sat in the second tier but never in the same place twice.

Meadows started the meeting, "I'd like everyone to welcome our two new logistics teammates." He pointed to two men sitting at the table to the left of Katori. "This is Dr. Winston Shepherd and Mr. Christoff Bobinski. Dr. Shepherd has several degrees and government certifications in logistics and support. Mr. Bobinski is world renowned in industrial construction, particularly under extreme conditions. Gentlemen, welcome to the team."

There were nods from around the table. Dr. Shepherd was a slightly overweight, medium-height man in his fifties, with a hawkish nose and thin, black hair combed carefully over a large bald spot. Bobinski was similar in age but with a gray beard, looked more like Sean Connery.

Josh couldn't help but think what a strange and eclectic team this was.

Meadows kicked it off. "So, where and how are we going to site this thing?"

Katori said, "We believe we've found the perfect location. Mount Howe is the closest exposed bedrock to the geographic South Pole. This site will allow us to build on solid ground instead of snow pack. That's good since we have to align the beam to within a gnat's eyelash, and we're powering it with a nuclear reactor which generates a lot of heat."

Meadows asked, "Don't we need to be right at the South Pole for the beam to swivel as the earth rotates?" He smiled at Chandra. "See, I've been paying attention."

Chandra grinned back. "Normally, yes, but it's only 300 kilometers from the Pole, and the top of Mount Howe is almost 9,000 feet above sea level. That height compensates for not being right at the pole. The mountain top, combined with the flattening of the atmosphere at the poles, also means there's 40% less air to get the beam through."

Katori continued, "There's also a major logistics advantage.

Turns out, they evaluated Mount Howe back in '89 as a potential airfield to support the South Pole base. A flat plain of smooth blue ice surrounds the mountain. That means with some surface prep, conventional wheeled aircraft can land there."

Meadows frowned in question.

Major Crowell jumped in. "At the South Pole base, they have to use special C-130s with skis. Being able to use large conventional cargo jets, like C-5s, vastly simplifies our construction transportation and logistics. The only reason they scrapped the idea was that it was too far to the South Pole."

"That's great. What about security?"

Josh said, "With the Antarctic Treaty, there's no way we'll get permission to put a nuclear reactor there without U.N. debate. Our international expert," Josh didn't use Carl's name, "has been working with Dr. Lopez and Dr. Chandra on a cover story." He nodded at them.

Chandra said, "Mount Howe would be a great location for an astronomical observatory for the same reason we want it."

Meadows asked, "So a new observatory is our cover story?"

Chandra laughed. "No, it would draw too much attention. Hundreds of astronomers would be fighting for observing time before it's even built."

Lopez added. "The cover story will be an ozone layer study. It's a little thin," she smiled at the obvious pun, "but should give us some time." She shook her head. "We're not going to keep this under wraps long. There are too many people involved and we'll be moving heavy equipment."

Meadows nodded. "Where are we going to stage out of?"

Katori said, "Falklands."

"Why?"

"Four reasons. It's one of the closest airfields to the South Pole. It's a stable satellite country of the U.K. The island is very isolated with a tiny population of only 3,000, yet they have a big commercial/military airfield able to support large cargo jets. Finally, we have a stroke of good luck. Turns out, we have some Boeing people already there."

Meadows looked surprised. "Seriously?"

Katori continued, "The Australians have a Super Hornet squadron deployed to the Falklands right now."

There were some curious looks around the table.

Meadows jumped in, finally in his area of expertise. "Of course. Despite Argentina's loss to the Brits during the Falklands War, they still claim that the Falklands are rightfully theirs, and recently purchased advanced Russian fighters. I'm guessing the U.K. made an arrangement with the Australians. I'll bet they're funding the deployment of the Super Hornets under the guise of a joint training exercise. It's a clear message to thwart any renewed Argentine interest in the islands."

Katori shrugged. "Bottom line, we have Boeing technical reps assigned to support our foreign military contracts on the Super Hornets. Two of our people are there now. They can easily run our staging office without drawing attention."

Meadows said, "Excellent. Let's look at the timeline."

Katori said, "It's going to be extremely tight. We have to have the facility on top of Mount Howe, ready to receive the energy-beam projector, in eight months. We also have to have an operating nuclear reactor by then. Fortunately, the Antarctic summer, with six months of daylight, begins in a few weeks."

Dr. Shepherd, who had been frowning the whole time, finally pulled his glasses off and said, "There's no way we can get a nuclear-powered base on top of a mountain in Antarctica in seven months. It will take a couple years, minimum."

There was a tense silence. Katori looked from Shepherd to Meadows. Meadows looked at Christoff Bobinski. "Mr. Bobinski, what do you think?"

With a heavy Russian accent, he asked, "What are budget constraints?"

Meadows looked directly at Josh.

Josh had watched Bobinski's face while Shepherd spoke and saw an almost imperceptible smile. Josh said, "None."

Shepherd inserted, "It doesn't matter what the budget is; you have to scrape a runway, build an access road up the mountain, and put a large facility on top. How are you going to do that in Antarctica?"

Meadows then looked at Bobinski with raised eyebrows, clearly giving him permission to speak.

Bobinski simply said, "D7E electric diesel hybrid bulldozers."

Shepherd asked, "How're you going to get them there?"

"One C-17 can carry two of them."

"How're you going to keep them from freezing? The temperature there gets down to 50 degrees below zero."

Meadows leaned over and whispered to Josh, "Fahrenheit or Celsius?"

Josh whispered back, "At that temperature, it doesn't matter."

Bobinski said, "Bulldozers will never be turned off."

Shepherd continued to argue, "There just isn't enough time."

Bobinski said, "We'll use the six months of daylight. Since the sun and bulldozers will be up 24 hours, so will we."

Shepherd said, "What about blizzards and white-out conditions?"

Chandra jumped in. "Antarctica actually only gets about an inch of precipitation a year. The blizzards are mostly ground snow blown around by high winds. Antarctica is more like a desert with sandstorms than a winter wonderland. With the energy-beam on the mountaintop, it will also be above most of the blowing snow."

Shepherd asked, "Where are you going to get enough C-17s?"

Katori laughed. "Dr. Shepherd, you're sitting in a Boeing conference room. We make 'em here."

Shepherd finally stopped arguing and shook his head.

Meadows wrapped up the meeting with more assignments.

Josh thought it was progressing beautifully but he knew the real technical and logistics challenges were ahead. Oddly, one of the things he was most concerned with didn't involve the program. He hadn't been able to reach Elizabeth. He really wanted to see her, particularly, after the Kelly catharsis. He'd called several times but always got her voicemail. Still trying to keep a low profile, he hadn't left messages or texts.

Smith stayed behind after the meeting. Speaking quietly, he said, "Captain Meadows, I've finished my background checks on the team personnel."

Smiling, Meadows said, "I hope you're not going to tell me

that Cho likes to paint his toe nails."

"No, but if he did, it wouldn't matter because he's an extrovert. He'd be the first to tell you. I only look for things that could be used to blackmail or entice."

"And?"

"It's a solid team. There are only two individuals who are of some concern: one, because of his financial situation, the other, because I can't find any background information on him at all. He's what we refer to in the intelligence community as a non-person."

Meadows frowned. "Who are you talking about?"

25

ANTARCTICA

Things were moving fast. They were working feverishly at Los Alamos and sending a team to survey the South Pole site. Meadows said that he would visit Los Alamos and shepherd the laser work, and he told Josh to go on the site survey to Antarctica.

With all the activity, it was probably good that he was no longer involved with Elizabeth. He'd finally left her a voicemail, asking if she was all right. By text, he'd received a simple reply, "I'm fine." He remembered her telling him that her parents took in strays all the time. It occurred to him that their relationship might have been nothing more than that. Maybe she was just a Good Samaritan like her parents and had moved on once she knew he didn't need her help anymore. Still, he had to admit it hurt, but he needed to keep his focus on the mission.

He met briefly with Meadows, Katori, Smith and Lopez.

Smith said, "We'll need a cover story for the Antarctic logistics flights."

Meadows smiled. "It's common knowledge that the Australians are interested in upgrading their Super Hornet's phased-array radar."

Katori jumped in. "It wouldn't be unusual for Boeing to send a team to install the new radar so they could test it under real-world conditions before buying. Since radar technology is highly classified, it would explain Boeing Phantom Works involvement and the logistics flights."

Smith and Lopez both nodded.

Meadows still smiling said, "Covert stuff's kind of fun."

After wrapping up the meeting, Josh and Lopez walked toward the parking lot together.

She casually asked, "How's Elizabeth?"

Josh frowned. "I think she's fine. I haven't talked to her in a couple months."

She stopped and turned to him. "I thought you two were kind of an item?"

He smiled to cover his hurt, "No, I think she's just an incredibly kind and generous person. Now that we're off and running, she's gotten back to her regular life."

With raised eyebrows, she said, "Really ...."

Not wanting to talk about it, he changed the subject. He needed Lopez's help on when and how to introduce this to the public, and didn't want to share it with the rest of the team yet. "Sheri, when I return from the Pole, there are some things I'd like to talk to you about ... privately."

Smiling, she said, "Let's have dinner when you get back."

⸺✸⸺

They flew to Antarctica in a Boeing C-17 ER Globemaster. The "ER" stood for Extended Range. In addition to the extra tanks, they'd also installed a giant fuel bladder in the cargo area.

Their mission was to survey the proposed site and set up a base camp. The team consisted of Josh, Katori, Bobinski and four of Bobinski's people: a civil engineer, a construction expert, and two burly construction crewmembers. They also had two full flight crews, an Air Force Loadmaster and a medic. Unlike the old days when military transports had nothing but uncomfortable web-seats, this one had a few regular airline seats. The only thing missing was sound insulation, windows and a flight attendant.

They stopped in Fort Meyers, Florida, to pick up Musk and load equipment. To keep a low profile, they used Private Sky Aviation, a trusted company that had hosted other classified government flights. The C-17 was quickly loaded with two snowcats, several snowmobiles, a large, portable Quonset hut and several boxes of equipment. From there, they flew to Antarctica with a short refueling stop in the Falklands.

Josh used the 8,500-mile flight to catch up on his reading. With his reduced need for sleep and ability to speed-read, he could finish a dozen books during the flight. On his tablet, he'd downloaded a wide range of titles including astrophysics, quantum mechanics, cosmology, anthropology, psychology and sociology. He had biographies of famous leaders and books on

Antarctica, cold weather survival and mountain climbing. His photographic memory and speed-reading only went so far. He still needed time to process what he read.

Halfway through the flight, he finished the fourth book. It was on quantum mechanics and required some thought. He decided he needed a break. The loud drone of the C-17's turbofan engines was like pink noise, and looking around, he saw all his fellow passengers were asleep. He hadn't been able to reach Jesse in a quite a while. Truthfully, he had been so busy he hadn't really tried. Knowing no one could hear him over the engines, he called Jesse.

He was no longer surprised his communication link worked inside an aircraft over the Atlantic. "Jesse, I've been reading a lot and thinking about what you said. May I ask some more questions?"

Science, art or religion?

He frowned. "Why would we want to talk about art? I mean it's cool and all but it's ... art. As for religion, it's mostly moral philosophies, historical stories, and superstitions propagated over time. I'd like to talk about science."

Science is that which you can do and understand. Art is that which you can do without understanding how, and religion is simply that which you can neither do nor understand.

"Huh ... that's an interesting way to look at it." He thought for a moment. "So if we treat a known bacterial infection with a specific antibiotic, that's obviously science. Acupuncture appears to have some effect but I don't think we're completely sure why. So, that might be art? Then we have people with untreatable diseases that are somehow miraculously cured. Guess that might be the spiritual stuff?" He paused again. "Let's start with the stuff we understand."

He sensed attention and began, "Quantum mechanics lies at the heart of physics, but if you follow it to its ultimate conclusion, the results border on the mystical. Nobel Prize-winning physicist Niels Bohr once said that anyone who isn't shocked by quantum mechanics hasn't understood it."

Yes?

He paused marshalling his thoughts. "OK, quantum mechanics says at the subatomic level, weird things happen, particles pop in and out of existence and can be in two different places at the same time. There's a thought experiment called 'Schrödinger's Cat' that illustrates one of the paradoxes that haunts physics. There's a cat in a sealed box with a particle detector attached to a vial of poison gas. The detector can detect a single particle's presence. The odds are fifty-fifty the particle will appear. If it detects the particle, it releases gas into the box and the cat dies. I suspect Schrödinger didn't like cats. If it doesn't detect the particle, the cat lives. But quantum mechanics says a subatomic particle can be both over here and over there, until observed. *Only by observing it*, is the particle locked into one location."

He shook his head. "That means until someone observes whether the particle is there ... the cat is both dead *and* alive, which is absurd. It suggests *reality isn't real* until an observer observes it." That doesn't make sense."

Then why do they believe it?

"Because 70 years of experimental results confirm quantum mechanics works. Technologies we use every day require it. In fact, without it, our laser wouldn't work. Niels Bohr summed it up with, 'Nothing is real until it's observed.' That can't be right ... can it?"

Their conversation ended when the Loadmaster passed out box lunches, waking up the passengers.

Fueled by a dry ham sandwich, quantum mechanics and his conversation with Jesse, he decided to dig deeper into the physics books and even start reading some of the books of the world's major religions.

26

MOUNT HOWE

Josh and the others crowded into the cockpit as the C-17 approached Mount Howe. It was mid-September, the end of the long dark Antarctic winter. The sun lit only the mountaintops, casting a shadow on the featureless, white plain.

As they circled, Petrov, one of Bobinski's men, took hundreds of pictures of the ridgeline with a telephoto lens. They were looking for the optimal site at the top and a way to get to it with heavy equipment. Bobinski asked the pilot to circle one more time and go lower.

She was an Air Force test pilot assigned to Boeing. "No problem. I'll go as low as you want, but we'll have to land soon to have enough fuel to make it back."

The landing was rough. It felt as if they were setting down on a cobble stone street. Just in case, they were prepared with equipment to change tires. The aircraft finally bumped to a stop, and the pilot shut the engines down. She kept the auxiliary turbine running to supply the aircraft with power and heat.

After everyone bundled up in arctic gear, the Loadmaster lowered the C-17's giant ramp. Musk was the first off. As Josh stepped off the ramp, Musk yelled over the turbine whine, "Welcome to the bottom of the world!"

Josh, feeling a little like the Michelin man, nodded. Their clothing was the best money could buy. It kept his body warm in the 25-below-zero temperature, but his face was partly exposed. Even without much wind, his cheeks stung and his eyes watered with tears quickly freezing to his face.

Musk, watching him, smiled. "It's actually spring-like temperatures for Antarctica."

After adjusting to breathing icicles, the next thing that

struck him was the eerie twilight. It was a perpetual sunrise with just enough light to read. Only the direction of the sunrise would change, rotating slowly around the horizon like the hour hand of a clock.

In the sky to the south, he saw the greenish glow of a faint aurora borealis. Correcting himself, he realized he was in the Southern Hemisphere and said softly, "aurora australis." High-energy particles captured from the sun spiraled down the earth's magnetic pole like water going down a drain. As the particles dove through the atmosphere, they collided with the air. The ghostly green glow was the oxygen molecule's funeral pyre. The crash zone of particles formed a giant circle, 2,000 miles in diameter, centered on the magnetic pole. The aurora was only visible in darkness and when the sun was angrily energetic.

Antarctica was alien enough without the twilight and ghostly glow. As he looked at the horizon and slowly turned, he saw vast plains stretching into the distance and merging with the gray horizon. He continued to turn until he saw the mountain ridgeline. It jutted out of the plain like a dull circular-saw blade cutting up through a piece of white plywood. Hundred-foot-tall snowdrifts looked like white caulk liberally applied to seal the ridgeline to the icy plain. The mountaintop was the only part high enough to receive direct sunlight. With the sun at his back, the mountaintop looked like a sculpture lit by a spotlight, majestic and surreal.

Looking down, he kicked a layer of dry, loose snow from the underlying ice sheet. He was standing on what looked like a beautiful blue lake, complete with wind ripples frozen in place. The "ripples" stuck up several inches, explaining the rough landing.

Bobinski, seeing Josh look down at the ice, said, "Zamboni!"

Josh said, "Pardon me?"

Bobinski came closer and asked, "Do you ice skate?"

"Badly. Yes, I know what a Zamboni is. They resurface ice rinks."

Bobinski said, "We use specially built Zamboni on steroids!"

Josh smiled, trying to picture it.

Bobinski continued, "It will scrape ice and fill with hot water until smooth. We create any size runway. Will last for years because of temperature."

"You've done this before?"

"Siberia is not so different." He paused and looked directly at Josh. "Why are you here?"

He'd read Bobinski's file and knew that the Russian had a deep distrust for the KGB and CIA. "You mean I'm about as useful as a bikini in Siberia?"

Bobinski's eyes narrowed. "Bikini we find use for."

Josh stopped smiling. "Mr. Bobinski, I'm not a spy. I'm actually one of the architects of this program, and I like to imagine I'm smart enough to know where I'm incompetent. I'm here to learn. I may ask questions because it affects other parts of the program, but you're in charge here and have the final say on all site decisions."

Bobinski shrugged, not looking very convinced

They turned to watch the snowcats, loaded with supplies, drive slowly down the C-17 ramp. Painted bright orange, the snowcats looked like large, jacked-up SUVs on tank tracks.

Before they climbed aboard, Bobinski said, "First we find location for base camp at foot of mountain. It must be big enough area to house workers, fuel depot and communication center. Then we study photographs and choose gentlest path to top."

The ridgeline had a series of small rounded peaks. They drove to the spot directly under the highest peak, Mount Howe, but the giant snowdrifts obscured the bedrock. Bobinski shook his head and directed them to drive parallel to the ridgeline until they found an area of exposed bedrock. It looked like a gentle ski slope of volcanic gravel. Its angle and location allowed prevailing winds to scour it free of snow.

They stopped and got out. Bobinski gave orders to his two engineers, Petrov and Olenev. Musk, who'd been scanning the ridgeline with binoculars, handed them to Bobinski and suggested a possible ascent point.

Josh, pointing to the area where Bobinski's men were working, asked, "Why this site?" He had lifted his goggles so Bobinski could see his face.

Bobinski studied him, probably to see if he was being micromanaged. Then replied, "We need to be on bedrock close to the mountain peak in case we need to run power lines up."

Josh nodded but asked, "Power lines?"

"Don't know if we can get reactors to top. Might put reactors down here. Run power up with cables."

Josh just nodded.

Petrov and Olenev set up the foundation perimeter, and along with the two Russian crewmembers and two Air Force crew, began pulling out parts for their new home. A sophisticated, partly inflatable Quonset hut, it was anchored to the ground by steel cables. Carbon graphite ribs; lightweight, polymer panels; and a double-layered, inflatable skin allowed for rapid assembly. The structure was large, about 15 by 30 feet, but with all of them working together, it went up quickly despite the steady, subzero wind.

Josh worked hard and quietly took orders from Bobinski's men. After several snowcat runs back to the C-17, they had installed generators, satellite communication dishes, and a small weather station. Inside, they put in heaters, folding tables and chairs, a small galley, laptop computers, communication equipment, and sleeping bags. It was a full day's work.

After they finished, they went inside.

Bobinski said, "Time to eat and get sleep. Tackle mountain tomorrow." They voraciously ate military pre-packaged field rations and climbed into their sleeping bags.

Josh was the first awake the next morning but still managed to finish reading two more books before he fell asleep the night before. He read a book on mountain climbing and a Lincoln biography. He wasn't sure which might be more relevant to his current situation.

After another hearty breakfast of military field rations and hot coffee, they sat around a laptop looking at photographs taken from the C-17. Bobinski and his team correlated the pictures into a 3-D representation of the mountain. Usually they used English, but when they got excited, they shifted to Russian. Bobinski would bring them back to English and explain anything that transpired. Finally, Bobinski, stroking his beard and speaking primarily to Musk said, "Best path up mountain is obvious from radar mapping and pictures, but may have dangerous areas."

Musk, pointing at a picture on the screen, said, "Should be

able to take the snowcat to here, maybe a little further. Then proceed on foot. There may be some loose slopes and small crevasses. The only way to be sure is to take a look."

Bobinski nodded, and turned to Josh. "We take both snowcats up mountain. You can come along if you stay out of way and help with equipment."

Josh just nodded.

The snowcats trundled off along the plain in the shadow of the mountain. Petrov drove the second snowcat with Katori in the passenger's seat. Wedged in the backseat, Josh sat between boxes of climbing and survey gear.

The C-17 and base camp were on a plateau 8,000 feet above sea level. That meant they only had to climb about 1,700 feet to get to the top of Mount Howe. But first, they had to drive several miles to find a slope gentle enough to start their ascent. The snowcat's suspension allowed the tall cab to sway continuously as they climbed. Noticing that Katori looked a little green, he was glad his new body wasn't susceptible to motion sickness.

They were two-thirds the way up the mountain when they hit an impasse. The mountain ridgeline was only about as wide as a football field, dropping off progressively on both sides to vertical cliffs. There were also large ripples in the ridgeline, as if someone had tried to compress it along its length. They hit one of the ripples that had split open, creating a small, rocky crevasse. It was too wide for the snowcats to traverse. Everyone got out.

Musk took over as the most experienced climber. He'd already interviewed everyone to determine their physical fitness and climbing experience. Although Josh won in the fitness department, he'd never climbed before. Musk chose Bobinski, Petrov and Josh, leaving Katori and Olenev behind with the snowcats.

Musk had already given them a climbing safety brief at the base camp, but he quickly summarized it. "We shouldn't have to do any exotic climbing, but we'll have to cross a couple of small crevasses. The slope won't be steep, but the combination of loose rock, high altitude and extreme cold is always dangerous." He smiled, obviously enjoying himself. "We're going where no one has been before! If you have any problems or questions, stop and ask. Don't be stoic or heroic."

Musk helped Josh and Petrov into their climbing harnesses, roping them together with 40 feet of separation. Then he showed them how to assemble and install a small metal footbridge across the crevasse. "Bridge" was a generous term. It looked more like a cheap aluminum ladder dropped across the gap and anchored to the rock. Josh, knowing they invited him along as a Sherpa, picked up the heaviest pack containing bridge parts and survey equipment.

The first test was crossing the bridge laden with the packs. With no fear of heights, Josh looked down as he crossed. It was just deep enough to kill them.

Musk led them across and took the lead. He put Bobinski, who also had mountain climbing experience, at the back. Josh and Petrov were in the middle.

They moved carefully up the slope until they hit a second crevasse, where they put up another bridge. On the other side, they took a break. Musk and Bobinski, who had been practicing and working out, were breathing hard. Even Petrov, a long-distance runner, was struggling. Barely winded, Josh loved his new body.

Musk tapped Josh on the shoulder. Josh turned to see him pointing silently at the sky near the horizon. The aurora had brightened considerably, with soft, undulating curtains of green fire. It was beautiful.

After a short rest, they continued their climb.

Finally, almost at the top, they stood on a gentle dome of what appeared to be exposed granite. On one side of the dome was a level rock shelf, naturally carved out of the mountain. Bobinski and Petrov pulled cameras and survey equipment out of the packs and started taking pictures and elevation readings. With nothing to do, Musk disconnected himself and Josh from Bobinski and Petrov. The two of them climbed the last 200 feet to the very top of the mountain.

As they reached the summit, they were initially facing back toward Bobinski and Petrov, and looking directly into the perpetual sunrise. The tiny C-17 looked like a toy on the plain 1,700 feet below. Josh felt like he was standing on an island – an island of orange, sunset-colored rock surrounded by an ocean of shadow. The plain blended into the sky at the horizon, making it difficult to tell where the earth stopped and the heavens began.

Musk said, "Do you realize we're the first to ever stand on top of this mountain? We're at the top ... of the bottom of the world."

Josh smiled. "I think there's a Country song in there somewhere."

They both slowly turned around until the sun was at their back and they faced the geographic South Pole.

As the ghostly green glow illuminated their faces, Musk said, "Oh my God!"

During the final climb, the ridgeline hid most of the light show. Now, standing on the peak, they saw an incredibly energetic aurora australis. Two 100-mile-high, luminous, gossamer curtains slowly rippled toward each other as if blowing in a gentle breeze. Beautiful bright white and ghostly green, they blended into a rich translucent red at the top. At the bottom of each curtain was a narrow band of rich purple, as if a cosmic interior designer added a royal fringe. It was both spellbinding and alien.

They stood transfixed for many minutes. Then, Musk pointed at a star barely visible through the aurora. "Isn't that Jupiter?"

It was the brightest star on the horizon, but still barely visible in the twilight.

Josh nodded and said quietly, "The comet should be between the orbits of Saturn and Jupiter right now."

Musk shook his head. "It's inconceivable that a mountain – bigger than we're standing on – could fall from the sky." He paused. Then looking back at the aurora, he added, "I feel like an ant on a giant stage ... looking up at the bottom of huge theatrical curtains closing after a performance."

Josh softly added, "Hope it's not the final act."

As they watched, the two colossal curtains of tortured particles finally met, becoming one. The sky vibrated with a riot of glacially slow, roiling sheets of color. Slowly twisting and turning, they looked as if someone was gently shaking them from above. It was one of the most beautiful things he'd ever seen.

Without looking away, Musk whispered, "Almost enough to

make you believe in God."

Interrupting their contemplation, Bobinski yelled up from below.

27

FREEFALL

Josh and Musk climbed back down to where Bobinski was.

Standing on the natural rock shelf, Bobinski declared, "This is perfect location for beam projector and control room."

They repacked their equipment and started down the mountain, frequently glancing up into the sky. With a downhill traverse, and no more bridge parts to shoulder, the trip went quickly. They crossed the last bridge and reached the snowcats.

Disconnecting the rope from their climbing harnesses, they gathered the equipment to load into the cats. Josh stood next to the metal bridge and finished coiling their climbing rope into a bag. Holding the end of the rope with the large metal carabiner clip, he smiled – yesterday, he thought a carabiner was just a key chain.

Looking up, he saw Petrov, free of his tether, venturing toward the edge of the ridgeline. With camera in hand, he was obviously trying to get a picture of the C-17 below with the aurora in the background. Looking through his camera's LCD, Petrov stepped on a large patch of ice. Like a Charlie Chaplin movie, his arms began to windmill rapidly.

Musk and Bobinski, standing next to the snowcats, watched the antics with amusement. Despite Petrov's comical contortions, gravity won and he finally landed on his back.

Assessing the situation, Josh's mind suddenly went into overdrive. His brain instantly projected the outcome. Petrov had fallen on a part of the ice sheet that wrapped the edge of the ridgeline like a frozen waterfall. The slope got progressively steeper for 30 feet, and then dropped off vertically to the plain, about 1,200 feet below. Petrov began sliding on his back toward the edge.

Josh was the closest to Petrov but still about 100 feet away. He tore off his gloves and clipped the end of the rope he was holding around one of the bridge's metal struts. Reaching into the rope bag, he snatched the other end.

Musk and Bobinski's expressions changed as they realized what was happening.

Josh sprinted toward Petrov as the climbing rope uncoiled from the bag behind him. Once again, as the adrenaline rose, time seemed to slow. With his freezing hands, he clipped the end of the rope to his harness. The rope was too long but he didn't have time to fix that.

Petrov looked like an upside down turtle used as a hockey puck. His arms and legs flailed as he clawed at the ice trying to right himself, but his heavy gloves prevented him from getting purchase.

Josh saw Musk running toward the metal bridge with Bobinski following. Musk had figured out what Josh was attempting.

Josh ran as fast as he could, but it wasn't fast enough. Petrov passed the point of no return and was about to go over the cliff. With all his strength, Josh launched himself into a dive calculated to intercept Petrov.

A detached part of him asked what he thought he was doing. If the bridge didn't hold, they were both dead. What would become of humanity's battle?

Petrov's torso slid over the edge as Josh slammed into him, grabbing his backpack and coat. The impact accelerated both of them over the cliff into freefall. Petrov screamed, clinging to Josh. Their momentum propelled them away from the cliff in an inverted bear hug. Josh was upside down, Petrov, right side up, their heads pressed into each other's chests.

They fell forever, or so it seemed with Josh's hyperactive time-sense.

One hundred feet down, the rope reached its end. Brutally jerking Josh to a violent stop, his harness cut into his torso squeezing the air from his lungs. Their bear hug broke as Petrov's weight almost pulled Josh's arms from their sockets. The metal bridge above clanged and shrieked against the rock like fingernails on a chalkboard, as Petrov slid toward his death.

At the last second, Josh caught him by his wrists. Attached only by their hands with Josh hanging upside down, they looked like a circus trapeze act. As if that wasn't bad enough, he glanced back at the face of the mountain – *not good!* His dive for Petrov pushed them far away from the cliff face. Now, their trapeze was rapidly swinging back toward the rock wall.

Josh quickly determined two things. The impact with the rock wall was going to hurt ... a lot. And even if they survived, in their current configuration, he'd never be able to hold onto Petrov.

He took as deep a breath as the torso allowed and used all his strength to pull Petrov back up into a bear hug. Twisting his torso so he'd be between the cliff and Petrov, Josh knew exactly how Wile E Coyote felt as he slammed back first into the cliff.

What little air was left exploded from his lungs as Petrov's head broke his ribs. It was like falling flat on his back from a ladder – with someone landing on top of him. As if that weren't enough, the bridge shrieked and slid again, slipping them another foot.

Josh was supporting the weight of two men. His harness squeezed his broken ribs, making it impossible to breath. Stunned and fighting for air, he managed a quick plea to Jesse, although he had no idea what good it would do.

Josh could only whisper. He told Petrov to climb up his body and grab the rope. Frozen with fear, Petrov stuck to him like Velcro. Josh knew he'd lose consciousness if Petrov couldn't transfer his weight to the rope. With the last of his air, he whispered, "Petrov ... bridge could fall any time ... climb ... now!"

Petrov finally looked up and pulled his gloves off. Slowly disentangling himself from the bear hug, he began to climb, using Josh's body as a ladder. Like a boa constrictor, Josh's harness squeezed him tighter. His vision faded. Petrov finally grabbed the rope, taking some pressure off and allowing Josh a shallow, painful breath. Then Petrov lost his grip, falling back on Josh and kicking him in the side. With broken ribs pushed against his lungs, he would have screamed if he could. With no air, Josh's consciousness slipped away bringing relief from the searing pain.

———✦———

Musk and Bobinski had reached the bridge and gotten their

weight on it just as the rope went taut.

Musk took control. He yelled to Olenev to connect two more ropes to the snowcat and throw them over the side. Then he motioned to Katori to switch places with him. As Katori added his weight to the bridge, Musk ran to the snowcat. He clipped the new rope to his harness and slid across the ice to the cliff edge. Leaning over, he was surprised to see Fuze *and* Petrov hanging 100 feet below. It was impossible. He couldn't believe anyone could hold onto a 200-pound man at the end of a 100-foot fall. He yelled down, "Are you all right?"

Petrov yelled back, "Dah ... not sure about Commander Fuze!"

Musk took the end of the new rope and clipped its carabiner around the rope holding Fuze and Petrov. Sliding it down toward them, he yelled, "Unclip the rope I'm sending down and attach it to your harness! We'll pull you up!" He knew Petrov didn't have the ability to tie it to Fuze. He needed to get Petrov's weight off the original rope before the bridge gave out.

He could see Petrov using Fuze's body as a shelf while he fumbled with the carabiner with freezing hands. Finally, Petrov clipped the new rope to his harness. Musk motioned Olenev to back the snowcat slowly away from the cliff. "Petrov, use your arms and legs to keep yourself off the cliff face as we pull you up!" He could see Fuze hanging limp in his harness.

They heard the metallic groan of the bridge, as the rope started bending the strut. Still perched at the edge of the cliff, Musk yanked his gloves off. He grabbed the second rope attached to the snowcat and used a Prusik knot to tie it around the rope holding Fuze. Tied correctly, it wouldn't allow the bridge rope to slide through it.

But before he could finish, the strut snapped, ripping the unfinished knot from his hand and over the edge. He held his breath until he saw his incomplete knot had grabbed and held.

Petrov's head appeared and Musk told Olenev to stop the snowcat. Petrov scrambled up over the ice slope to a level area.

Musk once again motioned Olenev to back the snowcat. He yelled down, "If you can hear me! We're pulling you up! Try to fend yourself off the cliff!"

Josh woke as his head banged sharply against rock. He opened his eyes and found himself hanging upside-down looking directly at the base of the mountain over 1,000 feet below him. He wasn't sure he wanted to be awake. As he scraped against the cliff, he was pleased to see he was moving in the right direction for a change. He slowly and painfully righted himself so that he was looking up instead of down. With broken ribs and freezing hands, he used his legs to reduce "cliff rash."

After what seemed like hours but was actually minutes, he reached the top.

Musk yelled to Olenev to slow the snowcat to a crawl and then stop. Grabbing Josh's arms, Musk and Bobinski carefully pulled him up over the edge and slid him up and beyond the ice sheet.

As soon as he was on relatively level ground, he rolled over on his side in a fetal position with his arms wrapped around his chest. Musk and Bobinski leaned over him. He felt Bobinski gently disconnect the rope from his harness and put his own gloves on Josh's frozen hands. Then he felt them wrap something around his head. Musk, trying to ascertain Josh's condition, held up three fingers and asked, "How many fingers do you see?"

"Three."

"Do you know where you are?"

"Disney World?"

Musk smiled and shook his head. "I can give you something for the pain. Are you allergic to anything?"

"Yes."

Musk leaned closer.

Josh whispered, "Gravity."

Musk and Bobinski both started laughing.

In a conspiratorial tone, Bobinski said, "Once we get you off mountain, I have special drink that will help with pain."

Musk put a pill in Josh's mouth and gave him some water, "We have to get you down. Can you walk to the snowcat?"

Josh nodded, grimacing. Slowly he rolled onto his stomach trying to get his knees under him. Bobinski and Musk, taking his arms, helped him stand.

Josh grunted in pain.

Musk warned. "He may have internal injuries; be careful

lifting him."

Josh shuffled like a little old man with Musk and Bobinski supporting him on each side.

They gently helped him up into the snowcat. Bobinski drove. Musk and Petrov sat on each side of Josh in the back. Bobinski radioed ahead to have the medic standing by and the C-17 prepared to leave.

Josh grunted, "We don't need to leave. Mission is priority. I'll be fine."

Bobinski said, "Nyet. I make decisions here, remember?"

28

MEDIC

There was no privacy in the Quonset hut. Everyone gathered around. Josh watched their faces as the Air Force medic cut off his shirt. Their flinches and grimaces didn't instill a lot of confidence. Looking down at himself, he saw huge red and purple bruises wrapping around his torso. He also had a deeper "head shaped" bruise over his rib cage and knew his head was bleeding. The medic began a thorough examination. He palpated Josh's chest, listened to his lungs with a stethoscope and checked him for concussion.

After asking him a few questions, the medic finally told Josh and the rest of the team gathered around, "I have good news and bad news. The good news is, you're going to live and don't need immediate hospitalization. The bad news is that you don't need hospitalization because there's no real treatment for broken ribs … oh, and your back looks worse than your front."

Josh, seeing the guilt on Petrov's face, winked at him and said, "I was really just trying to get out of carrying those dang bridge parts."

Petrov smiled and Bobinski laughed. "You're officially off active duty list. I prescribe old Russian cure." He reached into his pack and pulled out a bottle of … Jack Daniels?

Josh looked at Bobinski with surprise, and Musk said, "You're kidding!"

Smiling, Bobinski opened the bottle. "Only *real* American cultural contribution to world."

In a lot of pain, Josh wasn't about to turn down a shot of Jack. He started to stand but the medic said, "Not so fast. I still need to stitch up the holes in your head."

Musk couldn't resist. "He jumped off a cliff. You don't have

178

enough silk to stitch up the holes in his head."

They laughed as Bobinski toasted, "To holes in head!" They "clinked" plastic cups and drank in one swallow.

The medic, pointing at the bottle, said, "Go easy on that."

Bobinski said, "Of course," as he poured them another shot.

Despite the pain, Josh couldn't help but smile. Take some engineers, a Navy pilot, a Russian industrialist and a brilliant billionaire, throw them together into a death-defying adventure, and background, education, and culture evaporate. You end up with a bunch of boys, laughing and scratching. New comrades in arms, they stayed up, sipping Jack and sharing increasingly exaggerated tales.

Josh, wanting to maintain a low profile, made them all promise to play down his role in the rescue. He was relieved when they all agreed.

Mission complete, they flew back the next day. Josh, tired and in pain, slept most of the trip.

Meadows met the C-17 as it arrived in St. Louis. As Josh walked stiffly in from the flight line, Meadows came up to him and said, "I'd give you a big hug and kiss if you hadn't busted your ribs."

Josh frowned at Meadows. "Who else knows?"

Meadows, obviously enjoying himself said, "Oh, just me ... and everyone on the team."

Josh continued to frown as Meadows smiled. "Relax, Josh, news like this travels faster than Facebook, and it's great for team esprit de corps." He laughed. "You'd be on YouTube by now if Petrov hadn't dropped his camera over the cliff."

Josh said, "It wasn't that big a deal."

Meadows looked serious. "Yes it was. I'm very proud of you, and it's exactly the type of action that helps pull a team together against overwhelming odds. I'd put you in for the Navy Cross, if I knew who the heck you worked for."

Josh shook his head.

Meadows said, "Look, Josh, you put this program in my lap. As the Program Manager, I am recognizing your act on behalf of the entire team." He smiled again and added, "*And*, as a Navy Captain, I'm ordering you – Commander – to sit quietly while we sing your praises. Is that understood?"

Josh finally gave a half-smile. "Yes sir."

Josh didn't look forward to attending the team meeting the next day. He waited until just before it started and tried to slip in quietly, but as soon as they spotted him, they gave him a standing ovation. He was good at a lot of things; this wasn't one of them. He just shook his head and slipped into his seat. So much for keeping a low profile.

Smiling, Meadows said, "Commander Fuze is more comfortable hanging upside down from a cliff than being recognized."

The group laughed, and Josh, trying to be a good sport, nodded.

Meadows continued, "Seriously, the entire survey team did an outstanding job. Commander Fuze's act of courage may never be recognized outside of this group, but *we* will know and appreciate having served with men and women like him." Again, there was a strong round of applause.

Meadows finally said, "Now we have to get back to saving the other eight billion. Mr. Bobinski, can you give us your evaluation of the site please?"

Bobinski leaned forward and cleared his throat. "Site is suitable, but there are challenges. We can put in 20,000-foot runway that will allow us to land," he smiled, "*delicate* American cargo jets." There were good-natured groans from the Boeing engineers.

Bobinski, continued, "But cutting road to top of mountain will be difficult. Requires building bridges over crevasse." Bobinski paused. "Even with best equipment and men, road will take too much time."

Shepherd jumped in with satisfaction. "As I originally stated, it cannot be done in less than a year."

Josh and Meadows had agreed that Shepherd was a bureaucrat who always found reasons things couldn't be done, but it was good to have a devil's advocate asking the tough questions. It kept them honest.

Meadows gave Bobinski a small wink that Shepherd couldn't see.

Bobinski continued in a calm voice. "To make sure we stay

on timeline, we build road at same time we are lifting observatory components to top."

Shepherd looked at Bobinski suspiciously. "What do you mean ... lifting?"

Josh thought Bobinski couldn't have paid someone to be a better straight man.

Bobinski continued, "We use H-60 helicopters to lift components to mountaintop, where we put them together."

Smiling, Meadows added, "Some assembly required."

Bobinski continued, "Prefer good Russian-built helicopter, but H-60 is already designed to fit inside C-17 ... and *Sikorski* was, of course, Russian."

Shepherd whined, "You can't be serious. There's no way helicopters can lift heavy equipment to the top of that mountain."

Without missing a beat, Bobinski continued, "S model H-60 can lift 4,000 kilos and has 12,000-foot service ceiling. Payload is reduced by altitude, but cold, dry air increases turbine power output."

"What about the reactors? There's no way you're going to lift those things up the mountain with their lead shielding," Shepherd said with a smirk.

"Don't have to. Reactors stay at base of mountain. Will run power lines to top."

Meadows, without even looking at Shepherd, asked, "When do you need the helicopters?"

Bobinski said, "Antarctic summer starts in one week. We have six months to complete. Need helicopters yesterday."

They all looked at Shepherd to see if he had a rebuttal.

Shepherd just frowned, shaking his head.

Meadows said, "OK, who has contacts at Sikorski?"

Major Wendy Crowell raised her hand.

"Great. Major Crowell, your mission is to beg, borrow or steal two H-60s. If you run into problems, let me know. We'll shake some trees."

Crowell smiled and nodded.

Meadows continued, "Chris, is there anything else you need now?"

Bobinski smiled. "Nyet. If I need it, I buy it."

As they were breaking up, Chandra came by.

Not wanting to talk about the rescue, Josh said, "We saw an incredible aurora down there. Most amazing thing I've ever seen."

She nodded. "There was a powerful solar flare a couple days ago. When you blast that much energy through the atmosphere, you blow up a lot of air molecules. Wish I could have seen it." She paused and with a slight shake of her head, said, "That cliff rescue was amazing but a bit insane." With a wry smile, she added, "Anytime you'd like, I'd be happy to explain how that whole *gravity* thing works."

He rolled his eyes. "Thanks, but turns out I've already heard you lecture on gravity. When I was an undergrad, you came to our campus and gave a talk on 'Gravity Assisted Trajectories for the Saturn Cassini Mission.'"

She put her hand to her mouth. "Oh my God! I can't believe you remember that. I must have been in my thirties."

Josh shrugged. "You were. I was a sophomore and had a bit of a crush on you."

She grinned. "Glad to hear I had a *positive* influence on the minds of young college students." She patted him on the back. Seeing him wince, she said, "Oh ... sorry." She shook her head. "God bless you, Josh, you really took a beating didn't you?"

"I'm OK." Frowning slightly, he added, "This is totally off the subject, but you said, 'Oh my God' and 'God bless.' If you don't mind my asking, what does one of the *world's leading astrophysicists* think about spiritual stuff?"

She laughed. "Why? Did you see your life flash before you when you were hanging from the end of the rope?"

He shrugged with a half-smile.

She cocked her head slightly and said, "Not entirely sure what I believe. I think most of us have a little battle going on between our emotional and intellectual selves."

Josh nodded. "Yeah. Our emotional side looks for meaning in life, but our intellect says a supreme being isn't plausible."

She shook her head. "Actually, it's quite the reverse for many of us."

He looked surprised.

"Emotionally, I don't want to believe in a supreme being because I want to call the shots." Laughing, she said, "It's uncomfortable thinking something a lot smarter than me might be observing what an idiot I am."

Frowning, Josh said, "But ...?"

"Josh, before the 1960s, scientists believed the universe had been around forever. Then some crazy astrophysicists suggested it started 13 billion years ago. The idea that the universe had a beginning and started from nothing was so bizarre and mystical sounding most physicists made fun of it. In fact, the name, The Big Bang, was intended as a joke to show how absurd the idea was." She smiled. "Of course, the theory turned out to be correct. For those who believed a supreme being wasn't required, it was suddenly a bit awkward since *something* had to start the universe."

Josh said, "But quantum mechanics says particles can pop into existence out of nothing."

She gave him a challenging smile. "Yes, *but* The Big Bang didn't just create the *stuff in* the universe, it created the Universe itself, which includes space and time. Particles still have to have a *place* and *time* to pop *into.*"

Josh nodded thoughtfully. "OK ... but whatever started the universe doesn't have to be conscious. It could have been some kind of natural cause."

She nodded. "True, but whatever it was, it had to exist *outside* of space and time." With raised eyebrows, she asked, "Want to take a crack at describing what that might look like?" She paused. "On top of that, the universe appears to be *perfectly* fine-tuned to support life. If any of the dozens of physics constants were different by the *tiniest* amount – life couldn't exist."

Josh frowned. "What if there were multiple universes?"

"Actually, it would require *infinite* universes to get around the paradox. Problem is, by the definition of a universe, there's no way to see outside ours and prove others exist ... ever."

Her phone vibrated. Looking at it, she said, "Sorry, Josh, got another project meeting in a few minutes." She looked up with a smile. "To help *prevent us* from finding out if there is a God sooner than necessary."

Josh laughed.

As they were both leaving, he noticed Smith had stayed behind to talk to Meadows.

After Chandra and Fuze left, Smith frowned and said quietly to Meadows, "I'm not happy with Bobinski or Musk, and Fuze's dangerous actions put the program at risk."

Meadows looked surprised.

Smith exhaled and said, "It's my fault. I should have been down there with the survey team."

Meadows shook his head. "Tim, you can't be everywhere. It all worked out and helped pull the team together." He paused. "I think Fuze's '*dangerous* actions' demonstrate his dedication to the project and team. Are you still worried about his background?"

"Yes and you should be too."

III

PENETRATION

"Mr. President, the checks and balances have been working against us. They're designed to keep information from being extracted ... not inserted."

29

BIG BANG

With only a year and a half to impact, Josh knew it was time, probably past time, to figure out when and how to introduce this to the public. He needed to talk to Lopez privately. Broaching any of this at a team meeting would raise awkward questions, like why they were making decisions about notifying the public instead of, say ... the White House.

Lopez was back in Kansas City recording a TV special. He called her. She told him she'd be finished tomorrow, and they could meet for dinner.

With his need to get between St. Louis and places like Kansas City, not to mention his broken ribs, he decided this would be a good time to get a car. He loved performance cars, but ended up buying a two-year-old Ford sedan. He just needed reliable transportation that wouldn't draw attention. Of course, he did manage to find a Ford with a high-performance package. Using cash from Musk's account, it only took a few minutes to close the deal.

Sliding gingerly behind the wheel, he tried not to bump his ribs. It only hurt when he moved, breathed or sat still.

He actually enjoyed driving, particularly this time of year when the leaves were starting to change color. It also gave him time to think and it was the first time since Antarctica he had a real opportunity to talk to Jesse.

He spent a couple hours on the freeway running all the program's critical paths through his head. Finally, he asked, "Hey Jesse, can you talk?"

He immediately sensed the link and couldn't help but notice Jesse was almost always available. He probably didn't get a lot of sleep. "You sure you don't have access to some amazingly advanced laser technology you want to share?"

Silence.

"Just checking." He smiled and shook his head. "OK ... you asked me if there was an alternate interpretation of quantum mechanics. There is. If every time we *observe* something, a new universe is created, there would be an *infinite* number of branching universes. Schrodinger's Cat is alive in one universe and another universe branches off where his cat's deader than a doornail. Every possible outcome *will* happen, so no observer is needed to lock things into reality, and our fine-tuned universe might be inevitable."

Yes?

"It's a great idea. Though, I'm not excited to think in another universe I'm lying dead at the bottom of a cliff." He paused. "But I was talking to Chandra and there are problems with it."

Yes?

"If a bunch of universes are branching off, we're still stuck with what initiated the first universe. Even if there are infinite Big Bangs, we have a problem. The very definition of 'universe' means it's impossible to see outside *ours*. That means the idea of infinite universes is untestable, requiring it to be accepted on what amounts to blind faith." He paused. "Technically, it's just another religion."

I see your problem.

"That's it? That's all you're going to say?"

Silence.

"Thanks. That was really helpful ... not."

It was late afternoon when he hit Kansas City. He called Lopez and she invited him to her house for dinner. That was good since Lopez's celebrity status often meant fans interrupted their restaurant meetings. She promised a new Italian recipe. Despite his pain, he looked forward to dinner. Lopez didn't do anything halfway, and he suspected she was an exceptional chef. He told her he'd check into his hotel and then come over. In her usual direct manner, she said, "Food's almost done ... don't worry about the hotel."

Sheri's house was an imposing but elegant brick home in the best part of town. She met him at the large ornate doors wearing a chef's apron. The aroma of garlic and fresh bread wafted through the air as she invited him in. On the way to the kitchen, he saw a beautifully decorated home with marble floors, cathedral ceilings and crystal chandeliers. It looked immaculate ... until they passed the study. He knew she was an author and surmised that the study and its explosion of papers were off limits to her housekeeper. As they walked by, he nodded toward it and casually asked, "Suicide bomber?"

She laughed.

The kitchen was huge and equally impressive. Beautiful granite countertops and expensive cherry cabinets contrasted the large, commercial gas stove and subzero freezer. This was a cook's kitchen. There was a formal dining room, but the kitchen had a large island with a wrap-around granite bar. It made sense since most eating and parties ended up in the kitchen anyway.

Sheri handed him a glass of Chianti and put him to work cutting tomatoes for the salad. Pulling the lasagna out of the oven, she set it on the bar to cool. As she added the tomatoes to the salad, she asked, "How are you feeling? How are your ribs?"

Dismissively, he said, "They're fine."

She gave him a "yeah right" look, and topped off his wine glass.

She took the garlic bread out of the oven and pronounced the lasagna ready. Putting plates and silverware out, she motioned him to sit at one of the bar stools.

Lopez always wore tailored business suits or sports jackets, but as she pulled off her chef's apron, he saw a different side. Her clothes, while still elegant, were casual and much more feminine. He realized that in the hospital, he viewed her as an obstacle to overcome. Then, later, saw her as a potential ally to recruit. Now, seeing her in a silk blouse and form-fitting skirt, he realized Sheri was a very attractive woman. Opposite to Elizabeth in almost every way, Sheri was dark, petite and voluptuously curvy. Their personalities were also very different. Elizabeth was people-oriented. Sheri was definitely task-oriented, as was he. That similarity explained why he felt comfortable around her. Nevertheless, Sheri really was beautiful. As she sat down next to him, her loosely buttoned top drew his eyes. Suffice it to say, he'd need to keep his eyes above her impressive cleavage and cut himself off after his second glass of wine.

She caught his glance.

He quickly focused on his lasagna. As expected, she was a phenomenal chef.

After several minutes of concerted eating, punctuated by compliments to the chef, Sheri started the conversation. "Josh, what's the story on Tim Smith?"

Wiping delicious tomato sauce and cheese from his face, he said, "He's supposed to be one of the best security specialists the CIA has. Why?"

"Yes, I've heard he's extremely good at what he does. I've talked to him a few times. With his job, he has to remain detached, but there's ... something else there." She shook her head. "Josh, I'm not trying to be nosy." She paused. "But his *affect* is totally flat, and he almost exhibits symptoms of ...." She stopped and looked back at him. "I don't want to jump to conclusions. Can you tell me anything about his background?"

"Are you concerned about *him*, or his ability to carry out his job?"

"Both. As a psychiatrist, I can tell you our mental health affects everything we do."

He nodded. "Smith's job is to look after and protect the team, guess it wouldn't hurt to have someone looking after him ... and you're the most qualified." He paused. "Carl did give me some background. Obviously, we want to hold this in the strictest of confidence."

She nodded.

"Carl said Tim was one of the CIA's best field agents. His specialty has always been protection. He has a natural instinct and passion for it. When you think of protection, you don't usually think about killing people, but I guess it's like an offensive tackle protecting the quarterback. I gathered from Carl, Tim is quite deadly. He's killed a number of assassins and terrorists over the years."

He paused. "About a year ago he was involved in an operation in Turkey. They assigned him to protect a European Union Commissioner under a terrorist death threat. The commissioner he was protecting was married and neglected to tell Tim he was involved in an affair. Evidently, the

Commissioner's mistress tried to sneak into the house late one night. Dressed in black, she came in through a window, carrying something that looked like a gun. Tim shot and killed her."

He shook his head. "Tim was exonerated by the agency and the entire event was hushed up." He paused. "Carl also said that the woman Tim shot had two children." He shook his head again. "On the positive side, Carl said Tim is raising money for a trust fund for the children. Since he has no kids, he even made them beneficiaries of his life insurance."

One of Sheri's eyebrows went up, but she said nothing.

"Carl says he's as effective as he ever was, but, understandably, his heart isn't in it anymore. He told Carl he was going to retire. They're friends and Carl asked him to do this final job. Considering the nature of our mission, Carl thought it would be good for Tim and allow him to retire on a high note."

Sheri nodded and softly repeated, "Retire ...."

With a questioning look, he asked, "Does that help?"

She sighed. "Yes, unfortunately, it does."

Frowning, Josh said, "Sheri, I don't mean to sound insensitive, but with what we have at stake, do you think his condition could endanger the program?"

She shook her head. "I don't know." She sighed. "Everyone faces tragedies in different ways. I'll try to talk to him."

As he finished his second helping of lasagna, Sheri changed the subject. "OK, Josh, what can I help *you* with?" With an impish smile, she said, "Relationships?"

He smiled. "Is there anyone who doesn't struggle with relationships?"

"Yeah, dead people."

He laughed. "Not even sure that's true." Pausing, he said, "Actually, I really need your brain."

With a challenging smile, she said, "Just my brain?" And then quickly added, "Of course, what do you need?"

He caught the innuendo, but said, "How do we prepare the public for the inevitable discovery of a cataclysmic comet?"

She nodded. "I've been thinking about that a lot. I believe we need to leak the information slowly. I have an idea but I need to talk to Musk first. Give me a week, and I'll give you a plan."

He nodded. "You've got it."

She moved their empty plates to the sink and topped off their wine glasses. Then turned to him and said, "Now, off with your shirt. Let me take a look at those ribs."

He said with surprise, "You're a psychiatrist."

Sarcastically, she said, "Josh, *hello*. Psychiatrists have to go to medical school. I can handle broken ribs."

Seeing she wasn't backing down, he told her the truth. "Sorry – didn't mean to offend. The real reason is I don't drink much and haven't been with …." He shrugged. "Don't mean to be crass but you're seriously hot-looking and starting to look like dessert."

"Thanks for being honest *and* thank you for the compliment."

His phone rang. Looking at it, he said, "Sheri, this is Meadows. He doesn't usually call unless it's important. I need to take this."

"Of course."

He stood up and walked around her living room as he talked.

―✹―

Sheri smiled to herself. Dessert? She'd been thinking the same thing about him. His confession only made him more attractive, but it wasn't just his earnestness. He seemed like a tragic Greek hero – throwing himself over a cliff to save another, yet carrying a profound sadness. She had no idea what happened to him, but knew instinctively, and professionally, he'd faced death and carried a secret. He was a psychiatrist's dream. That, mixed with a great bod and a couple glasses of wine…. She didn't need his confession to confirm he was attracted to her, but there was something bothering him. It was just another challenge and she loved challenges.

As he returned and sat down, she asked, "Everything OK?"

He looked surprised. "Meadows just called to check up on me. He asked if I had had my ribs looked at." Winking, he added, "I told him I'm seeing a doctor."

With a disgusted smile, she shook her head. "Josh, he's right. You *really* need to have them looked at."

He folded his arms and shook his head.

She poured him another glass of wine. As she handed it to

him, she said, "Tell you what. If you're good and let me examine your chest," she gave him a mischievous smile, "Who knows, I might return the favor."

He unfolded his arms and with a smile said, "Been a long time since I played doctor."

As she started unbuttoning his shirt, her professional intuition made her say, "May I ask you a personal question?"

He nodded.

Watching him closely, she asked, "When was the last time you talked to Elizabeth?"

He looked down. "June 10th."

Bingo! She caught the flicker of pain that crossed his face. Here was one of his *internal* contusions. Some of her colleagues looked down on psychiatry, but diagnosing and treating *this* type of injury was often harder than fixing broken bones. Using the classic listening technique, she repeated, "June 10th?"

He nodded. "Right after we set up the meeting with Musk."

She stopped unbuttoning his shirt. Tapping one finger to her lips, she said, "Right after ... *we* had dinner." She realized indulging in "dessert" might cause serious complications. She sat back and asked, "Josh, did you try to contact her after that?"

"Yeah, I sent her a check in the mail about a week later."

"A check?"

"Yeah, paying her back for some money she loaned me while I was reestablishing my identity."

"You wrote a note with it?"

"Of course, I thanked her for everything."

"You *thanked* her for everything."

He nodded.

"That was it? That was all it said?"

Looking worried, he said slowly, "Yes ...."

"Josh, have you called her?"

"Several times but she never answered."

"Did you leave messages?"

"No ... except for the last time. A couple weeks ago, I finally left a message asking if she was all right. She texted me back."

Sheri raised her eyebrows in question.

"She said she was fine."

"*Fine?*" She couldn't help but give him the "flinch" look – the one you give someone who just missed the nail with the hammer and hit their thumb.

He sighed. "Fine doesn't mean fine, does it?"

She shook her head and said softly, "Josh, may I make an observation?"

"Please."

"When you were in the hospital, I gave you a battery of mental and psychological tests. You have some amazing abilities."

He shook his head, but she held up her hand and said, "Your IQ is off the top of the chart, and you have a photographic memory, don't you?"

He nodded.

"But as a psychiatrist, the thing that impresses me the most is your EQ or Emotional Quotient. You have outstanding people skills." She paused. "As a celebrity, I've had the opportunity to work with people who have exceptional talents, but I've rarely come across someone with all of this in one," she smiled, "rather impressive body. Do you have any idea how rare it is to have your IQ *and* EQ? Particularly, in a man?"

He laughed. "You're building me up because you're about to say I'm totally clueless with regard to Elizabeth."

"See? You're very perceptive and absolutely right. You're a complete blockhead with regard to Elizabeth, and I think totally missed the boat." Gently squeezing his arm, she added, "Don't be too hard on yourself, you're only human." Only partly joking, she added, "You ... *are* ... *human,* right?"

"Yeah, but your assessment of my EQ must be wrong."

"Not at all. You're exceptional at reading everyone except yourself. Don't feel bad, no one can do that. If they could, I wouldn't have a job."

"But I obviously can't read Elizabeth either."

Laughing, she said, "Part of it is simply that you have a handicap ... you're male." More seriously, she added, "Your real challenge is that you're emotionally attached. You're too close. It's like trying to read yourself."

He frowned, shaking his head.

"Josh, it's like looking out through a window at night. You can see outside clearly until you turn on the light inside. *That light is emotion.* Once it's on, you can't see outside anymore. In fact, the only thing you can see clearly … is your own reflection."

He nodded.

She had planned to let him stay … and not in the guest room, but looking at her watch, she said, "I didn't realize how late it was. Josh, you need sleep to heal." She started re-buttoning his shirt. "Can we talk more tomorrow? You're staying in Kansas City tonight, right?"

He nodded, looking surprised at the sudden transition. "Yes, at the airport Holiday Inn."

"Great, I'll call you tomorrow morning."

He stood up and thanked her for dinner.

As she walked him to the door, he moved slowly, obviously in significant pain. Poor guy, hurting inside and out, and she might have had something to do with the *inside*. She knew what she had to do. But as she closed the door, she shook her head with a slight smile. "Too bad."

30

RECOVERY

There was a knock on his hotel room door. Josh put his e-book down and frowned. It was after 11:00 pm. There was only one person who knew he was here.

He opened the door expecting Sheri, and found Elizabeth. Stunned, he just stood there.

Finally, raising her eyebrows and gesturing inside, she asked, "May I come in?"

"I'm sorry. Of course ... of course!"

As she entered, she held up a small black bag. "I'm here on business. I heard about your *accident* at the Pole."

"How did you know about that?"

"YouTube."

"YouTube?!"

"I'm kidding. Sheri called me. She said you refused to let her examine you and knew you wouldn't see a doctor." She went straight to the bathroom sink and started washing her hands. "So, let's get that shirt off and have a look."

"That won't be necessary."

Talking over her shoulder, she said without humor, "Josh, that's a direct order from your medical support team. Do we need to get Meadows involved?"

He frowned but started unbuttoning his shirt. As she came out of the bathroom, she saw him struggling and helped him pull the sleeves over his hands.

She shook her head as she saw his torso. "You look like you've been playing dodge ball with pipe wrenches."

He couldn't help but smile.

She opened her bag and put her stethoscope on. Frowning as she looked at his neck and head, she said, "Didn't they put any bandages on these lacerations?"

"Yeah, but I took them off to take a shower and ..."

She finished. "You couldn't get them back on *by yourself?*"

He shrugged.

She pointed at the giant black and purple bruise over the left side of his rib cage. "Let me guess, that's a likeness of Petrov?"

He laughed, followed by an, "Ouch."

She shook her head. "All right, this may hurt a bit but I need to feel your ribs. Sit down in that chair." She leaned over and gently ran her hands across his chest, sliding them over his rib cage and pushing in lightly.

It did hurt.

Nodding, she said, "It's your two middle ribs. They're the ones most likely to break." She warmed her stethoscope and told him to breathe deeply. She listened in several places on his chest and then went behind him to put it on his back. She whistled softly. "Yeah, that's going to leave a scar or two."

She didn't sound very sympathetic.

Pulling two pill bottles and some ointment out of her bag, she said, "Your lungs are clear. We could wrap your chest but that tends to restrict your breathing and can increase the chance of pneumonia. I'll put some antibiotic ointment on the lacerations." She went to the sink. "You have some major hematomas. I'll massage the tissue around the bruised areas to improve blood flow." She came back with six pills and a glass of water.

"What are these?"

"Just prescription strength ibuprofen for the pain, and melatonin."

"Melatonin?"

"It's something your body produces to help you sleep. It's an antioxidant and it's good for you. Doesn't matter how tough you are, you still need sleep to heal."

It *had* been difficult sleeping lately, for several reasons. One of them was standing in front of him. He gulped the pills down, saying, "Pills don't have much effect on me."

Moving behind him, she rubbed the ointment into the cuts on the back of his head and neck. It stung a little. Then she started to massage his shoulders, where his body took a lot of the impact.

"You're very tense," she said. "If we're going to promote

circulation, you're going to have to relax a little."

It hurt at first, but the awesome sensation of her hands quickly overshadowed the pain. "Elizabeth, I need to tell you something."

He heard, "Uh huh," from behind him.

"I think I owe you an apology. There may have been a ... a miscommunication."

She didn't respond.

"Sheri helped me understand that it's probably my fault."

He couldn't see her face and she still said nothing.

"I just learned that *fine* doesn't mean fine."

He heard her stifle a laugh.

Frowning, he said, "Sending that check without talking to you first was probably dumb." The massage pressure suddenly increased. "Ouch."

The pressure eased. "Apology accepted. Now shut up and relax."

He closed his eyes. His pain diminished. His *body* didn't hurt as much either. He forgot how good a massage could feel. It wasn't sexual; it was just incredibly relaxing and comforting.

She slowly moved around to face him and worked on his shoulders from the front. A detached part of him realized that this was the first time this body had ever experienced any significant human touch. After several minutes, she worked on his upper arms and then slowly worked across his chest. Moving around his side and down his chest, she gently massaged his stomach. His eyes opened. The massage was no longer increasing circulation just to his bruises. He reached out and gently touched her waist to pull her in, and then suddenly remembered. "Oh! I forgot. I have something for you!"

She looked a little surprised as he stood up and went over to his suitcase. He said, "It was a present I was going to send with the check, but I decided to wait and give it to you in person." He shook his head. "Not such a brilliant plan in retrospect." As he opened his suitcase, he saw her pick up his tablet.

Sitting on the edge of the bed, her face illuminated by the tablet, she said, "Have you read all these since I saw you last?"

Rummaging through his bag, he said, "All but two."

"There are over a *hundred* books in here!" Frowning and

then giggling, she said, "You read a book on Cosmetology?"

He looked up, laughing. *"Cosmology."*

"Oh."

He frowned. He was sure he'd put it in there somewhere.

Obviously, reading from the book, she said, "The Big Bang, that sounds ... interesting."

He found it! Pulling the small box from his bag, he said, "Ah, yeah, it's the theory on how the universe expanded from a tiny, infinitely dense point."

He heard her say under her breath, "Speaking of *infinitely dense* ...."

"What?" As he looked up, he caught her rolling her eyes, but she quickly smiled at him.

"Uh ... how do they know the universe came from an infinitely dense point?"

Setting the little box on the desk, he said, "They just looked at where the universe is now and kind of rolled it back in time. It's like playing a movie backwards. Ultimately, the universe ends up collapsing into a tiny dot called a singularity."

Frowning, she asked, "What was before the Big Bang?"

"Nothing, not even space or time."

She set the e-book down. "Then what caused it?"

He looked at her curiously. It was almost the same conversation he'd had with Chandra and Jesse. Frowning, he said, "Why do you ask?"

She shrugged. "Just curious."

Not wanting to get into quantum mechanics, he just said, "It's kind of complicated."

She smiled. "So, the universe started from absolutely nothing, blew up in a flash, and they don't know what was before it or what started it."

"Uh ... basically."

"Cool. Then I totally understand."

He looked at her with surprise. "You do?"

"Duh. 'The earth was without form and void, and darkness was on the face of the deep. And God said, let there be light; and there was light.'"

He shook his head with a smile. Of course, she'd bring it back to her simple religious beliefs. Then he frowned and shrugged. "I guess 'without form and void' isn't a bad description of nothingness. And The Big Bang was an explosion of pure energy. Light's energy." He smiled at her. "The physics description isn't really that much more informative than the biblical one."

Elizabeth patted his hand and said, "Be right back."

As she went to the bathroom, he picked up the little gift box and sat down in the overstuffed chair. He hadn't realized how big a hole there was in his life until he saw her at the door. His physical pain was hardly noticeable anymore. He wasn't going to make the same mistake twice. Injuries or no injuries, he couldn't think of anything better than holding her.

—✦—

Elizabeth came out of the bathroom with a mischievous grin ... only to find him asleep in the chair. She shook her head and mimicked him quietly. "Pills don't have much effect on me." Taking the pillow and blanket from the bed, she tucked him into the chair. As she did, she saw the little beat-up gift box in his hand. There was no way she was going to wait another three months. She carefully slipped it out of his fingers, leaned over and kissed him gently on the lips.

As she drove home, she knew Sheri was right. It was all a dumb misunderstanding, and it was as much her fault as his. It was well past midnight, but she had promised Sheri she'd call and tell her the outcome.

When Sheri answered, Elizabeth said, "You were right on both counts. Although brilliant, he *is* clueless and had no idea what he did. And yes, he lied about his injuries."

"How bad?"

"Nothing fatal, but he's a mess. Two broken ribs and probably fractured a couple more. He also has major bruising and lacerations covering half his torso. I gave him 800 milligrams of Motrin and 12 milligrams of melatonin."

"You still with him?"

Elizabeth laughed. "No! By the time I came out of the bathroom, he was sound asleep."

Sheri laughed. "Men."

"Thank you, Sheri! Can't tell you how much I appreciate your calling me and getting this straightened out."

"Glad to help. I'd love to get into that head of his someday. He's fascinatingly strange."

"Good strange or bad strange?"

Sheri laughed. "Well, I wouldn't kick him out of bed for eating crackers."

"Sheri!" Elizabeth laughed. "I'll take that as *good* strange."

Sheri said, "He's a keeper." She paused. "By the way, would you mind if I gave your number to Carl Casey's wife?"

"Carl's the CIA guy, right?"

"Yeah. Carl told me Kelly had a similar situation to yours. She lost her husband in an aircraft accident after being married for only a year. I've met her and think you guys would hit it off and might be good for each other."

"Sure. I'd love to talk to her." She paused. "Sheri, thanks again! You are a life saver."

"No problem. Get some sleep, girl."

As she hung up, she realized Sheri was right about Josh being strange. There was still the question of who he really was and where he came from. If he was schizophrenic, he was an extremely successful one. If he was a prophet, he wasn't like any she'd ever read about. In fact, he seemed theologically challenged. The whole thing was surreal.

After she got home, she opened the little gift box. Inside she found a painted Russian doll. Nested inside were seven progressively smaller dolls. As she opened the last one, she found a little wooden heart inside. Wrapped around it was a gold necklace. As she pulled it out, she saw a tiny handwritten note. "*Thank you for helping me find myself and believing in me. I love you. Josh.*" She tried not to cry as she realized he'd written the note months ago.

31

MIRROR

Lopez saw the limo pull up in front of her house. She grabbed her jacket and went outside. The driver held the door open for her. As she slid in, she leaned over and kissed Musk on the cheek. "Sure you can't stay for dinner?"

"Would absolutely love to but I've got to be in Ecuador tomorrow morning." He gently shook his head. "Sheri, you're more beautiful than when we met so long ago." He frowned. "Why was it that we didn't work out again?"

She laughed. "You're kidding?" She shook her head. "We're the exact same personality. Highly motivated and task-oriented ... eventually we would have had to kill each other."

He laughed, shaking his head. "Oh yeah, I forgot. Regardless, it's good to be working with you again." He paused. "On to saving the world. On the phone, you said you had a solution. I assume you were referring to how we're going to break this to the public?"

"Yes." Looking thoughtful, she started slowly. "We all have a fascination with the unknown. Did you know that the second biggest commercial holiday after Christmas is Halloween? People love mysteries and conspiracies."

Musk nodded. "OK."

"Instead of telling people directly what's going to happen, we leak it, and then deny it. It's weird but people are more likely to accept something if they believe it's a secret. The beauty of a conspiracy is that it can't be proven wrong, because anyone who attacks it ..."

Musk finished, "Must be part of the conspiracy."

She nodded. "It also allows people to get used to an idea a little at a time. Just like people, societies can go into shock if things happen too fast, which could be very dangerous."

Musk nodded. "Sounds good, but how do we get international exposure without ending up in the tabloids?"

She smiled. "That's where you come in. You've got a big reputable media department. We need *you* to start leaking some vague comet danger information to your media people. Tell them it came from a high-level U.S. government official on condition of anonymity. Coming from you, they'll accept it immediately. Then we have the U.S. government deny it."

Musk frowned. "Fuze was OK with this?"

"Yeah, he said government denial wouldn't be a problem."

He nodded. "Can do."

She frowned. "By the way, after spending time with him in Antarctica, what do you think of Josh?"

"He threw himself off a cliff; he's a complete lunatic." He smiled as he shook his head.

Sheri nodded. "Yeah, I love him too." Looking out the window, she added, "I have to admit, it's kind of fun being in on a conspiracy."

"*In* on a conspiracy? ... Sheri, you're creating it."

She smiled. "Yeah, there's got to be a bestseller in here somewhere."

It was late October, seven months since Josh woke up in the hospital and five months before they had to start deflecting the comet. As usual, he and Meadows were the first in the conference room. Sheri arrived next. He hadn't seen her since their dinner in Kansas City. He gave her a quick hug and whispered in her ear, "Thank you, Sheri, you are a goddess!" She winked and hugged him back.

The meeting came to order. Meadows said, "Katori's still at Los Alamos, but he said work's going well on the Comet Asteroid Tracking and Targeting Projector Beam Deflector .... Dang, that's way too long. What's a good nickname for this thing?"

One of the Air Force engineers said, "Let's use the Navy's naming system and call it, ComAstTraTarProBeaDef!"

Everyone laughed. The Navy's strange habit of using the first few letters of each word often ended in unpronounceable results. Without missing a beat, Meadows fired back. "No, no, let's use the Air Force's superior acronym system. We'll call it – let's see that would be – CAT P!" There were groans and more laughter. A lively discussion ensued. Finally, by adding "Laser" and ignoring order and grammar, they came up with "CAT BLasTar."

Josh said to Chandra, "Schrödinger would've been proud."

Chandra laughed but most of the rest of the group just gave them a blank look.

Meadows said, "OK, now that we've got the important work done, we can continue with the pesky technical details. Katori said they're building the first scale model for testing, and it appears to be ahead of schedule. How are we coming on the power source?"

Shepherd said, "We found the perfect small nuclear reactor. Made by a Los Alamos spin-off company called Hyperion, it's an easily transportable, sealed module about the size of a hot tub. With a small steam turbine, it can produce 25 megawatts of power and costs only $50 million."

Meadows said, "Awesome! When can we get it?"

"The first ones are being built now and should be ready next year."

Meadows, obviously holding back irritation, said, "Dr. Shepherd, we need to be feeding power to this thing in six months."

Surprisingly, Bobinski jumped to Shepherd's defense. "Shepherd's right. They are perfect for our purpose and we should put in priority order as soon as possible. Even offer bonus for faster production."

Meadows frowned but nodded.

Bobinski continued, "Until then, there are two small graphite-moderated reactors in Chukokta, Russia. They've produced 11 megawatts each since 1976. They're upgrading to newer reactors and will sell old ones to us with new uranium cores. They're big, heavy and need more assembly and monitoring, but they're robust, and we can buy them now. They can fill gap until modular reactors are ready."

For the first time, Shepherd didn't have a rebuttal. Although still frowning, he actually nodded his head.

Meadows said, "How soon can we get these and, not that it

really matters, but how much do they cost?"

Bobinski smiled. "We can have in one month. Negotiated special two-for-one price, $15 million for both reactors, but need additional $2 million in cash."

"Sounds great." Meadows paused. "Do I really want to ask what the cash is for?"

Bobinski continued matter-of-factly, "Cash ensures reactors delivered in good working condition."

Meadows asked, "Two million?"

"Offered two-week trip to Disney World to all plant workers and managers if reactors delivered on time and stay operational for 12 months. We also buy new computers and patrol cars for local police." He smiled. "They help avoid unnecessary paperwork and escort reactors to airfield where C-17 picks them up. Also paid local – how do you say – mob?"

Meadows said, unnecessarily, "Mob?"

"Yes, we pay mob to protect shipment from criminals."

Smiling, Meadows shook his head. "Glad you're on our side."

In a classified conference room at the National Reconnaissance Office, Northrop Grumman briefed the program status of their newest spy satellite. Dr. Jackie Jones wrapped up her PowerPoint presentation. The last slide highlighted the program's recent and significant schedule slips. At the bottom, it simply read, "Lead Engineers Tasked with Higher Priority Program." She knew that would stir up discussion.

The Deputy Director of NRO said, "What higher-priority program?"

Jones said, "We don't know, sir. It's black like ours, but it's important enough that it pulled our lead engineer and most of his team away."

The Deputy Director shook his head. "We're a Defense Category One, Top Secret Program. Who could have higher priority?"

She shrugged. "Just conjecture based on Dr. Cho's area of expertise ...."

"Air Force?"

"That would be my guess. He did their airborne laser."

He sighed. "If this continues, it's going to kill our schedule.

I'll talk to the Director."

Dr. Garrett Cho asked the test technician, "How much longer?"

"Capacitors will be at full charge in 20 minutes."

Just then, one of Cho's engineers came in with a box full of ICEEs. Cho loved the frozen drinks and had corrupted his team, which consisted of two engineers and two physicists, all under 26. While they were waiting, they sat around sucking the ICEEs. Cho lifted his drink and toasted, "Happy Thanksgiving!" They returned his toast with grins.

The youngest and skinniest, Greg Langlois, was an electrical engineer and software wizard. He asked Cho, "You think this one will work?"

Cho said, "Absolutely!"

Langlois smiled. "You always say that. What makes you so sure this time?"

Cho shrugged. "It has to. It's the last mirror."

Langlois said, "Uh oh."

Cho shook his head. "Relax, dude. We'll figure it out."

"No ... it's not that. I just got a brain freeze."

The optical engineer, Judy Lanier, laughed. She said, "That's not good. Your brain can't afford to work any slower than it already does."

One of the physicists added, "Brain freeze is a simple heat transfer problem. All we have to do is dunk your head in boiling water for a few minutes."

Lanier winked at Cho, then, very seriously said, "Greg, push your thumb against the roof of your mouth. The heat and pressure from your thumb will help."

As Langlois complied, the cell phones came out.

Knowing Langlois's image was about to become a screen saver, Cho laughed hard enough to send the drink up his nose.

His young team was irreverent and they frequently made fun of each other, but they worked well together and were very creative, particularly Langlois. He might be gullible, but he was the brightest of the bunch.

The test technician finally reported, "Doctor, the capacitors are at full charge. Ready to fire when you are."

The chamber looked like a small submarine with portholes.

Heavily armored, the walls were high-strength steel, several inches thick. The "portholes" were even thicker bulletproof glass.

After the final checks, the technician counted down, "Five, four, three, two, one."

There was a loud bang like a shotgun blast.

"Crap!" Cho said with real frustration. "There goes another one." He didn't have to see the test chamber to know what happened.

After it cooled, they opened it and Cho dutifully peered inside. He saw tiny beads of melted glass sprayed across the metal walls and windows. He pulled his head out and each of the others peered in. As Langlois pulled his head out, he asked, "Any other mirrors we could try?"

Cho shook his head, "No, this company has the best and most reflective mirrors in the world. This was their newest prototype."

Lanier added, "No mirrors can handle this much energy. We're vaporizing them and we're not even running at full power."

The physicist said, "Yes, but you have to be impressed by our laser's power conversion efficiency. We're cranking out some serious photons."

Lanier shook her head. "Unless we figure out how to get a tight beam out of the atmosphere, we're dead," she added softly, "maybe literally."

32

CIA

The Deputy Director of the CIA, Brian Davidson, rarely closed his office door. He wanted to make sure his people knew they had access to him in a world where access was tightly controlled. There was a knock on the doorframe. The Deputy looked up to see one of his directors.

"Sir, got a minute?"

"Sure, what's up?"

"Got a complaint from the Director of the NRO."

"A complaint?"

"Yeah, it appears our next-generation spy-satellite program is being delayed by some other super-secret program."

Davidson sighed. "What else is new? Do we know anything about the other program?"

"Well, NRO already checked with the Director of National Intelligence and she didn't know anything about it. DNI thought it might be Air Force, but the Air Force claims they don't know anything either. In fact, they're whining that one of their programs is affected too." He laughed. "Course, they immediately blamed the Navy." He smiled. "I think the Air Force-Navy football game must be coming up."

Looking back at his paperwork, Davidson said, "Black defense programs are usually the worst kept secrets. What's the rumor mill say?"

"Well, that's the weird part. Rumors are hinting at extraterrestrial stuff and the South Pole."

Davidson sat up in his chair, "What?"

"Yeah, normally we'd dismiss it like all the other silly rumors, but this program's sucked up several big name engineers and scientists."

Nodding, Davidson said, "Check your sources. If it still looks interesting, we'll take it to the boss."

It was early December. Josh noticed the meeting had ballooned to 40 people.

Meadows started it with, "OK, we're T minus three and a half months to our first operational firing. Dr. Lopez, how's our cover story holding up?"

"So far, so good, but there's a simple law about secrets." She glanced meaningfully around the room. "The chances of a leak ... go up exponentially with the number of people involved. It isn't a question of if ... but when."

Meadows nodded. "Dr. Katori, how's our Cat Blaster coming?"

Katori looked concerned. "We have a serious technical hurdle with the beam correction. Cho's still at Los Alamos trying to figure out options."

"What's up?"

"The scale model Blaster is performing beautifully. If we'd been able to do this a couple decades ago, we could've built an impenetrable missile defense. They still have to figure out how to scale it up and get the aiming system configured, but I'm not worried about that right now. The problem is the beam correction. We're using a concept from optical astronomy. They've used it for years to take better pictures by correcting for a light beam's passage through the atmosphere. "

Meadows said, "I understand the concept but can you explain the details?"

Katori said, "We're going to bounce the Blaster's beam off a deformable mirror. A guide laser, fired up through the atmosphere, tells the computer how to manipulate the mirror's surface to compensate for atmospheric distortion. Tiny servos in the back of the flexible mirror make tiny changes to its shape hundreds of times a second. It's a tried and true system."

Meadows said, "Sounds good. So what's the problem?"

"The problem is the power. The mirror has to reflect a billion watt beam in milliseconds."

"So ...?"

"Joe, no mirror is perfect. No mirror can reflect 100% of

incoming light. The best of the best can reflect a remarkable 99.99%."

Meadows nodded thoughtfully. "And if the mirror absorbs even one hundredth of a percent of a billion watts that's ..."

Katori finished, "Ten kilowatts and it's vaporized every mirror. Without beam correction, we can't focus it enough to hit the comet."

A discussion ensued among the engineers. The debate heated up. In each case, they discarded ideas due to physics, engineering, or time.

Finally, during a brief silence, Josh asked, "What causes thunder?"

Everyone stopped talking. Someone said "What?"

He repeated, "What causes thunder?"

All eyes turned toward him with expressions varying from confusion to irritation.

With a patronizing tone, one of the young engineers said what others were thinking. "Lightning?"

Josh smiled. "Really? The electric discharge generates the sound?"

The engineer looked a little less confident. "Well ... no, I think it's more like a ... a sonic boom."

Not letting up, Josh asked, "From?"

One of the physicists jumped in. "It's caused when the electric discharge superheats the air to tens of thousands of degrees. The hot air expands faster than the speed of sound creating a sonic boom and then falls back into the vacuum ...." His expression suddenly changed from lecture mode to interest. "A vacuum or *hole* in the air is created!"

The scientists and engineers looked at each other with raised eyebrows as several conversations began.

With a slight headshake, Meadows grinned at Josh.

Chandra held up her hand for silence. When it quieted down, she tentatively asked, "Is it possible that instead of correcting our beam, we could punch a *pilot* hole through the atmosphere, just before we fire the main beam?"

Katori added, "Fire the beam twice in rapid succession, with the first shot superheating the air and opening a vacuum tunnel for the second."

The physicist, who'd explained thunder, said, "It won't be a pure vacuum but it would be extremely low density. We'd have to optimize the laser frequency of the first shot for absorption by air molecules, but ... it *might* create a hole for a few milliseconds."

Chandra smiled. "Light's fast. That's all we need."

Katori scratched his head. "It's not impossible." He paused. "We'll have to think about how we fire it in rapid succession at two different frequencies. We'll need more power." He paused again. "We planned on using one reactor as the primary and the second as a backup, but maybe with both online ...."

Chandra raised her hand.

Meadows nodded.

"I think we need to adjourn so we can go chase this idea down."

Meadows nodded. "Class dismissed. Let me know what you figure out."

On the way out, Chandra gave Josh an approving smile and said, "You might be onto something."

Josh said, "I actually got the idea from you."

She frowned.

He said, "Remember when I told you about seeing the amazing aurora at the South Pole?"

She nodded.

"You said when you blast that much energy through the atmosphere ... you blow up a lot of air molecules."

She laughed. "We'll co-publish."

As they broke up, Sheri smiled to herself. She'd warned everyone about security leaks ... while she was busy working with Musk on creating a major press leak. But there was something else she needed to do. Catching Smith before he left, she asked, "May I talk to you for a moment?"

He nodded.

"I'd like to sit down with you, briefly, and compare notes on some of the team. I may have some psychological insights that could be useful in protecting the program and people in it." She thought to herself, *Including you.* She had to admit she also found him fascinating.

Smith frowned, but then nodded. "Actually, Dr. Lopez, there

is an area that I could use your help with." He paused, looking directly at her. "Of course, this would have to be kept in the strictest confidence."

"Tim, I'm a psychiatrist, we deal in secrets all the time. What can I help you with?"

He said quietly, "I'm having some challenges regarding the background of one of the members of this team."

"Which one?" But she knew who he was talking about.

Davidson read the report and decided to visit his boss.

The Director of the CIA was talking on the phone with his feet propped up on his desk. Seeing his Deputy at the door, he motioned him in.

Davidson came in and sat down, accustomed to waiting. Director "Buster" Johnson earned his nickname honestly. Looking a little like George C. Scott in the movie *Dr. Strangelove*, he was a short, swarthy man with a strong handshake and a temper to match. Like the general in the movie, he also had an irritating tendency to chew bubble gum.

Although he wasn't a lot taller than Buster, Davidson was different in almost every other characteristic. Unlike Buster, Davidson was trim with fine features and always dressed neatly with a tie. Even though he knew he'd never operate in the field again, he believed it was important to set the example. He was an avid runner and still competed in triathlons although pushing 60. He was also a patient man who rarely got excited and always enjoyed a good puzzle.

The Director finally got off the phone. "What's up?"

"Sir, we've got something a little odd going on and I wanted to bounce it off you."

Buster, chewing gum as usual, asked, "You mean that Iranian thing?"

"No sir, this is internal. Have you ever heard of a black program codenamed *Resurrect*?"

"Nope. What's it about or will you have to kill me?"

The Deputy smiled. "Well, that's the weird part. This appears to be a black program among black programs. It's been sucking up experts from other programs but we can't find any agency or military branch that claims it."

"Why should we care? Are they killing anyone or threatening to?"

"No. The reason we found out about it is that it's affecting our next-generation spy-satellite. Their best and brightest engineers are being funneled into it and off our program."

Buster laughed. "So we're really talking about a 'rice bowl' fight?"

"Possibly."

"Well, unless it threatens national security or we're given a mandate to investigate, let's just keep an eye on it. See what else you can find out ... quietly. Don't want to look like idiots by investigating a pet program of this administration, like that NASA fiasco last year."

Josh knew the schedule would continue to slide until they fixed the beam correction. Every day, the comet moved three million kilometers closer, making it that much harder to deflect. *These* issues, however, paled in comparison to his latest challenge – Elizabeth had invited him to her parents' home for Christmas.

He didn't want to go, but she pointed out there was little he could accomplish on Christmas Eve or Christmas Day. Even those toiling to save the world had to have a breather. She was right. The team needed to spend some time with their families, if for no other reason than to remind them of what they were trying to save.

Although he had talked to Elizabeth frequently since Sheri brought them back together, he'd only managed to meet her twice since then, and only for a quick lunch between events. He finally accepted Kelly's marriage, and his physical injuries had healed. He *really* wanted to see Elizabeth. Actually, he wanted to do more than just see her ... and her parents' house wasn't exactly what he had in mind.

33

CHRISTMAS

Two days before Christmas, Davidson was back in the Director's office. "Remember a couple weeks ago when I told you about that black program *Resurrect*?"

Buster frowned as he stuffed papers into his briefcase. "Uh, yeah I guess."

"My preliminary investigation shows a sizable program involving engineers and scientists from Boeing, Grumman and NASA. There are rumors about operations in Los Alamos and even Antarctica. I've talked to all the major agencies and military branches and no one appears to know anything about it. It may be so highly classified that they aren't talking, but it's unusual to have something this big without an obvious sponsor. My instinct says we should investigate further, but I'd like to confirm that the President isn't aware of it first."

Buster nodded vaguely. "I'll ask him, but it'll have to wait. I'm out of here. Short of DEFCON 1, I don't plan to be back until after Christmas." He slapped Davidson on the back. "Merry Christmas!"

Josh flew to Austin on Christmas Eve. He didn't expect snow but stepping outside the terminal, the almost 70-degree breeze caught him by surprise. Looking around, he immediately saw Elizabeth. She was leaning against her jeep wearing a light summer dress that fluttered softly in the breeze. He suddenly appreciated the warm weather.

After hugging her tightly, he threw his small bag in the back. Climbing into the passenger seat, he tentatively asked, "What did you tell your parents?"

"I just told them you were a military officer working on a

sensitive program. I also told them you didn't have any family, and I didn't want you to spend Christmas alone. They accepted it without question."

On the way to her parents' home, Elizabeth gave him a brief rundown on her family. He was happy just to sit and listen to her talk.

He quickly found her parents to be kind and open. He spent a lot of time playing with four of Elizabeth's very young nieces and nephews. Fighter pilots and small children played well together. He also discovered his new body made an exceptionally effective jungle gym.

Elizabeth's mother was much like her daughter, beautiful and gracious, with old world charm. He suspected that she was aware of the chemistry between him and Elizabeth. Women had that knack, a mother even more so, but she was very kind and never asked uncomfortable questions.

After dinner on Christmas Eve, Josh went for a walk to give Elizabeth time with her family. The dark tree-lined streets followed the rolling topography of the hills. It had cooled off after sunset, and he enjoyed the exercise as he randomly followed the serpentine streets.

There was no one out; everyone was with their family tonight. He appreciated Elizabeth and her parents, but it was hard not to think about the family he'd lost. Out there, somewhere were Kelly and Carl, celebrating their first Christmas with their daughter ... his daughter. It hurt to think about, but he no longer ran from the memories. Smiling sadly, he gave them all a silent toast, whispering, "Merry Christmas, Kelly, Carl and Caitlin." Wiping his eyes, he extended his toast. "Merry Christmas, Jesse." If it weren't for Jesse, he wouldn't be here to make a toast. He refused to let pity drive his thoughts, clearing his mind he asked, "Jesse, you there?"

After a few seconds, he sensed his presence.

"I know I've been a pain to work with and I apologize. Thank you for all that you've done for me." Not wanting to dwell on his past, he said, "Mind if I ask some more questions?"

He took Jesse's silence as a yes, and began, "Tomorrow's the biggest holiday of the world's largest religion. I've been reading some of the ancient religious texts, the Bible, Qur'an, Talmud and

Veda. They're pretty bizarre." He shrugged. "But then so is cosmology and quantum mechanics. If we set aside unprovable religious beliefs, including infinite universes, we have a paradox. Can you help me with it?"

How did the universe start?

"The Big Bang."

How did the Big Bang begin?

"Here we go again. From an infinitely small, infinitely dense point called a singularity."

Where did the singularity come from?

"Don't know. Since the Big Bang created space and time, it's like trying to give birth to a baby without the mother." He paused. "And if the singularity was birthed along with the laws of physics, it had to operate under quantum mechanics. That creates the paradox. To set the state, to lock the singularity into reality, we need an observer, which is impossible. Or we need infinite universes, which is unprovable."

How do you know there was no observer?

He shook his head. "Because nothing can exist outside of space and time!"

Then what initiated the Big Bang?

He walked for a few moments, thinking. He had been surprised to learn that the majority of the world's population believed in some type of supreme being. "You're not suggesting that some type of ... consciousness could have been the 'observer' that initiated The Big Bang?"

What does science say?

He shrugged. "Most scientists would probably say they can't exclude the possibility, but don't believe a supreme being is required to explain the universe."

What do you think?

"I believe that too, but unless we accept infinite universes on blind faith, our existence is mathematically impossible."

Yet here you are.

He took a deep breath. "Just seems awfully bio-centric to think that instead of *sentient life* being the result of inanimate matter ... *inanimate matter* might be the result of sentient life." With a wry smile, he added, "Yet, it's the one area where cutting-edge physics and our crazy spiritual beliefs appear to intersect."

He shook his head. "Just have a hard time imagining some *invisible entity* influencing the universe."

Dark Energy?

He laughed. "Touché"

Merry Christmas, Josh.

The President of the United States, Jeff Yager, was tired. It was only a couple weeks after Christmas, and he was already juggling marbles, bowling balls and nuclear weapons. As he wrapped up a discussion on North Korea with his Director of National Intelligence and the CIA Director, he looked down at his notebook and saw one more action he could check off. "Buster, you know that black program you asked me about a few days ago? The one that's messing with your spy satellite program?"

"Resurrect?"

"Yes. I checked with the cabinet, joint chiefs and NASA. None of them know anything about it."

Buster and the DNI both frowned.

Buster said, "I didn't expect that." He paused. "Then, we really need to get to the bottom of this!"

The President caught a slightly raised eyebrow from the DNI. They both knew Buster's reputation. His appointment was the result of political realities. Buster was a lawyer and a strong leader, but tended toward a "Fire, Ready, Aim" mentality.

Looking Buster in the eye, the President said, "Let's find out a little more before we start kicking in doors. Maybe it's a legacy project from a past administration. I'll check with them. If we don't get anything concrete, then you can go ahead with an investigation."

"Yes sir."

Davidson listened to Buster summarize the conversation with the President.

Buster finished with, "Let's go ahead and get a jump start on this. If the President finds out it's from a previous administration, we can stop the investigation."

Davidson said, "I'll call Lafferty at the Bureau."

"Wait a minute, this is our baby!"

He looked at Buster with some surprise. "What little we

know suggests it's all based in the U.S."

"Brian, I know what our jurisdiction is, but this is impacting our spy satellite and I hate telling the President I don't know about something in the black world. Besides you mentioned Antarctica, that's not FBI jurisdiction."

"The South Pole isn't really anyone's jurisdiction, but I'll broach the idea of keeping operational lead with Lafferty." He paused. "Sir, you may want to call the FBI Director yourself. I think Jay Jost will be more receptive if the request comes directly from you."

Buster nodded.

Davidson knew there was something strange going on but didn't want to spool up the Director, not yet. The intelligence world was painted in shades of gray, but Buster only saw the world in black and white. He looked right at Buster and said, "We'll need to proceed with kid gloves on this."

"Yeah, whatever."

34

PENETRATION

Davidson met with the Deputy Director of the FBI, Bart Lafferty. He knew Lafferty well, having worked with him on past projects. Like Davidson, Lafferty was a career agent who started on the streets and worked his way up. A big man, he fit the classic Irish cop profile with a mop of reddish hair going rapidly gray. Brian knew looks were deceiving; Lafferty was a Stanford grad and a gentleman.

Davidson ran through everything they knew.

Lafferty had no problem with the CIA keeping operational lead, and they agreed the first thing they needed was someone on the inside.

Lafferty said, "It'll be hard to spin-up an agent with enough technical background to pass 'em off as an insider."

Davidson agreed. "Let's find someone already in the program and 'turn' them."

"Brian, you guys have more experience in converting scientists and engineers to the dark side. What do you suggest?"

"We start at the top."

Lafferty gave him a questioning look.

"We need to befriend the program's senior office manager. We've already identified her. She's very experienced, and highly respected."

Lafferty shook his head. "Despite political correctness, they *are* almost always women." He paused. "Glass ceiling?"

Davidson shrugged. "I think it's because men suck at multi-tasking. Women are more competent at running the complexities of an office populated with people."

"But will she have access to the classified information we need?"

Davidson said, "Many office managers are read into the programs because they have to handle the administration, but that's not why we need her. Women are actually less likely to leak classified information. The reason we need her is that she can help us identify our mole. She has the most important information." He smiled. "She knows the office politics and where the skeletons are buried."

"So in the government and engineering world, who makes a good mole?"

"Human nature is the same whether pipe fitter or PhD. We look for people who either have something to hide or an ax to grind."

Lafferty shook his head. "You guys are sneaky."

Davidson smiled. "Why, thank you."

―�֍―

A couple weeks later, Davidson told Buster, "We should have our informant soon. Apparently, it hasn't been easy. Most of those involved are fiercely loyal to the program and its leaders."

"How'd you do it?"

"We established a relationship with the office manager. She's been extremely helpful."

Buster winked, "A little 'undercovers' work?"

Davidson shook his head. "Actually the office manager is a grandmother. All it took was inserting a young lady from the Bureau posing as a new office assistant. She made friends with the office matriarch and simply asked her who to watch out for. Never underestimate the power of women asking questions."

Buster looked disappointed.

―✖―

Kevin Yankovic was the CIA agent assigned to find an informant. Working with the FBI, their cover story was that he was from the Government Accounting Office. It wasn't unusual for the GAO to take an interest in government-funded programs at contractor facilities. Yankovic had an intuitive ability to read people, with the exception of his teenage daughter. The young FBI agent they'd inserted supplied him with a description of the major team players. After studying their profiles, he believed he had two potential candidates.

They borrowed the office of the local Defense Contract

Management Agency's Commanding Officer. As his first candidate arrived, Yankovic opened with a low threat approach. "Dr. Shepherd, thank you for seeing me on such short notice. I know you're a very busy man."

Shepherd nodded nervously.

"The reason I wanted to talk to you is that we are aware that you are part of a program that we're concerned about. Along with the FBI, we are investigating funding irregularities. We need to determine if there is a need for a criminal investigation. As the program's logistics expert, we wanted to talk to you first." Yankovic knew very well that in the government and contractor world, a GAO visit to your program was like an IRS audit of your tax return.

Shepherd fidgeted and didn't make eye contact.

Yankovic continued, "You know the program I'm speaking of?"

"Yes. Yes, of course." He paused, looking around. "I knew there was something wrong."

Yankovic leaned forward. "And why is that?"

"I have three degrees, 17 certifications and over 35 years of experience in my field, but they act like I don't know what I'm talking about. I told them their site was poor and their timeline was absolutely preposterous, but did they listen to me? No. They bring in some Ruski who has no degree and no certifications."

The reference to the Russian was interesting, but he had to let the fish run with the line. "Yes, I can certainly understand your frustration." He listened sympathetically as Shepherd continued to complain. He had one more interview but he was pretty sure he had his mole.

After 20 more minutes, Yankovic actually felt sorry for anyone who had to work with this guy. He called this type of personality the "all knowing black cloud." They never quite understood that, even though they were knowledgeable, no one wanted to listen to them. They were negative about everything and superior to everyone.

Davidson stopped by Buster's office. "We've got our informant and we're already getting some interesting intel. We probably need to call a meeting."

Buster said, "Who's our mole?"

Agency policy was never to use names, even in closed meetings. To reduce the risk of compromising their identity, they referred to them generically or with code names.

Davidson said, "He's one of the team's experts and sits in on most key meetings. The office manager told our agent, no one likes him. He believes that most of those on the program think he doesn't know what he's doing and it makes him look incompetent in front of his team." Looking at Buster, Davidson suddenly felt uncomfortable.

Buster nodded, oblivious to the parallel.

Two months after discovering the beam correction problem, Katori and Chandra called a meeting to discuss the progress. Smaller than usual, it included just the core engineers, physicists, Meadows, Smith and Josh.

Chandra started. "We tested Josh's crazy idea of burning a hole through the atmosphere. It worked! At least in the lab. We figured out the correct frequency and power needed; then we passed it to Katori's team to do the hard stuff."

Josh noticed Katori had bags under his eyes and looked like he'd been sleeping in his clothes. Cho, sitting next to him, didn't look much better.

"It's harder than we thought." Katori whispered, having lost his voice. "Two beams with different frequencies and power, fired from the same place within milliseconds." He paused for effect. "But we did it ... or at least we think we did. It was our youngest engineer, Greg Langlois, who came up with the solution."

Cho nodded. "It worked on our scale model Blaster at low power. We think it will work full scale but it'll require replacing components after each firing."

Meadows shook their hands. "Awesome! I'm impressed and proud of you and your team." Continuing gently, "What does this mean as far as our timeline?"

Katori rubbed his eyes. "We need to talk about that. This redesign put us behind schedule about six weeks."

Meadows glanced at Chandra.

She said, "These guys have been working their butts off, living on a few hours of sleep, but every day that passes makes the comet that much harder to deflect."

Meadows said, "Steve, Garrett, fantastic work! Please pass our congratulations to your team." Looking down at his program schedule, he added, "That pushes the first firing at the Pole back to May seventh, three months from today." Looking back at them, he said quietly, "I have to ask you to look carefully at your timeline and critical path. See if there's anything we can do to pull the schedule forward ... anything at all."

Davidson, sitting in Buster's office said, "The informant is giving us excellent information. This thing's bigger than we thought. They're trying to build the world's most powerful laser to deflect Earth-impacting comets, and they're going to put it near the South Pole. Our agent says that by all appearances it looks like a genuine program. They have highly respected engineers, military officers and astrophysicists on the team. They seem to have plenty of funding. We don't know the source, but our accountants don't see any illegal transfer of government funds or anything from offshore."

Buster nodded. "Sounds like a good program."

Davidson said, "Yes ...."

"But?"

"They're operating under a tight timeline due to a possible comet impact in a little over a year."

Buster laughed. "A comet hitting the earth? That's crazy."

"Actually, Chen from the Science Directorate says comets are a real threat." He paused. "What raises the warning flag is that the experts say there are no known comets that will come anywhere near the earth."

Buster shrugged. "Could they have detected a new one?"

"Our people say that if any observatory found a new one, everyone would know immediately, and this project claims they've known about it for almost a year."

"Where do they claim the information came from?"

"Our informant says no one knows. It's classified, even to them."

"Who's the ring leader?"

"Navy Captain Joe Meadows. He was captain of the aircraft carrier USS Ford." Looking at his folder, Davidson added, "He's a highly decorated officer with a good reputation. He'd be an admiral today if it hadn't been for a fire that destroyed some prototype fighters right after he assumed command. He works for NAVAIR, you know, Admiral Hendricks."

"Let me guess; Hendricks doesn't know anything about this."

"No, but that's not impossible. There are black programs that cross service and agency boundaries."

Buster said, "Could Meadows have been 'turned' by a foreign power because his career was ruined by the fire?"

"Anything's possible, but he holds the highest clearances and was in the PRP program."

"PRP?"

"Personnel Reliability Program. They continuously evaluate the stability of those who have particularly sensitive jobs, like carrying a live nuclear weapon in a single seat fighter. Meadows' profile and career indicate he's about as stable and ethical as they get. If he were on the other side, we wouldn't even think about trying to turn him."

Buster frowned. "He has to report to someone. This isn't rocket science."

Davidson smiled. "Actually, it is rocket science."

Buster didn't smile.

Davidson continued, "Short of bringing Meadows in for questioning, we can't be sure who he reports to. I don't think we want to do that yet. If we're investigating a genuine program, we risk compromising it, not to mention embarrassing ourselves. If it isn't genuine, then we tip our hand."

"Are there any other significant players?"

Davidson pushed several pictures across the desk to Buster. "Yes, but they read like a who's who of science and engineering. NASA's Dr. Victoria Chandra, Boeing's Dr. Steve Katori and the famous psychiatrist Dr. Sheri Lopez, to name a few. There are, however, two on the team who do have my interest. One is a Russian-born construction expert, Christoff Bobinski, and the other guy appears to run the funding side."

Buster frowned. "I don't care about the accountant. What about the Russian? What do we know about him?"

Davidson knew Buster was from a different era and had an

inherent distrust of their old Cold War adversaries. "Sir, the Russian is a naturalized American citizen and renowned construction expert. We actually have a dossier on him from the Cold War era. He had little use for the Communist Party. We're doing more background work on him but he'll be easy to track." Davidson paused. "I'm more interested in the accountant. We've broken a lot of terrorist operations by following the money trail."

"Who is he?"

"His name is Commander Josh Fuze."

"What do we have on him?"

"Absolutely nothing ... that's why I'm interested."

35

DOUBT

It was only two months to the first test firing of the Blaster. Chandra and Katori stopped Meadows and Josh after one of the technical meetings and asked if they could talk privately. They went to Meadows' office. Smith was already there.

Chandra began, "Joe, we trust your leadership and we're totally committed to this program but there are things that ... well, there have been some questions." She glanced guiltily at Josh.

Josh knew where this was going.

Meadows asked, "Like what?"

"Our NASA accountants say they've never seen this 'color' of money before. I know for the Antarctic operation, we're routing money through a private company to hide government involvement." She frowned. "But the funds to NASA and Los Alamos are also coming from a *private* company. Our government accountants are having anxiety attacks."

Katori added, "My key engineers, like Cho, are getting heavy pressure because they're letting their other programs slide and can't tell their bosses why. There are some seriously angry program managers out there gunning for us."

Chandra frowned. "Our team leads are asking why this program remains classified." She paused. "If the threat is real, why aren't we involving everyone to increase our resources?"

Meadows asked, "Are you having resource or funding challenges?"

Chandra said, "No. If we need something, we just buy it."

Katori nodded in agreement.

Meadows said, "So, we have a problem because ...?"

Chandra and Katori looked at each other sheepishly.

Josh knew this wasn't Meadows' battle. He caught Meadows' eye, and Meadows gave him a nod.

Josh began slowly, "Ken, Victoria, I understand your team's concerns. How are you feeling about the project personally?"

Katori smiled. "Don't worry about me. I'm having a blast. This must be what it was like to be part of the Apollo program."

Chandra said, "I completely agree ... it's just...."

Josh smiled. "Go ahead."

"Josh, I'd work on this project if you told me your fairy godmother gave you the tip, but we're almost a year from its arrival. It should be approaching the orbit of Jupiter. I've been keeping a tab on the major observatories. They haven't detected any new comets. It sure would help our team to have something more concrete." She looked at Katori. "Particularly, for those under the gun like Cho."

Josh nodded and made a decision.

"What if I can get you the coordinates and trajectory?"

"That would be fantastic! If it's 14 months out, we might be able to see it with the big scopes if we're looking in the right place."

Meadows asked, "How will you handle the inevitable questions of where the information came from?"

Chandra said, "Most astrophysicists who specialize in asteroids and comets aren't involved with planetary probes. With my background, they'll probably assume it came from one of our deep space probes. I doubt they'll question it as long as it's coming from me, but I don't really care what they think as long as we get search time at the big observatories." She frowned. "Josh, scientists and engineers like numbers. Give us coordinates, and we're good. When can I get them?"

Davidson had several Middle Eastern operations in progress and a congressional hearing, but he continued to follow the developments in the strange comet program. It was late February before he brought the results back to Buster.

Davidson dropped a surveillance photo on Buster's desk. "No one knows who Josh Fuze is or where he came from. Most of his team assumes he's CIA."

Buster studied the picture. "What do we know about him?"

"He doesn't have an office anywhere and lives in a small apartment in St. Louis. The only consistent thing we get is that he stays in the background, and everyone, including Meadows, respects him. He's probably mid-thirties and in excellent physical shape. No accent and knows both engineering and military lingo. We pulled his fingerprints off a glass, but they've turned up absolutely nothing. Since 9/11 that's almost impossible, particularly, for someone in the government or military-industrial complex."

Buster shook his head, "He has to have a government clearance. Can't we track him through that?"

Davidson shook his head. "He has a Boeing access clearance that should be tied directly to a government clearance, but it dead ends. There's no background check or history linked to it. The computer system has it tied to some dead military officer. If I didn't know better, I'd swear he's one of ours."

Buster frowned. "Could he be?"

"We have highly sensitive programs with deep cover agents, but I assure you, I'd know if this guy was on our payroll. I checked with the DNI and FBI. He doesn't belong to them either. Our informant says that the rumors suggest he's a former SEAL, but it's probably just because he saved an engineer from falling off a cliff."

"SEAL Team Six gets involved in some weird stuff."

Davidson shook his head, "It is possible his identity was erased but those programs almost always involve us, and the Navy isn't claiming him either."

Buster drummed his fingers on the table. "So you're telling me ... we've got a bunch of high-level military, engineers and scientists developing a powerful energy-beam weapon, *supposedly* to protect the world from an impending comet that no one should be able to predict. *And* one of the key players is a total mystery."

Davidson shrugged. "That pretty much sums it up."

Buster looked at his Deputy. "Could there be some super-secret government agency we're not aware of?"

Davidson said, "Sir, nothing's impossible but I've been in this business my entire life. I think I would have heard about an agency that could do all this. I suggest we run this by the

Administration one more time."

The President said, "I checked with the last two administrations. No one knows anything about it. How could someone infiltrate our military-industrial complex and create a fake program for God's sake? Don't we have security checks and balances to prevent this?"

Buster glanced at Davidson.

Davidson said, "Mr. President, those checks and balances have been working against us. They're designed to keep information from being extracted ... *not inserted*. If this thing isn't real, this guy's brilliant and knows our system inside out."

The President shook his head. "Get to the bottom of this, but," he looked Buster in the eye, "I don't want any cowboy coups. I want to know what they're really doing. If this is a genuine program, I want to know who's behind it. If it's not, I want to know who's behind it."

Buster said, "Yes sir."

Davidson added, "Sir, they have operations in Antarctica. We'll need support from the military."

The President said, "Antarctica ... I think that's under U.S. Pacific Command."

Davidson nodded. "Yes sir, Admiral Carroll Rea."

"I'll tell the Sec Def and Joint Chiefs this is a priority and to support you with whatever you need."

Buster said, "Thank you."

As they left the White House, Buster said, "Brian, this becomes the top priority for this agency."

Davidson nodded, and then said slowly, "Whoever they are, they breached our military-industrial complex." He paused. "We have to assume they might be able to do the same with other government agencies."

Buster's eyes narrowed. "You mean like ours. What are you suggesting?"

"I'd like to run this operation with extremely tight security and as few participants as possible. Use only senior personnel with top-level clearances and full compartmentalization. With your permission, I'll talk directly to the directors of National Intelligence, Homeland Security and the FBI, and ask them to do the same. I'd even like to have an internal cover story among our agencies and the White House. There've been too many leaks in the past with other programs."

"Good idea."

Davidson asked, "What do you want to call the operation?"

Buster frowned. "Well, everything points back to this Fuze character."

Davidson said wryly, "The Jackal's already taken."

Buster said, "He's predicting a comet's going to clobber the earth, a comet that can't be seen." He paused. "We'll call him the Prophet."

Davidson sighed. Operation codenames weren't supposed to describe the operation or subject, that's why they were *codenames*, but he needed to pick his battles with Buster carefully.

Davidson set up their first meeting in a special CIA conference room. He had checked that everyone on the team was a veteran with the highest security clearance. The internal cover story was a billion-dollar, international drug cartel operating out of southern South America.

Buster started the first official meeting of the Prophet Operations team. "What do we have?"

Davidson, holding up several reports said, "Their Antarctic base is further along than we thought. The structure on the mountain that will house the energy-beam projector is almost finished. At the base of the mountain, the two Russian reactors are in place but aren't up and running yet."

Buster said, "Russian reactors?!"

Davidson nodded to Dan Chen, the Deputy Director of the CIA's Science and Technology Directorate.

"They're small industrial reactors and don't use weapons grade uranium," Chen explained. "It's an old design. The Russian construction expert, Christoff Bobinski, procured them and is coordinating their installation."

Buster frowned. "Maybe, but I don't like Russian involvement, particularly, with anything nuclear. Plus, we're going to have an international incident on our hands when the world learns Americans are installing nuclear reactors at the

South Pole." He shook his head. "Tell me about this comet deflection beam thing."

Chen said, "They refer to it as the "Cat Blaster.""

Buster nodded. "Good name. I hate cats."

"It's based on the old strategic defense technology. It generates a tightly collimated, extremely high-power, laser beam capable of vaporizing what it hits."

"So they've created a weapon that can destroy anything!"

Chen said, "Sir, the equipment is huge. It's not portable or effective against ground targets. It really appears to be designed to put a lot of energy on a target in space."

"Can it shoot down airplanes?"

Chen shrugged. "It's certainly powerful and accurate enough." Looking at some notes, he added, "But they don't have any search or tracking radar."

The CIA Associate Director for Military Affairs Lieutenant General Norma Glosson, added, "There isn't a lot to shoot at near the South Pole, and there are faster, simpler ways to take out aircraft."

Buster nodded, chewing his gum vigorously. He suddenly said, "My God, they're going to use it to take out our space station and satellites. They could cripple us by hitting our imaging, GPS and communication. Bastards will probably take out DirectTV too. We'll be blind and deaf."

"DirectTV?" Then refocusing, Chen quickly said, "Sir, since this is a laser, it's a line of sight weapon. If it can't see it, it can't hit it. The energy-beam could easily take out satellites above it, but most of our satellites and the Space Station are in low, equatorial orbits. We do have imaging birds in polar orbit they could hit, along with southern hemisphere geosynchronous satellites."

Chen shuffled through several sheets and found what he was looking for. "However, our engineers say the system runs off capacitors that have to be charged between shots. They designed it for a single powerful shot with several hours of recharge time. They'd only be able to take out one satellite before we nailed him."

Still animated, Buster said, "I'm telling you, we may not know what the system can really do and putting it in Antarctica may be a ruse. We need to round these bastards up and sweat the information out of them."

Davidson jumped in. "Sir, this Cat Blaster is still in a government lab in Los Alamos, and our informant says they've got technical problems. We can round the players up and shut them down within hours. *But,* we still have no idea who the Prophet reports to. If we slam the door now, we may never know."

Buster sighed. "OK, but what contingency plan do we have if we guessed wrong?"

Davidson nodded at General Glosson.

"Sir, the Pole base is a geographically fixed and unarmored target. We can easily destroy it with a single bomb or missile. The issue is distance. Land-based aircraft would have to fly thousands of miles, but it is within the range of a ship-based Tomahawk cruise missile."

Buster, still chewing loudly, said, "Yeah. Now that's what I'm talking about."

Glosson continued, "They can be launched from a ship or sub off the Antarctic coast. We could blow anything off the top of that mountain within a few hours."

Buster said, "Norma, the President gave us authorization for full military support."

She nodded. "I'll call Admiral Rea and get a Tomahawk shooter assigned."

Once again, Davidson realized Buster didn't have the patience for intelligence work. He needed to bring him back from bombs to bugs. "Sir, I think the key to all this lies with the Prophet himself."

Buster asked, "Have we started surveillance yet?"

The FBI Deputy, Lafferty, said, "We just started. We're assuming we're watching an intelligence operative familiar with surveillance techniques. We're using the most subtle and least intrusive technology we have."

Buster grunted, "Let me know when you have something."

Josh had to get the comet's coordinates and trajectory. He went for an early evening run around the park by his apartment. Based on Chandra and Katori's comments about their program's impact on other programs, he suspected – no, he actually sensed – his rogue program was no longer operating under the radar. Although he might be able to communicate with Jesse without speaking, it was easier and more comfortable to talk to him out-loud.

Setting a steady running pace, he cleared his mind and very softly said, "Jesse, I need to know everything you know about the comet."

A picture immediately formed in his mind. He had no idea how that was possible, but he should have known Jesse wouldn't send him a picture on his cell phone. It looked like a potato shaped, charcoal briquette rotating against a black background. Along with the image, he got the dimensions, coordinates and trajectory.

He stumbled and almost fell, yelling, "Fifteen kilometers!"

Another runner coming from the opposite direction, smiled and said, "Fifteen K, way to go!"

Stepping off the trail, Josh leaned over, hands on his knees, to catch his breath. He'd assumed the comet was no bigger than the five kilometers of Shoemaker-Levy. Shaking his head, he said softly, "Jesse, a 15-kilometer comet could erase humanity."

Yes.

36

COMET

Josh called Meadows and asked for an immediate meeting with Chandra, Katori and Lopez.

Meadows asked, "Smith?"

"Sure."

The six of them gathered around a small table in Meadows' office.

As soon as Chandra sat down, Josh handed her a piece of paper. She looked at it, and then at him with raised eyebrows.

Josh nodded. "That's it. That's the enemy."

Chandra pulled out her phone. As she typed she said, "Looks like a very long period comet. I'm passing the coordinates to one of my colleagues at the Keck Observatory in Hawaii. Do we know its dimensions?"

Josh didn't say anything.

Chandra finally looked up from her phone.

Josh sighed. "It's 15 kilometers in diameter."

Chandra and Katori both said, "Fifteen kilometers!"

Chandra fired back, "Josh, a 15-kilometer comet is a planet killer! It's bigger than the one that wiped out the dinosaurs and 70% of all species on the planet!" She finished softly, "It'll be the end of most life on Earth, including us."

Josh said softly, "I know."

Meadows asked, "Josh, is it really 15 kilometers?"

He sighed. "Yes, I just found out."

Chandra said, "I need to go. We need to run some calculations."

Meadows nodded.

They got up to leave, but Katori remained seated. They all stopped and looked at him questioningly. Katori, staring through the table, said with a flat emotionless voice, "We designed the Blaster to deflect a five-kilometer comet."

Chandra added, "I'm sorry, Joe, since we didn't know how big it was, and you guys mentioned Shoemaker-Levy ..."

Katori interrupted, "We can't deflect a 15-kilometer comet."

Meadows said, "Can't we scale-up the Blaster or build a couple more?"

Katori, looking up at Meadows, shook his head. Looking very tired, he said, "Joe, the diameter is three times larger ... but the volume is the *cube* of the diameter. That means a 15-kilometer comet has *27 times* the mass." He continued softly, "Unfortunately, Newton's law applies. Increase the mass 27 times ..."

Meadows finished, "We'd need 27 Blasters."

There was silence.

Josh hadn't considered how much mass was involved, but he'd never intended for this program to be the entire solution. It was supposed to be the pilot program, the pump primer. No ... no, that was an excuse. He never asked Jesse how big it was, partly because he probably didn't really want to know. The devil was in the details, and he sucked at details. More accurately, he tended to ignore them. Didn't matter how good you were at seeing the forest, if you drove into a tree. His only solace was that there was no way he could have hidden a program big enough to produce 27 Blasters.

Finally, Meadows said, "We probably don't need to share this with the rest of the team just yet. We need them thinking clearly." Turning to Katori, he said gently, "Steve, it's important to start figuring out what it'll take to scale up."

Katori nodded mechanically.

Meadows put both of his hands on the table and said quietly, "Our job is to prove we can hit a comet. Do that, and all the world's resources will be at our disposal. We'll be able to build dozens of these things."

Chandra looked up at Josh and Meadows. "I know this sounds strange, but ... it just became real." She paused. "A year from now, we'll be successful and partying our brains out, or we'll be dead along with everyone we've ever known."

There was a moment of somber silence. Then Meadows

broke it with, "I vote for the party. *However,* to do that, we *have* to accelerate this program. What can we do?"

—⋆—

That night, Josh felt the weight of the world back on his shoulders. To deflect the comet, they needed to be firing 27 Blasters right *now*. Instead, they were still trying to produce one. Even if the Blaster worked, they might not have time to scale it up. Pacing in his small apartment, he finally decided to go out for a walk.

It was a cold, clear, spring night with no one around.

Under his breath, he said, "Jesse, I've pushed the 'secret source' as far as it'll go. I feel like the little Dutch boy with his finger in the dike. I may have an elevated sense of paranoia, but I also have elevated senses. Someone *is* watching me. I could sure use some help."

There will be a small precursor to the comet.

"That wasn't exactly what I had in mind." He paused. "What do you mean *precursor*?"

One again an image appeared in his mind, but somehow he knew this image was from the past – thousands of years ago. He saw a hundred-kilometer-wide, icy planet hurling into the inner solar system. As its highly elliptic orbit whipped it around the sun, heat and tidal forces tore it apart creating a cloud of comets and debris.

Josh nodded. "So the comet is surrounded by a cloud of debris the Earth will pass through?" He thought for a moment. "A spectacular meteor shower will get people's attention. How soon?"

Twenty-five days

"Good!" He exhaled sharply. Despite dark premonitions of his future, talking to Jesse lowered his blood pressure. He walked in silence for a few moments then said, "Jesse, I just realized I 'died' one year ago today." With a half-smile, he said, "I have a feeling that even if the world gets out of this in one piece, my prospects aren't that great. Guess this would be a good time to ask if you think there's life after death?"

You're alive.

He smiled. "*Outside* of being given a new body ... do you think consciousness survives death or does it just dissipate?"

What do you think?

"Why do I bother asking?" He knew the drill. "We'd all like to believe there's some type of life after death. Every religion believes it, in one form or another. But if that's true, where are all these conscious minds now?"

Where do your religions say they are?

"Most of them would say heaven."

Where's heaven?

"That's my question. If it exists, where is it? Why don't we see any evidence?"

How many dimensions are there?

He sighed. "Four. Three spatial and one of time."

Four?

He paused. "Well ... in an attempt to tie all the major forces together, Superstring theories require more dimensions."

How many?

"The leading contender, M-Theory, requires a total of 11."

Where are they?

"You mean the seven extra dimensions? ... I don't know."

Then how do you know they exist?

"They're required to make the equations balance ...." he finished weakly.

I see.

"You know, it's interesting, the Bible, Talmud, Qur'an and Veda all talk about seven heavens, seven levels of heaven or a heaven with seven spirits of God. And why are there seven days in a week?" He knew he was pulling a "Seinfeld," talking around Jesse's question. "I mean, it's easy to figure out where the day, month and year came from – but why seven days? Five would have divided into 365 better and matched the number of fingers on our hand."

Silence.

He took a deep breath. "OK, OK ... I admit it. If a physics equation suggests there are seven invisible dimensions – I'm good. If a religion suggests there's an invisible heaven – I got a problem." With a half-smile, he said, "I promise. I'll try and keep a more open mind." He laughed. "It really would be pretty funny if heaven is located in physics' seven missing dimensions."

It was one week since Josh had told them the size of the comet. He saw Katori was already in Meadows' office, sitting across the table from Meadows, doodling on a pad of paper.

After Chandra, Smith and Lopez came in, they closed the door.

Meadows nodded to Chandra.

Chandra looked at Josh. "They haven't found anything at those coordinates yet, but they just started looking."

Meadows nodded to Katori.

Katori tapped his pencil on the table, set it down and looked up. Not looking happy, he said, "We need to skip the test firing at Los Alamos ... do it at the Pole. It'll buy us back a few weeks. We fire it April 17 instead of May 7."

Meadows nodded. "We'll be going for broke."

Katori added, "We'll be testing everything at the same time: reactors, capacitors, tracking system, alignment system, software and the Blaster. Something we'd never do on a regular program because the risk's too high. We have to prove this thing works as soon as possible to have any chance of scaling it up in time."

Sheri added softly, "It's important for another reason. When the comet is identified, it's critical people have something to give them hope. Without hope, bad things can happen to societies."

Meadows said, "Like a stock market crash?"

"And worse. With the stakes so high, government statements or promises carry little weight. Many will assume we're lying to them to prevent panic."

Chandra shook her head. "People would really believe the government would lie about something this important?"

Sheri frowned. "I've been involved with several government-funded studies that asked the question – if there was nothing we could do about an apocalyptic disaster, would it cause more social damage and pain to tell people? Guess what the answer was?" She let the silence answer the question. "A successful demonstration could be just the beacon people can rally around."

Smith cleared his throat. All eyes went to him. He said quietly, "We may have another problem. I have indications that we're under surveillance."

Meadows looked surprised. "By who?"

Smith shook his head. "I don't know yet. They're extremely good and are keeping a very low profile."

"Terrorists?"

"I don't think so. They're too sophisticated and subtle."

Chandra said, "Who on earth could possibly be opposed to what we're doing?"

Sheri frowned and said slowly, "Put yourself inside the head of an outside observer. What do you see?"

Smith nodded at Sheri, but Chandra shook her head. "I don't understand."

Sheri said, "You might *see* the world's most powerful energy-beam weapon being developed."

Smith, glancing at Josh, added, "You might *assume* the comet is nothing but a cover story."

Chandra just said, "How twisted would that be?"

Meadows looked at Smith. "What should we do?"

"Nothing yet. I'm going to drop into the background and see if I can observe the observers. If I sense a threat, I'll bring in support. In the meantime, if you see anything out of the ordinary, *do not* call me. Text me using the security app I put on your phones."

Josh's brain was spinning. He felt like he was looking into one of those infinity mirrors that reflected back into itself forever. He was playing a game within a game. No, it wasn't a game. He was facing a powerful adversary, and like Jesse, it had no face.

He said to Meadows and Smith, "In light of this, I suggest we don't tell anyone about our plan to move the schedule up. Let's operate as if we're going to do the test firing in Los Alamos, and ship the Blaster to the Pole at the last minute."

Smith nodded. "That might be prudent."

Meadows nodded. "OK."

As they were breaking up, Josh said, "Oh, I almost forgot. We also found out there will be a small precursor to the comet. We're expecting a fragment big enough to put on an impressive light show. It should arrive within a few weeks."

Chandra nodded. "Makes sense if the comet was part of a Centaur or dwarf planet that broke up."

As Josh turned to leave, he noticed Smith watching him. In fact, it seemed like Smith's eyes were always on him.

Davidson started the second meeting by dropping a newspaper on the table with the headline, "Earth Under Threat From Comet?"

Buster picked it up, as Davidson said, "It says the information came from a high-level but undisclosed government source. It's not a front-page story but it's in several major papers and, of course, the tabloids. We also got a message from the President's Chief of Staff asking us what we know about it."

Buster slammed his hand on the table. "This is going to get rapidly out of control unless we shut them down."

CIA Operations Director Cindy Bishara said, "We also just found out from our informant that the Prophet's predicting the arrival of a smaller comet fragment." She looked down at her iPad. "It's supposed to arrive in a couple weeks."

Buster said, "Don't tell me, it's too small and too dark to be easily detected."

"Yup."

Lafferty asked, "Why would he do that? He'll expose himself as a fraud in a few weeks when the fragment doesn't show up. It doesn't make sense."

Davidson, looking thoughtful, asked, "When are they planning on test-firing this thing?"

Bishara looked at a paper and said, "The first full-power test is scheduled at Los Alamos in about two weeks."

Buster said, "Amazing coincidence! They're behind schedule, and he's using this imaginary comet fragment to scare his people into working faster."

Davidson nodded. "The informant also says Fuze is scheduled to go down to the Pole base before the first firing. Since all their logistics flights have to go through the Falklands for fuel, I recommend we let him get to the Falklands and arrest him there."

Buster frowned for a moment and then smiled. "Yes. The island's perfect. Nowhere to run and outside the U.S. we have more … options."

Davidson said, "I'll work through British SIS to get permission."

Buster added, "There may be hostiles at the Pole to protect

or take the equipment."

"We can have commandos assigned to secure the Pole base just in case," Davidson said, looking at Glosson.

She nodded. "I'll ask U.S. Pacific Command to assign an arctic-trained SEAL team."

Davidson asked Bishara, "What about communications when we arrest the Prophet?"

"To prevent him from warning anyone, the Brits can jam everything in and out of the Falklands once the operation starts."

Lafferty added, "We'll round up all the others in the U.S. at the same time."

The President said, "Buster, sounds like a good plan." He paused. "I have to tell you though, it still doesn't add up in my mind. Why would someone who's made these inroads into our system go to such an elaborate ruse? Stealing nuclear or biological weapons would have been easier."

Buster retorted, "He's using fear and playing on everyone's desire to be a hero and save the world. It's a brilliant strategy that keeps otherwise smart men from asking too many questions. Using our own capabilities against us, it'll make me ... make *us* ... appear not only weak, but stupid, to the rest of the world."

"Maybe, but it seems too much like a Mission Impossible plot."

A little too loud, Buster said, "If you know any agency that could be behind this, let me know!"

The President raised his eyebrows at Buster.

Buster sighed. "I'm sorry, sir. No one's claiming this joker, and I don't believe people understand what a threat he is."

The President said, "All right, you've got a green light, but if possible, I want this Prophet alive. We need to know what's in his head."

As they left the White House, Davidson got a secure text. "Sir, we've got a fingerprint match on the Prophet."

37

IDENTIFY

Waiting in Buster's office, Bishara immediately reported, "The fingerprints match a John Doe, found on the side of a road a year ago. He was naked and unconscious. They brought him to Kansas City Medical Center, where he remained in a coma for several days and then," Bishara looked up at Buster, "he woke up, claiming amnesia."

Buster said, "I knew it! He's a plant." Frowning he asked, "Why did it take so long to make the fingerprint connection?"

Bishara shook her head. "They fingerprinted him as a John Doe at the hospital but found no matches, so they contacted Homeland Security. The Bureau evaluated him as a potential threat, but guess who the evaluating psychiatrist was?"

Buster smiled. "Dr. Sheri Lopez."

"Yup. They kept him under surveillance for a while, but eventually closed the case ..."

Buster interrupted, "Based on Lopez's assessment."

Bishara nodded. "The problem was that when all this was done, he was still a John Doe. The computer made the fingerprint match, but with no identity attached, it ignored it. It's a software glitch. They're fixing it now." Bishara continued, "The medical report indicates the Prophet was remarkably healthy and extremely intelligent. The surveillance report says," she looked up with a raised eyebrow, "he lived with one of his nurses for several weeks, which explains some of the phone conversations we've tapped."

Buster nodded. "Bring her in when we pull the trigger." With a malicious smile, he added, "She may provide some leverage."

Elizabeth got a call from Josh. After some small talk, he said, "Things are going well but they're going to get a little crazy. I may not be able to talk to you for a while." There was a pause. "I don't want there to be any misunderstanding this time. I haven't been very good at showing it, but I *really* care about you."

She said, "Then why does this sound like an exit speech?"

"It's nothing of the kind." She heard some irritation in his voice and knew it was mostly because they couldn't talk openly on the phone. "In fact, I'm *really* looking forward to an intimate discussion on *certain* cosmology theories. It just would be *best* if you stayed there for now."

She smiled. So, he wasn't infinitely dense. She said, very positively, "You do whatever you need to do. I'll be fine here."

As soon as she got off the phone, she called Lesia, told her there was a family emergency and she'd have to be gone a week. Then she threw some clothes in a bag, dropped Toto off with a friend and headed to D.C.

Davidson entered the conference room. Buster was already there. "Sir, this is Carl Casey, from the European directorate. He's one of our key international law experts. Carl, tell him what you just told me."

"Sir, I was just brought into the Prophet Operation today, but I actually met this guy, Josh Fuze – the Prophet – almost a year ago."

"What?"

"Yes sir, he read me into his program."

Buster, looking incredulous, said, "Why didn't you tell someone!"

"Sir, I had no idea about *your* operation; I wasn't part of it. As for his program, I went through the normal paperwork channels. It was approved, and as you know ..."

Davidson finished, "You can't talk about it once you're read into it."

Carl continued, "I assumed CIA leadership was already involved."

Davidson laughed. "*We are* ... on the opposite side." He shook his head gently. "You gotta admire how this guy works."

Buster glared at Davidson and turned back to Carl. "Out

with it. What do you know about him?"

"Never met him before he contacted me a year ago. We shared a close friend. He knew details and stories that confirmed it. My wife and I have even had dinner with him. I'm positive he is, or was, a military officer. He speaks the lingo."

Buster's eyes narrowed. "Let's get a hold of this common friend."

Carl shook his head. "He was killed in an F-18 crash a year ago."

Buster said, sarcastically, "How convenient."

Frowning, Davidson asked, "Carl, what's the name of the pilot who died?"

"Commander Andy Logan."

Davidson flipped through some papers. Finally, finding it, he said, "Hmm. That's very interesting. In the computer, there's a link between the Prophet's security clearance and this deceased military officer. Could he be ...?"

Carl shook his head. "I was at the funeral. It was an open casket. Besides, this guy doesn't look anything like him."

Davidson continued, "Carl, what's your assessment of this man?"

Frowning, Carl said, "He's very intelligent, eloquent and likable, but intense. He seems like someone you'd have a beer with or follow into battle."

"Great! Can you tell us anything useful?" Buster said with a scowl.

Carl continued, "Sir, we're all skeptics by nature. If this guy's a fake, he's the best I've ever seen. Are we absolutely sure he's not for real?"

Buster's face got red. "This guy comes out of nowhere, fakes amnesia and uses a dead pilot's security clearance. What the hell do *you* think?"

The Deputy jumped in. "Sir, Carl's worked both analysis and operations. He's been involved with many interrogations and is a good judge of character."

Buster continued in a loud voice, "Am I the only one who's not living in Disney Land? This guy has us building the most powerful energy-beam weapon on the face of the earth!"

Davidson nodded to Carl, signaling him to sit down.

Buster continued to look shocked while vigorously chewing his gum.

During the uncomfortable silence, Bishara jumped in. "Sir, would you like to go over the plan for securing the Antarctic base?"

"*Yes!* Let's talk about something *useful.*"

"Sir?" Carl volunteered.

Buster gave him a "What now?" look.

"I assigned one of our people to his team to help with security. So, we have another operative inside his team."

Buster stopped frowning.

Davidson looked at Carl and said quietly, "A protector?"

Carl nodded. "Tim Smith."

Buster said, "Is this operative capable of taking the Prophet out?"

Davidson nodded, as Carl said, "*More* than capable."

Buster said, "Finally, some good news." He turned to Bishara, signaling her to continue.

Bishara said, "As you know, the plan is to send in a C-17 with an arctic-trained SEAL team and an AC-130 gunship."

Davidson added, "The last report said there are over a dozen people down there, mostly PhDs and engineers."

Bishara continued, "The SEALs will also have a nuclear expert with them to shut down the reactors."

Buster interrupted. "I want overkill on this Op. I believe there are other players tied to the Prophet who intend to sweep in and take the weapon, probably kidnap the technical people. We're not taking chances. I'd like to have fighters overhead just in case."

Davidson said, "Sir, we're using the AC-130 because it has the range." A CIA favorite, he didn't need General Glosson to explain the 130's capability. "They carry 25-millimeter Gatling guns that can fire almost a hundred half-pound, high-explosive rounds a second."

Buster smiled.

Glosson added, "The land-based fighters don't have the range, but we have an aircraft carrier battle group, the USS Reagan, on a port-call in Australia. They can deploy and be in striking range within a couple days. Her battle group also has a good-sized marine contingent that can be inserted by V-22 Ospreys, if needed."

Buster chewed loudly. "Yeah, there you go."

Davidson knew that Buster loved aircraft carriers, or more accurately, the ability to *direct* them.

Glosson continued, "The only way any bad guys can get in or out of there is by air. We can requisition an Air Force AWACS. With its radar, if it flies, we'll know."

Buster said, "Good. Do that! We'll want continuous coverage. After they finish testing the Blaster in Los Alamos, the Prophet could head down any time."

Carl cleared his throat. "Sir, the Blaster's on its way to the South Pole right now."

All eyes turned toward him.

Buster said, "What?"

He looked at his watch. "It should be arriving shortly."

Davidson said very clearly and slowly, "Carl, are you sure?"

"Yes sir, they were behind schedule. I think they made a last-minute decision to skip the Los Alamos test and do the first live test-firing at the Pole."

Buster pounded the table. "Damn it, I was right! He used the fear of a meteor shower to push up the schedule. When it doesn't show up – he'll be uncovered as a fraud. That means he's got to make his move soon." He gave Davidson an 'I told you so' look.

Davidson frowned. "This changes things." He turned to Glosson. "We need to put the C-130 and SEAL team on four-hour alert. Let's get the AWACS in theater now. Call U.S. Pacific Command. Tell him we need to pull the carrier battle group out of Australia and send them South. If Admiral Rea needs Presidential authorization, tell him it's on its way."

Glosson said, "Done."

He turned back to Buster. Shaking his head, he said, "I had hoped we'd know who was behind the Prophet by now." He paused. "But if the Blaster's down there, it could be fired," he glanced at Buster, "or taken, any time. I think we need to pick up the Prophet sooner than planned."

Buster nodded vigorously. "Absolutely, we need to slam this door shut now!"

Davidson looked around the room and said, "Let's figure out

how to take the Prophet without giving him a chance to warn anyone." He turned to Carl. "Where's our protector operative?"

Carl said, "I'll confirm it, but I think he's at the Pole now."

Davidson nodded. "So is our mole. They'll be our insurance policy in case the Prophet somehow gets word to the Pole base before we pick him up."

Turning to Lafferty, he said, "How fast can you put together a plan to capture the Prophet?"

Lafferty said, "That depends on whether we have to arrest all the participants at the same time. Remember, we're talking Elton Musk, Dr. Sheri Lopez and one of NASA's leading scientists. We'll need a couple of days to coordinate that."

Buster scowled. "No, we can't wait, I want him now. The others can wait."

Lafferty said, "We'll still need to get the warrants and coordinate the operation with local law enforcement. We can probably pull it together tonight and have him in custody early tomorrow morning. That's the best time to grab a suspect anyway."

Davidson asked, "When?"

"Let's do 5:00 am, St. Louis time."

Buster looked a little disappointed. "If that's the best we can do." He paused. "Where's my Tomahawk shooter?"

Glosson said, "USS Truxton is off the coast of Chili." She looked at her watch. "She can be in launch range in about 24 hours."

Buster said, "Excellent."

After the meeting, Carl caught Davidson. "Brian, I understand the Director's frustration, and you know I'm as skeptical as they come, but something doesn't add up."

"Yeah, there's a puzzle piece missing, but it's hard to argue with the fact that no agency's claimed him."

Carl sighed. "I know." He added with a half-smile, "Aiding and abetting an international terrorist probably isn't going to look good on my next evaluation."

Davidson gave him a smile. "Get in line."

Carl added, "By the way, I didn't want to say this in front of the Director, but our operative, the protector, is actually being funded ..."

Davidson finished, "By the Prophet?"

"I'm afraid so."

Davidson shook his head. "So, the CIA's not only protecting the Prophet, we're on his payroll." He laughed. "It'll be a shame if we have to kill him before I get to meet him."

38

RENDEZVOUS

Meadows answered the phone. "Hey Chandra, how's it going down there?"

She laughed. "We're freezing our butts off, but the installation is going well." She paused. "The reason I called is that I've been talking to my colleague at the Keck Observatory. Joe ... they didn't find anything at the coordinates Josh gave us."

Meadows sighed and then said, "Josh told us it was a low albedo comet. Could it be too dark to see?"

"It'd have to have a reflectivity of a fraction of one percent."

"Is that possible?"

There was a pause. "Yeah ... the IRAS-Araki-Alcock comet was probably that dark." She paused again. "Hmm. It's close enough now that it should have a decent IR signature."

Meadows knew she was thinking out-loud and waited.

She continued, "We really need an infrared space telescope, but we might be able to pick it up on the Chilean VISTA or the infrared scopes on Mauna Kea. I'll make some calls."

"Let me know what you find out."

"Joe, no offense to Josh, but at this point I'm hoping he's nuts."

After hanging up, Meadows drummed his fingers on his desk for several seconds. Then he picked up his phone and dialed. "Sheri? It's Joe. Need to talk with you and Smith as soon as possible."

Josh arrived back at his apartment to find Elizabeth on his laptop. She barely looked up, as she held up a small hand written note. "Your Internet access has been compromised."

Both angry and happy, he said, "Elizabeth you cannot ..."

She interrupted him as she stood up. "Give me a hug and tell me how beautiful I am."

He shook his head, walked over and hugged her. Looking down into her face, he kissed her and said, "You *are* incredibly beautiful, inside and out."

"See, that wasn't so hard." She stepped back and became all business, "Josh, what's happening?"

"Let's go for a walk." They grabbed jackets and went outside to the small park nearby. Not well lit, it was usually empty at night. Josh knew being outside wasn't a guarantee they couldn't be overheard – technology was such that few places were impervious to eavesdropping – but it would make it more difficult. Keeping his voice very low, he told her about the comet fragment.

She listened intently and became excited. "That's great news. In a few days, the whole world will be more open to the possibility of a comet."

Josh shook his head, "Sometimes I wish I could see the world the way you do."

She looked into his eyes. "You can."

Washington, D.C.

It was almost midnight. Lafferty took an FBI jet from Dulles to St. Louis. With the sensitivity of the case, the Director of the FBI had asked him to oversee it personally. He had to admit, he enjoyed being in the field again.

His phone rang. It was his on-scene commander. Lafferty said, "How's it going, Nate?"

"Good, sir, we've got the plan in place. We'll cordon off several blocks around the apartment and shut down his Internet and cell phone just before moving in. The state and local police will lock down the outside perimeter and we'll have a helicopter overhead just in case."

"Thanks, Nate. I know this is overkill but this guy did hijack the entire military-industrial complex."

"Well, the Godfather wouldn't get more assets."

"How's the surveillance going?"

Nate said, "As you know, we've got full audio inside and

cameras all over the apartment complex with an agent or camera watching every possible exit point. The subject left the Boeing Phantom Works an hour ago and drove to his apartment. The only unusual event was that his girlfriend arrived a couple hours earlier."

"Edvardsen?" He pulled her file out of his folder as Nate continued, "Yes sir. They went out for a short walk in the local park and just returned to the apartment."

Looking at her picture, he smiled slightly. "Well, she should certainly keep him occupied." His smile turned to a frown. "But if things don't go smoothly, she could be used as a hostage."

"We'll have a SWAT team in place. If he tries to use her as a shield, we should be able to take him out quickly."

"Thanks, Nate. I'm going to catch a catnap on the flight and be there in a few hours. Call me if anything develops."

As he set his phone down, Lafferty glanced back at the file picture of Edvardsen. He toasted Meadows with his cup of coffee. "Enjoy ... it'll be your last."

St. Louis

After they returned to his apartment, Josh watched Elizabeth disappear into the bathroom with her small travel bag. It was late but he needed to check a couple reports on the computer. His guilt was gone, his body healed, and there were no parents in sight. He felt like a teenager waiting for his first kiss. She finally came out ... but she wasn't wearing her usual negligee with the short silk bathrobe. Instead, she wore a pair of long flannel pajama bottoms and a t-shirt. He sighed. He didn't have to be Dr. Ruth to know she was dressing for sleep, not play.

As he watched her spread a blanket on the sofa, he thought she could make a burlap bag look sexy. Lost in his teenage fantasy, he realized he was being un-chivalrous. Standing up, he said, "Thanks for fixing this up for me. You're sleeping in my bedroom."

She frowned.

He said, "I often sleep on the sofa. Since I have to work late tonight, it works out well." He hadn't planned on working late.

She looked up at him and said, "I really don't mind."

"What type of cad would allow a beautiful woman to sleep on his sofa?" He added, "I'll change the sheets in the bedroom." He didn't want her sleeping out there simply because he knew he didn't have the discipline to watch her sleep.

She said a little abruptly, "Don't worry about the sheets. I'll take care of it."

After she went to bed, Josh worked on the computer for another hour and then tried to sleep. He just laid there and stared at the ceiling.

After midnight, he slid into a nebulous intersection of consciousness and dreams. He was partly aware of his surroundings, but his body felt like it was made of lead. The room closed in on him. The apartment, the city, the world, seemed to pulse in and out with his heartbeat, getting smaller and tighter with each beat. Then his perspective suddenly changed. He seemed to be outside himself, watching his body on the sofa. There were faint 'threads' radiating out from him in all directions. Each tied to an action. Do this – and that happens. Do that – and this happens. It was similar to his experience with Kelly at the restaurant. It was fascinating and terrifying, like seeing the future, or many futures. He realized he'd seen these threads in his dreams before and had unconsciously used them to drive his strategy and actions. He even saw situations where acting prudently created the wrong path. What he sensed – actually felt – were forces closing in on him.

He followed a thread that appeared to move him in the correct direction. His choices caused it to branch like a movie that had different endings. The further in the future it went, the more the threads overlapped. Like multiple TV channels interfering with each other, the correct path was harder and harder to distinguish. What he *could* see clearly was that staying where he was would result in failure. No, worse than that, staying would lead to death and destruction. He saw buildings and people on fire ... but not from the comet and not a year from now. He couldn't tell why or when, but it was soon, very soon. Even the paths that seemed to lead to a successful firing of the Blaster had an ominous similarity. They faded to black like the credits at the end of a movie. He wasn't sure what that meant but had his suspicions. Regardless, he knew what he had to do.

He came fully awake.

First, he contacted the brilliant young engineer, Greg Langlois. Good at improvising under pressure, he was certain he'd need that ability soon. It was 12:30 in the morning. He used the app that Smith loaded on his smart phone, to encrypt the text he sent.

Langlois answered immediately, saying that he was up, gaming.

Josh texted, "Problem. Pushing schedule up. Need your help. Can you leave for pole asap?"

"Yes"

"Be at flight ops in 1 hour?"

"k"

"Pack warm. Don't tell anyone."

Josh dressed quickly. He wrote and rewrote Elizabeth a short note and tiptoed into the bedroom. With the future he'd seen, he was certain this would be the last time he'd see her. Unlike Kelly, at least he could tell her how he felt, how much he appreciated her and apologize. If they succeeded but he didn't survive, he hoped she wouldn't hate him. If he failed, he knew she wouldn't hate him for long. He slipped the tiny note under her hand. Leaning over, he kissed her gently on the lips, etching her face into his memory. He softly said, "I love you." She smiled in her sleep as he left.

Using his *memory* of the future, he moved quickly. He turned the TV on and the living room lights off. The flickering of a late night movie dimly illuminated the apartment. He smiled as he realized it was **Invasion of the Body Snatchers**.

He dressed in black cargo pants, topsiders, a dark blue shirt and a black baseball cap. Scooping up his laptop, he threw it in his small bag and went to the front door. He grabbed the door handle and froze.

He closed his eyes for a moment ... then let go of the handle. He set the bag down. He sensed a rhythm. Silently, he walked to the sliding glass door that opened onto the tiny balcony. He inched it open. Glancing outside, he quickly slid through and closed it. He kept his body pressed against the wall next to the door. There were no buildings across the street from which to observe his apartment. With his excellent night vision, he looked down and scanned the dark parking lot. Looking closer, he noticed a van seemed to have a very slight red glow emanating from the side and part of the roof. He realized, with amazement, he was actually seeing a heat signature. He'd heard that there were people who had the ability to see very slightly into the infrared spectrum. Once again, he thanked Jesse for his genetically enhanced body. Without a doubt, inside that van sat his unnamed observers. Unfortunately, they probably had low light and infrared cameras and could see as well or better than he could. He needed to move fast. He took a deep breath and climbed onto the balcony's metal handrail where it met the wall.

The agent was glad that they were finally going to arrest this guy. He was tired of sitting in the van all night. He had two giant monitors with nine separate camera video feeds, and just like cable TV, there was nothing on. His partner sat next to him with headphones, monitoring the audio feed and playing solitaire on his phone. Even though they were both relieved every few hours, it got old continuously watching static video feeds. He started his zillionth scan of his low-level light cameras. Following a set pattern, he began with the hall and entrance cameras and then looked at all the exterior feeds. To the irritation of his partner, he always ran through them under his breath like a checklist. "Hall camera one and two, clear. Elevator camera, clear. Lobby entrance, clear."

Stretching, Josh was just able to get his fingers over the bottom edge of the balcony above. Doing a quick pull-up, he peeked over the balcony deck. Through the sliding glass door, he could see the upstairs apartment was dark. As he started to pull himself up, the rotting deck board under his left hand gave way. The end of the one-by-six broke off cleanly and fell. His body swung like a pendulum, hanging from the slipping fingertips of his right hand. Trying to hang on, he looked down. The piece of broken board hit the asphalt below.

The agent heard a noise outside. Standing up, he moved forward in the van and looked out the passenger-side window. Rolling it down, he stuck his head out and looked around. Listening carefully, he scanned the parking lot and the entrance to the apartment.

Hanging from the balcony, it was hard to be inconspicuous. His old body would never have been able to hold on with his fingertips. His new body was amazing but it wouldn't survive a four-story fall. Straining to keep his grip, he quietly pulled himself up with one arm until he could reach the railing with his other hand. He grabbed the metal railing, pulled himself up and quickly climbed over. He pressed himself against the wall next to the sliding glass door and froze. He caught his breath as he listened intently for any activity below.

The agent saw nothing. To his partner, who was looking up with interest, he said, "Heard something in the parking lot. Probably just a dog or cat."

His partner went back to his video console and completed his scan. "Stairwell exit one and two, clear. Balcony, clear. Side entrance, clear. Alley, clear." As expected, he saw nothing.

Josh reached over to the sliding glass door. Thankful that it was unlocked, he opened it slowly. Hearing nothing, he slipped inside with all his senses straining. He heard regular snoring coming from down the hall. He silently glided around the dark furniture to the front door. Unlocking and opening it, he peered out. The hall was empty. Normally, he'd go to the left toward the elevator. Instead, he went right, to the stairwell.

He went down the stairwell as fast as he could, bypassing the ground floor exit. The stairs continued down to a basement area. At the bottom, there was one locked door to an equipment/storage room. Sliding a credit card between the doorframe and door, he was able to open the simple lock. He entered a large, dim, windowless basement. It was dank, musty, and filled with boxes and rolls of carpet. Across the room was a small red exit sign. He went to it and slowly opened the door. It creaked loudly with lack of use.

Peering out, he saw he was in an outside stairwell, a walkout basement exit. He slipped out onto a set of concrete steps going up to ground level. Taking a few steps up, he poked his head up like a periscope. He was in an alley, illuminated by a single sodium vapor street light. Obviously failing, it buzzed loudly and flickered. Every 30 seconds it would dim for a few seconds and then relight.

Across the narrow alley, was a broken, chain-link fence. A large dumpster next to the fence provided some cover. Timing the light, he dove across the alley as the streetlight blinked. He quickly wiggled through a hole in the fence and found himself in a dark, poorly maintained parking lot. The lot surrounded a squat industrial building. Skirting the side of the building and staying in the shadows, he climbed over a tall fence and ran to the street. For the first time in months, he sensed no one watching him. He enjoyed the two-mile jog to the airport in the crisp night air.

It was 1:30 am when he arrived at Boeing Flight Ops, only a half hour before the weekly C-17 left for the Falklands. He saw Greg was already there. He was roughly Josh's height but only about 140 pounds. Standing in the corner with oddly contrasting clothes, he had a small duffel bag and wore a "geek" cap pulled over a bushy afro.

Geek caps were new to the market and still quite the fashion risk. A ball cap covered in form-fitting, flexible solar cells with a thin antenna on top. The cap charged electronic devices and provided better reception. Although clever and functional, the name was accurate. Greg also sported augmented reality glasses and keyboard-mouse gloves. This truly took computers to the street. Observers would see the user staring at nothing, wiggling their fingers in the air, and talking to themselves. Josh's sister had worked with autistic children; he couldn't help but notice the similarity.

He thanked Greg for coming on such short notice. As they walked out to the C-17, Josh looked at Greg's clothes and suspected he was color blind ... at least he hoped so. He was a good-looking kid, but his clothes and geek cap served several functions, including birth control. Josh promised himself, if they lived through this, he'd talk to Greg about women.

IV

IMPACT

The SEAL took his pistol out, pulled the slide back and put it to Petrov's head. Calmly, but with steel in his voice, he said, "Shut the power off or die."

39

CAPTURE

Elizabeth woke up suddenly, a little disoriented in the strange bed. It was early morning and still dark. As she got her bearings, her intuition said something was wrong. She turned on the bedside light and saw a small folded piece of paper lying on the blanket. Opening it, she read, *"Elizabeth, I'm sorry I have to go. I had a premonition I can't ignore. I'm catching the early morning flight to the Falklands. I apologize for leaving suddenly, but where I go, I cannot protect you. Cooperate with the authorities. You are everything that's good and noble about the human race and, I believe, the most beautiful woman in the world. Your belief in me is greater than I am. You deserve much better and you will find it. I love you. Josh*

Before she could react, the doorbell startled her. It was 5:20! Still clutching the note, she went to the door. Looking through the peephole, she saw a tall, dark-haired man with a black jacket. She asked, "Who is it?"

"FBI, we have some questions, ma'am."

"It's awfully early, can we talk later?" she asked, knowing full well that wasn't going to happen.

"No ma'am, this cannot wait. Would you please open the door?"

"I need to see some ID."

He held it up to the peephole. She folded up the little note from Josh, put it in her mouth and swallowed it. Taking a deep breath, she opened the door.

He came in pistol drawn, followed closely by four others. They wore black windbreakers with FBI on the back and wielded automatic weapons. By their bulk, she guessed they wore bulletproof vests. The man who spoke to her held her near the wall as the agents fanned out, moving rapidly through the small apartment.

They came back quickly and said, "He's not here."

After a female agent frisked her, the lead agent holstered his pistol and said, "Where is he?"

She shook her head and said honestly, "He was here when I went to sleep."

He watched her closely as she spoke. He didn't say anything but nodded to the female agent, who told her to put her hands behind her back.

As she was handcuffed, the male agent said, "We have a warrant for your arrest on the grounds of national security."

All Elizabeth could say was, "National security? You're kidding."

He didn't respond but spoke into a microphone. "He's not here. Bring in forensics. We're taking her out now."

The female agent brought Elizabeth's sandals out from the bedroom and dropped them in front of her, steadying her as she slipped them on. Elizabeth saw three more people come in with suitcases. One started taking pictures. Another picked up Josh's bag by the door and pulled out his laptop with a gloved hand.

They wrapped a blanket around Elizabeth's shoulders and led her outside. With an agent holding each arm, they took her down the stairwell and out the door. There were flashing blue lights everywhere and a helicopter overhead. Looking up, she saw its searchlight swinging back and forth.

It was surreal. She felt like she was in a police drama. A few curious apartment dwellers peeked out from their balconies. Flanked by the two agents, they put her in the backseat of a big black SUV.

Langley

Davidson was in Buster's office. It was 6:30 am eastern time when they got the call. They put Lafferty on the speakerphone.

Buster asked, "How'd it go?"

Lafferty said, "He wasn't in the apartment."

Seeing the veins on Buster's forehead start to bulge, Davidson quickly asked, "His car is still there?"

"Yes."

Frowning, Davidson fired back, "When did the surveillance team see him last?"

"Surveillance video shows him returning from a walk in the park with Elizabeth Edvardsen. They were clearly ID'd going inside at 10:05 pm. Inside audio confirms it."

Davidson persisted, "Could he have slipped out and taken another car?"

Lafferty said, "We had the entire building under surveillance. No cars left after 10 pm. We're going through the surveillance videos now. If he slipped out, we have a cordon around several city blocks and a helicopter with IR sensors. We'll find him. Edvardsen's in custody and on her way downtown for interrogation. We'll report back as soon as we have anything."

St. Louis

They drove to an old office building at the outskirts of the city. Still wrapped in a blanket, they took Elizabeth inside to a small room. The woman agent removed the handcuffs, sat her at a table across from two chairs and left.

With nothing else to do, she examined the room. It was nondescript. Maybe 10 by 10, beige linoleum floor, beige paint and white, acoustic ceiling tiles with industrial fluorescent lighting. The table was gray painted metal with no drawers and no sharp corners. There was a large mirror on the wall that faced her, probably, a one-way mirror. She tried to sit casually, but it was difficult wearing nothing but a t-shirt and pajama bottoms. She pulled the blanket around her.

Then she realized it was all a state of mind. She wasn't going to let her environment, which she couldn't control, affect her identity and belief, which she could. She sat upright, pretending she was wearing a suit, the blanket, a designer shawl. Still nervous but proud of what she was a part of, she knew she was right; they were wrong.

Langley

Davidson, tapping a pen against his leg, suddenly looked at

Buster. "May I use your computer?"

Buster slid his chair to one side.

Davidson grabbed the keyboard. They had access to the most sophisticated, high-resolution satellite system in the world ... but sometimes, you just didn't need it. Calling up Google Maps, he found the Prophet's apartment building and switched to satellite view. Slowly he zoomed out until he could see the airport.

He grabbed the phone and asked Bishara to come up to Buster's office. As she came through the door, Davidson motioned her around so she could see the screen. He pointed at the airport. "What's the schedule for their logistics flights to the Falklands?"

She scrolled through her tablet. "Looks like they've been running them every...." She looked up. "Monday and Thursday."

Buster, sharing the obvious, said, "That's today!"

Davidson fired back at Bishara, "What time?"

She looked back at her tablet. "Usually, it's early in the morning. It's a 12-hour flight. Let me check." She pointed to Buster's phone.

Buster nodded.

After a few seconds, she said, "Two o'clock. You sure?"

Before she could hang up, Davidson grabbed the phone. He looked at the clock as he waited for Lafferty to answer. It was almost 6:00 am St. Louis time.

"Bart, was Boeing Flight Ops under surveillance?"

"No, we pulled everyone in for his capture."

Davidson shook his head and then said with certainty, "He's on his way to the Falklands."

Lafferty said, "You sure?"

"I'd bet my retirement on it."

Buster said calmly, "Get the team together."

He glanced at Buster, surprised his boss hadn't exploded.

Buster, obviously reading Davidson's look, said, "If he's outside the U.S., he's no longer under FBI jurisdiction." He added with a slight smile, "Or U.S. law."

40

INTERROGATE

After a few minutes, two men came into the room and sat across the table from Elizabeth. They didn't introduce themselves. The bigger of the two was six-four and twice her weight. He looked like he came out of a mafia movie. With a large broken nose and a big bushy unibrow, the word "testosterone" came to mind.

She sighed, whispering a quick prayer under her breath.

The big one asked, "Do you know Josh Fuze?"

"Of course I do."

"Where is he?"

"I don't know. Why do you want him?"

"Just answer the questions."

"I haven't done anything wrong."

He leaned forward menacingly. "You're about to be charged as an accomplice to treason, espionage and conspiracy to commit terrorist acts against the United States. These charges carry the death penalty."

They were trying to scare her and it was working pretty well. "Josh Fuze is a good man," she said defiantly.

"Josh Fuze is a threat to this country and if you don't answer the questions we'll assume you are too!"

She shook her head and matched his volume. "You don't know what you're talking about, and I have the right to a lawyer!" She was worried but also angry, and refused to get emotional in front of them.

The second man had been watching her intently. He turned to Mr. Testosterone and nodded slightly. Silently the big man got up and left. Elizabeth noted that the second guy was the opposite of the first. Smaller and well groomed, he looked more like a corporate vice president. As he spoke, his voice and manner were much softer. She guessed they were using the "good cop, bad cop" approach.

The big FBI agent entered the dimly lit room, joining two women in suits and a tall, intense-looking man wearing a sports jacket. Watching the interrogation through the one-way mirror, the big agent said quietly, "Looking at her file, I didn't think that would work."

One of the women said softly, "She asked for a lawyer."

The tall man said, "Not yet. We need that information fast and you *know* we aren't worried about her Miranda rights."

The other woman looked at him with raised eyebrows, but said nothing.

Leaning forward, her interrogator said softly, "Elizabeth, Josh is in serious trouble. Time is of the essence. If you don't want to see him hurt or killed, we need you to tell us everything you know about him as soon as possible."

"Why, what are you trying to do to him?"

"Elizabeth, we need to stop him before he gets himself killed. You can help us prevent that."

This wiped out any questions about Josh having delusions of grandeur. Not only did the FBI think he was a national threat, they couldn't even catch him. She didn't doubt he was in trouble, but he was much more than they knew. "I don't believe that."

"Elizabeth, it's often those who are closest who don't see what's happening."

Elizabeth remembered her earlier pledge. They were not going to control her belief. She decided it was time to take the offensive. "You're making a huge mistake. He's trying to prevent a comet from wiping out life on Earth and if you interfere with him, you put yourself, your families and the entire human race at risk!"

Leaning back, he said, "Elizabeth, what do you really know about Josh?"

She knew … it was going to be a long night, but she also knew her rights. "I'm not afraid of what you can do to me, and I know Josh is doing the right thing. I also know I have a right to a lawyer."

The tall man behind the one-way mirror shook his head and

said quietly, "It's safe to say her relationship with the Prophet is real, at least from her perspective. Tony will stay in the 'What's good for Josh?' mode. It's time to play our last card." He nodded at one of the women. "Counselor, you know what's at stake. We don't want her. We want him."

Both women nodded.

As they left, the big agent said, "She's not a bimbo. She's very intelligent, yet she believes all this crap."

The tall man said, "The Prophet's fooled senior military officers, leading scientists and Elton Musk." Looking through the mirror, he shook his head. "About the *only* thing I am certain of at this point, is that the Prophet has good taste."

⸻✶⸻

Elizabeth looked up as the door opened. Two women in suits entered. The first was slim with an athletic build and short light brown hair. She was about Elizabeth's age and attractive but looked like she was all business. She came directly to Elizabeth and introduced herself as Rachel Hunter, her appointed federal defense attorney. Pulling one of the chairs around to Elizabeth's side of the table, she sat down next to her.

The second woman was a little shorter with long, beautiful, auburn hair and fair skin. Like her defender, this woman was impeccably dressed. Elizabeth's first impression was that she was cute and young, maybe mid-twenties.

Her newly appointed lawyer began by saying, "Elizabeth," she gestured across the table, "this is Amy Sobrero from the Federal District Attorney's office."

As Sobrero sat down across from her, Elizabeth realized the woman was closer to her own age. She guessed that this DA's beauty and apparent youth had probably caused more than one attorney to underestimate her.

Elizabeth's attorney said, "She's agreed to offer you immunity from prosecution *if* you will help the FBI with their investigation and tell them everything you know."

The DA had a disarming smile and said softly, "Ms. Edvardsen, we know that you wouldn't do anything to harm your country, and understand that you are an innocent victim in this case. All the FBI is trying to do is avert disaster. Your information may be critical to that effort *and* saving the life of Josh Fuze. We will grant you full and total immunity from prosecution regarding anything involved with this case." She slid a sheet of paper across to Elizabeth's attorney.

Picking it up, her attorney added, "The charges are very serious and this is an unusually generous offer. As your attorney, I would strongly recommend you accept it."

Elizabeth remembered the note, now resting in her stomach. Josh had told her to cooperate.

She would do just as he said ... kinda like when he told her to stay in Kansas City. Ignoring the paper and pen, she said, "I haven't done anything wrong, and Josh, not only hasn't done anything wrong, he's trying to save the world. This is a terrible mix-up. I will cooperate fully in an effort to help unscramble this insane situation."

She knew Josh created the "mix-up" intentionally, but it was still a mix-up. She'd "help" them understand that they were interfering in something they didn't grasp. She wouldn't tell them what she *really* believed. That would just solidify their belief that both of them were nuts, eliminating her ability to put doubt in their minds.

She decided to look at this as a game. Their goal was to wear her down with doubt, while pulling out information they could use against Josh. Her goal was to paint a picture that would make them question themselves.

Langley

The entire team assembled by 7:00 am. Lafferty, on speakerphone, said, "You were right. I talked to the flight ops personnel at Boeing. He arrived at 1:30 this morning along with a young software engineer named Greg Langlois. They took off at 2:05 am and are scheduled to arrive in the Falklands about 2:00 pm our time."

General Glosson said, "The C-17s are flown by Air Force test pilots. We can contact them by radio and have them diverted to wherever you want."

Buster asked, "Where are they now?"

Glosson looked at the ceiling as she did some quick calculations. "Probably over the Gulf of Mexico, but I can get their exact location in a few minutes."

Davidson looked at Buster and said, "Recommend we go with the original plan to capture him in the Falklands. Keep him isolated on an island where we have the upper hand. We're a little behind but we can have our team landing right after they do."

Buster said, "What if he doesn't go to the Falklands?"

Davidson turned to Glosson. "We need a tight watch on that aircraft. If it deviates from its planned route *at all*, we need to know and contact the pilot ASAP."

Buster nodded at Davidson. Davidson took that for approval and continued, "Otherwise, we let them proceed. Looking at Glosson, he asked, "How soon can we have our aircraft headed south?"

"We called in the aircraft crews and SEAL team as soon as we heard what happened in St Louis." She looked at her watch, "They should be launching within the hour. They're out of Hurlburt AFB in Florida, so, they're closer to the Falklands and can be there an hour or so after the Prophet's plane lands."

Bishara looked at the Deputy and said, "We have two of our people in the Falklands right now. Do you want them to capture the Prophet when he arrives?"

Davidson asked, "Are they experienced operatives?"

Bishara shook her head. "No. Their job was to coordinate the administrative side and act as a liaison with the locals."

"Can't risk it. Have them stay back. This guy's too good. Their only mission is to ensure the Prophet's C-17 stays put after it lands. We'll wait until we have the CIA/SEAL team in place before taking him.

Buster asked, "Do we have clearance to operate in country?"

Davidson said, "Yes, I've been working closely with Tony Collins, the SIS Chief."

Buster asked, "Do they understand how dangerous this situation is?"

Davidson nodded at his boss. "We probably have a closer working relationship with them than we do with most U.S. agencies. They know everything we know and have already coordinated with Scotland Yard and the British military in the Falklands."

Buster nodded. "Good."

From the speakerphone, Lafferty said, "When do you want to round up the rest of the players in St. Louis and Los Alamos?"

Davidson looked at Buster. "We know his girlfriend didn't contact anyone before we arrested her. No sense tipping our hand until we have him."

Buster nodded again.

Davidson said, "Bishara, as soon as our team lands in the Falklands, start jamming their cell phones. Bart, at the same time, let's pick up everyone else."

Lafferty said, "Our operatives know that the scientists and engineers are innocent pawns. When we pick them up, they'll be told they're being taken into *protective* custody."

Buster asked, "What about Lopez and Musk?"

Lafferty said, "We have all the legal warrants. We'll emphasize it's for their own protection."

Glosson added, "We have Presidential authority to use the carrier battle group. They're pulling out of Australia now and heading south. They should be within strike range in 24 hours."

Someone knocked and came into the room. He handed a note to the Deputy and left. As Davidson read the note, his eyebrows went up. "Just got word from the Keck Observatory in Hawaii. They think one of their infrared telescopes may have detected something at the coordinates the Prophet supplied. It's a weak signal and too early to plot a trajectory."

You could hear a pin drop as all eyes went to the Director.

Buster's face started turning red and his veins began to pop out. He released a string of expletives that would've made a sailor proud. Finally, winding down, he looked around the table and said in a controlled voice, "This guy's kept one step ahead of us the whole way. He's obviously planted the information."

Davidson said, softly, "It's a Caltech NASA observatory."

Barely keeping his temper in check, Buster said, "The Prophet's an expert at manipulating government agencies." He pointed at Carl Casey, almost smiling. "For God's sake, he's had us working for him!" He took a breath. "I want everyone from the observatory who knows about this picked up immediately for questioning. If there are any leaks, I want them discredited."

Davidson paused.

Buster slapped the table. "I mean right now! Do you

understand me? This jerk is *not* going to make a jackass out of me or this agency!"

Davidson said quietly, "Yes sir." He turned to the team and said, "All right, we know what to do, let's move."

As they broke up, Davidson saw Buster signal him to stay behind. He assumed it was for a butt chewing, but Buster looked unusually thoughtful.

"I'm sorry, Brian, I know you're just doing your job, trying to dot the i's and cross the t's." He paused. "I've decided ... I want you to personally take charge of the operation down in the Falklands. It's just too critical and I want my most experienced man on the scene."

Davidson was surprised. It was unusual for a Director or Deputy Director to leave the country except on official state business, and then only with full protection. The information in their heads was too valuable to risk. It was even more unusual for the Director to apologize. On the other hand, he'd love to get out of D.C. and back into the field. He also had to admit he wanted to be there personally when they captured and interrogated the Prophet. "Yes sir."

"Great." Buster paused. "There's something else I'd like you to do. After they finish interrogating his girlfriend, I want her down in the Falklands." He smiled, looking down at a sheet of paper. "The forensic team found a notepad in his apartment. They were able to reconstruct part of a message he wrote her before he left. *Apparently*, he has some feelings for her." He looked back up. "He's managed to stay ahead of us at every turn." His smile turned unpleasant. "I want to use her pretty little body as a negotiating chip in case something goes wrong."

Davidson frowned but nodded slowly. He didn't like what he was hearing and wasn't sure it was legal to take her out of the country, but he needed to have all his ducks in a row before challenging the Director again.

As Buster left and Davidson headed toward his office, Carl caught up with him.

Carl quietly asked, "Would you mind if I ran the observatory investigation? I'm not as vocal as the Director, but I'm not any fonder about being duped."

Davidson nodded.

41

FALKLANDS

Returning to his office, Davidson called Lafferty. He explained that Buster wanted Edvardsen in the Falklands for leverage. "Bart, this is outside my area of expertise, can we legally take a suspect, who's a U.S. citizen, out of the country?"

Lafferty said slowly, "I guess I don't understand why we would *want* to." He paused. "Brian, you've seen her file. She's never even had a speeding ticket. Her only crime was falling for her patient."

"If you tell me it's illegal, I'll tell him and we'll be done with it."

Lafferty sighed. "It's not *illegal,* but it is complicated." He paused. "The plan was to scare her into cooperating. We haven't officially charged her." He paused again. "Actually ... that could work to our advantage."

Davidson said, "I'm not following you."

"Brian, we don't have to arrest her and transport her. All we have to do is *ask* her."

Davidson said, "OK ...?"

"Look, she obviously cares for this guy and she's not a wimp. If you thought your significant other was in danger and someone offered to take you to where they were?"

Davidson nodded unnecessarily. "Got it. Can you make that happen?"

Lafferty said, "I'll take care of it."

Falklands

Josh and Greg arrived in the Falklands just before 3:00 pm local time. Although relieved that there wasn't anyone to meet them,

Josh felt very anxious. They had to wait for the C-17's aircrew to get crew rest before they could continue to the Antarctic base.

Looking around, Josh realized Mount Pleasant Royal Air Force Base was an impressive installation with state-of-the-art facilities, particularly considering the island's tiny population. They borrowed one of the Boeing cars and headed toward Port Stanley to get a hotel. Other than occasional sheep, they saw little sign of civilization through the wide-open tracks of treeless, rolling hills and windswept slopes. Josh decided he liked the Falkland's cool, windy desolation.

Langley

Bishara said, "Our on-site agent just reported they arrived. The pilot and crew are still with the aircraft. The Prophet and the young engineer left to get a hotel."

Buster asked, "Where are they going?"

"The only hotels are in Port Stanley about 30 miles from the base. We closed their aviation fuel account so they won't be able to refuel. *Our* C-17s will be landing in 15 minutes."

Davidson said, "Good. Make sure our two agents don't try anything heroic. Have them stay at the airport and contact us immediately if the Prophet returns." He turned to Buster. "Let's flip the switch on the U.S. portion of the operation and round everyone up."

Buster said, "Do it."

Lafferty, back from St. Louis, picked up his phone, and said, "Execute."

Falklands

The sky looked dark and foreboding, with an angry, gray overcast ... or maybe he was just projecting his mood. Josh felt anxious and the further he drove, the stronger it became. Finally, he was about to stop the car, when his cell phone buzzed. He looked down and saw a text message coming in. It was accessing the encryption app, so he pulled over and waited for it to decipher the text.

There was no sender or address. It simply read, "OK, they'll meet you at airport with Budweiser & then on to pole dancing.

Got to go. Will be tied up. Godspeed"

He understood immediately. It was Meadows. His signature "OK" authenticated it. "Budweiser" was clearly a SEAL team, either at the airport or inbound. "Pole dancing" probably meant they were going to go on to South Pole base and shut them down. "Tied up" was self-explanatory. The charade was over. They were coming to collect or eliminate him, and stop all they had done. Josh closed his eyes.

Greg asked, "Sir, you OK?"

"Give me a second to think."

From his thread visions, he knew what happened in the next hour would stop them in their tracks or allow them one more slim chance to continue. He cleared his mind. After a few seconds, an idea began to form. He knew what to do or at least try. Opening his eyes, he said, "Change of plans."

"What are we going to do?"

Josh did a wheel-spinning U-turn, as he handed his phone to Greg. "It's a warning message from Captain Meadows. Our program's been compromised. Believe it or not, there are forces trying to destroy it. I could use your help but from here on out, I'll be cutting corners and it could be dangerous, possibly very dangerous. If you want, I can drop you off at the base."

"No sir. I eat danger for breakfast."

Josh glanced at him with a raised eyebrow.

Greg smiled. "Sorry, movie line. What can I do to help?"

"You sure?"

He nodded.

"Greg, I don't suppose you have Internet access down here?"

Greg, still wearing his geek cap, whipped out his glasses and gloves. "Of course. If there's a tower, I can tap it."

After a few seconds he said, "I'm online."

"Log into the program site. We need to send a message to our team at the Antarctic base right away." Josh dictated, "'Program has been compromised by elements inside our own bureaucracy. They have access to our communications system. Ignore any command that doesn't have proper authentication. If approached in person by government agents, confirm their identity.' Sign it with my authentication code, 'Fuzed.'"

Greg repeated it back to Josh and then sent it.

"Greg, I also need to look up some information." He explained what he needed Greg to Google.

After a few seconds, Greg handed him his glasses. Josh was surprised he could read while seeing the road through glasses. He quickly found what he needed. Josh gave the glasses back and did several quick calculations in his head. He finally sighed and said, "This should be interesting." He drove back toward the airport as fast as the sedan would go.

Greg took off the video glasses. "Just lost the connection." He looked surprised. "Every cell signal on the island is gone."

Langley

Glosson said, "Sir, our first C-17 is on final approach. The second is five minutes behind it."

Bishara added, "Our agents report that the Prophet's C-17 hasn't been refueled, and the Brits are jamming voice and data transmissions in and out of the island. We've also taken over the satellite communication link to the Pole base. They can't send or receive anything without going through us."

Buster said quietly, "We've got him."

Falklands

As Josh and Greg approached the airport, they saw a C-17 taxiing in. They were still a mile and a half from the airport entrance but with his exceptional vision, he saw another C-17 parked ... next to theirs.

Langley

Bishara said, "Sir, our SEAL/CIA team and British Special Forces took control of the Prophet's C-17 and rounded up the crew and Boeing reps. The Capture Team is headed out now. Working with local law enforcement, they're putting up roadblocks on all roads around Port Stanley. There's one other small civilian airport and they've got that covered too."

Buster asked, "Do they have the Prophet's picture?"

"We're circulating it now, but on an island of 3,000 it's pretty easy to find 'Waldo.'"

Buster frowned, not getting it.

Bishara explained, "He'll be easy to identify. He's the one they don't recognize."

42

THEFT

Just before reaching the terminal where the C-17s were parked, Josh turned at a military hanger. There was a small guard gate at the entrance. As they approached, Josh said, "Not only could this be dangerous, but it could also get you in serious trouble." He smiled. "I won't hold it against you if you want to back out."

Greg swallowed. "No sir, I'm in."

"OK. Greg, do you have your Boeing badge?"

"Yes."

"Put it on and follow my lead." As they pulled up, Josh showed the guard his Boeing access badge, and said, "We've been called in for an emergency aircraft repair and need to get to the maintenance area immediately."

The guard looked puzzled. "You need to have a base badge."

Josh focused on "knowing" that the guard would let them pass, as three military vehicles with lights flashing and sirens blaring drove past the gate behind them. Coming from the main terminal, they were clearly, headed toward Port Stanley. Josh didn't turn around but caught a glimpse of U.S. military fatigues in his rearview mirror as they went by.

The guard looked up with interest, then turned back to Josh and waived them through. "Move along."

Josh looked at Greg.

Greg grinned back, and said, "That was like the scene where Obi-Wan Kenobi uses the force on the Storm Troopers."

Josh laughed. "Hate to admit it ... I was thinking the same thing."

They parked outside the hanger. As they walked toward the entrance, Josh looked at the six F-18 Super Hornets sitting on the tarmac and committed their tail numbers to memory. Just before they walked in the door, Josh turned to Greg. "This is one of those rare times when the ends do justify the means. But it could get us both in a lot of trouble." Continuing in a TV commentator voice, he added, "And although rare, side-effects may include bullets."

Greg's eyes got wide. Then he started laughing. "This is just like playing Splinter Cell Seven on Xbox. Did you know that after you jumped off that cliff, all of us young engineers nicknamed you James Bond?"

Josh couldn't help but smile. "OK, *Double-O-Six*, the single most important thing you can do is – say nothing and look like you know what you're doing. Ready?"

Greg nodded.

As they went inside, Josh looked at the plaque on the wall. It identified the RAAF Number 1 Squadron's Wing Commander as Bob Gulick. They went straight to the CO's office. Josh asked if the Wing Commander was in. The airman said, "Sir, he left for the day. Do you need to reach him?"

"No, we'll run down to maintenance and talk to the Flight Sergeant, uh ...."

"You mean Sergeant Laura Hawkins?"

"Yeah, Hawkins."

They headed down to the maintenance department and asked for Sergeant Hawkins. A tall serious-looking woman said, "That's me."

Josh introduced them. "We're the tiger team from Boeing. Commander Gulick wanted us to get our butts here ASAP. You probably just got the maintenance bulletin about the emergency software configuration issue." A software configuration error was a rare but scary problem in a fly-by-wire aircraft with dozens of interconnected computers.

The Flight Sergeant frowned and shook her head. "Crikey!"

Josh added, "Luckily it only affects a few aircraft. The ones that might have the problem are bureau numbers 5124637 and 5124644."

She said, "Yeah, those are ours, but I haven't seen the bulletin."

Josh smiled. "For once we're moving faster than the paper pushers."

She didn't smile. "Will this take them out of flight status?"

"Not if they pass a quick software check. Just need to do a power-on cockpit test. Can you give me the maintenance books on them?"

Without a thought, she handed them to him.

"There's a chance none of 'em will be affected, and we can all grab a pint." He winked at her.

She finally smiled back, nodding her head.

He went through the first book for show. He studied the second aircraft's book carefully, noting flight status, maintenance gripes and fuel. It was a two-seater configured as a tanker, with a refueling store hanging from the belly and two large drop-tanks on each wing. This allowed it to refuel other Hornets while airborne. With 30,000 pounds of gas onboard, it carried more than its own weight in fuel. He said, "We'll start with the tanker."

The Flight Sergeant said, "I'll see who I can pull off one of the birds to help you."

"That would be great but Greg here is a qualified Plane Captain."

Greg looked up at Josh with wide eyes.

She looked at their badges and said, "OK."

"Is there a place we can change into some coveralls?"

"There's a men's room down the hall on the right."

Langley

Bishara reported, "Our team just hit the hotel. They never checked in. They're searching for the car now."

Buster frowned but said, "We've got him bottled up on an island. No matter how good he is, he can't hide for long. I want more assets on the ground as soon as possible."

Davidson said, "We'll shut down the civilian airport and cover the seaports, I'm more concerned about the Blaster at the South Pole. Can we go ahead and send the SEAL team on to the Antarctic base?"

Buster said, "Absolutely."

Glosson nodded, "The second they're refueled, we'll have 'em airborne."

Falklands

Josh went down the hall with Greg in tow. Glancing back to make sure no one was looking, they walked past the men's room until he found the pilot locker room. With no flight ops going on, it was empty. "Greg, watch me and do as I do." Josh found and tried on several torso harnesses. With the survival vest integrated into them, they were bulky and hard to get into. He found one that was close.

Greg said, "You're going to jack an airplane!"

Josh said, "No ... we're going to jack an airplane." Seeing his face, Josh added, "If we live through this, I'll show you how to successfully meet women."

Greg nodded and started trying on a torso harness.

Josh found them helmets that would fit. Helping Greg get his legs into the correct loops in the harness, he thought Greg was an amazing kid. Most people would have freaked out by now.

"Now put your coat on over the outside to hide the torso harness."

They put their helmet, oxygen mask and gloves in a bag.

"Sir, I know you're a genius and all, and everybody thinks the world of you but ... can you really fly one of these?"

As Josh headed out the door, he said, "Not to worry, I had an Xbox too."

Greg shrugged and followed him.

The tanker-configured Super Hornet was easy to spot on the tarmac. It was the only two-seat fighter, and the only one with five large tanks hanging from its wings and belly.

Walking briskly but casually, they headed toward the jet. Josh pushed the button that opened the canopy. Then he released a latch that dropped a small rickety looking boarding ladder from under the wing's leading edge extension.

"Greg, climb up and get into the back seat."

Josh followed him up. He quickly connected Greg's oxygen mask and torso harness to the ejection seat, and set his intercom to 'Hot Mic.' Noticing that Greg was beginning to look panicky, Josh firmly said, "Look, Greg, I *do* know what I'm doing. Don't touch anything unless I tell you to." As he armed Greg's ejection seat, he added, "And *definitely* stay away from any control with yellow and black stripes on it. ... Got it?"

Greg swallowed and nodded.

"When you see me put on my helmet, put yours on." He patted Greg on the shoulder and smiled. "This is going to be fun."

Greg just looked at him with wide eyes.

Standing on top of the jet, Josh looked around and saw a couple airmen working on another aircraft. They were a hundred yards away and showed no interest. So far, what Josh and Greg were doing looked normal.

He climbed back down the ladder, and with a quick check to make sure no one was watching, pulled out all the flight safety pins and kicked the chocks away from the wheels.

He climbed back up, slipped into the front cockpit and strapped in. He was smart enough to know that he was dangerous without a checklist. As he lowered the canopy, he closed his eyes. With his IMAX memory, he was able to recall in detail the last time he started a Super Hornet. He turned the battery power on and started initializing the navigation system. He plugged the Pole base coordinates into the computer. No one would notice them until he started the Auxiliary Power Unit. The small APU turbine provided the "air" to start the engines, but was almost as loud as the engines themselves. Finally, looking around one more time, he put his helmet on and flipped the APU switch. In his rearview mirrors, he could see Greg do the same.

The APU cranked up with its characteristically loud howl. As soon as the ready light came on, he routed the APU's high-pressure air to crank the number two engine. As the engine slowly spun up, he listened to the radio, monitoring the ground control frequency. He saw one airman, a hundred yards away, watching them. He just stood there looking at them curiously.

As soon as the engine reached idle, he released the parking brake, pushed the throttle forward and began taxiing. He noticed the airman was now running back toward the hangar. The Australians used the squadron call sign "Phoenix." Appropriate.

He switched the high-pressure air over to start the other engine. Doing his best Australian accent, he called himself "Phoenix Seven," and requested taxi clearance. They cleared him to taxi, but then came back and said they didn't have a flight plan on him. It wasn't that uncommon to have late submissions or mix-ups. As he continued to taxi, he just said, "Sorry, mate. I'll get it straightened out on the squadron frequency, call you right back."

As soon as he said that, he switched to the tower frequency and listened. He taxied as fast as he could. Unfortunately, 30 tons of jet and fuel, perched atop three wheels, made the fighter handle like a three-legged pig on valium. He was almost to the runway when he saw a truck with flashing lights headed their way.

As he reached the runway, he did just like his mom taught him. He looked both ways for traffic. He saw a large cargo jet on final approach a couple miles out. He couldn't wait. They'd have to scramble to abort their approach. As he rolled onto the runway without a takeoff clearance, he keyed the mic and said "Sorry." Skipping the engine run-up checks, he pushed the throttles forward to full power. The tower, excitedly, said, "Phoenix Seven, you haven't been cleared for takeoff! There's an aircraft on approach, clear the runway immediately!"

Unlike his last takeoff, he couldn't afford to use the afterburners. They needed every drop of fuel. As his heavily loaded fighter lumbered down the runway, the truck with the flashing lights caught up to him. It ran parallel to him on the taxiway. He hoped the driver hadn't seen too many Rambo movies.

He heard a cockpit warning tone. Glancing down he saw the "Ladder" warning on his display. He *totally* forgot that the little boarding ladder was still down. It could only be stowed from the ground. As they accelerated, it would be ripped off the aircraft. He just hoped it wouldn't go down an engine intake.

He was a little clumsy on the controls as he lifted the fighter into the air but it came back fast. It felt good to be back in the cockpit.

There was a loud thump as the boarding ladder ripped off the aircraft. He checked his left engine indicators. Whew ... missed the intake.

As soon as he had his landing gear up, he turned south and accelerated to the optimum climb-out speed. He loved these jets. They took care of all the boring but important details so he didn't have to. He hated to admit it, but if it weren't for GPS, navigation computers and fuel calculators, he would have been lost at sea a long time ago.

He turned his IFF – Identify Friend or Foe – off. Without his radar repeater highlighting his position, the relatively stealthy jet would quickly disappear from the ground-based radar screens.

He keyed the intercom. "Greg, you all right?"

"Yes sir, this is totally wild. It's almost like Microsoft Flight Simulator 12.0."

Josh released his oxygen mask and let it hang by one bayonet fitting. Smiling, he replied, "Yes, they did a great job making these fighters feel as close to the game as possible."

Oblivious to the satire, Greg asked, "Do you think they noticed that we jacked a jet?"

43

ESCAPE

Bishara received a phone call during the meeting. After a few seconds, they heard her say, "Oh no! Are you sure? ... How long ago? ... But it can't... Oh. Keep me informed."

Seeing her expression, Buster said, "What is it, Cindy?"

"Uh ... someone just stole an FA-18 Super Hornet from the Australians."

Frowning, Buster asked, "What are Super Hornets doing in the Falklands?"

Davidson shook his head. "The U.K. asked the Aussies to deploy there as a warning after Argentina bought the Russian SU-27s."

Buster's eyes got big. "It's him, it's got to be!" Turning to Bishara, he yelled, "Tell them to shoot him down!"

She shook her head. "It's too late. By the time they figured out what was going on, he was outside their surface-to-air missile range, but they're scrambling another Hornet to intercept."

Buster continued to rant. "This is insane! How could he fly one? Where does he think he's going? He can't make it to the South Pole in a fighter!"

Bishara narrowed her eyes and said defensively, "Well ... actually, there *is* a chance ...."

Buster pointed a finger at his Deputy. "*You* told me that *we're* not using fighters because they don't have the range."

Bishara jumped in. "They just told me that this Super Hornet was fitted out as a tanker with extra drop tanks. Our Navy guys are running the numbers now, but there is a slight chance that if he flies a perfect flight profile ...."

Buster yelled, "Oh my God! Launch the C-17s. Where's my Tomahawk shooter and the carrier?!"

Davidson, trying to spin Buster back down, said, "We've already given the command to launch the C-17s with the SEAL team. They'll be taking off shortly."

Glosson added, "We've downloaded the target coordinates to the USS Truxton's launch computer. They're programmed and ready to fire on our command. The USS Reagan is preparing a strike package with tankers just in case. She can have fighters overhead shortly after the C-17s arrive at the Pole base and insert a Marine team by V-22, shortly after."

Buster was beginning to sweat. "We need to launch the Tomahawks now and be done with this."

There was silence in the room. Davidson said, "Sir, we can't do that. Most of the people down there are innocent civilians. Some are high-profile American scientists ..."

Buster interrupted, "If they're stupid enough to be duped into building this thing for him ...." His voice trailed off as all eyes were on him. He looked at Davidson angrily. "Then tell the SEAL team they're authorized to use deadly force. I want a termination order on the Prophet right now!"

Davidson continued in a quiet voice, "Sir, the Prophet's head of security is one of our contract agents. If by some miracle he survives the flight, our man can take him out quickly. He's one of our deadliest agents and the only guns down there are under his control. We've got him."

Buster sounded almost plaintive. "That's what we always think. Don't you see? At every turn he's made fools of us!" In a more controlled voice, he continued. "I'm not taking any more chances. I want a termination order on him, and I want it now!" He slammed his hand on the table.

Davidson glanced around and said quietly, "Yes sir. The President is involved with this operation, so we'll need Presidential authority for a termination order."

"Give the termination order to our agent on *my* authority. I'll get approval from the President." Buster's eyes narrowed. "I also want a million dollar bounty on his head."

Davidson said softly, "We'll have to go through the Attorney General and State Department to authorize that."

Buster said, "No, we don't." Sarcastically he added, "I'm a lawyer, remember?" Continuing as though completing a closing argument at a trial, "We've ascertained that the Prophet has no identity. Therefore, he's not an American citizen *and* he's now outside the U.S. Even so, we don't need a *public* bounty." He turned to Carl. "We simply offer *our* contract employees a large bonus."

Davidson knew targeting a foreign terrorist outside the U.S. was well within their authority, as was granting incentives for anti-terrorist operations.

Carl looked at Davidson for confirmation.

Davidson nodded.

Buster slapped his hand on the table again, "*And* I want that Tomahawk shooter ready to fire the second I give the word!"

"Yes sir."

Falklands

The SEAL team commander, Lieutenant Commander DeVries, was getting his men back together for the final leg to the Pole base, when the call came in on the C-17's encrypted satellite link.

He turned to his Senior Chief and told him about the stolen Hornet.

Shaking his head, the Chief responded, "Who're we chasing, Jason Bourne? Should we tell the Aussies who he is?"

"We don't even know who he is. They're scrambling a jet now and will hopefully shoot him down, but regardless, we've been ordered to press on to the South Pole ASAP. *And* ... we've been given unlimited Rules Of Engagement."

The Chief whistled. "Unlimited ROE." He shrugged. "Being able to shoot everybody makes the job easier, but I don't understand, aren't there American engineers and scientists down there?"

DeVries nodded. "There has to be a lot at stake." As the Chief ran off to round up the team, DeVries frowned and said quietly, "Or, it's personal."

Greg asked, "Won't they try and shoot us down or something?"

"We should be outside of their surface-to-air missile range by now." Josh said optimistically.

"What about sending another fighter after us?"

Josh said, "Uh, yeah ... that's a possibility."

Enthusiastically, Greg said, "But we can outrun them, right?"

Less enthusiastically, Josh said, "We could if we weren't flying a Bingo profile."

"What's a Bingo profile?"

"Bingo means minimum fuel. We're flying the perfect climb, cruise, and descent speeds to give us maximum range."

"So the speed for maximum range isn't really fast?"

"Greg, it's like when you're running out of gas in your car. You know going faster will just reduce your mileage."

"But ... a jet chasing us won't have that limit?"

Greg was sharp. "No. Another Hornet in burner can catch us, and we're configured as a tanker."

"What does that mean?"

"Greg, look at the wings. See all the tanks hanging under them?"

"Yeah."

"This fighter is setup to refuel other fighters. That gives us a lot more gas but also a lot more weight and drag. We're slower and less maneuverable until they're empty and we can jettison them."

"So they *can* catch us and out maneuver us."

"Yeah, but it'll take a while to scramble another jet, and we have two advantages. Super Hornets are stealthy – hard to find on radar. Plus, we're running away from them. That shrinks the range of their AMRAAM missiles. They'll have to get pretty close to shoot. I'm less worried about burning than freezing."

"Freezing?"

"Do you know how far our South Pole base is from the Falklands?"

"2,000 miles?"

"Actually, about 2,650."

"I didn't know fighters could fly that far."

"Me either."

There was silence from the back seat.

"Greg, normally they can't, but with five extra fuel tanks, it should give us a range of about 2,300 miles. We're also going to jettison the tanks as soon as they're empty. That'll buy us another 100, or so."

Greg said quietly, "That's still 250 short."

"Well, those numbers assume some fuel left for approach and landing."

"So we'll be almost empty when we land?"

Josh hesitated. "Yeah ... well, we probably need to talk about that." He paused. "Greg, do you like extreme sports?"

"Yeah, love to watch them."

"Ever wanted to try any of them, like bungee jumping or ... skydiving?"

"No, I'm more of a gamer."

He decided to bring it up later. "By the way, Greg, we've got another small challenge. The same guys who were trying to intercept us in the Falklands are almost certainly headed to the Polar base right now."

"I don't understand. We're trying to save the world. Are they terrorists?"

"I'm afraid it's much worse. They're from the government and they're here to help."

With obvious confusion, Greg said, "But you're from the government."

"Uh, in the government, the left hand doesn't always talk to the right hand. Normally, we could work this out with some emails and a couple conference calls, but we're a little short on time."

Australian Flight Lieutenant Tommy Harper was climbing in full afterburner. He followed the ground-based vector from the airport's radar, but they'd lost contact shortly after it took off. Using his jet's powerful radar, Harper picked up a very faint target moving due south at 35,000 feet. He was still 90 nautical miles away but closing fast. Looking at his fuel, he realized it was going to be close.

He called back to base. "Boss, I got him painted. He's headed due south, angels 35, doing about 500 knots."

Wing Commander Gulick replied, "Roger. How's your fuel?"

"I'll have to jettison my drops." He paused. "If I don't get within range in 10 minutes, I'll have to turn back."

"Keep pressing and you're cleared to jettison."

As he manned-up, they had told him it was two guys posing

as Boeing technicians. Before the attack on the World Trade Center, he'd never have thought terrorists had the sophistication to steal and fly an aircraft. As he blew his drops off, he asked, "What do you want me to do? What's my ROE?"

Gulick replied, "We're trying to figure that out now. Just be ready and try to get him on the radio." There was a pause. "Tommy ... we can't let them use that jet against us."

"Roger that." He shook his head. He had to either get them to turn around or take them out.

44

INTERCEPT

Elizabeth refused to sign the immunity from prosecution agreement.

After six hours of interrogation, they put her in a locked room. There were no windows, one cot, a toilet and a sink. She was still wearing her pajamas with her blanket around her. She thought it was late afternoon and realized she had had nothing to eat, but she wasn't hungry.

She paced around the room for a while, and then, emotionally exhausted, sat down on the cot. She wanted to cry but knew they were watching and she wouldn't give them the satisfaction.

Josh heard a low-pitched warbling tone. Greg said, "What's that?"

"We have company."

"The bad guys?"

"No, just some seriously pissed off Aussies."

He noticed that two of the drop tanks were empty, and happily jettisoned them into the ocean. With the new flight configuration, the computer recalculated his maximum range profile, allowing him to speed up a little and climb another 1,000 feet.

Loud and clear on Guard, the emergency radio frequency, he heard, "Super Hornet flying south, we're intercepting you. If you return to base, you won't be harmed."

Josh didn't respond. Their confusion about who was in the cockpit might still be an advantage.

Greg asked, "Have they launched a missile at us?"

"No, you'll hear a high-pitched warbling tone when they lock us up for missile launch."

"Can't we just stay out of their range by using afterburner?"

"Greg, with our burners lit, we'd go through 10 tons of fuel in twelve minutes. We wouldn't even make it to the Antarctic coast."

Greg volunteered, "We'd retain consciousness for 15 minutes in freezing water."

Josh shook his head. "Discovery Channel?"

"Titanic."

Southern Ocean

Flight Lieutenant Harper radioed back to base. "He's not responding. I don't have enough fuel to join on him, but I'll be in missile range in a couple minutes." He looked at his fuel gauge. "I'll have just enough time to squeeze off a missile before I'm *emergency fuel*. I need to know what you want me to do."

At the base, Commander Gulick said to the pilots around him, "Where the hell could he be going? He's heading south! There's nothing there." He shook his head in frustration.

"Boss, I'm at the edge of radio range. Can barely hear you. Need the ROE."

Gulick sighed. He had to make the call. His career was already over for losing the jet. "Haven't heard anything back from Command. On my authority, if they don't return, splash 'em."

Harper replied, "Roger." Then pulled off his oxygen mask and said to himself, "Root me!" Like all fighter pilots, he looked forward to testing himself in combat, but shooting one of his own bloody jets in the clacker wasn't what he had in mind.

He had a radar lock and selected his AMRAAM missile. The HUD immediately showed the range circle, indicating he was still out of range but closing. He flipped the Master Arm switch on. The missile launch button on his stick was now hot.

Josh heard the warning tone shift to a higher-pitched warble no pilot wanted to hear. The Aussie had locked him up in preparation for missile launch. He once again pictured in his head the course of action needed. At the same time, he heard another transmission. "Super Hornet headed south, this is your last chance. Return or I'm going to shoot you down."

Josh came up on the radio. "Aircraft in pursuit, break off your attack. I'm a U.S. government agent on a critical mission. Please contact the United States government immediately and they'll explain the situation. Really apologize for borrowing your aircraft, we'll replace it."

Harper used his other radio. "Boss, did you hear that transmission?"

He heard nothing but static.

It was going to be his call. If they were just crazy Boeing reps, they'd crash or eject in the ocean and freeze to death. Blowing them out of the sky would be merciful. But this guy didn't sound crazy, and he couldn't imagine any situation that would require stealing a fighter without a U.S. government heads-up. The transmission had to be a ploy to give 'em time to escape. In either case, the answer was clear. He came up on the Guard frequency and said, "Mate, that's bull and you know it. There's no way we can confirm that before I have to launch."

The computer determined the missile was now in-range. In his HUD, he had a "Shoot" cue. Harper, with his thumb over the launch button, thought to himself, this sucks. He keyed his mic. "Give me one good reason why I shouldn't put this AMRAAM up your ass?"

Josh had a flash of illogical insight. When he was an F-18 instructor, he flew with an Australian foreign exchange pilot. They'd become friends. The Australian Hornet community was tight and there was a chance this pilot might know his friend.

Josh replied, "I've been pinched on the butt by Mel Gordon's wife, Vivian."

There was a moment of silence, then laughter on the radio. "Fair dinkum? Vivian pinches everyone! That's how she says g'day."

Josh replied, "I know. She's an amazing lady, probably smarter than both of us combined."

The radar warning tone ceased.

"Ain't that the truth? Don't know what you're doing, mate, but hope you packed long underwear. Gotta go. Good luck."

Josh breathed a sigh of relief, adding, "Thanks. When we get back, I'll buy you a pint."

"You're on."

Greg said, "We made it!"

Josh said wryly, "Yup, all downhill from here." He checked the distance to the base. They were four hours away and the navigation computer was still telling him they didn't have enough fuel to make it.

"Greg, how much time do you need to get the tracking system software online?"

"About two hours."

"Can you do it faster?"

"Maybe cut a half hour off, but it'll take a few hours to charge up the capacitors from the reactor anyway."

"It's going to be really close. Tell you what, why don't you review anything you can. We still have a ways to go."

"I'll be ready when we get there."

"Good. By the way, can your computer fit inside one of your coat pockets just in case we have to move quickly?"

"Sure."

"When you're finished with it, why don't you go ahead and put it in there and button it up tight. Then see if you can get some sleep."

"OK."

Josh jettisoned another tank. Their predicted range improved, but the computer was still coming up short.

Mount Howe

As Smith helped him finish installing an access panel on one of the reactor control stations, Bobinski said, "Spah-see-boh,"

Smith replied, "You're welcome, but I'm afraid I wasn't much help."

Switching back to English, Bobinski said, "Every bit helps."

Smith's Iridium satellite phone rang. He pulled the oversized phone off his belt clip and answered, "Hello?"

He slowly walked away from Bobinski as he listened, but Bobinski heard him quietly ask, "Carl, are you *sure*?"

Frowning, Smith listened a little longer and then asked, "*How* much?"

Exhaling heavily, Smith said, "Yes ... yes, I know." Disconnecting, Smith just stood there for a second staring at the phone in his hand.

Bobinski asked, "Something wrong?"

Smith looked up and said, "Not yet." He grabbed his parka, picked up the small duffel bag he always carried with him, and headed toward the door.

Bobinski went back to work but watched Smith out of the corner of his eye. He saw Smith glance around, then pick up an adjustable wrench and put it into his bag. Pulling an automatic pistol from the bag, Smith checked the clip and slid it into his shoulder holster as he left.

45

METEOROID

Jesse hadn't responded to his calls in several days. He was relieved, when he finally reached him. "Thank God you're back again, but it may be too late. My house of cards is collapsing." He paused. "Isn't that comet fragment supposed to arrive soon?"

It enters the atmosphere in 10 hours.

"Any distractions would be welcome right now. Where's it headed?"

The coordinates and trajectory appeared in Josh's mind.

He plugged them into the Hornet's navigation computer. Expecting it to be over the ocean by statistical odds, he was surprised when the display put the coordinates almost on top of London. "Well, they're not going to be able to miss this. How big is it?"

Like the comet, he suddenly saw it in his mind – it looked like a slowly rotating, lumpy, black boulder. He immediately sensed it was about 70 meters across.

Startled, he said, "Oh my God! That's the size of a small building." Three times bigger than the Chelyabinsk meteor, he was fairly certain it could cause massive destruction. "We need to get the word out!"

He tried his UHF and VHF radios but got no response. He tried different frequencies and the emergency Guard channel, but knew he was in one of the few places in the world where there was no one in radio range. "This is a nightmare! You knew this thing was coming in over a city but didn't tell me. Why are you giving me this information now when we can't do anything about it?"

Can't you?

Josh paused and thought. "Are you suggesting ... we can

deflect it?"

Can you?

"I have no idea. They haven't finished installing it much less testing it! The tracking scope may not be able to see something this small, and the beam's probably not powerful enough for something this close. Even if it works, they'll shut us down or blow us up before we can fire it. Tens of thousands will die. We'll lose all credibility and never have time to stop the comet."

Is this the outcome you wish?

"Of course not!"

Then why are you rehearsing it?

Josh took a deep breath and slowed his breathing and anger. As he thought about it, he sighed and said, "It's my fault." He shook his head. "I never asked you how big the comet or fragment was until too late – absurdly obvious questions." He paused. "I don't want help ... I just want suggestions, and you've honored that. The result is we're playing catch-up with the survival of the human race hanging in the balance."

He envied Elizabeth her ability to believe without constant analysis. Maybe he could learn from her, but even as he thought that, he knew it was never going to happen. She'd been open, kind and trusting. He'd repaid her by withholding the truth and keeping her at arm's length. In retrospect, it was fortunate they'd never consummated their relationship. She had lost her first husband, and Josh's "fade to black" future was pretty obvious. Even if he survived, she'd learn he wasn't what she thought he was. Her feelings would die with her belief in him. He shook his head. One love believed him dead and soon another might wish him dead ... another great Country song.

With a small laugh, he said, "It's a bit late to ask for relationship advice, but I got nothing else to do until we're in radio range." He paused. "What do you do when someone loves you because they think you're something you're not?"

Have you claimed to be something you're not?

"I lied by omission. By not confronting her, I let her believe I was something I'm not."

What does she think you are?

He frowned. "Uh ... I'm not really sure."

What are you?

"I'm ... uh ...." He laughed. "As if it matters. I'm being chased by SEALs in a stolen fighter over Antarctica without enough fuel. Even Dr. Ruth wouldn't waste her time."

Bitching Betty disturbed his pitiful conversation with the casual announcement, "Bingo, Bingo."

He checked their distance to Mount Howe and reset the Bingo warning to 2,500 pounds of fuel. A headwind hadn't helped. The navigation computer was indicating they were going to be 150 miles short.

Greg woke up and said, "Did you say something?"

Josh said, "No. Did you get any sleep?"

"Yeah, but I had weird dreams. I was flying without an airplane."

"Interesting ... Greg, got some new information while you were sleeping. Turns out that one of the comet fragments is going to strike near London in about nine hours."

Greg asked, "Is it big enough to cause damage?"

"I think so, but Chandra will know for sure."

"Snap! Can we deflect it?"

"Don't know but it's going to be that much more critical that our test firing be done at full power."

Greg said, "It's going to be risky pushing full power through it on its first shot."

"Just make sure you're ready to go when we get there."

For several minutes, Josh tried the radios on various frequencies but still heard nothing.

Then Betty repeated, "Bingo. Bingo."

Greg asked, "Are we out of gas?"

"No, Betty's an alarmist. We still have 2,500 pounds left."

"How long will that last?"

"Another 20 minutes."

Greg asked, "Why is the computer warning system a female voice?"

Josh thought his question was a bit non sequitur, but realized Greg was a computer whiz. Explaining it would delay having to worry him about their impending method of debarkation. "Greg, years ago, before there were female fighter pilots, they did studies and discovered men respond better to women's voices."

"Why didn't they change it when women started flying fighters?"

"Hate to break it to you, but the studies showed that women *didn't* respond any better to men's voices."

"Well, *that's* not fair."

Josh laughed. "I agree."

He tried again to reach the Pole base on his UHF. "Base, this is Josh Fuze, over." He repeated his call several times. Finally, he got a static filled but understandable reply. "Commander Fuze, this is Major Crowell, we weren't expecting you."

"I know. Change of plans. Is Chandra there?"

"She's on top of the mountain."

"Please patch me through. This is an emergency."

A minute later Chandra's voice came on the radio. "This is Chandra, is that you, Josh?"

"Yes. Victoria, I just learned the comet fragment we're expecting is 70 meters across and will enter the earth's atmosphere in less than nine hours."

Chandra said, "Seventy meters? It could be bigger than Tunguska!"

Josh said, "Is that likely?"

"I'm afraid so. The Tunguska object created a 10-megaton blast and flattened everything in a 40 kilometer radius." She paused. "Where's it headed?"

"London."

"Oh my God, we have to evacuate London!"

Josh said, "Let me give you the coordinates so the observatories can back this up."

After he gave her the coordinates and trajectory, she said, "I can't reach the observatories. We're having communication problems." There was a pause. Then she said, "If these coordinates are right, the shockwave could level much of the city. It could kill hundreds of thousands. Josh, your source has informed the authorities already, right?"

Josh said, "No! We have the same problem you do. You've got to get this information out somehow."

"Josh ... we got word that the program's been compromised. Shortly after that, we received a strange message from people claiming to be from the government. They told us to stand down, but they didn't have the correct authentication passwords. We knew they weren't real and ignored them. Unfortunately, they killed our satellite link. We have no way to communicate!"

Josh said, "Keep trying. See if anyone has a satellite phone that's working." He paused. "Victoria ... *can we deflect it?*"

"Deflect it?"

He heard Katori in the background. "We don't even know if it will fire."

Cho said, "At this range the beam will be incredibly tight. It's powerful enough to vaporize a major divot out of it and create a decent jet plume."

Josh repeated, "Victoria, is it possible?" There was a longer pause. He knew she was running calculations on her laptop. It took 60 long seconds before she replied.

"No, Josh, I'm sorry. We can't. It's just not physically possible this late. Even if everything worked perfectly, the impulse from the gas jet isn't enough. It's just too close and the earth's too big to miss. I'm ... I'm sorry."

"It doesn't have to miss the *earth,* just London."

She replied immediately with excitement in her voice, "You're absolutely right! We only have to nudge it enough to get it over the ocean. If we can slow it down a tiny bit, we can shift its impact point a few hundred kilometers ...." There was another pause and then, "Yes, there *is* a chance ... if we hit it with everything we've got as soon as possible. It all depends on the coordinates being accurate and the fragment reflective enough that we can find it and track it. Sorry, don't have time to talk; gotta run some calculations."

Katori jumped on the radio. "Josh, we just finished installing it. Haven't checked out any of the circuits or even tried to charge the capacitors. If something goes wrong, it could destroy the Blaster, possibly blowing us up in the process."

Josh said softly, "I know, but there's too much at stake.

Even if we *can* get the word out, you know they can't evacuate everyone from a city in eight hours."

He could actually hear Katori sigh over the radio.

Josh added, "I have Greg Langlois with me for the software interface stuff."

Katori, sounding very tired, said, "Good. We'll need him.

Josh, I have to go. I need to find Bobinski and get the reactors online."

Josh said, "Major Crowell, are you still there?"

"Yes sir."

"Can you send a snowcat out about two miles due west of the base. We're going to need a ride."

"Did you say two miles *west* of the base?"

"Yes, and we're not dressed appropriately."

Crowell said, "I don't understand."

"I'll explain when we're on the ground."

Washington, D.C.

It was 9:30 pm. Davidson boarded the specially equipped Gulfstream G650 for the 12-hour flight from D.C. to the Falklands. It was the fastest, longest-range, executive jet on the market. They'd also specially modified it with extensive satellite communication and defensive systems. He'd only flown on it a few times, preferring to travel by more conventional and economical means. Buster had had no such reluctance, and had often used it as his personal airliner.

He began to have serious reservations about not being in the Ops Center when the SEAL team arrived at the South Pole. He suspected Buster wanted him out of the way. All he could do before he left was talk to a couple of the key team members. As concerned as he was, his job was to be the Director's Deputy. As long as Buster was giving legal directives, Davidson would support him ... whether he agreed with him or not.

46

EJECT

Greg asked, "Why aren't they meeting us at the airfield?"

Bitching Betty chose that time to say, "Fuel Low. Fuel Low."

Josh said, "That's why."

"We're out of gas?"

"No, we have another 10 minutes."

"How far are we from the base?"

Josh said, "About 20 minutes."

"Then how are we going to land?"

"Actually ... we're not. Greg, trying to land a fighter with no engines is tough under the best of conditions. Add darkness, insufficient altitude and an unlit ice runway, it's just too risky."

"What are we going to do?"

"We're still at 37,000 feet. We can glide there, but eventually we're going to have to step outside."

"We're going to eject!?"

"Yup, just like in **Top Gun**."

Greg said, "But in **Top Gun**, the guy in the backseat dies."

"Sorry ... bad example. Don't worry; it'll be a piece of cake."

"But I don't know how to eject."

Josh speaking slowly and calmly, said, "Don't have to. It's set for Command Eject. When I go, you go. Listen carefully, Greg. We still have plenty of time, but when I say get ready, I want you to put your head back against the headrest with your chin slightly elevated. Put your hands in your lap and extend your feet so that your thighs are touching the seat cushion. I'll do the rest."

"Why didn't you tell me this earlier?"

"Would have ruined your nap."

"But how do I use the parachute?"

"It'll open by itself, and you'll come down just fine. Just look at the horizon. Keep your feet together, knees slightly bent. When you hit the ground, just roll with it. Make sure your jacket's zipped up and your helmet and gloves are on tight. The departure's a bit of a rush."

"You've done this before?"

"Yup."

"Did you get hurt?"

Josh grimaced. "Uh ... after it was over, I felt like a new man. Don't worry, Greg, we'll be ejecting under perfect conditions. You'll be fine. This will be a great story to tell your kids and grandkids someday."

For the first time, Greg sounded plaintive and scared. "Commander Fuze, why is all this happening? It isn't fair! They can't be doing this to us. The government needs to do something about these people. Someone needs to ... sue someone!"

Josh stifled a laugh. Greg had been a real trooper but the pressure was catching up. He decided to try to take Greg's mind off the ejection by engaging him in philosophical discussion. He knew where to start.

"Greg, how do you think unfairness in our country and the world can be better addressed?"

"What!?"

"Greg, if you were king, what would you do to fix things?"

"Commander Fuze, you're just trying to take my mind off ejecting."

"Yup."

There was a pause. "Good idea." After another pause, Greg said, "I think too many people get to do anything they want and in the process hurt others. Everyone needs to operate under the same rules so no one has an unfair advantage."

Josh scanned his fuel gauge – it read zero. "Can you give me an example?"

"Yeah, when I was going to high school and college, jocks were treated differently. The academic standards didn't apply to them. Winning a stupid athletic event was more important than learning. Some slept through classes and flaunted it. No one should be able to do that."

Betty cheerfully said, "Engine Left, Engine Left." Josh watched as the RPM on the left engine started to drop.

Greg asked the obvious, "Are we out of gas now?"

"No, still have the right engine."

Betty corrected him, "Engine Right, Engine Right."

Josh said, "Now we're out of gas, but we'll glide for another 10 minutes." As the engines wound down, it was unnaturally quiet in the fighter's cockpit.

Greg, the consummate computer engineer, asked, "Will the flight control computers remain powered without the engines?"

"No worries. The engines are still windmilling with the air running down their intakes. That's enough to spin the generators and supply plenty of power and we have backup batteries." He shut down the radar and all unnecessary electronics to reduce the load on the generators.

"Greg, do you understand that no matter how hard we try to make things fair ... the universe isn't fair? It's not fair that a comet is on a collision course with Earth. It's not fair that we respond better to women's voices than they do to ours. How do we regulate that?"

"I understand, but we can control the unfair actions of *people.*"

Passing 25,000 feet, he checked the navigation computer and refined their heading. "OK. As king, what would you do to make sure all students are treated fairly?"

"I don't know ... I guess I'd have the teachers keep a closer watch on what was happening both in and out of the classroom and give them the power to take action."

"Let's say they assign someone to every student. They could follow you all day and make sure no one broke any rules or did anything unfair." Josh checked the distance to the base. With no drag-inducing tanks, they'd glide about seven feet forward for every foot they dropped, but they still had 50 miles to go. It would be *very* close.

Greg finally said, "That would suck. You'd always have someone looking over your shoulder. You'd have no freedom."

Josh smiled. "Reducing unfairness requires more control. The way to eliminate *all* unfairness would be with total control. There's your tradeoff – control and total fairness versus freedom."

Greg added, "Besides, what if the person following you

didn't like you?"

"Good point. Who gets to decide what's fair? Puts a lot of power in the hands of the regulators and enforcers, doesn't it? That's the paradox of government. If we seek security above all else, we achieve maximum security, which also happens to be the name for the tightest cell in a prison."

"Guess it has to be a balance."

"Greg, governments have struggled with that since the beginning of time. Figure out that perfect balance and I'll vote for you."

St. Louis

Elizabeth sat on the cot, head in hands, replaying every conversation she'd ever had with Josh. She'd maintained her position throughout the interrogation but it took a toll. They couldn't be right ... could they? She wasn't just some gullible mark. She couldn't, she wouldn't, believe that, but it was so hard to hear what they kept saying about Josh.

She heard the door open and looked up. The female FBI agent who'd handcuffed her introduced herself politely and asked Elizabeth to accompany her. Still holding onto her blanket, she followed mutely.

They went up in an elevator to what looked like a hotel suite. Inside, she was surprised to see they had a nice dinner waiting for her. She saw that they also had her purse, makeup bag, toiletries and clothes from Josh's apartment.

As she was eating the food, the woman agent surprised her by asking if she would accompany them on a flight to the Falklands.

She dropped her fork, and without hesitation pulled her pajamas off and grabbed her clothes.

Ten minutes later, she was on her way to the airport. They rode in another black, unmarked SUV with a police escort. It took them right onto the airport tarmac where she saw a large, sleek business jet with subdued U.S. government markings. Climbing the stairs and entering the executive jet, she realized it was several steps up from first class. In addition to her FBI escort, who followed her inside, there were two people already onboard.

One was obviously a flight attendant, who welcomed her and asked her what she'd like to drink. The attendant also told her there was a bed and bathroom in the back she could use after they were airborne.

The other individual was a tall, dark, serious-looking man. He wasn't wearing an FBI windbreaker but she could see a holster under his sports jacket. He introduced himself and called her ma'am but never smiled. She really wasn't sure if they were escorts or guards. She didn't care. She was going to see Josh.

After they took off, Elizabeth tried to stay awake but the combination of emotion, no sleep and hours of interrogation took their toll. No matter how hard she fought it, the drone of the jet engines lulled her into a deep sleep torn by nightmares.

Langley

The Prophet Operation team started to assemble in the Operations Center. Carl knew nothing would happen until the SEAL team arrived at the Pole.

By 10:00 pm, the entire team was present, minus Deputy Director Davidson. Carl initiated a STU-III encrypted call from the Ops Center to Davidson, who was now over the Atlantic.

"Thanks, Carl. I'd like to stay on the line during the entire operation if possible. Is Lafferty there?"

"Yes sir."

"Can you have him pickup, but stay on the line."

Carl brought Lafferty over and gave him another phone.

Davidson asked, "Bart, anything useful from Edvardsen?"

Lafferty said, "Just got off the phone with the interrogation team. Not much we didn't already know." He paused. "Brian, I have to tell you, my guys are some of the best. Edvardsen made a strong case for this crazy comet thing. My lead interrogator said, and I quote, 'She's not just the Prophet's play toy. She's very intelligent and made compelling arguments we're messing with something we don't understand. She even suggested the agency running this is beyond our security clearance.'"

"Dang it, Bart, I've felt the same, but as much as I hate to admit it, Buster's right. If the Prophet was for real, the responsible agency would have come forward and slapped our hand by now."

Lafferty sighed. "I know, just wanted to pass that on for what it's worth."

"Thanks, Bart. Carl, you still there?"

"Yes sir?"

"What have you found out about the observatory's claim?"

"As suspected, they were given the tip on where to look by Dr. Chandra."

"Figures."

Carl continued, "We squelched the information and put FBI personnel at the observatory to ensure it isn't leaked. However, the astrophysicist I talked to really thought they might have found *something* out there. He admitted, however, that the signal was barely detectable above background noise." He paused. "I hope you don't mind; I allowed them to pass the raw data to the IR observatory in Chile."

Someone handed Carl a paper. "Sir, hang on, I just got something in." After reading it, he said, "This is interesting. Even though we cut off the satellite communication to the Pole, Dr. Chandra is trying to transmit coordinates for that smaller meteoroid. She's claiming it's going to hit London in about eight hours with catastrophic consequences."

Davidson said, "Yeah right. It's more of the same, intended to cause panic and confusion." There was a long pause. Then Davidson said, "Carl … just to be on the safe side, go ahead and pass those coordinates to the Keck and Chilean observatories."

Mount Howe

It'd been six months since Josh had been to Mount Howe on the survey visit. Instead of spring with perpetual sunrise, it was now fall with perpetual sunset. The sun had set three weeks earlier making it very dark with only a little twilight in one corner of the sky.

They had only a few thousand feet of altitude to spare but they were going to make it. He could see the lights of the base camp with the mountain range silhouetted behind it. He put the Hornet into a gentle turn that would fly them right over the top of the mountain and then outbound over the base.

As they descended, he clearly saw a faint light on the mountaintop. With no engines, those on the mountain would be unaware of the Hornet gliding overhead. He looked at the outside temperature indicator. They weren't dressed for 30 degrees below zero. To keep them from freezing, he needed to get as close to the base and ground as possible, but far enough that the jet wouldn't hit anything.

"Greg, it's almost time. Remember what I told you. Make sure your coat, gloves, oxygen mask and helmet are on tight and your visor is down. Head firmly against the headrest with your chin slightly elevated and your feet on the rudder pedals. Keep your hands in your lap. I'll tell you before we eject."

Crossing the mountaintop, the radar altimeter indicated 2,000 feet above the ground. He pushed the fighter's nose down. When they were about a mile west of the base, he leveled off, slowing the jet into the heart of the ejection envelope. He set the autopilot, told Greg, "Here we go," and pulled the handle.

The Plexiglas canopy instantly blew off the jet as the back seat, with Greg, fired first. Josh didn't realize how loud it would be, but didn't have time to think about it as his seat followed a fraction of a second later. The ejection charge slapped him hard into the seat as the rocket motor ignited and blew him into the frigid night. Hitting 140 mph, subzero air was beyond cold. It was like a belly flop off a high-dive into ice water. At the apex of the seat's trajectory, the parachute deployed, ripping him out of the seat. What a rush! It was a new experience, since he remembered little of his last rocket ride.

He checked his parachute canopy, but had to lift his visor, which was rapidly fogging with ice. He looked around for Greg's chute in the weak twilight, but couldn't see him anywhere. Looking to his right, he saw the Hornet's faint green formation lights. The autopilot was still trying to carry out his last command and maintain altitude, but as the airspeed decayed, the fighter stalled and rolled over like a submissive dog. The beautiful jet quickly became nothing more than 20 tons of tumbling alloys and composites. It hit the ground with a bright flash. A delayed screeching boom echoed off the ice as residual fuel vapor in the tanks created a small orange fireball, punctuated by the detonation of the air-to-air missiles. Reflecting beautifully off the icy white plain, it provided enough illumination to locate Greg's parachute just below him.

Drifting in the cold still air, he looked up at Mount Howe. The twilight-illuminated mountain looked like a breathtaking but underexposed postcard. On the very top, he saw the silver dome that housed the Blaster. Looking at the bottom of the mountain, he could clearly see the lights of the base camp. There were two large Quonset huts and a snowcat garage. A half mile away, nestled at the foot of the mountain, a boxy building housed the nuclear reactors. He also saw headlights, a mile off, headed their way. He decided to enjoy the few seconds of solitude, knowing they might be his last.

Landing on the hard ice pack jolted him back to reality. He popped his parachute release fittings and jogged toward Greg's chute about a quarter mile away. From his survival vest, he pulled out a Velcro-wrapped, emergency strobe light. Switching it on, he stuck it to a matching Velcro patch on the top of his helmet. It would make it easy for the snowcat to see them in the dark.

In the eerie strobe illumination, he saw Greg's shape buried under his chute. Josh clawed through the canopy. Uncovering him, he saw that Greg had gotten his oxygen mask off and was smiling. All he said when he saw Josh was, "Wwwwait 'til the other gamers hear about this. But I ffforgot to look at the horizon and roll. I think I bbbbroke my ankle."

Josh released Greg's parachute fittings, bent over, loosened his shoe and felt his ankle. "Don't think it's broken, but it's probably badly sprained. Ride will be here soon." Greg was shivering violently so he wrapped Greg in the chute and sat down next to him with his arm around Greg's shoulder.

A couple minutes later, the snowcat pulled up and a man climbed out. It was hard to identify anyone in arctic gear. Without saying a word, he came over and helped Josh get Greg on his feet. As they put Greg in the back seat, Josh saw it was Tim Smith. Josh climbed in the front with Smith. Turning around, he asked Greg how he was doing.

Greg, still shivering violently, said, "Wwwwicked! My ffffirst ride in a fighter, first ejection and ffffirst parachute landing! Now we're going to ffffire the bbbaddest laser in the world!"

Josh knew Greg's adrenaline was still pumping. There was

nothing like facing death and winning. Smiling, he turned back and saw Smith looking at him seriously. He had worked with Smith for almost a year, but Smith *had been* a CIA operative. Josh felt stupid. Still another detail he hadn't really thought through. His only chance was if they hadn't contacted Smith.

47

MOLE

As soon as they got inside, all eyes were on him. They also had a video link with the mountaintop. Josh knew it was time for the proverbial "locker room talk" before the big game. Before he could start, one of the young engineers asked, "Did you really fly a fighter here?"

Before he could answer, Greg jumped in. "Yeah! It was *awesome!*"

"Where is it?"

Greg said, "Dude, it *totally* blew up."

"Sweet!"

Chandra, overhearing it on the video feed, just shook her head.

Josh, trying to put his serious face back on, said, "OK, this is it. This is what we've all been working for. We have to do it a lot faster than planned but we have the chance to save thousands, maybe hundreds of thousands, of lives. As you know, we also have another challenge. Our program's been compromised."

The same young engineer asked, "By who?"

"It's complicated, but there are elements in our own government," he thought, minor elements like the CIA and military, "who want to shut us down."

Major Crowell asked, "Why on earth would anyone want to do that?"

Josh shook his head. "I'm really not sure." His intuition told him. "Somehow someone got the idea we're going to use the Blaster to shoot down satellites. All I *am* sure of is that they're very serious and probably on their way. With the meteoroid inbound, we don't have time to unravel the insanity. We have to prove this thing does exactly what it's supposed to do. But to do that, we *have* to fire it the second the capacitors are charged. We won't have a second chance." He paused. "We're going to prove it works *and* save a city at the same time."

He shook his head again. "If we're visited, it will be by U.S. commandos with guns. Don't try to be a hero. They don't understand and probably won't want to hear your explanations."

"How do we know they're not terrorists?"

He thought to himself, *Define "terrorist,"* but said, "You'll have to trust me on this one. They're from the government. Do whatever you can to give us a chance to take out that meteoroid but don't get yourself killed. Do you understand?"

Most of them gave nervous nods.

"OK, what's the status?"

Bobinski appeared very relaxed. Josh knew he was an adrenaline junky and worked best under pressure. "Reactors coming up to full power and charging capacitors. One reactor is being cranky but we'll fix it. We're three hours from full charge."

With a skeptical look, Wooldridge said calmly, "Our biggest challenge is that we haven't been able to locate the comet fragment."

Katori on the video link said, "We also have an issue with the integration software between the tracking and the beam aiming system."

Josh said, "Meaning?"

"We're dead in the water unless we can get the software talking to the targeting servos."

Josh, looked at Greg, "Can you fix it?"

"Yeah, but I have to be at the control console on the mountaintop."

"Then let's get you up there ASAP."

Crowell said, "One of the helicopters is up there idling. I'll call them down to pick you up."

Josh nodded. "Can someone help Greg? He needs some warmer clothes and boots, and he's got a sprained ankle."

To the rest he said, "Show time!"

As Lanier, the young optics engineer, helped Greg hobble out the door, Josh heard her quietly ask, "James Bond flies fighters too?"

Greg said, "Totally! But..." he glanced back at Josh and

added quietly, "... not sure he knows how to land them."

Smiling, Josh put on a borrowed jacket and sat down on a stool to put on boots.

As everyone bundled up and left, he realized he was alone in the Quonset hut with Smith. Smith remained seated in a chair eight feet away, facing him. As Josh looked up, he saw Smith was watching him again. He also noticed the Iridium satellite phone attached to his belt. Josh raised his eyebrows and gave him a questioning look, as he slipped on a boot.

Smith said softly, with no emotion, "The program was bound to be compromised ... eventually."

Josh just nodded as sweat began to run down his back.

In the same calm voice, Smith said, "If you don't mind my asking ... how *do* you know the things you know?"

Josh quickly assessed his options. Despite his enhanced reflexes and martial arts training, his seated position and distance from Smith made him a sitting duck. A physical confrontation represented a low probability of his survival. It would be his last resort. He went through a series of possible responses. Too late, he realized he'd come to depend too much on his premonitions. They'd totally failed him here.

He needed to know what Smith knew. As he finished fastening one boot, he said, "The agency contacted you, didn't they?"

Smith nodded.

"They're having trouble figuring out who I'm working for."

Smith nodded again.

"They don't understand or believe in what we're doing."

Smith said softly, "*That* would be an understatement."

He noticed Smith was sitting with his right hand in his lap near the holster.

Josh sighed. Starting slowly, he said, "Tim, I..."

Before he could finish, he heard the door open behind him and glanced back. He'd never been so happy to see the scowling face of Winston Shepherd. Behind Shepherd was Drake Wooldridge.

Sheppard said, "Josh, the helicopter's landing now."

Josh hoped Smith wouldn't shoot him in front of Sheppard and Wooldridge. Standing up, with one boot still unfastened, he looked back at Smith ... and saw him holding the nine-millimeter pistol in his hand.

Checkmate. At least from a standing position with his boots on, he had a tiny chance. As he was preparing to make his move, from behind him, he heard the unmistakable metallic double click of a slide drawn back on an automatic pistol. Slowly looking over his shoulder, he saw Shepherd scowling ... but his arms were at his side and he was looking sideways at Wooldridge. Wooldridge held a 45 automatic pointed directly at Josh.

Shepherd said to Wooldridge, "You can't be serious."

Without looking at Shepherd, Wooldridge said, "Shut up, Shepherd, you're a moron." To Josh he said, "I am one of the world's leading experts in comets. Did you really think you could pull the wool over my eyes?" Wooldridge smiled smugly. "I've been working with the authorities for over two months now, and I'm putting an end to this charade." He gestured toward Smith, "We've been offered a very nice bonus for bringing you to justice, dead or alive."

Josh's heart sank. He didn't see this coming and there was no way he could take both of them. How stupid could he be? The hints had been there with Wooldridge. And Smith ... Smith worked for the CIA! He had to come up with a plan, but he was drawing a complete blank.

Smith stood up and casually walked around Josh toward Wooldridge. He kept his distance with his nine millimeter in front of him.

Josh slowly rotated to continue facing Smith as he moved to Wooldridge's side. Totally blindsided, his 'visions' were nothing more than dreams after all.

Stopping next to a smug Wooldridge, Smith said quietly to Josh, "You were saying?"

48

BLASTER

Josh sighed and said, "Tim, the meteoroid is real and ..."

Before he could finish, Smith knocked the barrel of Wooldridge's pistol up and away from Josh, and with an amazing flick of the wrist, snatched Wooldridge's gun, saying, "Give me that before you accidently shoot yourself."

A startled Wooldridge said, "I captured him. He's mine and so is the bonus, no one is going to ..."

With the same calm voice, Smith interrupted, "And shut up before *I* accidentally shoot you." Smith popped the clip out of Wooldridge's gun and handed it back to him.

Wooldridge looked at the clip with confusion. "It's empty."

Smith winked at Shepherd and said, "Thanks for the heads up."

Josh wasn't sure what transpired behind the scenes but it was the first time he'd *ever* seen Shepherd smile.

Smith holstered his pistol and said to Josh, "You've got a helicopter to catch. I'll join you in a second. Shepherd and I are going to introduce *Wooldridge* to some duct tape."

Josh realized he'd been holding his breath. As he released it, he gave Smith a questioning look.

Smith shrugged. "I'm retiring anyway."

Speechless, Josh headed to the helicopter.

He strapped in next to Greg. Smith joined them a minute later. Bundled up, they sat three across on a web seat. The helicopter had heat but it couldn't keep out the Antarctic cold. As the H-60 lifted off, he saw Greg's head bobbing in time to the helicopter's vibration.

It was a short flight to the top. Reviewing what just happened, he had a light-bulb moment. He never had a premonition about the confrontation with Smith because it *never was*. As he closed his eyes to think through the next step, he had another prescient moment. He saw a flash but it wasn't the Blaster, it was a very close muzzle flash. He opened his eyes just as the helicopter made its approach to the tiny mountaintop-landing pad.

Josh had seen pictures, but he'd never been to the finished facility. There were two structures – a control room and a dome housing the Blaster. The control room looked like a cross between a doublewide mobile home and one of his childhood Lego creations. Anchored to the ground with steel cables, it was 25 feet wide by 50 feet long with modular seams every 10 feet. An umbilical cord, thicker than his waist, stretched between the control room and the giant dome. The 40-foot-wide aluminum dome was open on one side with a little light coming from inside.

After they landed, the helicopter copilot caught Josh's eye and winked. It was Elton Musk! Of course, Musk, the adrenaline junky, angel investor, and pilot, wasn't going to miss the first firing. Josh just shook his head as he got out of the helicopter.

He walked toward the control room, but stopped to peer inside the dome. Open to the cold night air, the Blaster had to be at ambient temperature.

He'd seen pictures of all the Blaster's components, but never assembled. He wasn't sure what he was expecting ... probably Marvin the Martian's giant Disintegrator, but the reality was a bit different. The first thing he noticed was the noise. Right next to the entrance were several refrigerator-sized heat pumps. He knew they kept the mercury-cuprate superconductors at an Antarctic-embarrassing, minus 170 degrees. Following the thick metal hoses to the Blaster, he saw a cylindrical aluminum core, 15 feet in diameter and 15 feet tall. Pointed at the sky, it looked like it had beer kegs strapped around the perimeter. Thin metal cooling fins sprouted from the bottom and sides like a bad haircut. Attached to it with metal struts, was a large optical telescope with a video feed. They had bolted all of it to a massive, but rather standard-looking, telescope mount. He knew the mount could rotate the Blaster 360 degrees and elevate it in hair-thin, 10-thousandth-of-a-degree increments. The whole thing looked more like a giant, mutant hair dryer on life support, rather than the salvation of humanity, but to Josh, it was a thing of beauty.

He also saw someone in a parka crouched over a giant metal box with dozens of wrist-sized wires coming out of it. Although impossible to see a face, from the size, he was sure it was Cho.

They entered the control room through the only door. Josh immediately saw several giant computer monitors mounted on one wall. Facing the monitors were two rows of plastic folding tables and chairs. The kind you rent for a wedding reception. On the tables, sat a dozen laptops that controlled all the Blaster's many systems. Katori and Chandra were working intently on two of them. Cables went everywhere. The room was on the dim side to make the monitors easier to see. There were no windows except a small porthole in the door. It looked more like a laptop repair shop than a control center.

The back of the room had a massive metal wall that looked armored. On the other side, he knew, sat two dozen giant capacitors. The size of washing machines, they were being charged by the nuclear reactors at the foot of the mountain. Each could hold the equivalent of a lightning bolt worth of energy. More importantly, they could release all of that power to the Blaster in a millisecond.

The control room had a constant background noise. It was a combination of laptop fans, electric heaters, intercom static and a high-pitched hum from the capacitors on the other side of the wall. He also noticed the aroma of hot electronics mixed with stale coffee and a dash of "wet dog."

Katori and Chandra looked up as they entered.

Josh raised his eyebrows in question.

Chandra shook her head. "I'm sorry, Josh; we haven't been able to find anything at those coordinates."

Josh felt like he'd been punched in the stomach. It had all come down to this moment. There were only two possibilities. Their equipment wasn't capable of seeing the fragment or ... there wasn't one. If there wasn't one, he might be nothing more than a puppet in a much bigger game. He'd lied to these people and put them in mortal danger so they would create the most powerful weapon in the world ... for what? Maybe he really was public enemy number one.

With all eyes on him, Josh said, "I'm ... I'm sorry. I ..."

Before he could finish, Chandra said, "Wait a minute." Looking from her laptop to the main display at the front of the room, she said to herself, "What do we have here?"

Squinting, Josh tried to make something out on the screen. He saw nothing but dark shapes and an occasional glint among the static.

Looking back at the data on her laptop, Chandra tilted her head and then clapped her hands together. "By Jove, I think we found the little sucker!" She looked up at Josh. "And it's right where you said it would be!"

Josh's knees were weak as he let out a lungful of air in relief.

Chandra added, "Dang thing looks like a lump of coal. It's so dark, I can't keep the tracking scope locked. We'll have to wait until it gets closer."

Musk, looking at the digital clock on the wall, said, "It's going to enter the atmosphere in less than six hours."

Chandra rubbed her eyes. "I know, I know ... but you have to understand, this thing won't even cross the moon's orbit for another four hours."

Katori said to Josh, "One of the reactors kicked an over-temperature fault and dropped offline. So we're not charging as fast as we should. The capacitors are up to about 70%, but at this rate it could take three more hours."

Josh asked, "Can we fire it with less than 100% charge?"

Katori said, "Yes, but ..."

Chandra interrupted. "We'd have to fire it more than once. We don't have time."

Katori shook his head. "We'll be very lucky if it fires *once*."

Chandra added, "We need every erg of energy we've got. With each minute that passes, the chances of deflecting it get smaller."

Josh looked back at Katori. "Can we override the over-temp shutoff on the reactor?"

Katori looked up. "Maybe, but if the warning is real, the reactor could go critical and melt down."

Josh just looked at him.

Katori nodded. "Yeah, right ... London." Katori got Bobinski on the intercom. "Chris, we won't have enough power to pull this off unless we can keep that second reactor online."

"Dah, we will take off all failsafes and overrides."

Katori shook his head at Bobinski's comment, but then looked back at Josh. "*And*, the software interface between the tracking system and the aiming servos is still out of commission. Without that, we can't point the Blaster."

Greg, already on a laptop, said, "I'm on it."

Without looking up, Katori added, "Cho's outside getting frostbite. He's trying to align the Blaster to the tracking system and check the power circuit continuity."

Josh asked, "How much time until we can fire it?"

Katori ticked off on his fingers, "*If* we get the tracking system working, Chandra can hold a visual lock, *and* the second reactor comes back online ... the capacitors should be up to full power in one hour."

"Can we do anything to speed that up?"

Katori shook his head. "Sorry, Josh, we're still limited by the laws of physics."

Josh wondered about that.

Chandra said, "Let's do everything we can so that the second we're charged, we can fire."

Katori nodded. "I'm overriding all the safety interlocks and transferring control to the main panel over there." He pointed at a metal console near the front of the room, under the display screens. Looking at the wall display, Josh saw it was broken into three "windows" with various graphs and indicator boxes. They were all red.

Katori pointed to the first window on the screen. "Once the tracking system can see the target and has a stable lock, this box will turn green. The middle window will show when the Blaster is actually aligned with the tracking system. When it syncs, it will also turn green. The last window on the right is a bar graph of the capacitors' charge. When it hits 100%, and the other systems are green, it will be ready to initiate the firing command."

They all heard it at the same time – the unmistakable sound of a C-17 flying over. They looked at Josh.

Josh ignored it. "Can you set it so it'll fire automatically when the capacitors hit full charge?"

Katori said, "We can set the tracking scope lock and the projector's aiming system to fully automatic, but there's still one manual intervention required for safety. When the capacitors are at full power, someone *must* hit the interlock safety switch or the firing will be aborted."

Josh asked, "Where's that?"

He pointed to the console under the main display. "It's the big red button."

Josh smiled. "You're kidding. To fire this thing we actually have to push a big red button?"

Katori smiled sheepishly. "Yeah, well, it's actually a go-no-go button. The firing sequence is automatic, but we have to push the button to *allow* the firing sequence to continue. If we don't press it within five seconds after the capacitors reach full charge, the system aborts. But once it's pushed, it's impossible to stop the firing sequence."

Frowning, Josh said, "Shouldn't it be *green*?" He shook his head. "Never mind. Can we push it now?"

"No. For safety, it requires human intervention to fire, and it can't be pressed until we hit 100% charge."

On the intercom, they heard Bobinski report, "Second reactor is putting out 110% ... but she's running a little hot." There was a pause. "And, I think we have company soon."

Josh said to Bobinski and the others, "Obviously, things didn't get straightened out back home. These guys are here to shut us down. Chris, keep us powered as long as you can, but these guys are dangerous ... they know not what they do."

49

SEALS

Carl looked at the clock. It was 11:20 pm. The Op Center received confirmation that the C-17 had landed at the Polar base. The first objective was to cut off any escape and shut down the power, without which the Blaster was useless. The SEALs broke into three groups. The first would secure the other C-17. They would also commandeer the helicopter, so they could use it to get to the top of the mountain. The second team would secure the snowcats to prevent any escape and round up the staff. The third would go a half mile to the nuclear reactor building and shut down the power.

They were getting a live video feed from cameras on the C-17. With zoom lenses and low-light capability, they pointed a camera at each of the buildings and the top of the mountain. They could also hear all radio communication between the SEAL teams.

In less than 10 minutes, the first SEAL team reported they had taken control of the other C-17 and the helicopter without any resistance, and were putting their pilot into the H-60 to take the assault team to the mountaintop.

The second team reported the same. They secured the snowcats and captured the staff. The engineers were indignant and angry, but didn't put up a fight.

The third SEAL team had the furthest to go. After another 10 minutes, they reported that they had just secured the reactor building without any resistance and would shut down the power.

From the Op Center the operation was rather anticlimactic. Although they still had to secure the mountaintop, they now controlled the base and power. Stuck on the top of a mountain, surrounded by 300 kilometers of polar ice, there was no place for the Prophet to run.

Mount Howe

The Navy helicopter pilot that accompanied the first SEAL team was in the cockpit going through the startup procedures. Five fully armed SEALs were onboard. They carried the compact but deadly MP5 submachine guns for close-quarters work.

The pilot started the engines but when he tried to engage the rotors, nothing happened. Finally, he gave the cut signal to the SEAL Commander in the back. On the intercom, he said, "Sorry guys, this bird ain't going anywhere; transmission's frozen."

The SEAL Team Commander simply said to his team, "Plan B." He reported the problem via radio as they headed toward the snowcats.

Josh looked at Katori. "How much longer?"

Katori looked at his laptop. "Another 30 minutes to full charge."

Josh sighed and said quietly, "We don't have 30 minutes. Our friends will be up here in the other helo any time now."

Smith, standing at the back of the room with the helicopter pilot and Musk, cleared his throat. "I'm afraid someone may have disconnected the helicopter's transmission oil heater."

Musk and the helicopter pilot shook their heads with a smile as they looked at Smith.

Katori nodded. "They'll have to use the snowcats ... unless ... they also have issues?"

Smith nodded. "Regrettably."

Josh knew SEALs never showed up unprepared. They'd have brought their own vehicles. He looked at the capacitor charge. It might not matter. If they shut down the reactors, game over.

Langley

Carl heard the SEAL Commander report that the helicopter had a bad transmission and they would go up the mountain using the snowcats. Buster, frowning, began to pace, chewing his gum loudly. Carl relayed the situation to Davidson.

Mount Howe

"Which one of you is Christoff Bobinski?"

Bobinski and his men had been sipping coffee, with their feet propped up on the consoles, when the SEALS burst in. Now, they were all lying face down on the floor. Bobinski raised his hand.

The SEAL Team Leader said, "Get up, but don't make any sudden moves."

Bobinski stood up slowly. Having served in the Russian army, he knew he was facing a Navy SEAL. He also recognized the subdued rank insignia, Senior Chief Petty Officer.

The Senior Chief said slowly and clearly, "We have a nuclear engineer and reactor expert with us. I need you to shut down the reactors and kill the power to the mountaintop. Do you understand?"

Bobinski said, "Sure, but if we kill reactors, it will get very dark and cold."

The Senior Chief looked at his expert. The young engineer said, "There's a backup generator. If we need to, we can turn the reactors back on later."

Bobinski nodded and casually went over to the main control panel with the engineer. One SEAL went with them. The Senior Chief and the third SEAL stayed back, where they could cover everyone. He told Bobinski, "Shut it down but don't touch anything on that control panel without telling him." He pointed to his young engineer. To the engineer, he said, "Check every step."

Bobinski picked up a clipboard in Russian and referring to it said, "First we increase the cooling and make sure SCRAM interlocks are ready." The young engineer nodded as Bobinski leaned forward to comply.

After five minutes of the slow step-by-step process, the Senior Chief interrupted, "How long's this going to take?"

Bobinski stopped and turned around slowly. "To shut down safely by procedure, about hour."

The young engineer nodded. "That's probably reasonable for a normal shut down."

The SEAL team leader said, "That's not acceptable! We need this thing offline now. I know these things can be shut down in an emergency faster than that."

The engineer said, "Yes, we can SCRAM the reactor. That drops graphite control rods into the core, absorbing the neutrons and stopping the reaction, but we might not be able to get it started again."

The Senior Chief, looking at the young engineer like he was an idiot, said, "I don't care. SCRAM it!"

The engineer turned to Bobinski.

Bobinski shrugged his shoulders, "OK." He pointed at the large red button at the top of the control panel. The young engineer reached toward it. He looked back at the Senior Chief, and then pushed it.

A very loud alarm startled all of them.

After a few seconds the SEAL asked, "Is it shut down?"

The engineer, looking carefully at the control panel indicators, said, "No. The rods failed to drop. The alarm is indicating a SCRAM failure. If I'm reading this right, this reactor is at full power *and* it's over-temping!"

The Senior Chief said, "Shut that noise off!"

Bobinski, complied, shutting the alarm off, and said with a half-smile, "Dah, she's like Russian woman, hard to turn on, but once on, very hard to turn off."

The young engineer and Senior Chief weren't amused.

Bobinski continued more seriously. "We have trouble with reactors. They were damaged during transport. Cold weather hasn't helped."

The SEAL team leader said to both of them, "I don't care what you have to do, shut it down and shut it down now!"

The engineer looked at Bobinski almost pleadingly. Bobinski glanced quickly at one of the repeater monitors. It showed the capacitors were at 92% charge. "We must do emergency manual shutdown."

The young engineer said, "I assume the SCRAM button on the other reactor is also *malfunctioning*?"

Bobinski shrugged. "We can try it."

The Senior Chief leaned over to the engineer and said quietly, "Are they stringing us along?"

Frowning, he whispered back, "Remember Chernobyl? They really don't seem to worry that much about fail-safes. This thing appears to have *none*."

The SEAL said to Bobinski, "How long will the emergency manual shutdown take?"

Bobinski turned around slowly and said, "If you quit asking questions and pointing guns at us, we can shut it down in about 10 minutes." Bobinski thought, *10 maintenance minutes – which were very different than SEAL minutes.*

Langley

The SEALs reported that they were having technical difficulties with the reactor shut down, and the other team had discovered that the snowcats were missing parts. Carl heard Buster swear and spit out his gum. Buster then walked over to the control console where a Navy liaison officer sat. They talked quietly.

Mount Howe

It had been 20 minutes since the C-17 landed. The capacitors were at 94%, but they'd lost all contact with the base camp. Josh hated standing around waiting. He brought a cup of coffee to Chandra. "Victoria, I can't tell you how much I appreciate your trust. I know it hasn't been easy."

She turned to Josh with raised eyebrows. "Actually, the message I got said, and I quote, 'Fuze is dangerous and a threat to national security.'" She shrugged. "I've been in the government my entire career. I *know* things can go terribly wrong in a bureaucracy. But this *is* the weirdest program I've ever been a part of."

Josh, looking apologetic, didn't know what to say.

Chandra tapped her finger against her lips as if thinking. "Let's see ... listen to a faceless bureaucrat on a satellite link ... *or* believe a combat-decorated carrier captain and a madman who throws himself off cliffs to save people?" She shook her head. "That's a tough one."

Josh shook his head with a smile. "You and Katori are amazing, and the way you work under pressure...."

"Pressure?" She shook her head dismissively as she sat down at her computer. "I have three teenagers at home."

Southern Ocean

In the twilight off the Antarctic coast, the bow of the guided missile destroyer crashed through 20-foot swells. The Captain of the USS Truxton was standing in her ship's Combat Information Center when the message came in. As she read it, her body automatically swayed to compensate for the ship's pitch and roll. They were in the middle of one of the polar cyclones that frequented the Southern Ocean. The storm's wind and waves were within the ship's launch parameters, but it made for a rough ride. She checked and rechecked the authorization code, and then gave the order.

Two Tomahawk cruise missiles exploded out of the destroyer's deck cells. They climbed out of a boiling orange ball of flame, their fiery exhaust illuminating the ship's deck and the dark rolling sea around it. As the missiles jettisoned their rocket boosters, small wings popped out and their turbine engines spun up. They both turned south and accelerated.

The Captain sent back the launch confirmation. She grabbed a cup of coffee and sat down to watch the missile's progress on the big display. They had positioned themselves as close to the Antarctic coast as possible, but the cruise missiles still had a 700-mile journey. She looked at the countdown timer; in an hour and 15 minutes, the missiles would deliver two 1,000-pound, high-explosive warheads to their target with an accuracy measured in inches.

Her Executive Officer joined her. Watching the missiles' progress on the screen, he said what she was thinking. "I have a hard time imagining what we need to blow up at the South Pole ... but the CIA must know what they're doing." He handed her a piece of paper. "Check this message out. We're going to be joined by friends in this God forsaken place."

After reading it, the Captain looked up at her XO with surprise. "Reagan and her entire Carrier Battle Group?!"

Mount Howe

Fifteen minutes had elapsed. The Senior Chief was angry. "Forget about the reactors! I want the power to the mountaintop cut off!"

Bobinski said, "We can do that but it wouldn't be wise before we shut reactor down."

"And why is that?"

"Reactors are putting out 11 megawatts of power. If we don't shut down reactor first, where will that heat go?"

The engineer chimed in, "He's right. This thing's running in the red. It's over-temping at full power. It should have already shut itself down. If we pull the load suddenly, without any way to SCRAM it, it could go critical and melt the core."

The Senior Chief said, "What's the worst that can happen?"

The engineer looked at him incredulously. "A core meltdown ... with an explosive release of radioactive uranium. If the explosion doesn't kill us, we'll die of radiation poisoning before they can get us out of here. There's no place to run."

Frustrated, the Senior Chief let loose with a long string of expletives, finally ending with, "Just finish what you're doing!"

Bobinski smiled to himself. He started life as a language major and was impressed. He hadn't realized the grammatical versatility of the worst word in the English language. The SEAL had effectively used it as an interjection, noun, verb and adjective, all in one sentence.

Bobinski overheard the Senior Chief call his Commander. He reported that they had to shut the reactors down before they could cut the power. Bobinski was close enough that he heard the reply. "We're on our way to the top. I don't care what you have to do. The power *will be* off before we get there. Is that understood?"

50

CHECKMATE

It had been 30 minutes since the C-17 landed. Josh was startled when the door opened. Cho came inside, accompanied by a blast of bone-chilling air. He closed the door and pulled his parka hood back. Shivering, he said, "I aligned that sucker and she looks good but I didn't have time to check the continuity of all the power circuits."

Katori nodded.

Josh watched Cho pick his way back toward his laptop, gingerly squeezing his large frame between tables and cables. As he sat down, he said to no one in particular, "It's definitely going to work!" Then, with a quick furtive glance around, he made the sign of the cross over his chest.

The Senior Chief glanced at his watch and with a calm but deadly voice said to Bobinski, "It's been 20 minutes, why isn't it off?"

Before Bobinski could respond, the Senior Chief said, "I think you're lying." He looked at his engineer and said, "Kill the power."

The engineer shook his head and started to say, "That would be extremely dangerous ..."

Before he could finish, the Senior Chief walked over to Petrov, who was sitting in front of the power distribution panel. He asked, "Do you understand me?"

Petrov nodded and said, "Yes."

Slowly and clearly, he said, "Shut the power off now."

Petrov shook his head no.

The SEAL took his pistol out, pulled the slide back and put it to Petrov's head. Calmly, but with steel in his voice, he said, "Shut the power off or die."

Petrov saw the capacitor charge at 97%. Keeping eye contact with the SEAL, he slowly reached up on his control panel and flipped a breaker.

The lights in the control room went out.

In the dark, Bobinski flipped the SCRAM alarm override switch. As the ear splitting alarm began to howl, Bobinski yelled, "Oh my God! Reactor's going critical! She's melting down! Everyone to get out! Now!"

Josh, suddenly felt anxious. The heaters and the electronics made a lot of background noise, but he heard a sound outside. They were out of time. Instinctively, he moved to the wall on the hinge side of the door. With his sensitive hearing and a little more, he knew a split second before ....

The door burst open and two SEAL commandos rushed in with submachine guns in front of them. One went left, one right.

Once again, as his adrenaline flowed, time slowed. Josh moved behind the first SEAL with superhuman speed. With the agility of a magician, he unlatched and pulled the SEAL's pistol from its holster. As the man started to spin to his right, Josh had the nine-millimeter pressed against his neck.

Smith, almost as fast, dropped to the floor. In a jujitsu move, he came up under the second commando, with his pistol barrel just inside the bottom of the SEALs bulletproof vest.

Three more commandos spilled in.

Josh positioned himself carefully behind his SEAL to prevent them from getting a clean shot at him. Everyone froze.

Josh knew if Smith hadn't engaged, they would have shot right by the man Josh was holding. SEALs were never held hostage. Quickly, Josh said, "I'm the man you're looking for. I'm going to return this pistol to its owner. We are American citizens on a critical and highly classified mission that you are endangering. I ask that we all take a deep breath, and that you lower the barrel of your weapons from my people so we can talk." As he said that, he slowly rotated the pistol barrel up and away from the SEAL's neck. Turning it toward himself, he offered it handle-first to the SEAL. Smith did the same as he slowly stood up.

While he was acting, Josh's mind worked at phenomenal

speed. He knew there was no way they'd win a firefight against heavily armed SEALS. He only realized why he had done what he did, after the fact. Making a physical move that was almost impossible, and then identifying himself as their target, earned their respect, and he hoped, a few precious seconds.

Bobinski, the technicians and SEALS scrambled out of the building into the frigid cold. All the building lights in the base were out. The only illumination came from the C-17. The last out was the Senior Chief. Bobinski watched him look around.

Josh put his hands up. The SEAL he returned the gun to, frisked him and stepped back, and the other SEAL did the same to Smith. The SEAL Commander lowered his weapon slightly, and the other SEALs followed his lead.

As they frisked the others, Josh watched the monitor out of the corner of his eye. It showed that the tracking system had finally locked on to the meteoroid. It also indicated that the Blaster's aiming system was moving the Blaster into firing position. The power board was at 98%.

The officer said to him, "You are Josh Fuze?"

Josh said, "I am."

"My orders are to take you into custody immediately and shut down your operation. We are authorized to use deadly force."

Josh read the subdued insignia on his uniform. He was a Lieutenant Commander. Josh said quietly, "On whose authority, Commander?" Josh doubted they knew where their Command's orders came from, nor was it relevant, but he needed time.

The SEAL Commander said, "I am acting on orders authorized by National Command Authority. I appreciate the fact that you didn't put up a fight or attempt to flee and took responsibility, but my orders stand. As long as your people continue to cooperate, I give you my word they will not be harmed. We'll let the experts sort this out."

Josh said, "Thank you." He was dealing with an honorable warrior. He continued, "This operation is highly classified and intended to deflect a large incoming meteoroid. If we don't initiate the beam in the next few minutes, the meteoroid will destroy London. It's critical that you contact your Command Authority immediately."

"My orders are to secure this facility and take everyone into custody. I was told specifically to stop *all* operations immediately."

Josh saw the tracking scope sync. The aiming system was now showing green. If everything was working, the Blaster should be pointed in the right direction and slowly tracking the meteoroid. Three down, one more "green" to go. All they needed was full charge. He saw the indicator change to 99%. Just a couple minutes, that's all they needed.

Josh continued in a calm voice, "Doing that will result in the destruction of a major city. Your unit and command may take the blame. I know you're following orders, but you're an officer in the United States Navy ... *as was I*. You swore an oath to defend the Constitution of the United States against all enemies foreign and domestic. The U.S. and world are facing the most powerful enemy. It's closing at 40 kilometers per second. Every minute we waste, reduces the chance of our success. I'm asking you to exercise your authority as on-scene commander. Please contact your command and ask for an immediate review. You know as well as I, blue-on-blue engagements occur. Hundreds of thousands could die."

He could see the conflict in the officer's eyes, but the man shook his head and said, "I'm sorry. My orders are very clear. I promise to contact my command as soon as we've shut this operation down." He signaled to start rounding up the control staff.

This SEAL was not going to bend. He just needed a few more seconds. He'd try one last stall tactic. "We can shut it down but we have extremely high-voltage capacitors with tens of thousands of amps of power. If we don't shut them down properly, they could explode. Your people and mine could be seriously injured."

The SEAL Commander paused and then said, "We're shutting the reactors down now and have experts coming in behind us." He motioned with his gun for Josh to move toward the door.

He knew the SEAL was finished listening to his monolog. He was 10 feet from the panel with the red button. There were two tables in between and four SEALs with their weapons pointed in his direction. He had no choice – when it hit 100%, he'd have to make a run for the button and hope he could hit it before they cut him down.

Bobinski and his men had no coats. The Senior Chief told his team to move their shivering captives to the C-17 as he looked nervously over his shoulder at the reactor building. Bobinski heard him report over the radio that the power was finally off but the reactor could melt down. Bobinski couldn't hear the response, but the Senior Chief suddenly stopped, turned around and looked up. Seeing the lights on the mountaintop, he swore loudly, pulled his pistol and ran toward Petrov.

Mauna Kea

The VISTA Infrared telescope in Chile was the first to detect the meteoroid. They immediately sent messages to observatories across the world and to NORAD to plot the impact point.

Mount Howe

The charge indicator hit 100% and the display turned green. A buzzer went off and several lights changed color.

Chandra, on the far side of the room, gave him the needed distraction. Pointing to the display, she yelled, "Oh my God! Look at the capacitor board!"

All eyes turned to the board.

But before Josh could launch himself, Smith pushed the SEAL nearest him off balance. He knew Smith was going for the red button.

Once again, Josh's mind sped up. He saw the SEAL Commander was still looking at the board and the SEAL Smith pushed wouldn't recover fast enough, but the other two SEALs were swinging their submachine guns toward Smith. Smith would never make it.

Josh pushed off the wall behind him as the submachine guns fired at Smith.

Two bullets caught Josh in the stomach and spun him

around as a third grazed his arm.

Smith hit the red button and rolled on the floor, as a fourth bullet just missed his head and ricocheted off the armored metal wall.

Josh's trajectory sent him crashing into a table with laptops.

The SEAL Commander yelled, "Hold your fire! Hold your fire!"

Lying on the floor amidst a tangle of laptops and cables, Josh heard the warning siren and the sound of the capacitor primers release. The electronic hum rose to a shriek.

One SEAL shoved Smith to the floor with his boot, pushing the gun barrel to his head.

The Commander grabbed Greg Langlois and yelled, "Shut it down!"

Greg yelled back, "We can't stop it once it's started!"

On cue, the giant capacitors discharged like a fireworks grand finale.

From the tiny porthole window, a brilliant flash lit the control room as the high-pitched shriek ended in a wall-shaking, bone-rattling boom. It felt like a lightning bolt striking inside the control room.

In the blink of an eye, millions of amps excited trillions of photons into coherent, perfectly collimated lockstep. Reaching their exit threshold, they departed the Blaster at the speed of light. First, at a frequency absorbed by air molecules, the three-meter-wide beam superheated the air to incandescence. A millisecond later, the second more powerful train of photons followed the tunnel created by the first. The double beam was a beautiful, brilliant blue-green, so intense that stray reflections could damage unprotected eyes. As the beam left the atmosphere, the vacuum tunnel collapsed with a sonic boom. The photons crossed the distance to the incoming meteoroid in less than a second.

———✸———

As the Senior Chief dragged the shivering Petrov back toward the reactor building, the landscape lit up with a blinding blue-green flash followed seconds later by a thunderclap.

———✸———

In the control room, all sound stopped. Only the ringing in their ears remained, along with a smoky haze of black powder and burned insulation. The light coming through the small window faded to a green glow.

On the video feed from the dome's interior, they saw the Blaster's tellurium/sapphire core had exploded and the superconducting mercury cooling lines had burst. A colorful fire grew from the melted electrical components. An exterior camera, pointed above the dome, showed the sky. Disrupted air molecules along the beam's path fluoresced with a bright green glow. The long, narrow, artificial aurora pointed toward the deadly meteoroid, like an accusatory finger.

Into the silence, the SEAL Commander said, "What happened!?"

Greg's voice cracked as he spoke. "You just killed the best man I've ever known." With tears in his eyes, he said, "He was telling the truth. The beam fired like it was supposed to ... if it wasn't too late."

Lying on the floor, Josh whispered with a Monty Python accent, "Not quite dead yet."

The Commander nodded to one of his men, who went to Josh and bent down. Checking the wound and the spreading pool of blood, he said, "He's alive," he shook his head, "but it doesn't look good."

The Commander, in a softer voice, said, "Do what you can."

Josh felt pain but it seemed distant. He felt the blood soaking through his shirt. The bullets obviously missed his heart, but he wasn't sure what they did to his other organs.

Smith and Musk, daring the SEAL holding the gun to do anything, slid over to where Josh was lying. Josh felt Smith put pressure on the wound to slow the bleeding.

The SEAL said, "I'll be back with a medic bag."

Langley

Carl noticed Buster was chewing another piece of gum and watching the main screen with apparent calm. Suspicious, he walked over to the console with the Navy operator and asked how things were going.

The operator said, "Four minutes to impact."

Carl grabbed the phone next to the Navy officer and

switched the line to Davidson, praying he would still be online.

Davidson answered.

"Buster has Tomahawks four minutes out!"

Davidson said, "Give me the Navy guy!"

Carl handed the phone to the operator and said, "This is Deputy Director Davidson."

51

DEFLECT

As the SEAL Commander was trying to contact his Command, he heard the sound of a high-pitched jet engine getting rapidly louder. It had the unmistakable rising Doppler that indicated rapid closure. Recognizing the signature sound, he yelled, "Incoming! Hit the deck!"

As they threw themselves on the floor, the escalating turbine whine was joined by the sound of a second engine.

When it couldn't get any closer or louder, the Doppler pitch suddenly dropped. The sound receded, and a few seconds later, two deep reverberating booms echoed in the distance.

As they started to get up, Greg was the first to ask, "What was that!?"

With a frown, the SEAL Commander shook his head, "I think that was plan B."

As Katori stood up, he said, "*Those* were Tomahawk cruise missiles."

The SEAL Commander looked at him with surprise.

Katori said, "Before Boeing, I worked for Raytheon, the maker of those things. That's closer than I ever want to get."

Southern Ocean

The Navy Petty Officer sitting at the Tomahawk console said, "Wow! We *really* cut that close." He looked at his Captain. "I'm surprised the missiles picked up the satellite signal that close to the Pole."

She patted him on the shoulder. "Good job. That was the first *operational* test of the new Block IV redirect-in-flight capability." She added softly, "I wonder if we'll ever know what was going on."

Turning to the Communication Officer, she said, "Send the abort confirmation to Langley."

Langley

Still holding the phone and his breath, Carl reported to Davidson that they had been able to redirect the missiles.

Davidson asked him to patch him through to the Director of National Intelligence.

Carl said, "I can do better than that. The DNI came into the Ops Center a few minutes ago. She's standing against the back wall."

"Put her on."

After a short telephone conversation, Carl watched the DNI walk up behind Buster and say, "That was an incredibly dangerous backup plan!"

Buster spun around with irritation until he realized who was talking to him.

She continued, "Did you know that Elton Musk was on the mountaintop?"

His silence said it all.

She continued coldly, "You took a huge risk that the new Tomahawks could be redirected."

Without thinking, Buster said, "They can be redirected?"

Her eyes narrowed as she shook her head in disgust. Lifting her right hand, she motioned to two agents.

As Buster turned to look at the security agents, she said softly, "Please escort Mr. Johnson out of the Ops Center and pull his access on my authority." The men didn't even blink as they flanked the now silent Buster.

As they were escorting him out, a CIA analyst burst into the room, almost knocking Buster over. He yelled, "NORAD and NATO just announced an evacuation order for London. They're predicting a meteoroid impact in five hours!"

The Director of National Intelligence announced loudly, "This operation is now under my personal control. I'm ordering all forces to stand down and render assistance to the Pole base staff *immediately!*"

Mount Howe

The SEAL Commander received a communication. It had the correct authorization codes. It immediately rescinded the use of deadly force and told them they were to assist the personnel at the base in any way they could. He shook his head swearing. He could have used that information 10 minutes ago, before he blew the guy away.

Chandra, who had been staring at one of the monitors, suddenly pointed at her laptop screen, exclaiming, "We hit it! We actually hit the dang thing dead on!" She added, "The question is ... was it enough?" She started to move over to her laptop but a SEAL restrained her. She looked at the Commander like a mother ready to discipline an unruly child.

The Commander told his team, "We've just been ordered to stand down and assist these people in any way possible." He realized that whatever they were supposed to have stopped – they didn't and it was probably a good thing. He read the dossier and knew who Dr. Victoria Chandra was. "I'm sorry, Dr. Chandra. Is there anything we can do to help?"

She ignored him and moved to one of the laptops. Studying several tables of numbers and graphs, her fingers whizzed across the keyboard.

Cho, looking at the remote video feed from the dome, said, "Blaster's slagged."

Just then, the power and overhead lights went out and red emergency lights came on.

Katori said, unnecessarily, "There go the reactors."

The overhead monitors went dark. The laptops, on battery, remained active.

Katori turned to Chandra. "Did you get enough trajectory information before they cut the power?"

Chandra didn't answer but kept working. She stood up suddenly, startling the SEAL behind her, who raised his gun instinctively. Oblivious, she said, "It's impossible to be sure this early. Trajectory changes are so tiny, but there's a chance."

Cho blurted out, "You mean it worked?!"

Greg said, "Yeah, but it blew itself to bits."

"Who cares, we can build another. I can't believe it actually worked!"

Chandra and Katori both turned and looked at Cho with surprise.

Cho looked amazed. "You don't understand. These things *never* work the first time and certainly not at full power!" He did a little NFL touchdown victory spike, then stopped, looking apologetically toward Smith and Musk, kneeling next to Josh.

Cheyenne Mountain

NORAD was the first to notice the trajectory change. They recalculated and published the new impact point. They added a new evacuation order for low-lying areas on the southern coast of Ireland and the eastern coast of England, France and Spain. In addition to grounding or rerouting all air traffic in Western Europe, a new order went out to ships in the Eastern Atlantic. They were to move away from the impact area as fast as possible and prepare for a multi-megaton atmospheric blast with hurricane force winds and seas.

Mount Howe

Smith, still holding pressure on Josh's wound, leaned over and said quietly, "Josh, I'm sorry."

Josh whispered back weakly, "Are you serious? Chandra just said you *protected* hundreds of thousands of people." He winced but continued, "It was someone else's turn to protect you." He paused to take a painful breath. "I also know I ruined your plan to *retire* yourself." The emotion he saw on Smith's face confirmed that he had planned his own *accidental* death.

Josh was beginning to feel lightheaded, but needed to tell Smith one last thing. With his hand, he weakly motioned him closer.

Smith bent down.

Josh whispered, "This is important."

He leaned closer.

"Lopez thinks you're hot."

Surprised, Smith leaned back smiling and shaking his head.

Josh heard the SEAL Commander say on the radio that they were sending a critical casualty down by helicopter. The SEAL medic came back and took over. He sprayed the wound, put on a pressure bandage and gave him some type of shot.

Josh had the metallic taste of blood in his mouth – probably not a good sign. He began to feel fuzzy and disconnected ... he'd been here before. For him, the mission was over. He felt completely at peace for the first time since his return. He could finally let go ....

As they loaded the stretcher into the helicopter, it was too loud for the SEAL Commander to talk over the engines. He caught the medic's eye. The medic understood the unspoken question, and glancing briefly at the unconscious body on the stretcher, he shook his head.

52

IMPACT

Three hours after the Blaster fired, a Marine V-22 Osprey landed on the ice near the C-17. It offloaded a small Marine recon team. Twenty minutes later, it was airborne again, flying at its maximum speed through the Antarctic night. After taking on fuel from an airborne tanker, it continued on to a stormy ocean rendezvous.

Europe, Noon

With 24-hour news networks, social Internet sites and smart phones, few in Europe weren't looking skyward as the meteoroid entered the atmosphere. It created a beautiful white-orange streak almost as bright as the sun. Crossing Germany and the Netherlands in 30 seconds, and traveling 100 times faster than a bullet, it penetrated deep into the atmosphere. The intense heat and violent deceleration finally overcame the building-sized body. At 30,000 feet, 500 kilometers west of London, it exploded with the power of a 10-megaton bomb. The explosion echoed across Europe.

The Tunguska-sized blast damaged ships that couldn't move fast enough. The shockwave pushed the giant vessels like sailboats in a Category 5 hurricane, almost capsizing them. It created 10-foot-high tsunamis that inundated coastlines from Ireland to Spain and crossed the Atlantic to the United States. The damage would exceed hundreds of millions, but the advanced warning saved tens of thousands of lives.

Atlantic

She awoke and found herself lying in a small bed in a tiny but nicely trimmed cabin. Someone must have carried her there.

She got up, peered out the window and saw nothing but

ocean through the clouds far below. A clock on the wall said 9:30. She went to the door she thought pointed to the front of the jet and cracked it slightly. Peeking out, she saw the two agents sitting in chairs. The woman was working on a laptop, and the man was talking quietly on a phone connected to the wall. The flight attendant was working in the forward galley. She went to the back door of the cabin and found a small, well-equipped bathroom. It even had a little shower. She now understood the term "sweating the information out of someone." She felt very grubby and the mirror confirmed it. With their altitude, she thought she had time before they landed. In all of her travel fantasies, she never dreamed of showering at 40,000 feet.

They had placed her bag and clothes in the cabin. After a quick shower, she dressed and put on some basic make-up. She felt much better and realized she was starving. Tentatively, she opened the door to the main cabin and came out. The woman agent smiled and called to the flight attendant, who asked her what she wanted for breakfast.

"Whatever's easiest and fastest. I could eat anything right now."

The flight attendant winked as she handed her a large, warm sticky bun and a cup of coffee.

Elizabeth sat down at one of the small tables.

The woman agent came over and said very politely, "Ms. Edvardsen, I think you may want to check out the news." She swiveled one of the flat screen monitors toward her and gave her the remote control.

Elizabeth scanned through to find a news channel. It wasn't hard. It appeared this TV only carried news. Then she realized that breaking news had preempted every channel. She stopped at the news network she usually watched.

The flight attendant put a large, hot omelet in front of her.

She realized that between the interrogation and sleep, she lost an entire day. Apparently, she was coming in late to something everyone else already knew.

As it began to sink in, she clapped her hands over her mouth in excitement, tears in her eyes. Someone deflected a meteoroid bound for London. It landed in the Atlantic, saving hundreds of thousands of lives. Details were still coming in, but it was clear that a secret base at the South Pole had hit the comet with some type of energy beam. As if that weren't enough, there was a bigger story. There was a "mother" to this meteoroid. Detected much farther out, it also appeared to be on a collision course with the earth.

Elizabeth asked how soon they'd be landing.

The female agent said, "In about two hours, ma'am ... but there's been a slight change of plans. We'll be transferring you to another aircraft for the final flight."

"Final flight? Where to? Is that where Josh is?"

Elizabeth saw the two agents exchange a quick glance. Both looked uncomfortable. The male agent said quickly, "I'm sorry, ma'am; they'll explain it all to you when you arrive." He changed the subject to the weather in the Falklands.

She could tell there was something they weren't telling her but decided not to press it. She was elated that she and Josh had been totally vindicated. She wanted to do a victory dance and yell repeatedly, "I told you so!" But she would be a gracious winner. They probably already felt bad enough.

Southern Ocean

In the heavy rain and late morning twilight, the V-22 transitioned to vertical landing mode. With limited visibility and large ocean swells, the tired Marine pilot struggled to match his aircraft to the motion of the pitching deck. As he skillfully and firmly set the aircraft down, a crew rushed out in the driving rain to take the critical cargo.

Falklands

Elizabeth watched through the window as they landed in the Falklands. Heavily overcast, it was windy and cool as she stepped through the jet's door. They gave her an FBI windbreaker to wear. As she came down the steps, directly in front of her was a stubby, gray, twin-engine turboprop. It looked like a caricature of an airliner. An airliner designed by a committee, and considering its size, a committee that ran out of money. It was truly an ugly duckling compared to the sleek business jet she was leaving. On its side, it proudly wore "United States Navy" with "VRC-30" on the tail. The male agent, seeing her expression, reassured her. He said that although the Cod looked funny, it was only because it landed on aircraft carriers.

"Aircraft carriers?" This was getting stranger and stranger.

Misunderstanding her question, he told her it was one of the safest carrier-capable airplanes.

She suspected, "safe" and "carrier" was an oxymoron, but didn't care as long as it was taking her to Josh. The male agent – she still couldn't remember his name – accompanied her onboard the Navy aircraft. She sat in a rather makeshift-looking seat. A young woman in a flight suit gave her a quick safety brief and handed her a vest and soft helmet with a headset. The vest, with its integrated inflatable life preserver, didn't instill a lot of confidence. They told her it would be a three-hour flight. As the engines started, she understood why she wore the helmet.

Washington D.C.

The press grilled the world's leading astrophysicists in a huge video conference. The scientists reinforced each other, telling similar stories. They confirmed the comet's existence and estimated its size and trajectory. Without intervention, the world was scheduled to end in 11 months on March 21 at 10:00 am Greenwich Mean Time.

Southern Ocean

The surgical suite was located near the center of the ship, both to protect it from battle damage and because the ship's motion was muted near its center of gravity. Despite the ship's size and the Captain's attempts to maneuver it to reduce motion, the raging cyclone rocked the operating room like a cradle. The surgeon, however, had years of experience treating combat casualties from Afghanistan to the inner city of Los Angeles.

They had been in surgery for four hours. The surgeon knew too much time had elapsed before they could operate. The medics had chilled the patient's body during the long transport, but with the severity of the wounds, her patient's survival prospects were almost zero.

The anesthesiologist said, "His blood pressure's dropping."

The surgeon said, "We're almost finished."

"He's 60 over 40. I've already pushed five units. He's not responding to the drugs anymore."

"I can't stop here. Do what you can."

They both heard the cardiac monitor tone change.

The anesthesiologist shook his head. "He's tachycardic ... we're losing him."

The aircraft was small enough that she could see into the cockpit and out the aircraft's windshield. As they descended, it was easy to identify the aircraft carrier, even in the late afternoon twilight. It was the largest ship of a small flotilla, all headed in the same direction. As they made their approach, all she could think of was, there's no way they're going to get this thing ... on that. Getting closer, she could actually see the ship moving in the rough seas, and began to realize how big the carrier really was ... but still not big enough to land on.

The little turbo prop touched down hard and went from 120 miles per hour to a dead stop in 200 feet. To Elizabeth, it felt like a crash landing.

As the engines shutdown, a Petty Officer from the ship came onboard to escort her. Over the jet noise, he yelled, "Please follow me very closely until we're off the flight deck and inside the ship."

As she stepped off the aircraft and glanced around, she understood why. It was total chaos, or at least appeared that way. There were dozens of jets all around her. Some taxing, some parked just inches apart. One jet sat on the catapult at full power. She was mystified how they kept from running into each other. It was also loud. No, it was beyond loud. Her stomach and spine felt the rumble of afterburners from the fighter 100 feet away. There was a pervasive smell of jet exhaust, tinged with sea air. The steel deck she walked on looked like the skin of an avocado, dark and rough with a bit of an oily sheen. What amazed her was that all of these sights, sounds and smells were taking place in the middle of the Antarctic Ocean in an area the size of a parking lot.

As she tried to follow her Navy escort, she felt the motion of the ship and had to compensate constantly just to walk. The 20-knot wind added to the challenge, and her light clothes and windbreaker did little to stop the arctic chill.

Once inside with the large metal hatch closed, it was like stepping into another world. She removed her helmet and vest, and along with her FBI escort, followed a Navy Commander in khakis. They walked through a metal maze of passageways, hatches and ladder wells. She had a good sense of direction but knew she'd never find her way back without help. They finally brought her to a nicer looking part of the ship with wider passageways and shiny blue linoleum with stars. Her Navy escort took her to a locked door, entered a button combination in a small box on the wall and opened it. Inside was a small conventional-looking conference room. Her escort motioned her to enter but stayed outside. He said, "Would you please wait here, ma'am. There's coffee on the table and someone will be joining you shortly."

She nodded and went inside. She could still feel the ship gently rocking and rolling. It had to be rough out there to move something this big. She carefully poured herself a cup of coffee and sat down to wait.

Netherworld

Josh was back in the netherworld. He wasn't frightened this time. Sensing Jesse's presence, he asked, "Did we do it? Did we save London?"

Yes.

"Awesome!" Tentatively, Josh said, "I toasted another body, didn't I?"

Your body is dying.

"I'm not going to get another one, am I?"

No.

"Thank you for giving me another chance and saving our collective butts. I guess this is the end of our journey together."

Our journey is just beginning.

Josh's shadowy netherworld faded for the last time.

53

DÉJÀ VU

He tried to focus his eyes. It took a while, but when he could finally see clearly, it was white acoustic ceiling tiles again. Unlike last time, he felt a rocking motion and smelled the faint background odor of hydraulic fluid and jet fuel mixed with a tinge of methane. Josh recognized it instantly. It was like being home. He was onboard a ship, almost certainly an aircraft carrier.

He looked sideways and saw the familiar IV bag and EKG leads. He could also feel a small plastic tube blowing oxygen in his nose. He started to prop himself up but his stomach immediately let him know that was a bad idea. He felt like someone ran over him with a truck and punched him in the stomach for good measure. His head pounded, and he was very queasy. Despite that, he was in a great mood. He was alive, and they had proved it was possible to deflect a comet!

The biggest challenge was ahead but the secret was out and his part was over. It really didn't matter what happened to him now. He knew that if he survived, which was questionable, his best possible prospect was life in prison, but he could deal with that knowing he'd done everything he could.

A doctor came in to check his vitals and look at the wound, asking the usual questions about how he was feeling and if he needed any more pain medication. He felt pain but it was bearable and he didn't want to cloud his mind. He was just savoring being alive. Josh noticed the doctor's nametag. He was a Lieutenant Commander. Appropriate, he thought wryly. Shot by a Lieutenant Commander, and now another one had to fix him up. He also noticed the command pin on the nametag was USS Reagan. He'd done carrier qualifications onboard the Reagan.

The doctors and medical corpsman were polite and

attentive but left quickly and didn't talk. He also noticed an armed Marine in fatigues standing outside his room.

Within a few minutes, he had visitors. While he was recruiting his team, Josh had done his homework on who was who at the major federal agencies. He immediately recognized the Deputy Director of the CIA. Two serious looking, plain-clothed agents flanked him a few paces behind. They kept Josh in their view. He wondered if they thought he'd try to attack them with an IV bag.

The Deputy started by saying, "Sorry about shooting you, but it looks like you're doing remarkably well considering."

Josh smiled. "Apology accepted."

"Do you know who I am?"

"Deputy Director of the CIA Brian Davidson."

"Actually, Acting Director."

Josh frowned. "What happened to the Director?"

Davidson gave him a half smile and said quietly, "You did." He turned to the agents behind him and asked if they would please wait outside. They looked a little surprised but complied. He continued, "Buster is retiring due to ... health issues brought on by ... job stress."

"Sorry about that."

Davidson didn't smile. "Don't be. He wasn't cut out for the job. Now that we've established who I am, do you mind telling me who you are?"

"Who do you think I am?"

"Please don't answer my question with questions. Who do you work for?"

"You wouldn't believe me if I told you."

"What?" He smiled. "Extraterrestrials?"

"Do you believe in extraterrestrials?"

Davidson smiled. "There you go again." He paused. "Josh ... is that really your name?"

"Yes, actually it is."

"That thing you built near the South Pole did in fact give the meteoroid enough of a nudge. It missed London and hit the Atlantic – *spectacularly* – but with only a few lives lost. We need to thank you for saving a city and hundreds of thousands of lives. I'm just glad it's over."

Josh said, "It's just beginning."

"Yeah, we know. They've identified the fragment's mother and plotted her trajectory. It looks like we're right in the crosshairs as you predicted. The entire world knows now." He paused. "That doesn't answer the question of who *you* are or who you work for. There's no record of you existing prior to Kansas City Medical Center. We've looked hard, very hard. After 9/11, it's almost impossible to escape detection. All we can say for sure is who you're not. You don't belong to any government organization ... yet you have the knowledge of several."

"Kind of bold to say you know the membership of every government organization."

Davidson continued matter-of-factly, "Not really, that's my job. The only organizations that can make someone invisible, I'm a member of or in close contact with." He frowned. "It's not just that. You have information that shouldn't be possible. According to our experts, nothing can detect a dark comet as far out as you did. On top of that, your medical records from Kansas say you have perfect health ... too perfect. They've never come across a specimen like you, no fillings, inoculations or scars."

Glancing down at his stomach, Josh said, "No scars?" Looking back up, he said, "So, you think I'm an alien?"

"No. While in surgery, they poked around inside enough to know you're human ... not that they wouldn't have wanted to dissect you if you hadn't made it."

Josh raised his eyebrows at that comment. "So, what's your theory?"

"I don't know. That's why I'm asking. If you told me you were psychic or working for little green men, I'm not sure I'd question it."

"Does it matter?"

"Of course it does!"

"Why?"

"How are we to handle you?"

"You think I need to be handled?"

Davidson frowned but didn't answer.

Josh continued, "Do you trust me?"

"What?"

"Do you trust me?"

"It's my job *not* to trust."

"You didn't answer the question."

Davidson just shook his head. "It appears you just saved our butts despite our best efforts to stop you. You hijacked the military-industrial complex and had it doing your bidding, while holding the most powerful government agencies at bay." He stopped and looked behind him before adding, "Very impressive by the way."

He continued, "The people who worked for you, trust you completely. In fact, we heard the story about the cliff rescue. I'd have discounted it as exaggeration, but we got the same story from several eyewitnesses." He shook his head again. "Frankly, I'd love to see you working for us ... but I'm not entirely sure we shouldn't be working for you."

Josh smiled. "Why did you make the CIA your career?"

"What?" Davidson sighed. "I'm going to have to go back to remedial interrogation school." He pulled a chair up next to the bed and sat down. Finally smiling, he said, "What the heck. Josh, I was a history major. I remember it like it was yesterday. It was the day I discovered that World War I happened largely due to wrong assumptions and miscommunications. I believed, and still believe, that if we can ferret out the truth, if all the parties know what's really happening and why, we might prevent governments from making stupid mistakes – mistakes that cost thousands of lives. Maybe even stop wars that don't need to happen."

Josh said, "You're an idealist."

Davidson looked genuinely surprised. "I've been called a lot of things during my career, but it's been a very, very long time since anyone called me an *idealist.*" He smiled and shrugged. "Thank you."

Josh nodded. "We're not that different, you and I. If you have to *define* me, think of me as another cynical, idealistic soldier. Like you, I have discretion to operate autonomously, but still have to report to a higher authority. The human race has a huge challenge ahead. It's going to take the best we can be to survive. I helped, but I'm not Superman."

"You did a pretty good imitation."

Josh shook his head. "Superman wouldn't be hooked to an IV."

Davidson became serious. "You asked me if I trusted you, but trust goes both ways. Can you give me something, anything, to anchor you into … my world?"

Josh understood exactly what Davidson was asking. He needed something to make Josh Fuze appear human. He sighed. "I can't tell you much, but I can tell you that I grew up in the United States. I was educated as an engineer in an Ivy league school." He knew Davidson was a Yale graduate. "And I was a Navy pilot."

"Yeah, we kinda figured that out after you stole the Hornet. By the way, your landing sucked. The Australians are already asking when we're going to replace it."

Josh frowned, shaking his head. "A gallon just doesn't go as far as it used to."

Davidson laughed. "OK, you asked me if I trust you. I believe actions speak louder than words. Based on that, as hard as it is for me to say this, and it better never be repeated," he sighed, "yes, I do trust you."

"Thank you. I know *exactly* how hard that is to do."

"So where do we go from here?"

"I was nothing more than a catalyst. All the cards are on the table now. There's nothing more I can add."

Davidson nodded.

Josh continued, "Ultimately, the next step is your call. I have no identity. No one will miss me. I've broken enough laws that no one would blame you if I were to suffer *complications* from the surgery."

"You're not a very good poker player. You're not supposed to show all your cards."

"No, but I *am* a good judge of character."

Davidson smiled. "Yeah, you probably also realize that there's no way we could ever prosecute. To do that would require showing what you actually did. It would be *awkward* delaying the trial for a Medal of Honor ceremony." Continuing more seriously, "The problem is that you can't just fade into the shadows. There are people out there who know you and know what you did. There will be too many questions."

"Actually, not many people *do* know me or what role I played. Between your agency and the administration, I bet you can come up with a great story to explain all this."

"You're willing to let others take the credit for this?"

"Of course."

Davidson smiled. "Well *that* won't be a problem. That's something governments are very good at." He paused. "I noticed you didn't exactly live lavishly. You had a cheap one-bedroom apartment and drove a used Ford. I assume your finances aren't superhuman?"

Josh realized his "slush fund" from Musk would cease. He smiled and shook his head.

Davidson looked thoughtful for a moment and then said, "Tell you what. I'll create an account for $175,000 a year that you can draw on any time. By the way, that's what I make. Consider it a pension from the federal government for services rendered. If you don't deserve it, no one does."

Josh smiled. "A pension ... or a retainer fee?"

Davidson shrugged with a slight smile. "Whatever."

"I imagine, use of that account might be ... traceable?"

"Yeah, I figured you might think of that." He continued more seriously, "Josh, I can promise you as long as I'm around, that information will go to no one but me, but yes, I would like to be able to stay in touch with you."

"Thanks, I'll think about it." Josh realized there was one other thing he needed to do. "Brian, none of this could have happened without Carl Casey and Tim Smith. I don't know what happened behind the scenes, but I'm sure without Carl, I'd be dead or in a prison cell and London would be burning. Tim Smith actually *fired* the Blaster, knowing he would almost certainly be killed in the process."

Davidson added, "He *would have* been killed, if *you* hadn't gotten in the way."

"Both of these men risked everything to make this work."

Davidson nodded. "They're good men. The Distinguished Intelligence Cross presentation is actually the fun part of my job." Looking at his watch, he said, "I've got to go. I have to brief the President." He frowned. "But first I have to figure out what I'm going to say. You've created quite an opportunity and challenge for us." He put a card on the table next to Josh. It had nothing but a telephone number on it. "This is my direct line." As he turned to leave, he said, "Oh, we're assigning medical personnel to supervise your recovery."

"Thanks, but that won't be necessary."

As he left, he said over his shoulder, "It's the least we can do."

54

PROPOSAL

After waiting several hours, Elizabeth saw the door open. A slim man in his fifties entered, flanked by two men. Smiling, he walked over with his hand out, saying, "Ms. Edvardsen, it's a pleasure to meet you, I'm Brian Davidson." He added to the two men with him, "Will you please excuse us for a moment?"

As they left the room and closed the door, she shook his hand, not knowing what to expect. She assumed he was a government official but didn't know who he represented.

As if reading her mind, he said, "Ms. Edvardsen, I'm the Acting Director of the CIA, and I want to sincerely apologize to you for your incarceration and interrogation. We didn't understand what Josh was doing. We had good intentions but, as much as I hate to admit it, we were operating under some major misconceptions. I'm so sorry. Can you ever forgive us?"

This took her by surprise. He looked as if he was prepared to take a verbal beating. "Mr. Davidson, Josh is ... unique. I can imagine your situation quite easily. No apology necessary, officially or personally." She already liked this man.

With a look of relief, he smiled and said, "Please, call me Brian. We also owe you a huge debt of gratitude."

Surprised, she asked, "Me? Why?"

"You put enough doubt in your interrogators that we forwarded the meteoroid trajectory information to observatories and NORAD. The early warnings saved countless lives." He paused. "Would you like to see the Prophet?" He shook his head. "I'm sorry, I mean Josh."

She cocked her head and looked at him carefully. "Did you say ... prophet?"

"Slip of the tongue. That was just the project codename."

With a slightly apprehensive look, he continued, "I don't know if anyone told you, but Josh was ... injured during the South Pole operation."

"What happened!?"

Davidson frowned. "He's OK, but he was *accidentally* shot."

Her eyes got wide. "Shot!"

Speaking quickly, he added, "The bullets have been removed, and he's doing well. I've already been in to talk to him. He seems to have an unusually strong ..."

She interrupted him. "Can I see him?"

"Yes. Yes, of course."

Davidson accompanied her to the ship's sickbay. As they followed a Navy commander on a several-minute walk through the metal maze, Davidson continued to talk to her. They finally reached sickbay. It was a small but fully equipped hospital. She recognized most of the equipment and was impressed. It made sense if you had to handle serious combat casualties. At a private room with a Marine guard, Davidson stopped outside and waved her in.

Josh heard someone outside and looked up. He was shocked to see Elizabeth. She ran to his bed and gently grabbed his face in her hands. With tears in her eyes, she said, "Are you all right?"

Smiling and trying not to get emotional himself, he said, "I'm doing great, really."

She gave a small laugh but her voice quavered as she said, "What is it with you? Do I need to buy you Kevlar underwear?"

He laughed and then winced. "I can't believe you're here!"

She leaned forward and kissed him on the forehead. "How and where did you get shot?" She was already peeking under his sheet.

"I think I have an extra belly button or two."

With anger, she said, "Who did this to you?"

"It's not important and please don't hold it against anyone. Brian Davidson's a good guy. You can trust him."

He stopped and sighed. He realized it was time to come clean. It wouldn't get any easier with time. He'd rather have a root canal than what he was about to do, but they were alone. He didn't know if they would let him see her again, and he needed to be the one to tell her. He said softly, "Elizabeth ... I need to tell you something. It's something I should have told you long ago."

She took his hand and with a little smile said, "You really don't know anything about plumbing do you?"

He couldn't help but smile. It was true; sprinkler systems and faucets never worked the same after he "fixed" them.

He started and then stopped. Finally, he sighed. "Elizabeth, I'm so sorry ... I'm not what you think I am." There it was, finally out in the open.

She frowned and said slowly, "What do I think you are?"

He frowned. "I ... I'm not exactly sure."

She gave him a compassionate smile. "Then how do you know you're not what I think you are?"

A chill went down his spine at still another parallel Jesse conversation.

She shook her head, laughing softly. "You *really* don't get it, do you? You're cute but you are soooo dense. I would love you, even if you turned out to be a raging schizophrenic with delusions of grandeur. Don't you understand? It doesn't matter to me who you are or who you *think* you are." Looking around conspiratorially, she smiled, adding, "But we might be able to set aside the *delusions* of grandeur diagnosis." She continued, "Never underestimate a woman's intuition." She leaned over and kissed him gently.

As he was processing this, she said, "And I'm going to be sticking around until you're fully recovered."

Finally grasping at a subject he could comprehend, he asked weakly, "They'll let you take that much time off work?"

She grinned. "Brian – probably as a way to make amends – offered me a contract to be your personal nurse through your recovery ... to the tune of $250,000."

"Wow."

Looking mischievous, she said, "Look, it's not as though I really want to be around you, I just need the money to fix the plumbing in my condo." She winked. "The contract says that I must supervise your full medical recovery and ensure you re-establish all your physical abilities." She gave him an innocent look. "Course, I'm not entirely sure what *all* your physical abilities are."

Saving Josh from a response, a corpsman came in and said he'd have to check the wound and change the dressings. Josh watched Elizabeth, as she watched the corpsman examine him. He wasn't impulsive, but came to a sudden decision. As the corpsman left and Elizabeth came back over to his bed, he asked, "Elizabeth, you really aren't mad at me? I mean you're not just being nice because you feel sorry for my situation?"

She didn't say anything. She just smiled and shook her head and held his hand.

He decided to forge ahead. "Then, Elizabeth, could you do me a favor?"

She said, "Sure."

"If I survive and don't do life in prison, will you marry me?"

Her eyes got big.

He'd accomplished something rare. He rendered her speechless.

Finally, with damp eyes, she said, "Let me think about it." Then, with a big smile, immediately added, "Yes!"

Before she could kiss him, one of the agents came in and said that she was needed. She said, "Just a second." And leaned over and gave him a long kiss.

As Elizabeth left Josh's room, the agent said to her, "I'll escort you back to the Director and then show you to your stateroom. You can return here any time you wish." He handed her a plastic ID on a neck strap, and said, "Ms. Edvardsen, this will take care of you while you're on the ship." Then he handed her a manila envelope and explained. "There's a State Department passport and a government credit card for expenses." As they walked, she took the maroon colored passport out and looked inside. She frowned, shaking her head. "They couldn't have found a better picture?"

The agent brought her back to the small conference room. Several people surrounded Davidson, but as soon as he saw her, he disengaged and came over. "Ms. Edvardsen, is there anything we can do for you?"

She said, "Just call me Elizabeth. You've been great, and I really appreciate your honesty. I don't hold what happened to Josh against you. I can't, because he doesn't. In fact, he said you were a good guy and to trust you." She paused. "But if you don't mind my asking, how did he get shot?"

Davidson surprised, said, "He didn't tell you?"

"No," she shook her head in disbelief. "He said it wasn't important."

Davidson started slowly, "Let's just say, the individual responsible won't cause any more trouble. He's currently under sedation."

Elizabeth looked at him closely. "You introduced yourself as *Acting* Director."

Davidson gave her a half smile.

Raising an eyebrow, she asked, "What will happen to the ... individual responsible?"

"Nothing *dramatic* unfortunately, but he's been removed from his position and will retire from government service ... under supervision."

She nodded silently.

He looked her in the eye. "Elizabeth, may I ask *you* a question?"

She nodded again.

Glancing around, he quietly asked, "Who *is* he and how was he able to find and figure out how to move a 15-kilometer mountain?"

With a slight smile, she tilted her head and said, "'I tell you the truth. If you have the faith of a mustard seed, you can say to this mountain, move from here to there and it will move. Nothing will be impossible for you.'" She winked.

Frowning, his eyes unconsciously glanced upward. Then he shook his head with a half-smile and said, "Uh, yeah ... OK." Quickly changing the subject, he said, "Well, gotta go. I have a lot of creative explaining to do." As they shook hands, he added, "Take care of him, Elizabeth. We may need him again."

EPILOGUE: HEADLINES

CIA Director Johnson Resigns Over Health Issues
President Yager said, "Mr. Johnson will be missed but Acting Director Davidson has my complete confidence." ...

Millennium Comet Officially Named Chandra-Wooldridge
With humility, Dr. Wooldridge stated, "I certainly don't want to take all the credit, but ..."

Australians Sacrifice Super Hornet to Save the Queen
Squadron Commander and courageous pilot *to be knighted ...*

Strategic Defense Initiative Cover Story for Deflection?
Department of Defense spokesman refused to confirm or deny ...

Meadows Appointed U.N. Director of Planetary Defense
Admiral Joe Meadows earned his second star, as the 10th Blaster became operational on Mount Howe ...

Elton Musk Declines Invitation to Run for President
With his usual elfish grin, Musk responded, "Why on earth would I want to have those limits?" ...

Josh said, "It's out of my hands now. I can disappear."
Can you?
"Are you suggesting there's another threat out there?
Silence.
"What could be more dangerous than a giant comet?"
You.

Preview of the second book of the *Fuzed Trilogy* follows

AUTHOR'S NOTE

This is a work of fiction. Unfortunately, the science behind the story isn't fiction. NASA estimates 95% of the largest asteroids have been found. However, that undiscovered 5% represents thousands of asteroids big enough to incinerate a continent or wipe out almost all life on Earth. Additionally, there are *hundreds of thousands* of smaller undiscovered asteroids big enough to destroy a city or, with an ocean impact, inundate coastal cities with 500-foot tsunamis.

After the asteroid blew up over Chelyabinsk, Russia, astrophysicists reevaluated the impact rate. They used data from the Nuclear Test Ban Treaty monitoring system, which *listens* for nuclear detonations in the atmosphere. The results were surprising. Here's the conclusion from a paper published in Nature this year:

> *"We performed a global survey of airbursts of 1 kiloton or more (including Chelyabinsk), and find the number of impactors with diameters of tens of meters may be an order of magnitude higher." (1)*

This means that impacts big enough to obliterate a city are **10** times more likely than we thought ... but it gets worse. Comets may be an even larger threat. New research suggests the dinosaur killer may have been a comet, not an asteroid. Our belief that comets are rare is based on counting observable comets. But what if many, if not most, comets turn out to be "burned out" or dark comets? With surfaces as dark as fresh asphalt, they're extremely difficult to detect, and may explain why the impact rate is much higher than expected. Here's a quote from a publication of the prestigious Royal Astronomical Society:

> *"Current detection and deflection strategies involve the assumption that decades or centuries of warning will be available following the discovery of a threat asteroid.*

However, if the major impact hazard indeed comes from this essentially undetectable population (of dark comets), the warning time of an impact is likely to be at most a few days."
(2)

All we know with certainty is that impacts have happened and will again. We now know the probability of any of us dying from an impact is statistically greater than being killed by lightning, earthquakes or even food poisoning. The difference is that everyone we know could die with us. With a year or less to respond, the survival of humanity (and potentially most life on Earth) depends on having a deflection solution in place. Currently, we have none. We're playing Russian Roulette. Dr. Ed Lu, former astronaut and CEO of the B612 Foundation, summed it up. Referring to the Las Vegas truism that "the house always wins," he said, "We're not the house."

We're putting our money where our mouth is and contributing a portion of the profits from the Fuzed Series, books, upcoming movie and video game, to non-profits working to protect humanity, such as the B612 Foundation. B612 is building an infrared space telescope to find all the Earth-threatening asteroids within a few years. For more information on real-world threats, the intersection of physics and metaphysics, or a preview of the rest of the series, visit us at Fuzed.org.

By the way, asteroids and comets aren't the only threat to our existence. Books two and three of the series cover the next two most probable and dangerous threats to our world. A preview of the first chapter of the book two, **IMAGINE**, follows.

1) Brown, P.G., et. al. (2013) **500-Kiloton Airburst Chelyabinsk and an Enhanced Hazard for Small Impactors** (Nature, DOI 10.1038/Nature/12741)

2) Napier, W.M., J. T. Wickramasinghe, J.T., Wickramasinghe, N.C., **Extreme Albedo Comets and the Impact Hazard** (2004) (Mon. Not. R. Astron. Soc. 355, 191–195, 2004)

PREVIEW

IMAGINE

Book Two of the Fuzed Trilogy

1

THE END

On the northeast coast of South America, a man and woman stand alone on a cliff top overlooking the Atlantic. The muted sound of surf rises from below as they hold hands and gaze across the ocean. Silhouetted by the setting sun, hair tousled by a tropical breeze – it would be remarkably romantic ... if not for the end of the world.

Admiral Joe Meadows said, "You're right. It all rides on this last shot." He paused. "Thank you, Mr. President, I'll pass your words on to the team." As he set the phone down, he looked out over his Antarctic base. His office, wrapped in heavily insulated glass, sat just below the airfield tower. The panoramic perch reminded him of the bridge of an aircraft carrier. Peering through the Antarctic twilight, he saw the last cargo jet land on the ice runway in 40-knot, 40-below-zero winds.

     He poured himself a cup of coffee. It was both beautiful and a bit surreal. Embedded in the ice, the taxi light's blue glow illuminated the snow swirling around the huge Russian jet. It was the last of an international bucket brigade that had built the nuclear-powered base of 10,000 engineers, scientists and construction workers. He shook his head. They'd failed. Although they *had* prevented a direct hit, the comet would still graze the earth.

     The elevator 'dinged.' He turned to see his highly efficient taskmaster, also known as his Flag Aide, bounding out. Lieutenant Molly Cardoso was dark, wiry and always in motion. Studying her smart phone intently, she answered his unasked question. "We still have a few minutes before we have to be down at the Control Center, sir."

     Looking back out the window, he put both hands around

his warm coffee cup. "You'd think after 10 months, I'd get used to the cold."

"I'll have them check the heating system."

He shook his head with a small smile. "It's fine, Molly." He nodded toward the three-story, windowless building, nestled at the base of the mountain. "Nuclear reactor's putting out plenty of power. In fact, it's starting to melt the ice." He paused. "It's probably just the 8,000-foot elevation." The reflection of his face in the window contradicted him. He'd gone from captain to three star admiral in ten months. The crushing responsibility and lack of sleep had taken its toll. No longer looking like a defensive lineman, he'd lost weight and let gray hair grow on his normally clean-shaven head. Did he really look that tired? The reflection of genuine concern on the face of his young aide confirmed it.

Turning back to her, he smiled. "Molly, you keep up with the news. How's the world reacting?"

"Well ... the conspiracy theorists still don't believe there's a comet or Antarctic base. We're just actors in a studio. Then there are those convinced the world's ending and are partying their brains out." She smiled. "But the majority accept the situation with cautious hope." She paused – unusual for her – and then added, "Things once important become trivial. Things trivial become important."

"Why, Molly, you have the heart of a poet."

"Doubt it, sir. I hate poetry." She looked at her watch.

Getting the hint, Meadows grabbed his coffee cup, took a last look outside and followed her to the elevator.

As the doors closed and the elevator headed down to the control center, she said, "Sir, you're scheduled for a short talk to the team as soon as we arrive. It'll be televised across the base, and," she looked at him meaningfully, "picked up by the press and broadcast around the world."

He gave her a tired grin. "I promise, Molly, I won't tell any more *sea stories*." He paused. "Have you talked to your folks recently?"

"Talked to my dad in LA yesterday. He's fine." She hesitated. "Wasn't able to talk to mom. She flew back to Venezuela to be with my grandparents."

Meadows frowned.

She sighed. "She knows about the comet's trajectory. I told her if things don't go according to plan ...." She looked down. "She said it's where she was needed." Meadows gently squeezed her shoulder.

As the elevator doors opened and they walked to the Control Center, she quickly attached a wireless lapel mic and snatched his coffee cup.

It looked like NASA's Mission Control. The front wall was a giant display with status information and live views of the laser domes on top of Mount Howe, which towered 1,700 feet above the base. Ninety silver domes dotted the mountaintop like mushrooms. Inside them were the world's most powerful and accurate lasers, poised for a final salvo.

Facing the giant display were rows of monitoring stations, occupied by two dozen engineers. Above and behind, was a glassed-in press gallery. There was a subdued but constant buzz of voices and keyboard clicks.

As Meadows moved toward the front of the room, he saw his Deputy Director and Chief Scientist, Dr. Victoria Chandra, standing near the center of the room. Six feet tall with long black hair and an intense visage, she was hard to miss. She was conferring with the Control Center Director and her astrophysics team: former astronaut and B612 Foundation CEO Dr. Ed Lu, Scottish extraterrestrial impact expert Dr. Bill Napier and legendary comet finder Dr. Carolyn Shoemaker.

Meadows exchanged a quick head nod with Elton Musk, who was standing quietly near the back of the room. If it hadn't been for his initial surreptitious funding and construction support, none of this would have been possible. But Musk had also been instrumental in the rapid production and installation of the 90 lasers. He had a brilliant knack for out-of-the-box thinking and problem solving.

Over the loud speaker, a calm voice said, *"T-minus 60 minutes."*

That was his cue. As he stepped up in front of the main display, the room quieted.

"I'll make this fast. You have more important things to do than listen to speeches. After 10 months of back-breaking work, around the clock, in the harshest possible environment ... you've delayed the Millennium Comet three minutes." He paused. "Doesn't sound like much, but it allows the earth to move 6,000 kilometers in its orbit, and out of the comet's crosshairs. Although it *will* still graze the atmosphere, you, and the millions who've supported us, have prevented a direct impact that would have erased almost all life on Earth." As he looked around the room, he continued, "I'm incredibly proud of each and every one of you."

There was a round of spirited applause.

He glanced at the display behind him. "We're 59 minutes from our final salvo ... the most critical to date. You're about to stop the rotation and stabilize the attitude of a 15-kilometer mountain. *Nothing* must stop us."

He paused. "Just got off the phone with the Secretary-General of the United Nations and the President of the United States. They, along with all the world's leaders and citizens, send their heart-felt thanks and prayers for our success." He paused again. "We're a truly international team and come from many belief sets, but at this point, I don't think any of us would believe it unreasonable to request supernatural help. Please join me in a quiet prayer."

After the prayer, Meadows moved through the Control Center, patting backs and shaking hands. He knew everyone by name. Finally working his way to the back, he grabbed a fresh cup of coffee for himself and Chandra.

Nodding to Lu, Napier and Shoemaker, he said, "graduation day," and handed the coffee to Chandra.

She gave him a small smile as he asked the same question he'd asked her every day for the past 10 months. "So, how are we looking?"

Over the loudspeaker, *"T-minus 30 minutes."*

She took the cup of coffee and nodded to Napier.

With a strong Scottish brogue, he said, "Latest projections have it penetrating 50 kilometers into the atmosphere and coming within 70 kilometers of the surface. Computer models still show multiple earthquakes, tsunamis, major meteoroid damage and a very powerful electromagnetic pulse, but they're all events we're expecting and hopefully prepared for."

Meadows looked at Dr. Ed Lu. "Comet orientation?"

Lu shook his head. "I hate having to wait until the last

minute, but we can't fire until our potato-shaped comet's *skinny face* is forward. We're going to hit it one last time with everything we've got. It should stop the rotation and lock it in the optimum orientation for atmospheric entry."

Meadows looked at Chandra.

She exhaled sharply and said very quietly, "Even firing all of them, it's barely enough to stop the rotation." She shook her head. "And we've never fired them all at the same time."

Meadows nodded with a frown. "Yeah, we barely finished installing the last of the extra capacitors and the power conduits last night. Haven't had time to test 'em." He paused and then asked Lu, "What are the odds it'll hold together when it hits the atmosphere?"

"With the correct orientation, it'll have 15% less drag."

Meadows said, "Ed, I know you've done a lot of atmospheric entries yourself," he raised an eyebrow, "but optimistic press release aside?"

Lu looked him in the eye. "Joe, you know the story. We're dealing with a mountain composed of ice and rock, moving 100 times faster than a rifle bullet." He shook his head. "There's no way it'll hold together through a dozen G's of deceleration at 4,500 degrees. All we can hope for ..." he blew out a lungful of air, "is it'll hold together *long* enough that the pieces won't hit us or explode in the atmosphere."

"T-minus 15 minutes. Target data upload complete."

"And if they do?"

Napier, staring past them, inserted, "The latest simulations say that if even part of it hits the ground or explodes in the atmosphere ... we're talking a 10-million-megaton blast."

Meadows gave a slight shrug. "Better than a two-*billion*-megaton direct hit."

Nodding, Napier quietly added, "Yes, but that's still a *thousand* times all the nuclear weapons in the world combined. It would melt the mile of ice this base sits on and scorch half the planet. The other half of the world would eventually freeze and starve."

Before Meadows could respond, the Control Center Director, Carlos Comulada, turned around and interrupted. "We've got a problem!" With one hand on his headset, he pointed at a display. It showed a schematic of the ninety Blasters, but three branches of ten Blasters each were blinking red. "Just lost the power conduit to 30 Blasters. Probably wind damage. We're clocking 70-knot gusts on the mountaintop. I sent in the emergency team."

Meadows signaled Musk to join them.

"T-minus 10 minutes. Targeting servos aligned."

Meadows asked, "Can we re-aim the other Blasters to compensate?"

Chandra said, "Sixty Blasters aren't enough." Calling up data on one of the consoles, she added, "Even if we re-target them, we've *got* to get at least 20 back online or we have no chance of stopping the comet's rotation."

Joining them, Musk asked, "Can we delay the firing?"

Lu and Napier shook their heads emphatically, as Chandra said, "Absolutely not! We have to hit it right when it's in the optimum orientation."

Comulada looked at them. "They have six minutes to evaluate, repair and evacuate."

Meadows noticed the press had sensed something and were pointing cameras their way. Lu leaned in and whispered, "If it hits the atmosphere with *any* angular momentum, our simulations say it'll tear itself apart within seconds."

"T-minus six minutes. Capacitors at 100% charge."

One of the mountaintop cameras was now displaying a damaged dome, ripped apart by the wind. Next to it, they could just make out shadowy figures in the twilight. Struggling against the subzero, hurricane-force wind, the repair team hunched over an outside power junction box.

"T-minus four minutes. Core super-cooling has commenced."

Comulada turned back to Chandra, "We've got to re-aim the remaining Blasters before the automated firing sequence locks them out."

Chandra closed her eyes. When she opened them, she said, rapidly, "Retarget, assuming we get 20 of the dead blasters back online."

Comulada's eyes narrowed. "You sure? If we end up with only 60, re-targeting for 80 will make things worse."

Chandra snapped, "Do it!" Stepping forward, she added quietly, "Carlos, if it's rotating when it hits the atmosphere, we're toast. We've got to go for broke."

Comulada finished keying in the changes just as they heard, *"T-minus two minutes. Targeting coordinates locked in."*

Meadows shook his head. It all hinged on the frostbitten crew on the mountaintop.

"T-minus one minute. Dome doors opening. Computer-controlled tracking initiated."

Chandra began to pace.

Meadows stared intently at the screen with Musk and Comulada.

"T-minus 30 seconds. Capacitor initiators armed."

Comulada pointed excitedly at the screen. "They got one circuit working. That's 10 Blasters back online!"

Lu shook his head. "Not enough."

Musk said, "Reroute the power intended for the dead Blasters to all the others!"

Comulado frowned. "They can't handle that much power. We'll melt their cores and blow 'em apart."

Musk said, "Melt 'em!" Turning to Meadows and Chandra, he added, "They only have to fire one more time."

Nodding, Meadows and Chandra simultaneously said, "Do it!"

Comulada nodded. "Rerouting power."

"T-minus 20 seconds. Targets locked. Abort disabled."

At the front of the Control Room, the display of the Blaster's status changed. Twenty Blasters went black. The remaining 70 changed from green to flashing yellow, with a "128% Power" next to each.

There was a buzz around the room and in the press gallery. Over the noise, Meadows told Comulada, "The Blasters may explode. Tell the repair crew to take cover inside the dome of one of the dead Blasters!"

Comulada nodded, speaking quickly into his headset.

"T-minus 15 seconds."

On screen, they saw the shadowy figures running toward one of the domes.

"T-minus ten, nine ..."

As they reached the dome, Meadows said quietly to Chandra, "Whatever the outcome, it's been an honor and privilege to serve with you."

"*Six, five ...*"

She whispered back, "Honor's all mine." She paused. "Just wish Josh had lived to see this."

"*Two, one ...*"

Blindingly beautiful, blue-green lasers lit the Antarctic plain like a flash photograph. Seventy beams stabbed at the comet in what might be humanity's last act of defiance.

Standing on the cliff top, Elizabeth pointed northeast across the ocean. "Look!"

Close to the horizon, Josh saw a pinpoint of light, sparkling like a tiny green firefly in the distance. He said, "That was it ... our last shot."

She just nodded. Still staring at the horizon, she slipped her hand back in his.

Watching her out of the corner of his eye, he thought once again – what a beautiful combination of exotic Indian eyes, olive skin and blonde hair. He glanced down at their hands. His skin was a few shades darker. Most would identify him as multi-racial, but they often did a double take when they saw his eyes. He thought the flecks of color embedded in gray were weird, but Elizabeth had told him his eyes were what first attracted her. That was good enough for him.

She asked, "How close will it get?"

Looking back at the horizon, he said, "It'll enter the atmosphere over the Caribbean and cross South America coming within 70 kilometers – about 40 miles – of the surface."

"No, I mean how close will it get to *us*?"

He pulled his eyes from the horizon. With a half-smile, he said, "Did you bring your sunglasses?"

She just looked at him.

"Sorry. It'll cross the coastline about 10 miles north of us, moving 200 times faster than the speed of sound." He smiled. "We have ringside seats."

"Is it safe?"

He shrugged. "As long as it doesn't break up when it hits the atmosphere."

"And if it does?"

Josh stopped smiling and looked back at the horizon. "We'll be the lucky ones. We won't be crushed, drowned, asphyxiated or starve to death."

She shook her head. "Let me guess ... because we'll be incinerated?"

He finished, "Along with everyone in North and South America."

Looking back at the horizon with a half-smile, she said, "Kind of an epic buzz kill on the ringside seats."

ABOUT THE AUTHOR

Commander Dave Stevens was a nuclear-weapons-trained Navy fighter pilot. He served as the Strike Operations Officer for the Persian Gulf during the Iraqi invasion of Kuwait. With a Top Secret clearance, he led classified defense programs, test-piloted new F-18 fighters and earned an aviation patent. He's been to over 30 countries, 10 miles above the earth, 600 feet below the Atlantic and survived hundreds of his *own* carrier landings. Dave holds engineering degrees from Cornell and the University of Michigan with graduate work in astrophysics and human factors. As an author and international speaker, he uses an extensive network of subject matter experts – from astronauts and astrophysicists to intelligence operatives and Special Forces – to entertain and educate.

Proof

Made in the USA
Charleston, SC
02 May 2015